Praise for Tyler R. Tichelaar's

"So much is asked of saviors that we can forget the beating heart behind the legends. Tyler Tichelaar understands the contradiction between our expectation of heroes and their lonely destiny. In exploring the Arthurian legend, he shows himself once more the master of the complexities of the human heart."

— Diana M. Deluca, Ph.D., and author of *Extraordinary Things* and *A Dream of Shadows*

"What if you discovered the famous legends you'd heard and believed all your life didn't happen the way they'd always been told? In *Melusine's Gift*, readers will join Adam and Anne Delaney as they hear the truth right from the mouths of the characters who lived the tales. Readers unfamiliar with Melusine's place in history will be drawn into her world, while the captivating web of multi-layered stories within stories combine and complement to obliterate the preconceived notions of those who consider themselves experts on her legend. I loved *Melusine's Gift* even more than *Arthur's Legacy* and can't wait for the twists and turns of *Ogier's Prayer.*"

— Jenifer Brady, author of the *Abby's Camp Days* series

"*Arthur's Legacy* is absolutely mesmerizing! Rich with fully-realized characters, legends, history and life-affirming viewpoints, it drew me into its world so fully...."

— Roslyn McGrath, author of *Goddess Heart Rising* and *The Third Mary*

"If you like medieval fiction, then this story should be right up your alley. It certainly was mine. The author knows how to turn a phrase. His characters are well-developed and interesting. Highly recommended."

— Sara Knight, The Drunken Druid

"*Arthur's Legacy* is a fresh new take on the ancient and wondrous myth of Arthur. Works of this kind are hugely important because they keep the legends alive and bring them into the 21st century. Strongly recommended for all who love the old and the new in mythic fiction."

— John Matthews, author of *King Arthur: Dark Age Warrior and Mythic Hero*

"What if the story of King Arthur was not quite what you thought? And what if its repercussions echoed down the centuries and across the seas? Casting a fresh, inventive and sometimes controversial eye over the rich tradition of Arthurian legend, especially its Welsh roots, in *Arthur's Legacy* Tyler Tichelaar has crafted an intriguing blend of action-packed time-slip fantasy adventure, moving love story, multi-layered mystery, and unusual spiritual exploration."

— Sophie Masson, editor of *The Road to Camelot*

"Tyler has clothed the stereotyped characters of myth with real, three-dimensional personalities, and has given strengths and faults to each. This is what makes the story so engrossing."

— Bob Rich, Ph.D., and author of *Ascending Spiral*

MELUSINE'S GIFT

MELUSINE'S GIFT

THE CHILDREN OF ARTHUR, BOOK TWO

TYLER R. TICHELAAR

Melusine's Gift: The Children of Arthur, Book Two

Marquette Fiction
1202 Pine Street
Marquette, MI 49855
www.MarquetteFiction.com
www.ChildrenofArthur.com

ISBN-13: 978-0-9791790-9-9
ISBN-10: 0-9791790-9-2

Library of Congress Control Number: 2014920813

This is a work of fiction. All of the characters, names, incidents, organizations, and dialogue in this novel are either the products of the author's imagination or are used fictitiously.

Printed in the United States of America
Publication managed by Superior Book Productions
www.SuperiorBookProductions.com

"My son, eat thou honey, because it is good; and the honeycomb, which is sweet to thy taste: So shall the knowledge of wisdom be unto thy soul: when thou hast found it, then there shall be a reward, and thy expectation shall not be cut off."

— Proverbs 24: 13-14

CONTENTS

PROLOGUE 1
PART I: LUSIGNAN, FRANCE, JUNE 1995 9
Chapter 1: A Honeymoon 11
Chapter 2: Romance 19
Chapter 3: Melusine 29
Chapter 4: The Creep 47
Chapter 5: Adam's Dream 59
Chapter 6: Anne's Turn 65
PART II: MEDIEVAL FRANCE, EIGHTH CENTURY 75
Chapter 1: Roland's Tale 77
Chapter 2: Bertha's Tale 91
Chapter 3: Milon's Tale 97
Chapter 4: Bertha's Tale Continues 125
Chapter 5: Roland's Tale Continues 137
Chapter 6: Raimond's Tale 151
Chapter 7: Merlin Interrupts 175
Chapter 8: Raimond's Tale Continues 179
Chapter 9: Roland Interrupts 201
Chapter 10: Melusine's Tale 205
Chapter 11: Morgan le Fay's Tale 223
Chapter 12: Melusine's Tale Continues 239
Chapter 13: Pressyne's Tale 247
Chapter 14: Melusine's Tale Continues 263
Chapter 15: Raimond's Tale Continues 295
Chapter 16: Merlin Illuminates 301
Chapter 17: Roland Replies 307
EPILOGUE 309
An Interview with Tyler R. Tichelaar about *Melusine's Gift* 313
Acknowledgments 323
The Children of Arthur Series 325
Sneak Peek at *Ogier's Prayer: The Children of Arthur, Book Three* 327
About the Author 337

PROLOGUE

RONCESVAUX PASS IN THE PYRENEES
BETWEEN FRANCE AND SPAIN
AUGUST 15, 778 A.D.

WHEN ROLAND WOKE, he felt immense relief—he had been dreaming—or had he been? His body was still exhausted. Was it true? Had they been ambushed? He remembered marching with the army, and then—yes, there had definitely been a battle. He remembered the feel of his sword as he slid it out of a Saracen throat and the sight of the blood squirting out, and then—and then a great soaring pain through his whole body, but most of all in his chest, as another Saracen sliced—but—was he dead then?

His eyes bolted open, and he tried to sit up, but the pain soared through his chest again so that he was quickly afraid to move and hurt himself worse. He bit his tongue, trying to keep from screaming over the agonizing pain that shot through his body.

After a moment, when the pain lessened, Roland looked about him, conscious that it was now night. He strained his eyes to see anything he could about him, but he could only make out shadows—of what he knew not. Where was he? Lying on the battlefield, not quite dead? Was the enemy still near? He closed his eyes again, fearing that if an enemy warrior or a grave robber should come and see he lived, he would be struck dead. He listened, waiting to hear footsteps, but all he heard was the great squawking of birds—carrion birds come to feast on the dead. In a moment, no doubt, they would be nibbling on him. He had to get up and make his way to shelter somehow—to see whether any of King Charles' brave men remained to look after the dead and wounded—or were they all dead or wounded?

"Be still."

He jerked in fright at the unexpected voice. He had not heard anyone approach, but it sounded like a male voice, and an elderly one. It spoke to him in French, not the Saracen tongue, and not the tongue of the surrounding provinces—rather the French of Paris, the French of King Charles' court.

"It's all right. You're safe now."

He slowly opened his eyes; it took a minute for them to adjust. It was growing dark, the sun nearly set now. Beside him knelt a shadowy figure.

"Lie still; your wounds mustn't be exasperated further. I've given you some medicine to help with the pain—that is what woke you, when I poured it down your throat. It should numb the pain in a few more minutes."

"My men, what of them?"

"Most are slaughtered; a few escaped; a few were taken prisoners."

"Oliver and Ogier, what of them?"

The old man hesitated a moment, then said, "Ogier survived."

Roland struggled to hold back his grief over the death of Oliver, his companion since childhood. After a moment, he asked the old man, "Can I speak to Ogier?"

"Ogier is gone now. The king and his men all thought you dead. They could not find your body. You were buried beneath the corpse of the Saracen who tried to slay you; he fell dead upon you when another struck him from behind. He covered your body, protecting it from further harm, but hiding it from view. Nevertheless, Ogier is the one of all King Charles' court whom you will see again when the time is right."

"Right for what?"

"That is too difficult a question to answer at this moment, but it will all be revealed."

"If my body was buried beneath another," Roland asked, "how did you find me?"

"I have my ways. I watched the battle from up in the mountains. I kept an eye on you."

"Thank you. Then you were not with the army?"

"No."

"But you know me and my companions?" Roland tried to read the old man's eyes in the dim light as his own eyes finally began to focus in the darkness.

"Yes, I know you, Roland, King Charles' nephew," the man solemnly replied.

A bolt of fear swept through Roland's body. How did the old man know him if he were not with the army? Roland knew he wore nothing to distinguish himself as the king's nephew.

"How do you know who I am?" he asked.

"Why, all your life I have watched you—I knew you when you were yet in your mother's womb."

"Who are you?" Roland asked, fearing he might have fallen into the hands of a sorcerer.

"I have many names," said the man, leaning back. "You would be surprised by them all."

Roland's eyes widened as the man spoke. Although the sun had set and there was no candle or other source of light, the man's face suddenly became illuminated. He was bearded—a long white beard, his hair long and falling about his shoulders—and his eyes were ancient, wise, and mesmerizing.

"Who are you?" Roland repeated, his eyes growing with amazement.

"I am of your father's people, the Britons," the man replied, "although perhaps even you yourself do not know of that aspect of your heritage after all these generations, but no matter, I am many other things as well."

"I don't understand," Roland replied. "Where did you come from? How did you get here, and what is your interest in me?"

"Most recently, I have resided in the Forest of Broceliande. In a cave where it is said by mortals that I sleep; if you think upon it, you will know me."

Roland barely dared think the name that came into his mind, but as he stared at the old man, trying to regain his ability to speak amid his astonishment, a glow slowly lit the old man's face, emanating from a ball the man held up near his chin. Roland had never seen this man before, and yet, he knew instinctively who he was, and finally, the name came to his tongue.

"Mer-lin?"

The ancient wizard nodded, and then the light diminished from his face.

"But—but," Roland stuttered in confusion, "I thought you were enchanted, in a cave, unable to.... Oh, how can this be? It doesn't make sense. Am I dreaming? I don't understand. Am I dead? Is that why you are here?"

"I am very much alive, brave Roland, and so are you. It is foolish, the stories men sometimes tell—that a great enchanter like I, one with such wisdom to live for centuries, could fall for a mere mortal woman barely past her youth and allow her to enchant and trap me. You mortals want to think romantic love is everything and even the greatest of wizards will fall for it, but it is not so. Most of the stories you have heard about me have been tainted by the fears of men and bear little resemblance to the truth, but just wait until you have lived long enough to hear the stories they will create about you."

"Can I have some water?" Roland asked, beginning to cough from the dryness in his throat.

"You are thirsty. That is the healing potion taking effect. I gave it to you before you woke. Wait a few more moments and we will be ready to leave."

"Leave? How? Do you think I'll be able to walk?"

"You will be healed completely; you may feel some bodily exhaustion for a day or two, but after that, you will be your old self."

"I don't believe this. I can't be alive; I must be dead or at least dreaming."

Merlin placed a drinking flask to his lips.

"Here, this will make you feel alive still."

The water was cold and felt wonderful on Roland's parched lips. He had not tasted water since early that morning before the ambush that had caused his companions' deaths.

"Will you take me to the army, to my uncle the king?" Roland asked when he had drunk his fill, and far more than he would have imagined could fill the small flask.

"No," said Merlin. "You have other work to do."

"I will need my sword and a horse and my men to pursue the Saracens."

"No, your fighting days have passed," said Merlin. "You have a more important task now."

"I am the king's nephew, one of his paladins; I fight by King Charles' side. There is no more important task."

"Do you think that I, who served the great King Arthur, do not know better than you?" Merlin asked. "You men and your wars. Trust me. You need not worry about your honor. Your uncle the king will claim to have your body so he may give you a fitting burial in the great tomb of the Kings of France at Blaye. Your great deeds will be remembered in song and story for more than a thousand years to come. You have no need to worry."

"What of Alda, my betrothed?"

"She—I'm sorry to say that she will be heartbroken to know you are dead; she will go to an early grave. It is sad, but you will see her in the next life, though it will be many, many years from now."

"I need to go to her. I cannot break her heart that way."

"No, you will not be returning to France," Merlin repeated.

"Who are you to tell me where I may go?" snapped Roland, his strength having now been restored to him, and with it came the full pain of knowing that he would never again see his dead companions and his fiancée.

"I serve a higher power than you or your king," said Merlin, "and now it is time for you to do the same."

"What do you want with me, wizard?" Roland demanded. "I'll have none of your trickery."

Roland sat up in anger, but although he winced in anticipation of pain at the effort, he was amazed to feel his chest and stomach whole again.

"Trickery, hey?" said Merlin. "I suppose my healing you was trickery."

Roland looked only amazed, and perhaps he felt a bit of fear, for swords he knew of, battles he could fight, but from sorcery he did not know how to defend himself, and sorcery that called him to serve a higher power than his king—that was frightening indeed.

"You will know soon enough what is wanted of you," said Merlin, rising to his feet. "Come; you are able to stand and walk now. We must hurry before the Saracens return."

"Where are you taking me?" asked Roland, first kneeling and then standing, amazed by his sudden renewed vigor; unbelievably, he felt stronger than he had before the battle.

"We go south, to your grandfather," said Merlin, turning and beginning to walk away.

"My grandfather? I know no grandfather."

"No, you wouldn't; he retired to the monastery at Montserrat before you were born," Merlin called over his shoulder.

"I don't understand," said Roland.

"Your father's father," said Merlin, turning back to look at Roland, "Raimond, the former Count of Poitou."

"I did not know my father's father lived. My father died before I was born so I never met my grandfather."

"Come; you have much to learn that you were never told before. You, my boy, are far more than the nephew of a king—even if that king will soon title himself Holy Roman Emperor. You come from a far more ancient line. It is time you learn the truth of your family."

"The truth of my family?" Roland whispered to himself. What was it Merlin had said at first, that he was of "his father's people"—that he was a Briton? But how could any of that be? He knew his father had been born in France, and Raimond of Poitou—he remembered hearing the name—from his mother's lips when he was a child, after his father had died. But he had dim memories of what his mother had said, not remembering much beyond that revelation that she was the king's sister, that he was the nephew to the great King Charles of the Franks. There had been something more—about his father's past and about a strange legend that his grandmother...but his thoughts felt all muddled. He could not remember it all at the moment....

And Merlin was walking off into the darkness.

Roland quickly ran after him, no longer doubting that he was healed and well.

"Here is a horse," said Merlin when Roland was beside him again. In actuality, there were two horses hidden behind a rock in the pass. In another moment, the wizard and the warrior were mounted and galloping south, toward the monastery of Montserrat—where secrets were kept that Roland could scarcely imagine.

PART I

LUSIGNAN, FRANCE

JUNE 1995

CHAPTER 1

A HONEYMOON

"STOP WORRYING," SAID Adam as he pulled their Porsche Convertible up to the motel. "Everything will be just fine."

"But it's the first time I've been away from the boys, and they're just babies," Anne replied.

"The twins are in good hands with my mom and grandma, and your father will also be looking in on them; if anything goes wrong, we can be home in just a few hours. France is only across the channel— we're probably closer to home than if we had gone to Scotland."

"I know," said Anne as Adam put the car in park. "I'm just a worrier."

"So am I," Adam replied, "but this is the first time we've been alone since Dad died—that's a whole year. We deserve these few days to ourselves."

"Yes, and I'm glad for it," said Anne, squeezing his hand. "I'm just not used to being away from the boys." She opened her car door and added, "Let me go into the motel office and check on the reservation since you don't speak French. I'll be back in a minute to tell you where to park the car."

Adam leaned over to give his wife a kiss before he let her leave his sight. Then as he watched Anne go inside the motel's main office building, he again felt overcome by his love for her and how fortunate he was to have her in his life. His American upbringing made him almost want to shout, "Yeehaw!" at the prospect of an entire week alone with her. After all the stress they had been under for the last twelve months, he could think of nothing he desired more.

The past year had been a long and difficult one for them both, although filled with astounding revelations. First, the American-born Adam had discovered he was the illegitimate son of an English earl, Bram Delaney. He had immediately traveled to England to meet his father, only to have Bram die soon after. Just prior to meeting his father, Adam had met Anne, fallen inexplicably in love with her at first sight, and gotten her pregnant; then he had been shocked to discover she was his half-sister. The situation would have been disastrous if Anne had not finally told their father what had happened; fearing his reaction, she was surprised when Bram had overcome his self-pride and admitted that Anne was not his daughter, but the child of his late wife and his best friend, Cedric Harker; Cedric and Anne's mother had committed adultery while Bram had been away on a business trip. Bram had long known the truth, but he had kept it a secret all these years. This revelation had meant Adam and Anne could marry, and with Cedric's legal help, Anne was able to inherit the estate and pass the title to her husband, technically the rightful heir, but Adam had not wanted to disparage his father or Anne's parents, so the truth was kept quiet. Although Adam had gone by his mother's last name of Morgan all his life, he had changed it to Delaney after finding his father, so now everyone was led to believe Adam was Anne's distant cousin—distant enough to marry Anne, who was considered Bram's heir. Regardless, once they married, Adam and Anne became the Earl and Countess of Delaney.

The grief over Bram's death and the red tape of settling the estate inheritance and title had cast a damper on Adam and Anne's marriage until everything had brightened with the birth of their twin sons in early February; then their lives suddenly revolved around all the happiness and work that babies bring. But Adam kept pressing Anne to go on a honeymoon, and she kept saying she wanted to wait until Lance and Tristan—the twins, named for popular figures from Arthurian romance because the Delaneys claimed descent from King Arthur—were older. But now summer had arrived, and the newlyweds badly needed some time just to themselves.

Adam's mother and grandmother had come from the States to visit, and they had agreed to watch the twins so Adam and Anne could finally take a late but much desired honeymoon. Anne had been reluctant to go somewhere distant like Hawaii or New Zealand or any of the other places Adam had suggested, so they had finally settled on a quiet week in the French countryside, close enough that they could return home quickly if needed. They had found a motel on the edge of the town of Lusignan in Poitou, from which they planned to take several day trips, but they also planned to spend a lot of time relaxing and just being alone together. "And making passionate love!" Adam added after Anne described her vision of their honeymoon, and although she didn't admit it, neither did she deny that was part of the plan.

Now after all the mess and confusion of the past year, Adam sat in the car counting his blessings. He truly believed everything that had happened was meant to be. He felt confirmed in this belief for several reasons, including ones he had not yet told Anne; he had been meaning to tell her those reasons, but he feared she might think him a bit crazy, so he had been waiting for the right time—and finding time to be alone to talk with her had not been easy since the twins were born. Plus, he still found it hard to believe that just prior to his father's death, he had actually met the great wizard, Merlin, and it was even harder to believe he had dreamed the history of Camelot as if he had lived it, then been told by King Arthur himself that he and his children would play a role in bringing about King Arthur's return.

Who could possibly believe such a story? No matter how Adam tried to wrap his brain around it all, and even though he believed what Merlin had said, he had not been able to find words to explain it to Anne. But he was hoping that now, during this week together, he could tell her everything without their being interrupted. It was a lot to tell, but she would need to know it all if, as Merlin had said, they and their children would somehow be involved in King Arthur's return.

But first things first...as soon as he got Anne alone in the room, Adam had more urgent plans than to tell her about his dream. Waiting in the car, he was already becoming impatient to be alone with her; Anne had only been gone a couple of minutes, but it felt as if she were taking forever—perhaps he should have gone inside with her to make sure the desk clerk didn't give her any trouble.

As Adam looked toward the door, anticipating Anne's exit, he saw a professorial-looking man—complete with a white bushy mustache and a corduroy jacket with fake elbow patches—emerge from the motel office. For a moment, the man paused; he turned to look at Adam, tipped his equally professorial-looking hat at him, and then disappeared around the side of the motel.

"It can't be!" gasped Adam. He was tempted to jump out of the car and chase after Merle—the name by which he had first known Merlin in his twentieth-century disguise—but then Adam saw another man exit the motel office and quickly follow Merle. This man wore a black hat and a long black coat—it looked almost like a cape—and it was far too warm to wear in June. "He looks like the proverbial villain," Adam thought, but then his attention went back to Merle.

"What is he doing here?" Adam wondered. Had Merle followed him here on his honeymoon because it was time to reveal more to him about his family's role in bringing about King Arthur's return? If so, Adam knew he had made a mistake in not telling Anne everything a long time ago. He would have to tell her tonight, as soon as possible, although it would take hours to explain everything—his dream of Camelot had been so vivid that Adam could recall entire chunks of the conversations he had heard, as well as all the details of battles, weddings, births, romances, and all manner of events. He would have to tell Anne everything—and soon, before Merlin showed up and gave her the shock of her lifetime.

Anne now exited the motel office, and in a moment, she was climbing back into the car.

"We're in Room 6," she said. "Just drive around the back."

"Okay," Adam said, starting up the car.

"It's the funniest thing," said Anne as Adam drove them around the building. "The man at the front desk was so friendly, as if he had known me all my life; he even greeted me by name, but I guess the motel doesn't have many guests right now so he could guess who I was."

"That's weird," said Adam, feeling certain Merle must have been the motel clerk. Who else would know who she was?

"There was one other guest," said Anne. "He had a strange accent—Eastern European maybe—and he was in this dark long coat. He insisted the man at the desk personally show him to his room."

"Oh, yes, I saw them come out, I think," said Adam, certain now that Anne had spoken to Merle.

"I spent an extra minute looking at a poster about an exhibit at the museum here," said Anne. "Apparently, there's some interesting legend about this town—I'd like to find out more. I know how much Devin likes legends; I'm sure he'd like it if we brought him back a book about it." Devin was Adam's scholarly cousin, back in Michigan, studying for a master's degree in medieval history.

By now, Adam had pulled their vehicle in front of Room 6.

"Speaking of legends," said Anne, opening her car door, "we haven't talked about it in forever, but someday we have to do something about that old manuscript we found. We've kept putting it off ever since Dad died."

"Oh, yes," said Adam, getting out of the car. "Maybe when we get back home."

He said it dismissively. He was not sure he wanted to research that manuscript any more, even if it did reveal his family's descent from King Arthur. Merlin had told him to keep it a secret, which was one more reason why he had to tell Anne about the dream and how it concerned them and their sons.

"I'll unlock the room door while you get the luggage," said Anne. "I'm so excited to be here. For some reason, I've always wanted to come back to this town after I drove through it last year with Morgan. She said she felt the appeal of it too, but neither of us could explain it at the time. I miss her. I wish I knew why she doesn't return my phone calls anymore, but she's probably just busy like us."

Adam was already pulling the luggage out of the trunk. When he did not reply to Anne's comment or offer her consolation over her apparently lost friend, she walked to the room door and unlocked it. Adam was right behind her with two suitcases by the time she got it open, but before she could enter the room, he set the suitcases down and unexpectedly lifted her into his arms, saying, "It's our honeymoon, isn't it, Mrs. Delaney? Let me carry you over the threshold." Anne giggled and didn't object when he kissed her, carried her into the room, and laid her gently on the bed. But when she started to suspect he intended to have his way with her right there with the door wide open, she exclaimed, "Stop, silly! What about the luggage?"

"What about it?" he laughed.

"You left it out in the parking lot, and I need to use the bathroom first anyway."

"All right," he said, reluctantly crawling off her.

For a moment, lost in amorous joy, Adam had forgotten the anxiety he felt when he saw Merle. It instantly returned, however, when he stepped outside to find the man in the long black coat standing by the car and looking at their luggage.

"Hello!" Adam called out in a surly voice.

"Oh, there you are," said the man. "I was afraid someone would take your luggage before you came out, so I thought I better keep an eye on it for you."

"Thank you," said Adam, frowning. "I can handle it now."

"Are you staying long?" asked the man, in what Adam was sure was an Eastern European accent, as Anne had surmised.

"Just a few days," Adam said politely. But he did not encourage conversation by inquiring into the man's own stay at the motel.

The stranger waited a moment, presumably for Adam to say more, but when Adam gave no hint of being friendly, the man said, "Well, enjoy your visit," and walked away.

"Thank you," Adam replied, waiting for the stranger to disappear around the side of the building before he collected the luggage and returned inside the motel room.

"Adam, dear," Anne called from inside the bathroom, "I'm starving. I know food isn't your first priority right now, but can we go have dinner somewhere?"

Adam set down the luggage, shut the room door, and walked into the bathroom where Anne was washing her face. Nestling his face in the back of her hair, he whispered, "I don't know what you're thinking. What possible priority could I have other than food?"

"I promise you'll have all you crave later," she laughed, "but right now I'm craving some fine French cuisine."

"All right, then," said Adam, stepping back from her. "Dinner first. Should I go ask at the front desk where we should eat?"

"No, let's just walk through the town and stumble on something. That way we can get a sense of our surroundings."

"Okay," Adam agreed. "Whatever my beautiful bride wants."

CHAPTER 2

ROMANCE

SOON ADAM AND Anne were walking down the city streets on a quest for somewhere to eat. After a few minutes, they came to a little restaurant where they went in and enjoyed some simple but delicious French cuisine.

Both were tired, and Adam was trying to figure out how to bring up the topic of his dream of King Arthur, so they said little during dinner, but by the time they had finished eating, the meal had revived their spirits.

"Look at us," Anne laughed. "We're finally on our honeymoon and we've been acting like we have no energy."

"I'm saving mine up for later," said Adam, grinning.

"Oh, I'm sure you'll have plenty for later," Anne replied. "But it's early. It's not eight o'clock yet, and it will still be daylight for a couple of hours since it's almost the summer solstice. We can't go to bed already. And besides, you know I like moonlight for lovemaking."

"Well, I ate plenty," said Adam, "so what do you say we go for a walk and explore the town and countryside a bit more?" He knew he was just procrastinating having to tell her about Merlin.

The town wasn't very large. Only about three thousand people lived in Lusignan, so within an hour, Adam and Anne had walked well outside the town limits into the countryside; then they decided they should turn back before it got dark.

"It doesn't look like there's much of anything to do here," Adam said.

"No," said Anne, "but it's a sweet little town. And it feels so peaceful after dealing with all the reporters and the fuss this past year over us being married and having children—as if there haven't been plenty of Americans marrying into English nobility in the past, but I guess there were no royal scandals to cover this year, so the media needed something to write about. Still...it's a relief being here; I wouldn't mind a month of hiding in a quiet little town like this."

"Well, we only have a few days," said Adam, who now felt almost relieved that they wouldn't be here long—maybe it was just a coincidence that he had seen Merle, and hopefully, the wizard wouldn't show up again, but that said, Merle had been working the motel's front desk—that couldn't be a coincidence.

"I wish we could stay longer," Anne replied. "If the boys were here, it would be perfect. I miss them so much already."

"We'll call when we get back to the motel to make sure they're okay," said Adam, "but I'm sure they're fine. Mom and Grandma will take good care of them, and if they don't, I'm sure your father will have something to say about it."

"Yes, I'm sure he will," said Anne, still not completely used to the idea that Cedric was her father. "I've never seen him so happy as he is with his grandsons. He's so proud of them."

"I'm glad it's worked out for all of us," said Adam. "I'm even slowly starting to warm up to him myself."

Anne smiled and linked her arm in Adam's. "I'm glad," she said. "Cedric will never take Dad's place, but as my biological father and your father's best friend, I want us to have a good relationship with him. He's always been kind to me, despite his cantankerous ways, and your father loved him enough to forgive him, so I want him to feel like part of the family."

"I want whatever you want," Adam replied, "and our children should know at least one grandfather and one grandmother."

"Plus your grandmother," said Anne. "A great-grandmother is nice to know also."

Once they were back at the motel, Anne made a long distance call to Delaney Castle while Adam went to brush his teeth. After a minute, the housekeeper had put her on the phone with Adam's mother.

"Did you have a safe trip?" Mary asked.

"Yes, we're fine," Anne replied. "The drive through the chunnel was a bit unnerving—I don't think I'll ever get used to it—but Adam was right that it was perfectly safe, and if we had flown as I wanted, we wouldn't have had such a nice drive through the French countryside, which is just so beautiful at this time of the year."

"I don't know how I let the two of you go to France without me," Mary said. "I've always wanted to spend a romantic evening in Paris. Only, now that the only man I ever truly loved is gone, I don't know that I'll ever have that experience."

For a moment, Anne thought how nice it would be if her father and Adam's mother would fall in love, but somehow, Cedric did not seem like the type to fall in love, least of all with Mary since he had not approved of Bram's brief relationship with her. In fact, Anne still had a hard time imagining how Cedric and her mother had ever managed to get together—she could not imagine why any woman would choose him over Bram, but then, her mother had died when she was born, so she had never known her well enough to speculate on her choice.

"How are the boys?" Anne asked her mother-in-law.

"Oh, they're fine," said Mary. "They've been sleeping peacefully for hours."

"I wish they would do that for me," Anne replied.

"Oh, they will in time," said Mary. "They're only going on five months right now, but before you know it, they'll be twenty years old and you'll wish they were still babies. I can't tell you how much I regret not being part of Adam's life while he was growing up. Trust me; the day will come when you'll wish they still needed you."

"I know," said Anne. "I can't believe how old they are already. It seems like just yesterday I met Adam, and other than losing Dad, I never thought my life could become so perfect so quickly."

"Mine either, dear," Mary said. "I'm so glad I came back into Adam's life; I just wish I had gotten to see Bram again before he passed, but I'm so happy that you and Adam can now have what his father and I never did."

"And I think we're blessed to have you and Elizabeth in our lives," Anne replied. "I wish I could have known Adam's grandfather too."

"He would have loved you, dear, and your boys, but everything works out for the best in the long run."

"I know it does," said Anne, catching Adam winking at her from the bathroom with his toothbrush in his mouth. "Well, I better go. Adam keeps reminding me that it's our honeymoon."

"Give him my love. I don't expect him to talk to his mother on his honeymoon."

"We love you," Anne said. "Thank you for being there for us."

"My pleasure," said Mary before hanging up the phone.

"How are Lance and Tristan?" Adam asked, coming out of the bathroom. "I still love their names. I just love saying them. Lance and Tristan Delaney."

"They're fine," said Anne, digging in her suitcase with her back to him. "They were sleeping."

"When we get home," said Adam, "we'll have to buy a toy Round Table for the boys."

"You're never going to let up on me for choosing those names, are you?" laughed Anne.

"No," Adam replied, going up to her. While in the bathroom, he had taken off his shirt—all the better to seduce her. As he wrapped his naked arms around her, she gave into their protective masculine strength.

"But I'm sure," she said, "that their father will prove tonight that he's worthy of siring two Knights of the Round Table."

"I'll see what I can do," he replied as she turned around to press her lips to his.

After a few lingering kisses, Adam reached over to turn off the light.

"I was going to take a shower first," Anne said.

"Sounds like a plan for both of us," said Adam, taking her hand and leading her into the bathroom.

Adam could not remember ever having been so happy. Anne made him feel like more than a man, like a god, and she could put Aphrodite to shame as far as he was concerned. He had always thought love such a cliché until he had met her. As they stood together in the shower, he washing her back, he could not believe the curve of her neck, the beauty of her shoulders, the softness of her skin, and words completely failed when she turned around to let him view her from the front. Then it was all he could do to stay calm as they turned off the water and toweled each other off before retiring to the bed.

He had felt so much eagerness all day to be alone with her, but now, instead of feeling rushed, their lovemaking was long and gentle, not so much passionate as endearing and even spiritual. Adam had never dreamt he could feel so good for such a long time. Half the night seemed to pass before he finally could wait no longer to take her, feeling as if he had finally connected with the other half of his soul.

In ecstasy, Anne clutched his back, moaning with pleasure....

They had reached the very height of pleasure. Adam felt as if he could never again know such bliss.

And then Anne screamed out:

"Raymond!"

Immediately, Adam stopped, his deep longing instantly quenched.

"Raymond?" he exclaimed. "Who the hell is Raymond?" He pulled back, startled by the sudden jealousy surging through him.

"I—I don't know," said Anne, completely confused. "Oh, honey, it's nothing. I don't even know where that name came from. Oh, don't be angry. I love you. I don't think I've ever even met a Raymond in my entire life."

But Adam pushed himself back on the bed, feeling uncertain, a bit hurt, even a little angry, although he tried to control the anger.

"Is he an old boyfriend?" Adam asked. "Because it's pretty sad when I'm on my honeymoon and my wife fantasizes about an old boyfriend." He could hear his voice trembling, his anger suppressing a tear he felt trying to escape from his eye.

"No, I swear," said Anne. "I've never even known anyone named Raymond. It's just...it's weird. You wouldn't believe me if I told you."

"Believe what?" he asked, sitting back on the bed, staring at her, trying to stay calm as he reminded himself that they had two adorable twin boys.

"It's just, well, for a moment," said Anne, searching for the right words, "when you looked at me, just before I cried out, you...it was like you had a different face, and—"

"Well, it's dark in here, after all..." said Adam, feeling confused.

"No, I could see your face clearly, but it was like you had a beard like Ray...like someone named Raymond had. This sounds crazy, but... it was like you were someone I knew in another life or something."

"You're starting to freak me out now," said Adam, moving to his side of the bed and pulling the sheet over himself. Anne was hurt by his withdrawal; she longed to reach out toward him, but she feared he would push her away.

"Adam, I...please believe me. I love only you. Don't make a big deal out of this."

"What am I supposed to think?" he asked; it was on the tip of his tongue to remark how her mother had cheated on his father, but he held back, trying to give her the benefit of the doubt, although he felt their honeymoon had been ruined....

"Adam," she pled, "it's as if for just a minute I wasn't myself any longer—like I was inhabiting someone else's body and seeing things through her eyes. Please believe me; I don't know how else to explain it. It was like I was in a movie, watching someone else making love, but only—"

Suddenly, Adam's body language changed. "What do you mean?" he asked, turning toward her, his eyes looking straight into hers. "What do you mean, like watching a movie?"

"It was such a...there aren't words to explain it," Anne stumbled, "but I had such a weird feeling, maybe like déjà-vu. I just felt as if…." But she felt lost for words; she turned her eyes down, disturbed by how Adam's eyes were probing her, not with anger but intense curiosity. And then after a moment, she said, looking at him again. "Maybe, do you think…well, maybe that the motel could be haunted?"

"Haunted?"

"Yes, like bewitched, like a ghost is playing with us somehow?"

"Do you feel frightened?" he asked, sliding over to put his arm around her. "Do you feel something is trying to hurt you?"

"No, no, I felt.... I was in your arms and I felt great joy, even when I saw Raymond's face—that sounds so weird—but I felt as if I were glad to see him.... I just don't know how to explain it."

"I suppose it could be a ghost," he said, staring into her eyes, wondering whether….

"Don't stare at me as if I'm crazy," she said. "I swear I wasn't thinking of someone else. I don't know anyone named Raymond, and there isn't any man in this world I would rather be with."

He brushed the hair out of her eyes, seeing how his behavior was hurting her.

"I believe you," he said, at least half-meaning it.

"You do?" she asked, her eyes pleading.

He wanted to believe her. To relieve her fears, he kissed her.

"Yes," he said. "We don't know what our minds are capable of, and who's to say we haven't been reincarnated, or maybe we have memories of ancestors, or—"

"That could be it," said Anne. "I don't really think it was a ghost. It felt instead like suddenly I was living a long time ago, maybe a thousand years ago, and I was inside a castle or some ancient building."

The more Anne said, the more Adam did believe her. He felt

frightened to believe her, but at the same time, he was relieved; for just a second, he almost told her about his dream of Camelot from a year ago, but then she said, "I need to use the bathroom; to splash some water on my face or something, and then I hope you'll want to try again."

"You can count on that," he laughed awkwardly as she got up from the bed.

It took Adam a minute to shake off the strange feelings of anger and confusion—to wonder whether she had just had a similar experience to what he'd had a year ago—it had been at the solstice then too; could Anne's experience be a coincidence? Was it really similar to his? Adam didn't remember anyone named Raymond in the Arthurian legend. And Adam thought that if he did resemble this Raymond, why did no one in his dream of King Arthur resemble Anne? It was all very strange, but if Anne had experienced something similar to his own dream—and Adam found, no matter how he tried to argue otherwise with himself, that he did believe in his dream—then what Anne had said must also be true.

But he would think about it later. When Anne came back out of the bathroom, they both admitted they were too tired to do more than cuddle. Adam still felt some resentment, but by the time he fell asleep, he had forgiven her. He knew in his heart she would never betray him, but if she ever called out that name again....

CHAPTER 3

MELUSINE

ADAM AND ANNE slept late, then made love again in the morning, any discomfort from last night's incident all but forgotten.

As they finished a late breakfast at the nearby restaurant, Anne said she would like to visit the town's museum.

"I thought we'd take a drive to the nearby winery," Adam objected.

"Oh, we can do that too," said Anne.

"But museums can be so dull," said Adam. "Devin has dragged me through so many of them over the years."

"I know, but this one doesn't look very big," Anne replied. "We won't stay long—just half an hour—and then we can go for a ride through the countryside. I'd just like to know a little bit about this place. As I said, I'm not sure why, but I just feel such an attraction to it."

"All right," said Adam, thinking it better she was attracted to a place than another man, "but then we're going to go find a romantic winery and a little café where we can have lunch."

"We just ate," laughed Anne.

"Well, I need to keep up my strength."

"Trust me, honey," said Anne, patting his arm, "you don't need to work on that. You have more stamina than anyone I know."

Adam grinned, feeling a bit foolish, but pleased nevertheless. He could barely keep his hands off her now that they were alone and away from the stress of everything back in England that they had dealt with for the last year.

As they approached the museum, it looked more like a tourism office, but a sign in front of the building did say there was an exhibit.

"Maybe they'll have a brochure for the nearest winery," said Adam, looking around.

"I didn't know you even liked wine," Anne replied.

"Visiting a winery just sounds like something romantic to do, and I'm all about romance," Adam said.

"Well, you know you don't need to get me drunk to get me in bed," Anne laughed. "I'm all yours."

"I know, but I want to romance you to show you how much I appreciate you," said Adam as he opened the museum's door.

The building turned out to be empty of people other than a man behind the front desk.

"*Bonjour,*" the museum guide greeted them.

"*Bonjour,*" Anne and Adam replied.

"Ah, Americans," he smiled.

"*Non, Anglais,*" Anne replied. Adam was going to object that he was American, but now that he was an English earl, it didn't seem to matter that much—he wasn't going to give up his U.S. citizenship, but other than that, he might as well be English. His wife and children were British citizens after all.

"What brings you to Lusignan?" the guide asked in English, for which Adam was grateful.

"I passed through this area last year," said Anne, "and I just thought the town was so charming that I wanted to come back and see it in more detail."

"Ah," said the man, "then you are not here because of Melusine?"

"I'm sorry," Anne replied, feeling confused, "but I guess not since I don't know what '*melusine*' means in French."

"It does not mean anything in French," said the guide. "Melusine is a person, or rather, *le f*ée." And the man held up a brochure on the counter that depicted a woman in medieval dress with wings sprouting out of her back.

Anne shook her head, not knowing who this odd looking creature was.

"I'm afraid I never heard of her," she admitted.

"Where are you staying?" asked the guide.

Adam let Anne reply since her French was far superior to his.

"At *Le Motel de la Fée*," she said, pronouncing the motel name perfectly.

"Ah," he replied, perhaps sensing Adam's French was not good and continuing in English. "And do you know why the motel has such a name?"

"No, actually, I was wondering that," Anne replied.

"Did you notice the street names when you were out walking?"

"Um, no, not particularly."

"Perhaps, however, you noticed there is a *Rue de la Fée Melusine*."

"Oh," said Anne. "I think I did see that. So Melusine must have been some sort of local fairy back in medieval times, then?"

"Yes, but not just any fairy—she is the greatest fairy in the history of France, perhaps in all the world."

"Strange," said Anne, again looking at the picture, "I don't think I ever heard of her, and yet she seems strangely familiar."

"She was the founder of Lusignan," the guide continued. "Our town grew up around the great castle she built here, but it was torn down eventually; it stood where the park is. We also have a *Rue Raymondin*, named for her husband."

"What's the name of the rue again?" Adam asked, stunned by the name.

"*Rue Raymondin*," the man replied. Before Adam could ask whether *Raymondin* was the same name as Raymond in English, another gentleman entered the building, diverting the man's attention. "*Excusez-moi*," the guide apologized before turning to the newcomer.

"Oh look, Adam," said Anne, pulling him toward the exhibit. "All of this is about Melusine."

Adam looked at the exhibit, but his eyes quickly glazed over since everything was written in French. He did pay attention, however, to the medieval illustrations of Melusine, one showing her with dragon-like wings, and another depicting her in a tub of water with a mermaid tail and showing no sign of modesty. But he was more interested in her husband being named Raymond—it sounded like Raymond anyway, despite the French pronunciation. That Anne had called out that name last night while they were making love now made Adam shiver. What could it mean? Why had Anne seen a vision of this fairy's husband?

"Oh, you're just being paranoid," he told himself. "It was probably just something subconscious; she saw the Raymond street name out of the corner of her eye when we were walking around the town last night, and it came out on some subconscious level—it was her brain trying to process it when she was in a transformed state—of ecstasy, but that's still transformed, kind of like sleep. Anyway, it means nothing." He wanted to believe he was being foolish to think it could be something more, but because his dream of Camelot had seemed so real, real to the point where he had felt he was practically in King Arthur's mind, he felt unsure.

"Hmm," said Anne, as she finished reading about Melusine in French. "That's all really interesting."

"Is it?" asked Adam. "Why, if she were a fairy, did she have a mermaid tail?"

"Well, from what I can figure out—I guess my French isn't as good as I thought," said Anne, "but I guess she was a fairy and her husband didn't know it. Then one day he found out the truth, and she turned into a serpent-like woman and flew away. It isn't a story with much detail really—maybe there's more to it, but it seems kind of fragmented—and silly, actually."

Anne walked away to look at the tourist brochures while Adam continued to look at the picture of Melusine. He couldn't help noticing how closely her womanly figure resembled Anne's.

"Oh, look, Adam!" exclaimed Anne, calling away his attention. "Here's information about a local winery."

She said it a bit too enthusiastically, enough to make Adam realize something was disturbing her. He suspected she had read something upsetting about Melusine's story that she wasn't telling him. He wished he could ask the museum guide more about this mermaid fairy or whatever she was, but the man was busy waiting on the other gentleman, and Adam also sensed that to discuss Melusine further might somehow upset Anne.

"Let's get going," Anne said, stuffing the brochures into her purse before Adam could think what to do next. The whole thing was silly anyway, Adam told himself. Who had ever heard of Melusine? What a ridiculous name. Her legend surely wasn't as well-known as King Arthur's.

"Adam, are you ready?" Anne asked, looking anxious to leave.

"Sure, if you are," he said, following her outside and then quietly walking beside her down the street to their motel and car.

"So where are we off to?" asked Adam as they climbed into the Porsche.

Anne pulled out the brochures she had collected at the museum. Adam had only seen her take the one for the winery, but now he noticed she had also taken the one about Melusine that the guide had first shown her.

Anne quickly stuffed the Melusine brochure into her purse, and then after spending a minute looking at the brochure for the winery, she gave Adam directions for how to reach it.

"Isn't the view marvelous?" she said as they left behind Lusignan. "I wouldn't mind living in a charming little town like this in the French countryside."

"We already live in a charming little town in the English countryside," Adam replied.

"Well, yes, but in a giant mansion," said Anne. "We could just buy a quaint little cottage somewhere around here."

"What does it matter how big our house is?" Adam laughed. "We don't have to clean it."

"You're right, and we are providing jobs for a lot of people with the estate and the tours," said Anne. "I know we're lucky, but it's a lot of responsibility too. Sometimes I think I wouldn't mind living in a quiet little cottage in the forest with my handsome woodcutter husband."

"Who do you think you are, Snow White?" Adam laughed.

"Oh, I don't know...Snow White was a princess after all," said Anne. "I'm just a countess, but then, the fairy Melusine was also a countess, and she met her husband, Count Raimond, in the forest."

Adam found that comment disturbing; again, he had a flashback to his memories of King Arthur, but he tried to laugh off Anne's remark by saying, "I wouldn't be surprised if you were a fairy. You've certainly cast your spell over me."

"And I plan to bewitch you some more tonight," said Anne.

That was fine with Adam...so long as she remembered his name.

As they continued driving, Anne wouldn't let up on the cottage idea. All the way to the winery, she kept joking about how she could be like Marie Antoinette, building a little hamlet for herself where she could play at being a milkmaid. "We should go to Versailles while we're here in France," she suggested, "to see the hamlet there. You might find that you'd like me as a milkmaid."

"It's fine for a queen to play at being a milkmaid," said Adam, "but my wife is a countess, and countesses are definitely too wise to play milkmaid. They should do something more romantic, like pose for paintings."

"And I suppose you'll be the painter?" Anne asked.

"You guessed it," said Adam, grinning, "and my favorite subject is the female nude."

"You're terrible," she laughed. "Whatever happened to you? You were a nice, conservative young man when I met you."

"That was before you seduced and corrupted me," he said. "Now you've spoiled me, so I will never fall out of love with your body...or you."

He leaned over to kiss her quickly. For a moment, his head blocked her view, but when he pulled back, Anne had time to exclaim, "Watch the road!"

Adam turned the steering wheel in time to avoid hitting a rabbit on the run.

"Oh, the poor thing," said Anne, relieved they had not hit it. "It must be terrible to be a little bunny and always so scared of the rest of the world."

But Adam was thinking that rabbits probably didn't have as many worries as he did, and after all, weren't rabbits famous for copulating? Being a rabbit wouldn't be so bad.

"So how far is it to the winery?" Adam asked.

"Just about an hour. I'll tell you where to turn," said Anne. "What a treat to have nothing more pressing to do than drive around and visit a winery."

"I can't think of a better thing to do," said Adam. "We deserve to enjoy ourselves, and there's no one I would rather spend time with."

Anne squeezed his leg. "I'm looking forward to us enjoying the rest of our lives together; I'm sure the worst is behind us now."

"I hope so," said Adam. "I'm sure there will be dark days now and then, but on this vacation, we can just relax and be free from all our worries."

Their conversation shifted to their dreams for the future. As they continued driving toward the winery, Anne talked about rooms of the castle she wanted to redecorate and what they would do to entertain Devin when he came to visit, and whether they could convince Adam's mother and grandmother to extend their visit in England. As far as Adam was concerned, his family had no reason to stay in the United States, but his grandmother, Elizabeth Morgan, insisted she didn't want to leave her home where she had so many memories of her late husband, and Adam's mother, Mary, felt she should stay close to her mother now that she was getting older. As for Adam's cousin, Devin, he was halfway through an M.A. program in the States, but Adam hoped to convince him to come to England to continue his studies for his Ph.D.

"It's hard to believe my life is in England now," Adam said. "Not much more than a year ago, I thought I was going to have a business career in New York, and now I have more money than I probably would have made in a lifetime working there, not to mention all these companies and organizations that want me on their boards to fill Dad's shoes—something I feel I can never do—and then all these investments to keep track of, as well as the various houses we own. I'm still trying to remember all their names and locations."

"You know, Dad relied on Uncle Cedric for so much of that," said Anne, who still couldn't get used to referring to Cedric as her father. "I'm sure he'll keep helping you with everything."

"He's been very helpful," said Adam. "I know he wasn't too fond of me at first, but we all seem to be getting along now."

"My life is more perfect now than I ever could have imagined it," Anne confessed. "I think for the first time in years, there's nothing I consciously feel I'm lacking or wanting."

"I hope you'll always be content," said Adam, "but we always need something to want or strive toward or life would become stagnant."

As he spoke, Adam thought how life always changes, and again, he thought about what Merlin had predicted for his family's future— their role in bringing about King Arthur's return in some way—and he suspected that meant it could not possibly be a coincidence that he had seen Merlin yesterday.

"Turn left here," said Anne as they came to a bend in the road. "The winery should be just a few more miles."

Adam did as she directed. Soon they were touring the winery as the noon hour approached. They were actually taken by the tour guide out into the vineyard itself where they could smell the grapes and the fragrances of early summer all around them. Then they went to the tasting room to try the various vintages before they came away with far more bottles of wine than they needed and an appetite for lunch.

They quickly found a nearby café and had a huge but long and relaxing meal, complete with French pastries for dessert. But Adam passed on drinking more wine since he was driving.

"Now where should we go?" he asked when they got back into their vehicle. "Should we go look for a chateau or some other place to tour?"

"Oh, no, I don't want to be around crowds of people," said Anne. "It's such a beautiful day. Let's just drive around. Who knows what we might stumble upon, and I just like feeling the wind in my hair and being alone with you."

"Good enough," said Adam, putting down the convertible roof before they headed out to explore the French countryside.

The scenery was beautiful, although they scarcely paid attention to where they were or where they were going. It was late June, so everything was green and lush and warm. If England were a garden, France felt to them like a long picnic among the rosebushes.

Eventually, they saw a sign telling them they had entered Vendée, which was a province or a county—they weren't quite sure which, not being overly familiar with how France distinguished its various regions.

"I hope we're not lost," said Adam. "I don't want to get too far from our motel and have to find my way back in the dark."

"We can just check into a hotel somewhere else then," said Anne. "It would be kind of exciting—spontaneous."

"That's true," said Adam, "as long as I get to be with my beautiful wife tonight."

"Don't worry about that," said Anne.

Soon after, another road sign told them they were heading into a village named Vouvant, and since it was now late afternoon, when they would usually be having tea back home, Anne suggested they stop and have a snack.

"This isn't England, you know," said Adam. "The French aren't going to concede to your teatime ritual. And we already had a big lunch."

"It's such a charming village, though," said Anne. "It wouldn't hurt for us to walk around a bit. We can't be more than two hours from Lusignan. And I want to enjoy all the French pastries I can while we're here. We can have tea and a pastry, look around for an hour, and still drive back to the motel in time for a late supper."

"Your wish is my command, milady," Adam replied, driving into the village and looking for somewhere to park. After a minute, he found a place to leave the car only fifty feet from a little café. In a few more minutes, they were inside having *tay* despite the French waitress' disapproving looks over their beverage choice.

The café was dark and quiet, and since it was between regular mealtimes, completely empty of customers. Adam and Anne feared they might be disturbing the employees, who certainly made them feel that way, but they talked pleasantly to each other in English anyway, ignoring the French women's irritated glances.

"It's a charming town, even if the locals don't seem to like us," said Anne.

"I imagine we're ruining their downtime," Adam replied.

"I don't care if they're irritated so long as I get to eat these delicious French pastries," said Anne. "They're far too rich for everyday tea, but when in France...."

Adam laughed. "You can't use that line because the French don't have a teatime ritual like you English."

"Like *we* English," said Anne. "I'm not going to tolerate any superior American attitude from you, Lord Delaney."

"Are you Lord Delaney?" asked the waitress, overhearing as she approached them.

"*Oui*," said Anne. "He is my husband, the Earl of Delaney."

"Oh," exclaimed the girl, suddenly no longer uppity but friendly. "I thought you looked familiar. We have read all about you in the papers, about your fabulous fairy tale romance, how you were born an American but now are a rich earl."

Adam felt overwhelmed. His marriage to Anne had made all the gossip papers in England, but he had not expected that his fame had spread to the continent.

"You are much more handsome, *monsieur*, than your picture," giggled the girl, and then she ran back into the kitchen.

In less than a minute, she was back with all the other waitresses and even the male chef, and she shoved a French magazine into Adam's face which had a whole spread about Adam and Anne, including photos of them and Delaney Castle.

"I love England," said the waitress, "and we were all very fond of Lord Delaney. He used to visit us here every now and then. He loved Vouvant."

"You mean my father, Bram Delaney?" asked Anne.

"*Oui, madame*," said an older Frenchwoman. "He told us he and his wife spent their honeymoon in this area."

"Dad did tell me," Anne confirmed to Adam, "that he and my mother spent time in the French countryside on their honeymoon."

"I remember your mother; she was a beautiful lady," said the older woman. "You are the spitting image of her, your ladyship."

"Thank you," said Anne, astonished to meet people in this remote place who had known her parents.

"Oh, yes," continued the woman, "we were heartbroken when we heard she had died; she was such a beautiful lady, and we were always glad to see his lordship when he would be in the area. We were so sad to hear he had passed away."

Adam and Anne did not know what to say to such an outpouring of appreciation for Bram and Anne's mother; they found it hard to believe they had even stumbled upon a town their parents had once visited.

"Please, what attracted my parents to this place originally? Do you know?" asked Anne of the older woman. "I had no idea they had ever been here."

"My cooking!" exclaimed the male chef.

But only Adam laughed while the rest ignored him. The woman explained, "Your father thought the town beautiful, and he was always interested in history and local legends. He used to come to see the Tour Melusine, and sometimes he would stay here and use it as his central place to visit other areas like Brittany and Tours."

For a second, Adam felt troubled—what was this Tour Melusine? But Anne, as if reading his mind, changed the subject by saying, "Thank you for making us feel so welcome. I'm so happy we happened to stop here."

A few more pleasantries were exchanged, and then Adam and Anne left the restaurant. The staff's French accents had made their English a bit hard to understand, so Anne had talked to them mostly in French, which had left Adam clueless about much that was said, but he was not completely surprised when, upon leaving the restaurant, Anne said, "Adam, I want to go find this Tour Melusine."

"What is it?" he asked. "I mean—is it like a bus tour of places associated with Melusine?"

"No," said Anne. "*Tour* is French for 'tower.' The café owner—the older Frenchwoman who remembered my mother—she told me how to get there."

"All right," said Adam, "but we should head back soon so we get back to the motel and restaurant before suppertime."

"We will," said Anne.

It didn't take long to reach the Tour Melusine. In a few minutes, they were standing before the ruin of a castle whose only remnant was the old watchtower.

"The woman at the restaurant said Melusine built this tower just like she did the castle of Lusignan," said Anne. "She was a fairy, you know, so it must have been built by magic."

Adam recalled how last year in the ruins of Delaney Castle they had discovered the medieval manuscript that claimed the Delaneys were descended from King Arthur. Now he wondered what strange incident this castle's ruins might bring about for them. He felt rather resistant to explore it; he just wanted to enjoy his time with his wife, not explore history's mysteries.

"There's Melusine," said Anne, pointing up to something resembling a weather vane, a metal figure sticking out of the tower roof. "Can you see her serpent tail?"

"I thought Melusine looked more like a mermaid," said Adam, observing the strange metal statue.

"Well, her wings are more like a serpent or a dragon's," said Anne. "If only we could find out the truth about who or what she was."

"This tower isn't much in the way of ruins," said Adam, not liking the serious tone in Anne's voice; she seemed more interested in this Melusine character than she should be; for some reason, he found it disturbing—he had a flashback to the Raymond incident of the night before. "I think the ruins at Delaney Castle are far more impressive," he said dismissively.

"Only because you're so obsessed with King Arthur," Anne laughed, taking his hand and pulling him toward the building.

"Obsessed with King Arthur?" he muttered, wondering why she would say such a thing when he had avoided mentioning King Arthur for the last year. And she had been the one to suggest naming the boys Tristan and Lance; he had been stunned by the suggestion, feeling it was somehow a partial fulfillment of Merlin's prophecy, but he had remained silent about saying more, knowing if he objected to the boys' names, Anne would suspect something.

Melusine's Tower looked to be about four stories high with a steep staircase to the second floor. Inside were vaulted ceilings but nothing much to see. Adam and Anne were able to walk all the way to the top floor, and then they looked out upon the countryside.

"Wouldn't you just love to be a fair damsel, looking out from this tower to wait for your knight errant to come?" Anne asked.

"No," said Adam.

"No?"

"No. I'd rather be the knight errant, on my way home after having slain a dragon, and bringing back with me dragon steaks for the damsel to cook for supper."

"Whatever," laughed Anne, having picked up on Adam's American slang. She was silent a moment and then said, "I don't know why, but it feels so peaceful here. I feel so content, almost like I belong here."

"I don't know why either," said Adam. "This tower is nothing special compared to our castle back home."

"Maybe it's just because we're in France and it's our honeymoon so it seems romantic. But then, neither do I know of any towers back in

England that were built by a fairy."

"They claim Merlin built Stonehenge," said Adam.

"That's not quite the same thing," Anne replied.

Adam patiently waited another minute as Anne looked out at the countryside before she said she was ready to descend back to firm ground. Then they walked around to the tower's other side. Anne kept stopping to look at the walls, and finally, she insisted Adam take her photo in front of it.

"This tower just doesn't do anything for you, does it?" she asked once the photo was taken.

"No," he admitted. "I find it kind of creepy, all those old stones falling apart and it standing here all solitary in this park."

"But you have to imagine what it was like when it was an entire castle," said Anne. "That's what makes it romantic."

"I guess my imagination just isn't that good," said Adam.

"I don't believe that," Anne smirked. "You must be getting tired or hungry or something. After all, you only ate one pastry at tea while I had two."

"I've gained a few extra pounds since we got married. I don't want to gain more."

"That's from the stress of settling the inheritance and title and everything," said Anne. "And you're not twenty anymore. You just need to get back into an exercise routine. We'll do that together when we get home. I could lose a little of the baby fat from the pregnancy myself."

"It's a deal," said Adam, "but let's head back now so we reach the motel and restaurant before it gets too crowded for supper."

"All right," said Anne, wrapping her arm around his waist and letting him lead her away from the tower. Adam was glad to leave, feeling rather creeped out by the building, as if Melusine might be perched on its roof and watching them.

On the drive back to the motel, Anne read the brochures she had picked up that morning.

"I wonder how much of it is true," she said after a while.

"What?" Adam asked.

"The legend of Melusine—she couldn't really have been part mermaid or serpent."

"No, I suppose not," said Adam. "She probably just had a bad skin condition or something that made her skin look like fish scales."

"Oh, I hope not," said Anne. "That would be the lamest thing to inspire a great legend."

By now, Adam's stomach was growling again.

"All I know," he said, "is she better stay away if she knows what's good for her because I'm in the mood for a big plate of fish."

Anne rolled her eyes, but she couldn't help laughing, and she put her hand in his as they drove the last few miles to Lusignan.

CHAPTER 4

THE CREEP

"I'M EXHAUSTED," ANNE said as she and Adam finished dinner at the restaurant adjacent to the motel. After a minute of discussion, they decided to return to their room and call it an early night. Soon Anne was in the bathroom washing her hair, but Adam was feeling restless.

"I'm going to go have a drink at the bar," said Adam, standing in the bathroom doorway, "and give Devin a call, and then I'll be back."

"Okay," said Anne, lifting her head from the sink to look at him. "Don't be long. I was hoping to get some cuddling time in for myself before I give you what you want."

Her smile was so bold and brilliant that for a moment, Adam felt complete happiness, as if he had not a care in the world; it was a feeling of relief he had not felt all day as the strange story of Melusine nagged at him.

"I promise you'll get all the cuddling you want," Adam replied. "I just thought Devin would get a kick out of hearing about the places we saw today."

Adam only had to step over to give Anne a kiss on the lips to feel himself becoming aroused. "I won't be long," he promised. "You know how I love the smell of your hair after you wash it."

"You love the smell of the strawberry shampoo, not my hair," she laughed, pushing him away.

As Adam left the room, he told himself he had been worrying over nothing. Everything in his life was perfect; this Melusine stuff was unnerving him for no reason—her legend was famous all over this part of France, just like King Arthur's legend was all over England; that they kept bumping into places associated with Melusine was just a coincidence...but the connections to King Arthur that he had experienced in England hadn't been coincidences, had they? And Arthur's story was far more popular than Melusine's. And he had seen Merle—he was convinced about that—but they hadn't seen him at all since they first arrived, so maybe that was just a coincidence, too. Besides, the wizard could have plenty of other reasons for being in Lusignan.

Adam had planned to go down to the bar and call Devin from a quiet corner, but his nervous thoughts now made him desire privacy, so he went out to the Porsche, put up the convertible roof, and then sat inside the car and took out Anne's cell phone. He still wasn't used to this new technology, but he had more money than he knew what to do with now, and Anne had told him that having a cell phone would be convenient for her when she went up to London without him, so he had bought her one for her last birthday and occasionally used it himself.

After dismissing the thought that he should look through Anne's contacts on the phone to see whether she had any old boyfriends named Raymond listed, Adam took a deep breath and dialed Devin's number.

Devin was Adam's best friend and his cousin. They had grown up together, raised in the same house by their grandparents. They had supported one another through everything, and Devin had helped Adam locate Bram once he knew his identity. Soon after, Devin had followed Adam to England to be there for him through his father's illness. And even though Devin now was back in the States, they still spoke on the phone every few days and continually emailed one another. Plus, Devin had been the only one Adam had told about his strange dream of King Arthur, so now he thought perhaps Devin would be able to give him advice about this odd Melusine situation.

"Hello?" Devin answered on the second ring.

Adam felt more nervous upon hearing his cousin's voice. He didn't know how to begin to say what was consuming his thoughts.

"Hello?" Devin repeated.

"Devin, it's Adam."

"Hey, how are you?" asked Devin, obviously pleased. "I didn't expect to hear from you. I thought you were on your honeymoon."

"We are," said Adam.

"Taking a break then from all the sex?" Devin laughed.

"Yeah, something like that," said Adam. "Actually, I just called to tell you about some of the cool places we've visited. It seems like there's history everywhere in France just like in England. And you being the expert on all things medieval, I thought you'd like to know about some of it."

"Sure," Devin laughed. "I'd have gone on that honeymoon to France with you if you'd have let me."

"Well, maybe when you come to visit next month, we can run over to France for a little while."

"Yeah, but you'll have already been and…well, okay. I keep forgetting you're filthy rich now so you can afford to go anywhere you want."

"Yes, I keep forgetting that myself," said Adam, "but anyway, we're staying in this little town called Lusignan, and it has this really weird legend, so I was wondering if you knew anything about it."

"Lusignan?" Devin repeated. "Then you must mean the legend of Melusine."

"You mean you actually know about her?"

"Oh, sure," said Devin. "Everyone interested in the Middle Ages knows something about Melusine. She was the alleged ancestress of half the royal and noble houses of Europe; they all wanted to claim they were descended from her."

"Really?" said Adam. "Why? I mean, she was some sort of half-serpent or something."

"Well, she was actually a fairy, or rather a half-fairy," said Devin. "Her father was human."

"Yeah, I don't understand that," Adam replied. "I've only picked up bits and pieces of the story since everything is in French around here. I think Anne understands it, but can you tell me about the whole thing? I'm trying to make sense out of it."

"Sure, but why don't you just have Anne explain it to you?" asked Devin.

"She's busy washing her hair right now, and I have better things to do with her when she's finished than hear about an old legend."

Devin laughed. "All right, well, here are the basics: There was a woman, or more likely she was a fairy, named Pressyne, and she married Elynas, the King of Albany, which is an old name for Scotland. Pressyne made Elynas promise that he would never interrupt her or enter the room when she was giving birth to her children, or maybe it was feeding her children—it might have been both; it probably depended on which version of the legend it was—I can't quite remember. Anyway, whichever it was, he agreed to the promise, but Elynas had a son from an earlier marriage and this son convinced him to break his oath, so Elynas entered the room soon after Pressyne had given birth to three girls—I guess they were triplets. Their names were Melusine, Melior, and Palatyne. Pressyne was furious when Elynas broke his promise so she immediately left with her children and took them to the Isle of Avalon to be raised."

"Avalon!" exclaimed Adam.

"Yes, Avalon," said Devin.

"King Arthur's Avalon?" Adam asked.

"I guess so. The romancers probably just stole the name from the Arthurian legend, but anyway, the three girls were raised in Avalon. Then when they were grown, Pressyne told them about their father and how he had betrayed her trust. The girls were so angry that they decided to get revenge on him for their mother. They went to Albany and used their fairy powers, at least that's how I assume they pulled it off, to—"

"Wait," Adam interrupted. "They had magic powers?"

"Yes, I assume so since they grew up in Avalon and because of what happened next," said Devin. "They went to Albany, and they trapped their father in a cave by rolling a giant stone over it. When their mother found out what they had done, she was so furious that she cursed each of the girls. Melusine was made to turn into a serpent every Saturday from the waist down. I forget exactly what the other punishments were, but one of the girls, I think, had to guard a cave, and the other had to watch over a hawk, or something like that. I believe there are also elaborate stories attached to both of the sisters, but neither of them had any children that I know of so Melusine is the one who usually gets the attention."

"But what does Melusine have to do with Lusignan?" Adam asked.

"Well, Melusine was cursed as I said, but the curse could be lifted if she won the love of a man who would promise never to see her on Saturdays when she transformed into a serpent or mermaid—it's kind of like a repeat of the earlier story about her father and mother really. Anyway, she became something like the water fairy of a fountain in the forest near Lusignan. One day, this young nobleman named Raimond was out hunting and got lost. When he came to the fountain, he saw Melusine there and instantly fell in love with her. I think there are more details than that about their courtship, but I don't remember all of them; it's been a while since I read the story."

"That's okay," said Adam. "So what happened next?"

"Well, Melusine agreed to marry Raimond on condition that he would never see her on a Saturday because that was the day she turned into a serpent from the waist down—sometimes she is depicted to look more like a mermaid, but I think she was really a serpent because later in the story, she's able to fly like a dragon. Anyway, they got married and Melusine used her fairy powers to build all kinds of castles including the one at Lusignan which was the biggest in France—I doubt anyone named Melusine lived or really built it, but because it was so big, it was attributed to her fairy powers."

"Yeah," Adam confirmed, "the man at the museum told us it was pulled down and stood where the park is now. But did Raimond know Melusine was a fairy?" Adam asked.

"No," said Devin, "but he must have wondered. I imagine she had workers to build the castles so no one got too suspicious, but she must have at least made the process go smoother and faster. Anyway,

Melusine and Raimond were very happy for many years, and they had a whole bunch of children, but every child that was born had some sort of birth defect; I think one had warts with hair growing out of them, and another had a third eye, and they even had a son named Horrible, if you can imagine that. He was so horrible that I think he killed his nursemaid when he was just a boy, so Melusine had him destroyed because she feared he would grow up to be a monster."

"That's twisted," said Adam.

"Yeah, well, the rest of the kids, other than the weird blemishes, all grew up to be great knights and kings. Most of the medieval royalty of Europe would later claim to be descended from them, although I never really understood why they would want to when the children were deformed. The most famous child was named Geoffrey Great-Tooth because he had a tooth like a boar's. He was a great warrior and a killer of giants, but he had a brother—I forget the brother's name—who became a monk, and for some reason, Geoffrey was so furious about his brother becoming a monk that he burned down a monastery and his brother died in the fire."

"Wow, he had some issues," Adam laughed.

"Just before that happened," Devin continued, "Raimond's cousin told him he thought Melusine must be committing adultery on the Saturday nights when Raimond wasn't allowed to see her. Raimond grew so suspicious that he broke his promise and entered the room where Melusine locked herself up every Saturday. And when he entered the room, he saw her with her serpent's tail. I can't remember whether he told Melusine he had seen her or whether she knew he had seen her, but you can imagine he was surprised by what he saw. But he also felt horrible because he loved his wife so much and he had broken his promise so he didn't tell anyone what he had seen.

"But after Geoffrey killed his brother by burning down the monastery, Raimond was so upset that he blamed Melusine for the incident by calling her a 'serpent' and claiming she was the reason why their children had turned out to be such monsters. Melusine was heartbroken by Raimond's betrayal and told him she could no longer stay with him. She gave him two golden rings and then she flew out the castle window and was last seen flying through the air, her serpent tail trailing behind her."

"That's sad," said Adam. "I kind of feel sorry for her."

"She then became a sort of family ghost," Devin continued. "After that, it was said that whenever the Lord of Lusignan was about to die or the castle was to change hands, she could be heard crying and be seen flying around the castle tower until the castle was finally torn down, I think sometime in the 1500s."

"What a crazy story," said Adam. "So why would anyone want to be descended from Melusine if she were some sort of weird serpent woman?"

"That I can't say," said Devin. "A lot of people think it's because she had fairy blood in her, which somehow made her powerful or gave her some sort of special bloodline people wanted to claim they belonged to. The story we have wasn't written down until the late 1300s by Jean d'Arras, but Melusine probably lived in the eighth century if she lived at all, so who knows how much of the true story was lost over the centuries? It's like the King Arthur legend in that way. If she lived at all, I suspect a lot of the story we have was embellished and the real story is mostly forgotten. People spread lies about her for whatever reason, making her out to be something she wasn't."

"But if she were a fairy—"

"Yeah, but fairies aren't real," Devin replied.

"I don't know," said Adam, only half-joking for Devin's sake. "In England, there are some people who would argue that they're real."

"Sure, it's fun to think of fairies," said Devin, "but no one has ever really seen one or can prove they exist."

Adam didn't want to argue the point; he was fine with believing fairies weren't real. That they might be real kind of creeped him out. Instead, he asked, "What was the significance of those golden rings you said Melusine gave to Raimond?"

"Oh, they meant something. I forget what. I think they were supposed to protect the wearer from being slain in battle—something along the lines of how King Arthur's scabbard protected him—typical fairy tale stuff."

"I suppose. Anything else I should know?" Adam asked, thinking Anne must be done washing her hair by now so he had better get back to the room. He was also telling himself he had been foolish to be worried. Melusine's story was just too far-fetched to be true. At least King Arthur's legend had plenty of realistic elements to it, but seriously, fairies and women who turned into serpents and deformed children who killed giants—it was just too hard to believe any of that could be relevant to him. That Anne seemed taken with this legend and that they had just happened to come to this place associated with the legend had to be a coincidence.

"No, I think I told you the basic gist of it," said Devin. "The only other thing I remember is that Raimond felt a lot of guilt over disclosing his wife's secret, so he retired to the monastery at Montserrat, which is in Spain today, but I think the country was Arragon back then, which was its own kingdom at the time. Montserrat would be a cool place for us to visit too—it was also believed to be the place where the Holy Grail was secretly kept."

"Oh," said Adam, again surprised by another connection to King Arthur. "Well, thanks, Devin. I better get going. I'll call you when I get back to England."

"Great. I'm going to buy my plane ticket this week, so I'll let you know my flight plans when I do. My summer class is ending in a few days, though, so I have to focus on studying for my final exam first."

"Okay," said Adam. "Good luck. I'm sure you'll ace it."

"Thanks," said Devin, not arguing. He was a straight A student, and although no one in the family understood why he'd want to study the medieval period, they all knew someday he would be a distinguished professor and scholar. "Enjoy the rest of your honeymoon."

"I'll definitely do that," said Adam, ending the call. He wanted to enjoy his honeymoon, but he wished he could shake this weird haunted feeling hanging over him—all the more reason to get back to his bride.

Adam was just about to open the car door when he saw the strange man in the long black coat walking through the parking lot—the same man he had spoken to yesterday.

Adam watched the man for a second, and then anger surged up in him when the man stopped in front of Adam's own room door, lit a cigarette, and then proceeded to smoke it. Adam was about to get out of the car and tell the man to move along when he was enraged to see the man place his ear up against the door as if trying to listen to what was going on inside.

Adam's sudden and angry leap out of the car startled the strange man, but as Adam slammed the car door, the man took off running. Adam bolted after him, but when he reached the end of the motel's grounds, the man had already disappeared into the darkness.

Disappointed that he hadn't caught the man, and thinking being married was not conducive to his staying in shape, Adam returned to the room. When he entered it, he expected to find Anne lying in bed, maybe watching TV while she waited for him, but when he didn't see her in the bed, he looked toward the bathroom. The bathroom door was wide open—and Adam realized he was alone in the room.

"Anne!" he called, but there was no answer. Obviously the room was empty. Had she left while he was outside, maybe to go down to the office for a minute? She must have, and he had been too engrossed in his conversation with Devin to notice. Maybe she was out looking for him right now? Should he wait for her, or—wait—that creep was outside. However suspicious Adam thought the man looked before, after he had listened at their door, he definitely fit the description of a creep now. With that man wandering about outside, Adam quickly became concerned for Anne's safety.

Cursing himself for not having watched the door while he talked on the phone to Devin, Adam rushed back outside and scanned the parking area, then ran around the corner of the motel. Soon he had run around the entire building, making a circle in his search for Anne. When he didn't see her outside, he ran to the office, but it was locked and its lights were out. What motel office closed this early at night? It was barely even dark out yet—not even ten o'clock.

Quickly, Adam returned to the room, but again it was empty, and not only empty, but the front door was wide open! Had he forgotten to close it in his worrying about Anne's safety? No, and it was not only empty, but his suitcase had been rummaged through—he remembered it had been closed and standing up on the floor when he had come back in the room not two minutes ago.

"That damn creep!" he shouted, infuriated, but also a bit scared. Where was Anne? Was this creep a common thief, or was his wife really in some danger? Was the man still in the room? Had he heard

Adam coming and hidden in the bathroom?

Adam ran into the bathroom. He had barely looked inside it when he heard the closet door in the bedroom slide open, and from the corner of his eye, he saw the sinister man run out through the room's open door.

Adam was soon in pursuit. He had chased the creep for a block before he considered that he might be wiser to call the police. But now he remembered leaving the cell phone on the car seat when he had jumped out of the car so quickly. If he went back for it now, this thief or Peeping Tom, or whatever he was, would escape.

Adam was young and strong. He had played football in high school and had always worked out until this past year; he should have been able to catch the creep, who appeared to be in his forties—there was no way that man should be able to outrun him, yet Adam was surprised when he could not catch up with him as they ran through Lusignan's silent, deserted streets. But Adam did not lose sight of him, and when the man came to the Promenade de Blossac, Adam saw him start up the promontory to the statue and the park that Adam had observed during his walk with Anne the night before.

Adam continued to follow the man up the promontory, but just as he reached the top, he saw the man jump over a railing. Realizing he might break his leg if he also jumped, Adam stopped to catch his breath and try to spot the villain, but even by straining his eyes, he could see no one in the darkness below.

Turning to look at the route from which he had just come, in case the man somehow resurfaced there, Adam was surprised to see another figure in the distance. Stepping a few paces closer, he realized it was a woman. It was Anne! What was she doing out here, so far from the motel, and all alone?

CHAPTER 5

ADAM'S DREAM

"ANNE!" ADAM SHOUTED, suddenly racing toward her. "Anne!" Why didn't she turn around when he called? Then he saw another woman step out from behind a tree near where Anne stood. Adam slowed his steps, wondering who this other woman was. He suddenly felt nervous, and all his fears and confusion from the afternoon returned to him. What was going on? What was his wife doing out here at night? She was in her pajamas, for crying out loud—a negligee that no one but her husband had a right to see her in! And this other woman, why she—she looked like some kind of a druid. And what did that creep he had been chasing have to do with all this? What the hell was going on?

Adam felt like screaming as he took a step forward, only to find his legs would not move.

"Halt, Adam, Arthur's son!"

The commanding voice was one Adam knew all too well, one he had feared hearing, but he now felt relieved to know Merlin was involved in whatever was happening to Anne—that answer was better than her being kidnapped by some creep.

"I thought this might be your doing," Adam said, his voice shaking, after he turned around to see Merlin standing behind him.

"Then you are wise indeed," Merlin smiled, mocking him.

"What is this all about?" Adam demanded, certain now that Merlin was responsible for all the strange things that had been happening since he and Anne had arrived in France. "And where have you been all this time? Everything has been such a mess, and I haven't been sure what to do."

Adam was surprised to hear the words coming out of his mouth. He had felt so happy the last few days with Anne; he loved her dearly, and all the stress of the past year had been resolved; he was now the Earl of Delaney, and he had his wonderful sons, so why now did he feel he had been so upset and worried all this time? Suddenly, he felt so very confused about everything in his life.

"You didn't need me," Merlin replied. "That is why I have been absent for the past year. The technicalities of assuming your new role in the aristocracy were not something for which you needed my help."

"But why didn't you come to visit at least, or to warn me of what would happen when I left Cadbury Hill and returned home to find my father dead?"

"Foretelling the death of a loved one is not something that can easily be told," said Merlin, "and it would not have eased your pain any."

Adam accepted that as true, but he still felt frustrated.

"Then what makes you come now?" he asked.

"There is work to be done soon," Merlin replied, grinning, "but first, there is more information you must know. Actually, it is Anne this time who must learn another story, much as you learned Arthur's."

Adam felt his body relax at these words. He had known his vision of Camelot would not be the end but only the beginning of many strange and marvelous events to come. He knew he had been meant to learn something, but already the words spoken to him by King Arthur were beginning to fade from his memory. Amid all the hectic activities of the past year, he had in quiet moments pondered what it had all meant, and he had also longed for Merlin to come back and give him additional guidance. He had felt a deep pining for more knowledge, yet he had doubted whether any of it could have been true. So now that Merlin was standing before him, Adam felt both relieved and alarmed.

"Will you put Anne through the same kind of trance as you did me?" he asked. "Is she also descended from King Arthur?"

"She will experience now what you experienced, but a different story, one that is important for her gender. King Arthur is the great hero, the masculine ideal, the father of his people, and yet very human. There are also great mothers in your lineage—Anne shall hear the tale of one of the greatest, one whose name has been maligned by the foolish fears that men have of women. But only when the masculine and feminine come together can life flourish, so her tale is equally important to Arthur's."

Adam did not know what to say; he stared at Anne, standing there with another woman in the night air. "I've sensed something was up with Anne," he told Merlin, "that some strange power was at work much like I sensed when I first met you and came to England. We actually tried to find you and Morgan to invite you to our wedding. Anne really had a hard time understanding why her friend Morgan disappeared so quickly."

"My boy, we had more important things than weddings to stage."

"Stage? What do you mean?" asked Adam.

"It's time for you and Anne to begin to play out your destined roles, to enter into your kingdom, to bring about a new Camelot upon the earth. Morgana and I and many others have been working toward that for you, as your humble servants."

"Our kingdom? I'm an earl, not a king."

"You are the direct descendant of King Arthur in multiple ways and more directly his heir than anyone else. You and Anne, and your sons as well, will be called upon to act. The time is fast approaching."

"Then I didn't just dream it all, all that stuff about Camelot?" asked Adam, nervous that someone might overhear them talking, yet relieved to know he was not crazy.

"Be patient, my boy," said Merle. "The time is not yet come, but much will be revealed in the next few days—some of it within just the next few hours. You have no idea how many stories and secrets from the past have yet to be made known to you so you can fully appreciate and live up to your lineage."

"I trust..." said Adam, wanting to trust and yet feeling frightened as he watched Anne standing there. She looked so vulnerable as she spoke to the woman he now realized must be Morgana, King Arthur's sister, whom they had previously known as Morgan, Anne's incognito friend. "I trust," Adam said, despite his faltering voice, "that you know what you are doing, Merlin, but will you help me to bring Anne back to the motel?"

"No. Do not fear. Morgana will take her where she needs to be, to what she needs to experience, learn, and absorb until it is part of her. Go back to the motel now. I have come to stop you from worrying or interrupting what it is Anne must now experience."

"But—but what about that creep who was in our room, and—"

"Shh, all is well," said Merlin, and when he shushed Adam, it felt like a gentle breeze, blowing away the worries in Adam's soul.

Adam stood silent, realizing all that Merlin had just said was true. He watched as Anne took Morgana's hand and was led into a castle—a castle that had inexplicably appeared before his eyes, the ancient castle of Lusignan risen again.

"Return back to the motel now, my boy," said Merlin, gently placing his hand on Adam's shoulder. "When the time is right, everything will be revealed to you."

Adam reluctantly turned and walked back to the motel. He walked as if in a daze. When he reached the room, he decided he would shower because the night had been humid and he was warm and sticky from running after the creep. He undressed, stepped into the shower, and turned on the water.

The steam had completely filled the room by the time he turned off the faucet. It was thick like the fog he had experienced when he had visited Avalon, and it had a sort of hypnotic effect on him as he dried himself off, then wrapped a towel around his waist. He had barely left the bathroom and stepped toward the bed when he felt himself becoming incredibly sleepy, and then he lay down upon the bed and began to dream everything his wife was now experiencing.

CHAPTER 6

ANNE'S TURN

WHEN ANNE FIRST saw her old friend Morgan, dressed in a long blue robe like something a fairy princess or druid might wear and wandering about the park at night, she did not know what to think.

"Morgan!" she exclaimed. "Is it really you?"

"Yes," Morgan replied, looking her straight in the eye and smiling.

Anne felt put off by how Morgan seemed to stare at her; her old friend appeared different somehow. In the past, they would have run up to each other and hugged, but something had changed in the last year, and Anne had no idea why. She had telephoned Morgan several times, never receiving a response; after a few months, she had given up, fearing either something had happened to Morgan, or for some unknown reason, her friend was angry with her, though Anne could not imagine why. She had been with Morgan the night the two of them had met Adam and Merle and ended up spending the night with them. The next morning, stunned by Adam's sudden departure before she woke, Anne had been comforted by Morgan during breakfast. Then they had traveled on the continent together for over a month, even driving through Lusignan, and all had been well between them. Morgan had been the first to know Anne was pregnant when she missed her period during that trip, and Morgan had listened to her concerns about finding Adam again and telling her father about the baby. But then as soon as Anne returned home, she had never heard from Morgan again.

Anne had mailed her wedding invitation to Morgan's London flat when she couldn't reach her on the telephone, only to have the invitation returned by the Royal Mail as undeliverable. Even the joy of her twin sons being born had left Anne wishing her friend were there to play aunt to them, even be their godmother, but instead, when Anne again attempted without success to locate her friend, Adam's mother had been made godmother and Devin godfather.

Now, after a year of wondering why she had lost her best friend, Anne found Morgan inexplicably standing before her. Morgan had no way of knowing she would be in France. Yet it seemed too much of a coincidence that now they would be standing here in a park in France in the middle of the night staring at each other. And Anne could not even explain how she had come to be standing here in her nightgown. The last thing she remembered, she had been washing her hair, and now, as if she had sleepwalked, she found herself in a park blocks from the motel. In the back of her mind, she knew Adam would be worrying about her, but she could not lose the chance to find out why Morgan had apparently dropped her as a friend.

"Where have you been, Morgan?" she nearly cried. "I've tried to reach you so many times, I…are you angry at me? Did I do something wrong?"

"No," said Morgan. "I've just been very busy, and I knew you were also busy with getting married and having babies."

Anne wondered how Morgan knew these things—she must have

read about them in the British tabloids. But then why had she not contacted her? Had Morgan not approved of the marriage? But Anne never would have suspected her friend of being a snob—not after the fling she'd had with Merle. She just couldn't understand why her friend had dropped her so suddenly, and now, what was she doing in Lusignan, and dressed like a druid?

"Your mind is racing," said Morgan. "I can see it on your face. The answers to your questions are more complicated, and yet simpler, than you think."

"How did we get here?" Anne asked, suddenly feeling chilled in her nightgown and hoping nobody else saw her in it.

"You're here on your honeymoon," said Morgan, stepping closer to Anne and taking her hand, which made Anne feel relief, as if there were still some friendship between them. "You were drawn to come here."

"I was," Anne admitted. "It's funny; I still don't understand why, but I felt drawn to come to this town."

Morgan drew her toward a park bench where they both sat down.

"You look..." Anne tried to find the right words. "You look so radiant, Morgan. I know I haven't seen you in a long time, but your skin looks so healthy, so...I don't know, almost ageless."

"There's good reason for that," Morgan replied, reaching up to brush Anne's hair gently as a mother would brush aside the locks on her daughter's forehead.

Anne was surprised by the sudden tenderness. She waited for Morgan to explain herself, explain the reason she looked so well, but instead, Morgan said, "I think you do understand why you are here, and why I am now here as well. You are just a little too frightened yet to admit it."

Anne did not reply. She did feel a little frightened; Morgan seemed so odd, and yet it was also comforting to be with her.

"Come," Morgan said. "We are old friends; older friends than you know. I have always watched over you, even long before you knew my name. You need not be frightened. You know why you are here; at least you suspect why."

Still Anne did not reply. After several moments, as she stared out at the park and felt the breeze upon her face, she thought she saw something move among the trees, something loom up. And then the scene changed before her eyes. Great towers appeared, castle walls with turrets and arched windows—the most tremendous and wonderful castle she had ever seen suddenly stood before her.

"You have had some coincidences in the last day—random coincidences," said Morgan, nudging Anne to confess she knew what Morgan was talking about.

"You mean...Melusine," whispered Anne, her eyes glowing in disbelief at all around her.

"Yes, Melusine, the fairy Melusine, your own ancestress," said Morgan, still gently stroking Anne's hair.

But Anne now turned and stared at her with fear.

"It's not surprising that you are afraid," said Morgan. "Many feared Melusine because they did not understand her, but there is nothing to fear."

"I wasn't even sure she was real," Anne replied. "How can she be my ancestress?"

"Your husband, Adam, is the descendant of King Arthur, so why should you not be the descendant of Melusine? In truth, you are both descended from both of them. What part of that knowledge seems unreal or impossible to you?"

"Are you referring to the manuscript we found—the one that says the Earls of Delaney are descended from King Arthur?" asked Anne. "But we just thought that a forgery, a fanciful wish to tie the Delaney family to King Arthur."

"There are many who would like to be King Arthur's descendants, and there are many who have sought to claim descent from Melusine. The royal family of England, for example, has long tried to claim descent from both illustrious figures."

"Then Melusine was a real person?" Anne asked.

"Oh, yes, or at least, she was real. I wouldn't quite say she was a person, at least not fully human."

"I don't understand," said Anne.

"That is why I am here," Morgan replied. "To explain it all to you. Are you ready to hear?"

Anne was not sure she was ready, but her fear could not overcome her curiosity; she felt a sudden great surge of longing in her breast to understand what was going on, for she sensed that something significant was happening; she could feel it all through her body, as if every nerve, every sense in her was working overtime to adapt and prepare for something stunning to happen.

"You are Melusine's descendant," Morgan repeated, "through your mother's line. You have felt some unspoken sense of being less than your husband because of your parents, because you are not Bram Delaney's child. However, through both your parents, your lineage is as significant as your husband's, and you should well be proud of the great and brave Melusine from whom you descend, a woman who was once a child who sat at my very knee and whom I trained long ago in Avalon."

These words sent what felt like a lightning bolt through Anne's thoughts; she jumped to her feet as an image appeared in her head based on Morgan's words—of the fairy Melusine being trained in Avalon by Morgan le....

She took a step back in fear. Was Morgan crazy? Was she crazy herself? How could this be? Why Morgan was no older than she was.

"I need to get back to the motel," Anne muttered, turning to leave. "Adam must be crazy with worry."

But she had only taken a few steps when Morgan unexpectedly stood in her path, yet Anne had not seen her move.

Now terrified, Anne let out a scream. What other response could she make? How was any of this possible?

"You know me, Evelyn Anne Delaney," said Morgan. "Listen deeply to your own heart; you have always known me, although you have only allowed yourself to see me through a veil until the time was right. You know who I am."

Again, Anne feared to speak. Had it not been enough to hear she was descended from a fairy serpent-woman who lived centuries ago? How could it be possible that her best friend from college was…

"Morgan le Fay!" she gasped.

"Yes," said Morgan. "Although I went by Morgana in my early years. I am sister to King Arthur, and your husband is my descendant as well as Arthur's. But you need not worry about Adam; he is safe. Merlin is with him. Aha—I can see from your expression that you've finally put two and two together. Yes, Merle is the great enchanter Merlin, and he has become your husband's friend and mentor this past year, revealing to him much that the two of you need to know before your destinies are fulfilled. Adam has been troubled about how to tell you all of this, but now much will be explained to you."

"But what do you mean by our 'destinies'?" asked Anne. "You're confusing me."

Morgan laughed. "You have to understand that Merlin and I enjoy being a bit mysterious—it's more amusing that way, and we have to reveal these secrets gradually to you or you might find them too overwhelming. Do you forgive me for being so mysterious?"

"I...I suppose so," said Anne as Morgan stepped to her side and slid her arm around her shoulder. "But please explain it all to me," Anne begged, looking into her friend's eyes.

"I will, my dear," Morgan replied. "You see, because you and Adam are both Melusine's descendants and Arthur's descendants, your marriage is very significant; one marked by the stars, you might say. You and your children have a great destiny to fulfill, a destiny that requires you to understand the story of Melusine."

Morgan now began to guide Anne across the park and toward the phantom castle that had appeared just moments before.

"Come, my dear," said Morgan. "We will enter here. Be not frightened. It is a gateway between worlds to where you shall hear the story your heart and soul crave, but it would be long and tedious for you to hear it all from me. I've arranged for you to learn it from many of your ancestors. I promise you will not be disappointed, and although the tale does have its dark moments, in the end, all will be understood, so you have no need to fear."

Anne felt confused, hopeful, anxious, and content, all inexplicably at the same time. A giant pair of double doors now opened inward and she allowed Morgan to lead her into the castle's courtyard. There they were greeted by perhaps the most handsome man, excepting Adam, whom Anne had ever seen. He was tall, lean, but muscular, his cheeks ruddy, his eyes dark, his hair curly, and he was dressed in the garments of a young medieval nobleman, which complemented his manly physique and, though she knew not why, made Anne feel he must be "the flower of knighthood."

"Welcome, fair daughter," he said, approaching, first bowing, and then kneeling to take her hand and kiss it.

A thrill passed through Anne, and then she blushed to think any man could have such an effect upon her save for Adam.

"Be not alarmed," he said, rising to his feet. "You are here to be told a marvelous tale from my lips, nothing more."

As he stood before her, Anne could feel her heart beating; he was so handsome, so stunning, so perfectly masculine and noble in his mannerisms, but her anxiety was from concern over what he might reveal to her.

"Your sons shall look a bit like me someday," he laughed, aware of how Anne admired him. "You may be surprised to learn my identity, but a few more words first, before I reveal it to you. Come."

He extended his arms, one to each woman, and then led them into the door of a tower in the castle's center.

"This castle belonged to our ancestress, Melusine; your many times great-grandmother, Anne, but simply my grandmother, although I never knew her in my own lifetime. I did know my grandfather, her husband, Count Raimond, from whom I first heard her story."

They had now entered a large chamber, a sort of banquet hall strung with medieval tapestries, one of which represented what Anne recognized as a scene from Melusine's life, the pivotal moment when her husband discovered her secret.

"That moment depicted in the tapestry," said the handsome young man, observing how Anne gazed at the exquisite embroidery, "resulted in my grandfather retiring to the monastery of Montserrat where I first met him."

"Please, I don't understand," said Anne, turning to him and

searching his ebony eyes for answers. "Who are you, sir?"

"I am Roland, commonly known as nephew of Charlemagne, but also son to his sister, the Princess Bertha and her husband Sir Milon. My father was Melusine's youngest son, a mere infant when the pivotal moment of her secret was revealed; hence, I never knew her."

"You mean you're *the* Roland—from *The Song of Roland*?" asked Anne, vaguely remembering having heard of him from a Western Civilization class in college—or was it a French class?

"Yes," Roland nodded. "I am the subject of that old medieval poem."

"But," said Anne, "I thought Roland—I thought you died in battle, in the Pyrenees, slain by the Moors—isn't that what happened?"

"That is what the storybooks say, yes," said Roland, "but Merlin came to my rescue and carried me away to another destiny. The world was left to believe I had died, but my adventures had only begun at that time, and they first led me to Arragon, to the monastery where I first heard from my grandfather the story that now you will hear."

"It will be a long story," interrupted Morgan, "so let us have some nourishment." With a wave of her hand, goblets appeared on the long banquet table before them, complete with a pitcher filled with wine, a decanter of water, and plates of grapes, bread, and cheese. "Eat as you feel the need," said Morgan. "We will be here all night."

"All night?" exclaimed Anne. "But Adam will be worried. I...."

"Fear not," said Morgan. "Merlin is seeing to Adam. He will know all is well. You see, Adam once spent hours dreaming of Camelot, so he will understand. You have nothing to fear, no reason to be worried. When we are finished here, then action may be required, but for now, you may relax and listen and learn, for your life will be changed once this tale is told."

"I feel afraid," said Anne, her attention turning from Morgan back to Roland, "but somehow, as strange as this experience is, it all does seem vaguely familiar, as if I were meant to be here, even that I should randomly visit Melusine's Tower in another town miles from here, or learn that my father and mother used to vacation in this area, and…."

And then Anne found herself crying. She could not have explained why. But it was the same feeling as the joy that had spread through her that first night Adam had made love to her—a feeling of great relief, of happiness, of purpose, of life coursing through her, of being on the right path in her life.

"I'm ready," she said. "Thank you. I am half-afraid of what you will tell me, but somehow I trust all shall be well, and I feel humbled and honored to be here in your presence, both of your presences."

"Then we shall begin," said Roland. "Look at the tapestries." His voice was deep and strong, and as he began to tell his tale, Anne turned to watch the tapestries, which seemed to come to life; they transformed into the equivalent of a motion picture in 3-D, but far more enhanced, like a virtual reality, and Anne felt as if she were truly present in each story and scene that Roland described, his words meeting her ears and stirring her soul.

PART II

MEDIEVAL FRANCE

EIGHTH CENTURY

CHAPTER 1

ROLAND'S TALE

I DID NOT die at the Battle of Roncesvaux Pass, although all the tales written and songs sung about me claim I did. At times, I have almost wished I had, for I dearly miss my companions, particularly my good friend Oliver, who died valiantly on that ill-fated day. And I mourned when I learned that Alda, my betrothed, died of a broken heart when she thought my own life ended. Today, it seems hard to imagine a woman dying of a broken heart, but in those days, women's lives were narrow and she could not conceive of living without love, for true love was rare between men and women in a time when most marriages were arranged. Alda and I had truly loved one another, so she must have felt that with my loss, her choice lay in dying or in submitting herself to a husband she could never love so well as she did me. I am both honored and heartbroken that she chose death.

I also regretted that, though I lived, I would not return to the service of my uncle, the great King Charles, the famous Charlemagne of history. He and his empire have never been surpassed in glory, for although later men such as Napoleon and Hitler created their empires, they were ignoble men and consequently could not hold onto those empires for long. King Charles, for I never called him Charlemagne, had his faults, but his intentions were always guided by a desire to spread learning and holiness, even if he did not fully understand what they truly were. I longed to help my uncle in this great quest to create a better world, but when Merlin saved me on the battlefield, he told me I had a different quest to fulfill.

No one could have been more surprised than I to discover I was still alive after our army was attacked in the mountain pass. I remember the agony of the sword that pierced into my flesh and then the feeling of falling as all went black, but when I woke, confused and uncertain whether I was even truly alive, I found Merlin bending over me, his face glowing as he spoke. My head was seemingly filled with fog so that I thought I must be dreaming when he told me his name, for while I had heard tales of the great wizard all my life, I believed he was buried deep in his cave below the Forest of Broceliande. I never expected I would see him for myself, much less that he would come to me, speaking of a role I must play in trying to save the human race from all ill.

I could scarce understand what was to come, yet I quickly found myself following Merlin on horse out of Roncesvaux Pass, into the kingdom of Arragon, and on to the monastery at Montserrat.

Our journey was long and would have been tedious had Merlin not given me a miraculous elixir that not only healed my battle wounds but relieved me of all the fatigue I otherwise would have felt. We traveled swiftly, and I was amazed both by my own endurance and that of my steed, but most of all, by the stamina of the great wizard himself, who appeared with long flowing white beard as if he were a man of seventy or eighty, and yet he possessed the vivacity of a man half that age in his eyes and step. He was astonishing, and even now, more than twelve centuries later, I still have never ceased to wonder when I am in his presence.

We traveled through the night and all the next day, and as we drew closer to Monsterrat, I recalled tales I had heard of it, for it was a holy place for retreat even then. In later years, I would hear stories of shepherd boys who, in the hills surrounding it, had seen a blinding light and heard celestial music ringing through the air; some say the Blessed Virgin herself appeared to them, and the Black Virgin statue was then found there on the mountain, a sign that a monastery should be built on that great peak. But I did not hear these tales until years after my visit, and when I first climbed the mountain, already chapels, hermitages, and a small monastery had been built, while the great monastery would not be constructed for another century.

And then there were the tales of the Holy Grail being there—some to this day claim Montserrat was the great Montsalvat of Arthurian legend—but of that I am not qualified to speak, for even I am not akin after all these centuries to all the great mysteries; nor would I wish to be, for it is far better sometimes to know they remain enigmas.

But one mystery intrigued me enough to want to know its truth— the mystery of my own family's origins. I hoped, if I were truly to meet my grandfather at Montserrat as Merlin had said I would, that perhaps I would learn something of the father I had never known beyond what little my mother had told me. I wanted to ask Merlin about my father, but as we traveled, he was silent, so I sensed I was not to question him. Instead, I struggled to remember what my mother had told me of my father—told me on that marvelous day long ago when I would first meet my uncle, the king, and my life would change forever—the day that I had once thought was the greatest day of my life, but now, as I rode behind Merlin, I wondered whether my greatest day did not yet lie in my future—for even being the great King Charles' nephew seemed small compared to going on a quest with the legendary wizard.

Still, my thoughts went back to my boyhood as we traveled. Before I met King Charles, my mother and I had lived in poverty, residing in what was hardly more than a cave carved into a hillside near the town of Sutri, just north of Rome. It was the only world I had ever known, so at that young age, I had not thought to question my mother concerning why we were so poor or why we lived in Italy, even though I had heard her on more than one occasion speak the Frankish tongue. I had not even known the language was different, since she often spoke it to me and I had thought it everyday language in Italy, until one day a friend of hers commented on her speech in my presence; then she explained to me that she had come from the land of the Franks with my father to live in Italy. When I asked why we lived in Italy, however, she told me I was still too young to learn the reason.

Some months later, when I was maybe ten years old, I woke one night to hear my mother crying softly. At first, I thought I should let her know I was awake and try to comfort her, but it somewhat frightened me to hear her cry, for she had always been so cheerful; only later would I understand how she had held up her courage all those years for my sake. I had gone to bed that night hungry, and I realized quickly she was crying because I had gone without. Then I heard her say, "My poor Roland. If only I can persevere just a few years more until you are old enough and strong enough that King Charles will welcome you. I know the time will not be long before he travels to Rome to meet with the Pope, and when that happens, on that day I will make sure you see him and your life will be changed forever."

I was so surprised by her words and that she would keep such a wish a secret from me that I dared not reveal I had heard her, although I pondered long why she would think the great King Charles should be interested in me. Considering our poverty, I could not foresee why I should experience anything so grand as to have a king show me favor. Surely, I thought, what I had heard her say had all been in my dreams, for what persuasion could I or my mother have with a king?

It would be several years before I would know the meaning of my mother's words, and although I tried to dismiss them, I never could forget them. Now and then, I even pondered the possibility that they might come true.

Then came the summer when I was twelve. That year, news spread throughout the town that King Charles the Great of the Franks was indeed traveling to Rome to meet with the Pope, and he would pass through Sutri upon his way.

You can imagine my elation and excitement, but my mother only looked troubled at the news, and I dared not ask her why.

I remember well that afternoon when I first saw King Charles. I was sitting in the cleft of a broken rock on a hill about a mile outside of Sutri, overlooking the dusty road leading into the town, for it was said King Charles would stay at the castle of Sutri that evening. I sat watching for him, expecting to see him and his knights pass by at any moment.

I remember listening to the faint sound of the monks chanting from the nearby monastery, their voices coming to me on the breeze as I waited. I had felt the heat of the hot Italian sun before I had arrived, so now it felt pleasant to sit in the shade of a tree that towered over the cleft, but the pleasantness soon grew into anxious waiting. As a boy of twelve, every minute seemed like an hour in my great longing to see the mighty king. To pass the time, I imagined what King Charles would look like, and how I might gain an audience with him, and I wondered whether he would laugh at me if I told him the words my mother had said—that my life would change the day I would meet the great King Charles of the Franks.

After a little time, my friend Oliver appeared, coming through the woods behind me.

"I didn't think you would ever get here," I told him.

"I had trouble getting away from the castle," he replied, "but I was determined to come and join you so we would be the first to see King Charles. I couldn't let you have that honor all to yourself."

As he finished his speech, Oliver elbowed me playfully and then sat down beside me.

"You haven't seen any sign yet of the king's party, have you?" Oliver asked.

"No," I replied. "He must be coming soon. It seems like I have been here for hours."

"They said he would arrive in time for supper, but that's still a couple of hours off."

"Even if he does not come until after dark," I said, staring up the road, "I am determined not to move from this place until I see him."

"Roland...?" Oliver hesitated.

"What?" I snapped, for I knew what he was going to say. He was the only one to whom I had confided my mother's words, and while he had not laughed over them, he had appeared skeptical, thinking it likely I had dreamt rather than truly heard them.

"Do you really think you're sitting here and waiting to see King Charles will make any difference?" he asked.

"I don't know," I said, "but in my heart, I feel our fates are entwined."

"I just don't understand," Oliver persisted, "how seeing him will change anything for you. Why, the streets of Sutri soon will be lined with people, all of whom want to see him, but they don't expect it to change their lives."

"No," I admitted, continuing to look down the road so he would not read my intentions in my eyes.

"I hope you don't have some half-crazy plan, such as running up to him," Oliver said. "Why, King Charles will be heavily guarded, and his knights will quickly block your path, if not run you through with their swords. You're lucky you're still a boy or you'd likely be killed for sure if you attempted to get that close to him."

"I am not a boy," I said. "I am taller than any other youth my age in Sutri, including you. You know that many a time I have pinned you to the ground when we have wrestled, and I could have done far worse if you were not my bosom friend."

"Yes, I know," Oliver admitted, not liking to be reminded that he had been bested, although I knew he did not hold it against me.

"I am old enough to be a squire," I continued. "I can become squire to one of King Charles' great knights, and that will be the beginning of the changing of my life, and my chance to make something of myself so that I may care better for my mother as well."

"I hope it is so," said Oliver. "You know if you were nobly born, you would be a page at the castle like I am."

"Yes," I said softly, regretting how I had lorded it over him a moment before. "I do not envy you that, Oliver. You deserve it, and it is not your fault that you were high born and I was not. But even high born men have ancestors who had to prove themselves, and I am determined to prove myself if only King Charles will give me the chance. Then my descendants shall someday be proud to be high born because of me."

Oliver was silent for a moment as I resumed my watch down the road, but then I heard his voice break as he spoke.

"I—I do not want you to go with King Charles. You are my bosom friend. I—"

Before he could complete his sentence, we heard a trumpet blast. Within a second, we were both on our feet, leaning forward toward the sound.

"Can you see anything?" Oliver asked, his tone now changed, a sign he was ashamed to have betrayed his emotions.

"No, not yet," I said, straining my eyes. "They could still be a few miles off—the wind may have carried the sound."

"But surely they would blare the trumpets when they approach the town," Oliver reasoned. "They must be very close indeed."

We waited in silence for a minute, and then gradually, we heard the slightest noise, so low and faint that we did not know for sure whether we heard it or not, but then it grew and grew until we were certain of it, and then suddenly, came a great pounding of hooves. Holding our breaths, Oliver and I waited as the thundering noise grew louder and louder. Next came a blasting blare of trumpets, and then four mounted knights raced past us to clear a path for the king.

And then we saw it! I will never forget that moment. It was not the great flashing glory of a king, but rather the dust of the road flying up from the four knights who had passed us, and out of that dust came first the sound and then the sight of the heavy tread of warhorses, and a great rattling of arms and armor, and then above the dust, rising like a great creature out of the ocean, broke forth brightly-colored banners announcing the majestic company.

And finally, what I had expected appeared—a brilliant flashing of shields and armor in the sunlight—a blinding glare of glory.

Oliver and I were so excited and out of breath that we jumped up and down. We looked at each other with mutual joy and threw our arms around each other's shoulders, barely able to breathe from the excitement soaring through every inch of our bodies.

Next, like a torrent of roiling, white capped waves during a storm, in a moment unlike any other that lives in my memory, the full host of King Charles passed before us, with horns trumpeting, minstrels singing, and great, noble, and tall knights, who embodied what I knew deep in my heart I would one day be. Banners flew, and one great knight, spotting Oliver and me, turned toward us and waved. His action must have caught the eye of his companions behind him, for soon every knight waved to us as he passed, and a voice in my heart said, "They wave to you, Roland, not because you are a boy, but because they sense deep down that you are one of them; they greet you as a comrade well met."

"They must be the greatest army in the world!" exclaimed Oliver, finally able to speak.

"They are!" I shouted above the noise. "They are the great conquering army. King Charles has defeated the Lombards, and now he goes to receive the thanks and blessing of the Pope."

And now came the great vanguard of the procession. Two dozen heralds rode past, one bearing the golden eagle of Rome and another the silken banner of France. Their armor glittered like gold in the sunlight; even their shields sparkled and shone like mirrors such that I could see my reflection in them as they passed.

By then, Oliver and I, overcome by it all, had jumped down from the rock and stood along the road, so close that we were only a few feet from the horses, so close that my neck began to ache from looking up at the men, and I could almost reach up to touch the knights' knees as they passed.

A group of milk white horses passed, covered in cloth-of-gold with glistening red and blue saddles. I knew one of their riders had to be King Charles, but I did not know which, so I had to ask Oliver, "Which is King Charles?" for Oliver had seen the king once before when he had traveled with his father, the Governor of Sutri, to King Charles' court, and since then, he had filled my head with many stories of that court's wonders.

"Those are still just heralds," Oliver said. "King Charles is far greater and more grand than any of them."

And then came more knights, a great group of guards. Seemingly hundreds of them, their war steeds tall, powerful, huffing beasts, and the knights themselves dressed in armor, but with their arms bare so that their thick arms bulged with such strength that I both feared and longed to be one of them.

The knights were followed by an assembly of bishops, monks, and priests, many carrying crosses and all chanting prayers together.

"That is Bishop Turpin!" exclaimed Oliver. "He is one of King Charles' peers, and they say he is as good with a sword as he is at chanting a Mass—and there is the king!"

"Where?" I shouted. But I needed no answer, for then I saw him.

Even though he wore no helmet or crown, I knew King Charles. I could not have helped but to recognize him, for although his armor was not much finer than that of his knights, his posture alone declared him a king. He rode, looking straight forward, intent on his purpose, as if a million grand designs were being worked out in his brilliant mind while he was fully confident of his God-given right to rule. In his left hand, he carried a lance of steel, while his right hand held the reins of his magnificent white steed. His golden hair fell in waves upon his steel-covered shoulders. I stood in awe of him until he turned to look down at me, and for just a moment, I met his eyes and saw there strength and goodness, courage and wisdom, and I felt confirmed again in knowing that somehow my destiny lay with this man.

King Charles passed on, but I looked after him until he had disappeared into the distant cloud of dust, and I felt my heart almost cease to beat as if it could not bear any more grandness.

"Wasn't that magnificent!" exclaimed Oliver as the last of the host disappeared a few minutes later.

I was speechless.

"Roland, have you ever seen anything like it?" asked Oliver. "I saw great King Charles in his throne room, and that was overwhelming, but I don't think anything could be so grand as to see our magnificent king on his steed, surrounded by his warriors and paladins. Not only is he the greatest king who ever lived, but he must be the bravest and strongest and noblest knight in all the world!"

Still I stared after the company of knights, barely listening to Oliver's words until he put his hand on my shoulder, shook me, and said, "Roland, are you daft? What is wrong with you?"

"Nothing," I said, coming to my senses. "It was good to see you, Oliver. Thank you for coming. I have to get home now."

I did not want to talk more, for I did not want the splendid moment to end. Instead, I ran into the forest and continued to run until I was sure Oliver would not find me, and then I found a tree and climbed it and sat in its crook; from there I could see the walls of Sutri in the distance and imagine what it must be like at this moment in the city streets as Charles the Great passed, and I relived the moment of seeing him over and over again, telling myself that it had to mean something that our eyes had met right at the moment when he passed me.

And finally, as the sun went down, realizing my mother would be worried sick about me, I climbed down from the tree and went home, my heart full, my lips ready to burst with the desire to share my thoughts.

I had scarcely opened the door to our cottage, built half into the cave, when my mother jumped up. Grabbing me, she cried out, "Oh, Roland, there you are. I was so worried about you. Your supper has long gone cold. Why didn't you—"

"I saw him, Mother!" I told her. "I saw the great King Charles!"

She stepped back from me, looking at me curiously for a moment, and then she said, "Come; I'll get you your supper."

"I saw him, Mother. You know what that means," I told her, walking toward the table, unable any longer to keep the secret. "You did not know that I knew, but I heard you one night. I heard you say that the day I saw King Charles, that day my life would change. I feared it might not be true, but deep down, I knew it was. I thought perhaps there was some great secret, but now I think perhaps you just knew— you knew what a powerful effect it would have on me, that it would seep into my very soul and make me want more than anything to be a worthy knight, to be one of King Charles' peers. I do not know yet how I will be," I said, "but I will find a way, Mother. I just know I will. I feel it is my destiny."

My mother had walked to the fire where she had prepared to spoon my stew into a bowl, but now she stopped to look back at me, and after a moment, she said softly, "You have grown so fast, Roland. I thought this day would never come. I have long hoped and prayed for it because I feared we would starve before you had grown old enough, but now it is here, and I wish it would have held off just a bit longer."

"I am grown, Mother. I am old enough to be a squire, to serve one of the king's knights and to train for knighthood myself. Tell me,

Mother, how may I do this? I know there must be a way if I only search hard enough."

"You know it," she said, her back to me as she prepared my supper, "because it is your destiny."

I dared not ask her what she meant. I feared she did not mean what I hoped—that she knew a way I might become a knight.

"Come, Roland. Sit down and eat your stew," she said, setting the bowl on the table in front of me. Then she sat down across from me, and with tears in her eyes, she said, "There is something you must know. Something I have kept from you until I thought you old enough to hear it. I know every young man must dream of becoming a great knight someday and of serving King Charles, yet most never succeed. You, however, are the exception. I do not know how it will happen, but you will find the way because it is your birthright."

I had been about to eat my first bite of stew, but now my hands grew still as I stared into her eyes. I was amazed by her words and wondered what they could mean.

"You asked me many years ago, Roland," she continued, "about how I came to live here in Sutri since I spoke the Frankish tongue, and you have asked me about how your father died, and I promised to tell you when you were older. I did not tell you sooner from fear you would depart from me if I did, but I know now that I can wait no longer. Your father was a great man, a true knight, and it is time that you know his story."

"Please tell me, Mother," I said. "I have always felt my father must have been a knight. I just know he must have been, but tell me all. I have a right to know about my father, and what he has to do with King Charles. I hope he was one of King Charles' knights, but I will wait for your words and be grateful for anything you tell me."

And then my mother told me the story of her and my father's love and of my birth. I will retell it in her own words and refrain from mentioning all the times I gasped and interrupted her with questions as I listened in amazement to all she said.

CHAPTER 2

BERTHA'S TALE

Y OU MAY FIND this hard to believe, Roland, but your mother was
once a fine lady, and your father a great knight, although he was
raised in humble circumstances. And it was because of our love that
you, my poor son, have been forced to grow up in such poverty. Had
I instead loved a man of whom my brother would have approved, it
would have been far different for us all, but it was not to be, for once
the heart discovers it is in love, it will do anything to have that love
fulfilled, even face poverty or death, for it can think of nothing else.

I was born a fine lady, a noble lady, the daughter of a king. I see
in your eyes that you feel great joy over that statement, and I can
understand that, although it has brought me little joy truly. My father
was King Pepin, and hence, my brother is the great King Charles
whom you saw today. Yes, that means you are King Charles' nephew.

All my life, I grew up in fine palaces and was petted and favored
and treated royally until my father's death. And then I lived in my
brother's palace at Aix, and I believe everyone at court loved me second
only to Charles himself. When I came of age to be married, I dreamed

of love and romance and a handsome knight who would woo and win me and be my great hero for the rest of our lives so that only love and happiness would fill our days.

And then one day, my brother called me to him and told me he would marry me to Duke Ganelon of Mayence. I knew hardly anything about Ganelon, although he had been to court several times. I had never spoken to him, and I did not know that he had even taken notice of me. The duke was not bad looking or odious to me in any way, but neither did I feel any great attraction to him. His castle was hundreds of miles from Aix, but Charles assured me I would visit the court often since Duke Ganelon would come there on business and he would be made one of the king's peers once we were wed. But I was resistant. My brother told me he would give me seven days to get used to the idea, but that I could not choose otherwise. Charles was always headstrong and hot-tempered, qualities that make him a good king, for he does not let anyone refuse him anything he wants, but they are not qualities that make for a good brother. Still, I knew that after the seven days, I would be forced to wed Ganelon.

I became distraught and despaired that I would never know happiness. I feared I would spend my life being miserable, forced to be property to a husband I did not love, to spend my days overseeing a castle far from home, to be nothing but a brood mare to bear my husband's children. I admit I even considered the great sin of taking my life, for I was still young and brash and did not understand that with patience all things change, for good times will turn to bad and then to good again.

Then, when only three of the seven days remained before I would be forced into marriage, there arrived at court the handsome, tall, gallant Sir Milon, who was nothing less than the very man I had seen in my dreams. That night he sat in the banquet hall, and the second I saw him, I knew he was the man destined to be my husband, and when the bard sang his tale of the love of Tristram and Iseult, our eyes met, and I could see in Sir Milon's eyes a wisdom and understanding of what was in my heart. I knew then that I loved him and would follow him wherever he would take me, even if it meant I were never again to see the court at Aix or my brother Charles.

That night, I could scarcely sleep. I felt so passionately in love with Milon, yet I did not know how to profess my love to him, for a noble lady could never confess her feelings to a man, especially a stranger, and even more so, one beneath her station, for he was but a knight, while I was the king's sister. Finally, because I knew how servants gossip about their betters, I asked my lady-in-waiting, "Did you notice that handsome young knight in the banquet hall? I have never seen him before; do you know anything of him?"

"They say he just arrived to court last night, milady," she replied, "and that he has asked the king to make him one of his own knights. King Charles is much taken with him and has consented. No one seems to know who he is or where he came from, but while he does not appear to be wealthy, it is clear he must be of good birth."

"Order him to come to me," I said. "I would question him."

My lady-in-waiting looked askance at me, for it is not appropriate for a young lady, much less a princess, to have a man summoned to her chamber, but because I was the king's sister, it was unlikely anyone save my brother would deny me what I demanded.

Within the hour, Sir Milon was before me. I bid my lady-in-waiting to stay in the next room. I knew from past experience, having myself attempted to eavesdrop on others' private conversations, that she would be able to hear the murmuring of our words but not make out their meaning, which would both ensure my privacy and verify that no knight had taken advantage of me.

Once my lady-in-waiting had departed, Sir Milon knelt before me. When I gave him my hand to kiss, it was all I could do not to caress his ruddy cheek and declare my love for him at that very moment.

I hesitated before speaking, although I had pondered how best to proceed all the hour I had waited for him. Just from looking at him, I was certain he was the noblest man in the world, and yet, I also knew from the bards' songs that love can be fickle and inconstant. To be certain that he would not hurt or betray me, I began by questioning him about his past.

"Tell me your story," I demanded of him. "I want to know every detail of your life—your birth and origins and how you came to this court. I want no palaver, no omissions. I want the full story, for I have great need of trusting you, but I cannot do so until I know whether truth and loyalty make up a portion of your character."

When he smiled in response, my heart leapt within me, and I felt as if all other parts of me would completely melt away into nothingness. I knew then that whatever he said, I would ask him to be my champion, to protect me from my brother's wishes and wrath. I think I even knew that I could never endure being separated from this noble man, for already, I truly believed him to be the knight I had seen in my dreams, the man with whom I was destined to spend my life, and yet I tried to remain mentally steadfast and look for signs of guile or weakness of character within him. Still, if I did not trust him, in two more days I would be miserable.

"I will try with all humility to satisfy milady's request," he replied. "My story is humble, but not without its mystery and interest, so I will strive to entertain you."

"I do not seek to be entertained, but to be convinced I can trust you," I replied.

He nodded in understanding, and then he began his tale, and with each sentence he spoke, I became more and more pleased and taken with him, lost in the spell of his eyes and his words.

CHAPTER 3

MILON'S TALE

MILADY, I WILL be completely honest with you in saying that what I have to tell cannot all be confirmed, for my own history is one of mystery. My beginnings were humble, but as you shall hear, I have reason to believe I am of noble blood.

My earliest memory is of growing up in a small hut in the forest, raised by my nurse. I called her "Nurse" for that was the name she taught me to use, but in truth, she was more like a mother to me, and I do not recall any other mother, or any father either, for that matter. I often wondered whether she was really my mother, but something about her made me dare not call her such, and the few other children I knew seemed somehow more attached to their parents than I felt toward my nurse. As I said, she was loving, yet I always felt some indescribable distance between us. It was more something I sensed than understood until I grew older and began to question what had become of my parents.

My life really did not seem to begin until I was about ten years old. It was then that a knight passed through the forest where we lived with a few other scattered families as distant neighbors. At that time, I had never seen a knight before. I had once heard one of my friends who lived in the forest, Jean, tell me about a knight he had seen pass through the village a few miles from us, so I knew by his description what a knight was, but I had never expected that seeing one would be such a wonderful, awe-inspiring sight. I was completely overcome by this warrior's dazzling appearance on his tremendous horse. I had just been walking along the road by myself, returning from the nearby stream with a bucket of water for Nurse when I heard his horse approaching from behind me. When I turned around, there he was but a few yards from me.

"Whoa!" he called out to his horse as it stepped up beside me.

"Hello, boy," he said to me. "Might I trouble you for some water?"

"Yes, yes, sir," I replied, so stunned that if you had seen me, you might have thought I was speaking to an angel. I lifted up the bucket of water, but it was so heavy that I could not lift it far above my chest. Just when I thought I would drop it—I was raising it by the handle—the knight reached down and grasped the handle, and I found myself being lifted up into the air; within seconds, the knight had clutched me in his other hand and set me facing him upon his horse. Then he drank his fill from my bucket while I watched him in astonishment.

"Is it far to the stream, boy?" he asked when he lowered the bucket from his lips.

"About half a mile, sir," I replied, simultaneously terrified and elated to be on a horse several feet above the ground.

"If you point out the direction to me," he replied, "I will give you a ride there since I seem to have drunk all your water."

"Yes, sir," I said, wincing at the cold steel of his armor as his massive legs pressed against my own. "It's over that way, sir."

I pointed and he led his horse in that direction, one arm wrapped around me to prevent my falling while I held the bucket he had returned to me. When we came to the stream, he told me to take my hand in his, and then he picked me up again, swung me over the side of the horse, and set me on the ground, which made me think he must be the strongest man in the world. Once my feet were back on the earth, I marveled at how the sun shone on his armor, blinding me from seeing him as he continued to speak to me. I felt as if I were being addressed by St. Michael.

"Thank you, boy," he said to me.

"Thank you, sir," I replied.

And then in a second, he had kicked his horse into a gallop, and I was left by the stream with an empty bucket and a desire above all else to become a great knight.

When I told my friend, Jean, about my encounter, he listened quietly, then assured me that it had indeed been a knight I had seen, and when I confessed to him how I wished nothing more than to become a knight, he told me he had the same fervent wish.

We were still boys so we could do little about fulfilling our dream than to play at being knights, but playing led to our fashioning swords and shields for ourselves. Jean's father was the local blacksmith, so he had his father make us each a sword. His father thought it harmless child's play, little realizing what owning swords would mean to us. But without ceasing, we practiced with them every day, often coming home with cuts and bruises that made us wince, but congratulating ourselves on how we had drawn each other's blood. Nurse frequently railed at me for harming myself, but if I were going to be a knight, I told her I would not be mollycoddled by a woman who was not even my mother. She then gave me a funny look, making me fear I had gone too far, for she did care for me, but she did not reply, only turned her back to finish cooking our gruel. She never again complained about my knightly exertions, and I continued my training, as I called it.

As time went by, I became larger and stronger. Jean and I continually climbed trees, leapt ditches, and lifted every stone and log that came in our way to enhance our dexterity and strength so we would someday be matchless in battle. We were self-trained, and therefore, sorely lacking in many knightly skills and qualities, but we thought for certain we were prepared to seek our fortune in the world as soon as the opportunity arose—when that would be, neither of us could guess, but we were determined it would come.

Then when I was fifteen, Nurse became very ill, and one morning, she did not get out of her bed. I did all the chores about the cottage then, and I fed and cared for her to the best of my ability. But while in the past she had been sick for only a day or two, this time, she was not to get better.

I grieved that she was going to leave me, but I also believed great things awaited me, and it would be easier to seek them with her gone; at first, I felt guilt over such heartless and improper thoughts, but all guilt left me the night she died. That evening, she called me to her bedside.

"I have a secret to tell you," she said. "I cannot go to my grave with it on my conscience, and I hope and pray you will not be angry with me over it."

I did not know what to say in response. I had loved her, but I felt I could not promise not to be angry until I knew what that secret was.

"Let me help you sit up," I said instead, "so I can hear you better. And I will fetch you some water to clear your throat."

When this task was completed, she began to speak, her face filled with anxiety.

"My dear Milon," she said, "what I have done, I did with the belief it was the only choice I had at the time, and I did it for your own safety. Perhaps you will not think so, but you did not witness the terrible wrath of your brother and the horrible things that happened at your father's castle when you were but a babe."

I need not tell you how astonished I was by these words. I had never suspected I had a brother, and to hear that my father had a castle—did it mean he was a king? What was this secret she had, and what danger did she think I had been in?

"What are you saying?" I exclaimed. "Tell me. Tell me everything. I cannot bear not to know."

She grimaced and drew in a deep breath, then coughed. In panic, I held the cup of water to her lips, my head spinning, fearing she would not be able to finish speaking.

Once she had drunk, she said, "I will be brief, for I feel my strength failing quickly, and I do not know how long I will last."

And then she paused again as I feared she would die before I knew her story that was so vital to my wellbeing and future.

"Please, tell me," I begged of her, "what is my family name? Who were my father, my mother, and this brother you mention? What castle do you speak of? Please tell me. My life depends upon it."

"I don't know that your life does depend upon it," she frowned. "I think you would be wiser to stay away from such a family, but you are old enough now to make your own decisions. I pray when I have told you all, you will not rush off but stay here with me until I draw my last breath. It will not be long, probably a few hours at most. Certainly not more than a few days, but do not leave me at the last, Milon. I am frightened of death, and I wish you to fetch the priest for me after I have finished what I have to tell you."

"Yes," I said. "Yes, I will do so." I was ready to agree to anything if only she would tell me the great secret of my birth.

"I have loved you, Milon. What I have done was only done out of love."

I nodded as she looked at me. I saw the fear on her face, the fear that my anger would get the best of me before she had finished.

"Nurse," I said, seeing I must relieve her fears if I wanted her to continue, "you are the only mother I have ever known. If you have wronged me, I cannot believe you did it on purpose. You have cared for me all my life; I forgive you before I even know whether you need forgiveness, for I cannot believe you did wrong. Please, quit worrying now and tell me what I feel I must know if I am ever to be happy in this world."

"I don't know where to begin," she confessed. "I don't know how to explain it all to you so you will understand. You are wise for your age, and I am proud of how strong you have grown. You have been a good boy. Now I entreat you to be a good man. To fight for right and protect those who have no protector, and never to let anger get the best of you. I have watched you repress the anger I have seen flash in your eyes on occasion; you have some self-control, yet I fear your anger, for anger was your brother's downfall, and ultimately, his anger is why you are here with me. I feared for your safety if I left you with a grief-stricken father or a brother who had already shed your other brother's blood."

Horror filled me at this statement. I had a brother, and he had murdered another brother!

"Tell me my father's name, my mother's name," I implored. "And the names of my brothers."

"I do not know that you would know their names if you heard them," she replied, "although doubtless Jean and the other children about the wood have heard stories they may have told you without my knowledge. We are only a couple of days' journey from where you were born. You are of the great and noble family that resides in the marvelous castle of Lusignan. Have you heard of it?"

Lusignan! Who had not heard of Lusignan? Yet who could believe the tales told of it? I did not half-know whether or not it was a real place, having never seen it myself, for I had never traveled more than five miles from our hut. I believed it existed, but the tales told of it were so....

"Yes," I said. "I have heard of it. I have heard...."

But I dared not say what I had heard.

"You have heard of the Lady Melusine?" asked Nurse.

"Yes," I admitted, dreading what she would say next.

"Melusine was your mother," said Nurse, speaking the words I had feared to hear, words I could not even fully comprehend. "Before I say more," she continued, "let me assure you that she was a beautiful, gracious woman, and her husband, Count Raimond, was your father. Perhaps he is still, for I do not know whether he yet lives—for that matter, I do not know whether your mother still lives."

"I don't understand," I said. "I have heard...stories...of Melusine. They...can they be true?"

"I do not know the truth behind them all, but I know people say your parents had a great argument, causing your mother to depart. No one saw her leave by the castle door. I heard later from my fellow servants that she was seen flying from the castle window. It is hard to know what to believe based on what idle tongues have said. I only know what I saw myself."

"So you were a servant then to my parents?" I asked. "But how did I come to be raised by you?"

"I was your nurse. I was nurse to you and to all your brothers—your brothers, Geoffrey and Fromont, they lived to adulthood…and then there was your brother Horrible—I know not what became of him."

"Tell me of my brothers," I begged.

For a moment, she looked as if a chill had come over her—I knew not whether it was from death creeping closer to her, or from thought of my brothers, but she continued her tale.

"Your oldest brother, Geoffrey, was a great warrior and a giant killer; he was no friend of the Holy Mother Church, and he became so enraged when your second born brother, Fromont, became a monk that he burned down the local monastery, killing Fromont and most of the monks in the fire. It was because of that event that your father called your mother a serpent, blaming her for the deformity and behavior of your brothers—Fromont looked perfectly normal, but Geoffrey had great protruding teeth, besides a fiery temper—and as for your brother, Horrible, he was a violent nasty child. It was all I could do just to get him dressed each day, and one day when he was no more than four, he threw a stone from a castle window and killed one of the serving girls who was working below. We were all horrified by his behavior, and your mother feared he would grow up to be a monster. He was a hideously ugly child, born with three eyes, such that your parents had to search far and wide for a wet nurse for him, for your mother was always off on her building campaigns—she built castles like most women produce children—and so another wet nurse was needed. Thankfully, I was too old by that point to serve the purpose, so a woman was found who had lost her babe. That woman claimed she did not care how ugly Horrible was; she was thankful to have a child to feed, but that was before she saw him. I am surprised she remained then, for he was a terrible child, constantly demanding her milk, and born with sharp teeth. One day, he bit off her nipple in his eagerness and greed. The poor woman died from the wound for the doctor could not stop the bleeding right away and it quickly grew infected. When another wet nurse was found, Horrible did the same thing to her. That nurse ran away from the castle in horror and was never seen again, but I suspect she bled to death somewhere in the forest. Everyone at the court spoke of what evil omens these events were. After that, Horrible was forced to drink from a cup for no woman would go near him. Nor did it help that he had a terrible temper and was as strong as a boy of twelve by the time he was five. Everyone feared him, even your parents, I believe. And then one night, he disappeared and was never seen again; some say your father had him taken away in the night and drowned him; others feared he had escaped the castle on his own and gone to live as a monster in the wood. I...I do not...."

Here Nurse began coughing, so I gave her some more water. After she drank, she sighed and said she needed to lie back down so I helped her do so.

"I don't know what to say," I told her as she lay there. "How am I supposed to believe these frightful tales, or even that I am of such a noble yet strange family?"

"I can only tell you," she replied, "that I witnessed these things with my own eyes."

"But I still don't understand how you and I came to live apart from my family."

"I could not leave you in the castle after your brother Geoffrey had killed his own brother and your mother had abandoned you like that. Your father, the count, was overcome with grief after your mother's disappearance and seemed inconsolable."

"But how did I come to be here?" I demanded. "I have heard of Geoffrey of Lusignan, that he still lives and rules at the castle, so how did I come to be separated from my family? Did you...did you... kidnap me?"

She appeared troubled as her eye met mine.

"No, my dear boy. I...I don't know how to explain this. I have often wondered whether I did not just dream it, only, there is one reason why I have to believe it truly happened. It was a dreadful day when your mother disappeared. Your father, when he came out of that room alone, his face was white as a sheet. He was in great horror and distress, and it was hours before he would speak. Finally, he said your mother had told him she must leave and had flown out the window. None of us could believe this, and some of the servants went to make sure she had not fallen and lay dead in the courtyard below, but there was no sign of her. Within a few hours, stories began to pour in from the neighboring town and countryside that she had been seen flying through the air, although others believed only a large bird had been mistaken for her. Some even feared your father had murdered her and disposed of her body, though none of us previously would have doubted his great love and devotion to her.

"We were all so filled with distress, and your father most of all; he looked as if madness were settling upon him, and so I feared what would become of you if you remained in his or your brother's care. Late that night, after the castle was quiet, I went to your chamber to watch over you. I swear that was my only intention at that time—just to watch over you. I felt a need to protect you, for I feared yet that your father might have killed your mother, and I could not trust Geoffrey after he had caused Fromont's death. And again, I wondered whether your father might not have also been responsible for Horrible's death given the recent events. How could I not be filled with fear after all these violent and strange happenings? And you were such an innocent, sweet child."

She paused to catch her breath and gather her thoughts. I felt my blood racing inside of me, anxious to hear the end of her tale.

"I don't know how to speak the rest of it," she said. "It was just all so strange. I was sitting there in your room, watching over you. It was right about midnight when suddenly a woman appeared in a beam of moonlight before the window. I was too astonished to move or stop her when I saw her approach your crib. She looked so like your dear, beautiful mother, but she had great wings like those of an angel sprouting from her back.

"I held in my breath as she bent over the crib. Could she be your mother? I was so awestruck by her great wings and her mysterious appearance that I was frozen in place, unable to speak.

"After a minute, she sensed I was in the room, though hidden in the shadows. Then she stood tall and, looking at me, said, 'Nurse, watch over my son. Protect him. Do not let harm come to him.' Her voice confirmed she was your mother, but I remained frozen to my chair, for I had never seen a winged creature like her before. Then she stepped toward me and said, 'Put out your hand.' I did so, too frightened not to obey. In my hand, she placed a golden ring. 'Give this ring to my son when he is older,' she said. 'So long as he possesses it, he shall never be in danger of losing in battle or in law.' Later, upon examining it, I saw it must have been some ancient pagan ring, for carved into it was the image of a serpent swallowing its tail, and ever since, I have shuddered just to look at it, for I fear it signifies that your mother was some type of serpent. At that moment, however, all I could do was reply, 'Yes, milady.'

"'Do not fail me, Nurse,' she continued. 'You have always been true to me, more true than my own husband. Take the child away. Raise him where he will be safe and far from his brother's evil influences. I want no harm to come to him. Through him and his descendants I still have great hope that the pain of the past can be healed.'

"She spoke with such great sadness, and as the moonlight shown upon her face, she looked as if she bore the weight of all the world upon her. Then she moved toward the window, but she paused to turn around once more and say, 'Do not fail me, Nurse. Go now before daybreak. Protect my son, my last hope.'

"And then she was gone so quickly that I know not whether she flew out the window or simply evaporated into the air. I just know that I never saw her again.

"I sat there for some time until the coldness of the ring in my hand brought me to my senses and I realized I had not been dreaming. Then remembering your mother's words, I went back to my chamber, bringing you with me, afraid to leave you for even a moment. I collected what few belongings I could carry along with you, and quickly, I took my departure from the castle. You might wonder that I could escape without being seen, but I knew of a secret passage out of the castle, known only to me and a few others, for your mother, when she had built the magnificent castle, had designed it for easy escape should it ever be attacked. I had been entrusted with the secret so I could make certain her children came to no harm. I do not know whether she foresaw then that someday the passage would be necessary.

"I traveled with you for two days until I came to this forest where my brother was a woodcutter. He lived in this cottage. He died of sickness that first year we were here, and I feared then you would also become ill, but I believe you must lead a charmed life for you have never been ill a day in your life and have grown into a strapping young man now. We have lived here ever since, living on the food of the forest and what little money I could make with sewing and other small tasks. I have loved you all this time, and I have kept my promise to your mother, although I have never understood what exactly she was.

"I hope you will believe me. I swear to you that every word is true. Dear Milon, you do believe me, don't you? Please say you do so that my conscience is at rest and I can die in peace."

Truly, I knew not what to say, for such a tale was astounding to me, but somehow I stammered out, "Yes, be at peace. I believe you."

She spoke with such earnestness that while I questioned her tale, I sensed that she sincerely believed it. Her face relaxed when I said I believed her, and she reached for my hand, which I willingly gave her.

"I feel the pain leaving me," she said, "and numbness settling into my limbs."

She was struggling now to breathe, but she fought still to speak. "I swear my words are true."

"I will go fetch the priest as you asked," I told her.

"No, do not leave me. My soul is at rest now. If you believe me, I have nothing to fear from my Maker."

She took only a few more breaths. Then she closed her eyes. In a minute, she had breathed her last. I felt her grasp on my hand weaken until I knew her life was no more.

I did not know what to do then. I sat there beside her for a while. I believe I shed a few tears, far less than she perhaps deserved after caring for me all those years, but my thoughts, I'm afraid, were less upon her death than the revelation I had received from her lips.

After a little while, I walked to the village church and fetched the priest who came and gave her last rites, and the next day, she was buried and I was left all alone in the world.

"What will you do now?" Jean asked me after the funeral. I told him I did not know, and indeed, I didn't. I felt too overcome with wonder at the tale of my origins to do anything yet but ponder what I had learned, and I had not yet felt able to share the tale with him. But then he said, "Milon, don't you see? This is your chance to go into the world—to become a knight and win your fortune."

His words shot hope and excitement into my heart, and I came close to telling him then the tale of my birth and that I was of great and noble lineage, but I feared that if he questioned me further and I confessed I was the son of the serpent woman Melusine, that he would then fear me, and in truth, I somewhat feared myself because of it. So all I said to Jean was, "Will you come with me? We will ride to the king's court. To the court of the new King Charles himself and ask to serve him."

But Jean sadly refused me. He told me he had gotten a girl in the village with child, a girl I knew was hardly more than a child herself; she had lost her parents the previous winter so she had no one else to support her. Jean said he would marry her and remain to care for her and their child. I could only think how his dream of knighthood had been dashed due to his own folly.

"I have sinned," he told me. "I am not worthy of knighthood, but you, Milon, you are pure and noble still. Surely, King Charles will make you one of his peers. Go forth and live the dream for both of us."

He clasped my hand and wished me well, and so I promised him I would do as he suggested, but in truth, milady, I had no idea how I could bring about such a change in my position. How could I think myself worthy to be a knight when I came from such a family? I feared that although I had committed no sin myself, that the sins of my parents and brother would be held against me. With such a family, who was I to think myself worthy of being one of King Charles' knights?

I spent that last night in my and Nurse's cottage, and then I collected what few things I wished to take with me and prepared to depart.

I felt more was intended for me in life than to spend the remainder of my days in a peasant's hut in the forest, but I knew not where I would go. As I prepared to leave, I remembered that Nurse had hidden a small number of coins in a chink in the cottage wall. She thought I did not know about them, but as she had aged and grown slower, I had spied on her once or twice, not out of malice but from concern to see how she fared when I was not present. I now retrieved the coins, disappointed to find they were only a few pennies. Feeling deeper into the hole with my fingers to make sure I missed nothing, I was surprised to feel something more—a ring! "Truly, it couldn't be," I thought, but when I pulled it forth, it was indeed a ring—a golden ring, and when I brought it into the light, I saw engraved upon it the image of the serpent swallowing its tail, as my nurse had described; doubtless, it was the very ring my mother had given Nurse for me, and that made me realize at least most of her tale must have been true. I felt strange about wearing it, but the ring had been intended for me, and it was the only thing of value I had ever owned. I slipped it on, and instantly, I felt comforted by it, as if my mother, perhaps, or some other guiding force, was now with me.

Yet the ring also frightened me—the serpent image reminded me of what kind of half-beast my mother might have been—one who had birthed deformed or mad or wicked children. And how was I to know whether I was any different from my brothers? I was in no way deformed, but who was to say I did not have a streak of evil in my heart that I had yet to realize? But I knew full well I had never done anything exceptionally ill, other than engage in boyish squabbles with my playmates as all children do. I also believed myself perhaps morally superior to others, for I had grown to be the biggest and strongest boy in the forest and nearby village, far stronger even than Jean, who could best almost anyone, and more than one girl in the village had cast her eyes upon me, but I had always shied away from womanly affection, for I had heard that knights were to be pure and virtuous, and I would not by any means allow a woman to tempt me until I had achieved my goal of knighthood, and then I sought only to be with a noble woman of goodly birth and virtuous ways. It is strange, now that I think of it, that I should aspire so highly in love and marriage while yet a peasant boy of the forest, but perhaps I suspected even then that noble blood flowed through my veins.

That I seemingly had none of my family's shortcomings made me wonder whether my mother's great sin, whatever it might have been, had finally been forgiven, and so now I might be a good and noble son and perhaps redeem my family's reputation.

And so I departed from the forest, knowing not where I would go, but determined that I would make my fortune in the world and find some means to become a great knight. With me, I brought the sword that Jean's father had forged for me several years back, and though it was a simple weapon compared to those that true knights wielded, for Jean's father was mostly a maker of horseshoes and farming tools, still, it was something by which I could protect myself and show my skill when needed.

Little did I suspect my sword would come in handy that very day, for I was not more than a few hours walk from the village when I grew hungry, and although I had little food, I sat down in the shade of a tree and drew forth the bit of bread, cheese, and fruit I had and my flagon of water and prepared myself a meal. As for my next meal, I trusted that the few coins I had would buy me food when I came to a village, and after that, I hoped to perform some labor to earn my meals.

While I sat there in the shade, eating and trying to guess what adventure might occur that would lead to my achieving knighthood, it was my good fortune that a real knight—in appearance, though perhaps not in his heart—came riding by, and seeing me beneath the tree alongside the road, he stopped his horse a few yards from me and called out, "Give me a bite to eat!"

I was stunned by his demanding tone, but rising to my feet, I simply replied, "Good sir, I only have a bit of bread and cheese. I am sorry, but I have eaten all but a bite or two of it."

"Don't lie to me!" he thundered. "Give it here. Hurry. I am starved."

Astonished by his commanding words, I replied, "I do not lie," and I placed the last bite of food I had in my mouth, swallowed it down, and showed him my empty hands.

"Come, churl. I'll have no more of your rudeness or I'll have to teach you a lesson."

"It is you who deserve a lesson, sir," I replied, "for knights are to serve the weak and aid the oppressed, not try to steal food from poor men and defame their characters."

Hearing these words, he quickly dismounted and drew his sword. But by that time, I had grabbed my own sword from the ground and prepared for his attack.

I will not bore you, milady, with the skill and dexterity I displayed in fighting him, and I admit were I not so angered by his rudeness, I might have been doubtful of my skill, for never had I fought a true knight before, but while his skill was great, his blows were not overly strong, perhaps due to his hunger, but I think more likely from a false confidence he had, for within two minutes, I had whacked his sword with my own until his had shattered; what my sword lacked in swiftness, it certainly made up for in its heavy weight, and in another moment, this churlish knight was on the ground, at my mercy, and begging for his life.

"I am no murderer," I told him, "but it is my greatest desire to be made a knight myself."

"I will knight you if you so wish," he replied, his eyes still filled with fear.

"That I do not," I said, "for I will only be knighted by one gallant and noble."

"I am son of a baron," the knight stated, to which I scornfully replied, "Perhaps you are of noble blood, but not of noble manners, which are the true sign of nobility. I will spare your life, but rather than accepting knighthood from you, I will accept your horse and your armor, for as a knight, I shall have need of it, and although I have destroyed your sword, I see you have a dagger on your person that I will leave with you so you are not rendered defenseless."

He scowled at my terms, but he could see I was serious and dared not deny me. Once he had his armor removed, I bade him go on his way; I would not risk setting down my sword to put on the armor while he was near in case he should try to stab me in the back. I waited there under the tree until he had disappeared on foot, and then I donned his armor and mounted his horse.

I had never ridden a horse before, and I had a hard time of it, but the beast was gentle, unlike its former master. By the end of the day, I was sore from riding and just trying to stay on the horse, but I knew better than to complain, for I was now better off than I had been when the day began.

I slept that night under the trees, not wanting to spend what few pennies I had at an inn, and I fell asleep wondering whether I truly was more skilled than the knight I had defeated, or whether it was the ring I wore that had indeed, as my mother had told my nurse, prevented its wearer from being defeated in battle.

My tale has grown longer than I planned, milady, and I do not wish to become tedious, but I can see from your brow that you are still curious and have many questions for me, so I will not bore you with further details of my journey. I will simply tell you that I soon learned I was not far from the Castle of Lusignan. Although I had not initially thought to make it my destination, it was not surprising to me that I was riding toward it, for Nurse had said we were only a couple of days from the great castle. Once I knew it was near, although I felt trepidation over the thought, I deemed it best to travel there to see whether my brother Geoffrey yet lived and reigned as count over the surrounding countryside.

I cannot describe to you what I felt when first I saw those towering walls. With all respect, milady, it would be easy to fit two or even three of your brother's palaces inside Lusignan's courtyard. It is truly the largest castle in all of France, and to think that my mother was responsible for its construction was a marvelous thought to me, as you can well imagine.

I did not know what I would do or say once I reached the castle, but somehow I found myself boldly riding up to its gates and demanding entry of the guards. They refused me, of course, but I requested then that they tell Geoffrey, Lord of Lusignan, that his brother was being kept outside his walls and wished to speak with him.

I felt great trepidation once I had dared to utter these words. In truth, one of the guards seemed troubled by the statement, and he had a page boy sent to relay the message. The boy quickly disappeared behind the castle wall while I waited upon my horse with the guards staring crossly at me. It was an awkward experience, and I was just considering whether I might yet gallop off on my horse when a priest came out and muttered something to the guards. Then I was told I must disarm myself before I would be allowed to enter.

I quickly handed over my sword, not wishing to offer resistance, for despite what I had heard of my brother and his anger, I still wore the ring and believed it would keep me safe.

The priest now bade me follow him. He led me across a large courtyard and through a side door into the main castle; then we passed through many a hall and winding passage until we came to a council chamber. The priest opened a great door and stepped inside, and before I could follow him, he announced to the room's occupant, "My lord, here is the knight who would speak with thee."

I stepped into the room to find seated before me the man I knew immediately must be my brother. And the scowl on his face made it clear he was not pleased to see me.

"How dare you claim relation to me?" he demanded. "Who are you and what do you want of me?"

"My name is Milon," I replied, trying to prevent my voice from trembling. "I do not know rightly why I have come except that the woman who raised me and whom I knew simply as 'Nurse' told me on her deathbed that I am of the House of Lusignan. She told me that she stole me away one night while I was yet a babe, but now that she has passed away, I, who never knew anything of my family or my origins before, have come to see whether her story be true."

"Milon?" Geoffrey muttered, his face growing pale. "You claim to be my brother, Milon, who disappeared as a babe?"

He stood up from his chair and bid me come closer, and as I did so, he stepped toward me and looked me directly in the face.

"Aye, you would be about the right age I should guess," he said, and then walking around me, he sized me up, remarking, "You are tall and strong and well-built like a warrior. You might indeed be my brother, but then so might a thousand men your age who are strongly built, nor is it impossible, seeing as I am childless, wifeless, and without an heir, that many would like to lay claim to being my lost brother and thereby gain my castle and lands when I am gone. Is that your plan?"

"No, sir, it is not," I hotly replied. "It is my plan to be virtuous and honest and to be knighted, and since you are my brother and of noble lineage, perhaps you are the one who may so knight me."

"What? You are not even a knight! Where then did you get that armor?" he demanded, half-laughing and half-mocking me.

I explained to him how I had acquired my armor. Then he laughed as if he enjoyed my tale, but a moment later, he rose from his chair and stepped up into my face, his nose not an inch from mine, and a growl rumbled from his throat as he flared his nostrils and his eyes bore into mine. I was not about to give way, though I knew from Nurse that he had murdered our brother, as well as killed a giant. Without even a flinch, I returned his stare, seeing in his eyes much pain and grief. And then a look of shock and fear crept across his face as he stepped back and said, "Who are you, really? You have the strangest eyes. They remind me of my mother's eyes. How can I believe you are truly whom you say?"

"I do not know how to prove it to you," I replied as he slowly retreated to his seat, clearly disturbed to have found familiarity in my face. "I can scarcely believe we are brothers myself, having only learned the story of my family's origins a few days ago. I do, however, carry with me this ring that my nurse claimed my mother gave to her, telling her to give it to me when I came of age."

And I boldly stepped toward him and lifted my hand before his eyes so he could see the ring on my finger.

Geoffrey seemed almost speechless when he first saw the ring, but after a moment, he asked, "Might I see it for myself?"

I did not want to take it off, for I did not know whether to trust him, but I also realized that if he wished it, he could call his guards and keep me his prisoner in that room, and since I had surrendered my sword at the gate, I figured the ring could do little to protect me at this moment, so I drew it from my finger. As I placed it in his open palm, I noticed that he wore a similar gold ring, which made me step back with surprise.

But his surprise was even greater, for when he held my ring up close to his eye and looked at its serpent image, he exclaimed, "It is indeed my mother's ring!" And excitedly, he then took off his own ring and held it out to me so I could see the same engraving of a snake upon it.

"These were my mother and father's wedding rings," he said. "When my father entered the monastery at Montserrat, he gave me his, and he told me that our mother left behind her own for Milon. I have always wondered what became of it, for it disappeared the same night as did he. Now...I guess I have my answer."

I was silent as he returned the ring to me and I replaced it on my finger. He also slid his ring back on his finger before he continued.

"I know not what to say. I have always wondered what became of my brother Milon. I had thought perhaps my mother had returned and stolen him away in the night, but it is true that his nurse disappeared that same night after my mother's departure. Is it possible that now, after all these years, standing before me is my brother?"

"I believe so," I said slowly, "and even more so, I want to believe it is true, for to my knowledge, I have no other family in the world."

As I spoke, my voice cracked with emotion, which surprised me as much if not more than it surprised Geoffrey, for I had been so set in my goal to achieve knighthood that I had not taken time to grieve over my nurse, or even to say goodbye to my friend Jean and all the small world I had known. I was a brave and strong young knight, or so I wanted to be, but now I also felt a longing for a true brother.

Looking kindly upon me, Geoffrey said, "I see truth in your eyes, Milon, and I hear it in your voice, but you know not what you ask if you think me any suitable excuse for a brother. Do you know the story of your parentage? Do you know the crimes I myself have committed?"

"I have heard bits and pieces of these from my nurse," I replied, "but I only know her version of these tales, and I would prefer to hear them from my own brother's lips. I have also heard tell how you are a prodigious knight, and from the people in your domains as I journeyed here, I learned that you are a great and good lord who has mended his ways and done much for the Holy Mother Church and the poor."

"You speak true, young man," he said, nodding as he considered my words. "Perhaps in time, we shall come to know one another as brothers, if you truly can overlook my faults and flaws. I would not mind having a brother again; I have no other kin, save our father, who lives in a hermitage, in exile from the world; he will not even allow me to see him, although occasionally he will send word to me."

He paused, deep in thought, as I felt my heart leap with joy and longing to know my father yet lived.

"Whether we shall tell him of your existence," Geoffrey continued, "is something we must let time decide. It is late in the day now and I prefer to dine alone. I do not wish to be unfriendly or inhospitable, however, so I will give you shelter for the night...and for as long as we deem it mutually beneficial for you to stay. My servants shall see to your meals and other needs. I will now retire to my own chamber and my private thoughts for this evening. You have given me a shock, and while I do believe your words, I need time to come to terms with them...Brother."

I was stunned by his last word, so stunned I could not speak. I simply bowed my head in obeisance and tried to stifle a tear—to think that this great and powerful knight would call me his brother.

"Thank you, milord," I finally replied.

Then Geoffrey hollered to a servant, "See to my brother's chambers and find him suitable apparel. Fulfill his every need." And looking one last time at me, he said, "We will meet again at breakfast."

I bowed and slowly walked backward from the room. Not until the door had closed behind me—and the priest who had greeted me initially, said, "Sir Milon, come this way," which I let pass despite my not yet being a knight—did I recall that the kindness of Geoffrey calling me his "brother" might mean little considering what he had done to our brother Fromont.

I soon learned that I had nothing to fear, for despite his initial and understandable trepidation, Geoffrey was all I could have desired in a brother.

The next day, he showed me all about the castle, and the day following, he took me riding across all his vast domains, and when I was more than thoroughly impressed, he said to me, "All this, Brother, may someday be yours, for I am now grown far past my youth and do not know how long I will be of this world, while you are young, hearty, and hale. Doubtless, someday in the not too distant future, you shall find yourself a beautiful young wife and have a brood of children to fill this castle with the laughter and happiness I remember it held in my childhood."

"I did not seek you out, Brother," I replied, "so that I might be your heir."

"No, but the property must be kept in the family," he said, "and you are the only family I now have. I pray that you live to succeed me, for nothing but misfortune seems to strike this family because of the strange curse upon our mother."

Before I could ask what curse—assuming he meant her supposed serpent form, but not realizing it had resulted from a curse—he quickly added, "But we will not talk about that now. I am deathly sick of thinking about it."

"Brother," I cautiously replied, "I do not know the whole story. I would hear it from you."

His nostrils flared at my request, but he quickly regained his self-control and responded, "Someday perhaps I will tell you all, but we have more important things at hand now. If you are to succeed me, there is much for you to learn, for you have been absent from this castle the better part of twenty years, and no offense intended, but you have the manners of a kitchen boy. We must turn you into a true and valiant knight, and then we must send you out on a quest—perhaps to join the great King Charles and become one of his paladins—to earn your spurs and prove yourself worthy to be my heir and the next Count of Forez and Lusignan."

I was pleased with this speech and dearly longed to prove my manhood by doing great and gallant deeds, and eventually, even to win by my prowess the heart of a lady fair.

My brother Geoffrey soon had me engaged in a rigorous training program. His own knights served as my teachers, and save, milady, for your brother King Charles' paladins, I believe they are the finest knights in France, for as you have doubtless heard, my brother was a great warrior in his youth, and he has trained most of his knights himself so that they truly are skilled in swordplay and all manner of physical exertions.

And finally, when I had been bested about a hundred times by them (for my brother told me I could not wear the gold ring that would protect me while training), I became far more skilled. I had thought myself hardy and strong before, but now my muscles hardened and my speed and agility became astonishing. I trained twelve or more hours a day, and when I was not training, I was put to work in the stables or some other task about the castle. Whatever my brother Geoffrey insisted I do, I carried out his orders, no matter how sore my body became, no matter how foolish the task seemed, for I knew he intended it for my good.

At night, I would collapse on my bed, exhausted, and I would sleep like a babe, but just before I would drift to sleep, or in the morning when I would wake and dress for the day, I would often spend a minute or two wondering how my brother could be the great and terrible warrior he was said to be, with a fiery temper that would result in his killing his own brother, for while he had his gruff moments, he was certainly no warmongering Attila the Hun. I could not understand it, but I could see that he must have greatly changed since the day he had caused our brother Fromont's death. At times, a great sadness would come over him when we had sat at table a little too long and he had drunk more wine than he should, but he would say little to me at these times. He also showed me little affection, but his smile when I entered the room told me all I had to know—that I had a brother who was glad of my company, and that was enough for me.

After two years of rigorous training, I was delighted when Geoffrey informed me, "Milon, you have truly earned knighthood, and I am proud to grant it to you, but you are not done yet. You must go out into the world now and make a name for yourself so that the people hereabouts will be ready to acknowledge you as their lord when I am gone, whenever that day may come. They would do so regardless of any deeds you may accomplish, but they would not respect you, and to have the love and respect of your people is the greatest thing to which any lord can aspire. Do you understand?"

"Yes, brother," I said, "although I grieve to leave you."

"That cannot be helped," he replied, "but I know you will return now and then whenever you are able, perhaps when you are marching with King Charles' army through this part of the country, and if, in the meantime, I need your services or I grow ill and think my time has come, I will send for you."

My tale has gone on too long now, milady, and I do not wish to bore you further. Let me close simply by saying that my brother gave me his blessing, and he bid me always to carry the gold ring from my mother to keep me safe. Should you have any doubt about any of my story, here is that ring to verify that I have told you the truth. I bear it with me wherever I go, and I believe it will help to make me a great asset to your brother's army, for I do believe I truly am undefeatable.

CHAPTER 4

BERTHA'S TALE CONTINUES

ROLAND, WHEN YOUR father, the brave and handsome Sir Milon, finished speaking, such a smile lit his face at the thought that he was undefeatable that I was quite charmed with him. And he did indeed have a gold ring in his hand, which he placed in mine and allowed me to admire. It was a beautiful thick ring with the image of a serpent swallowing its tail engraved upon it. But it was a ring from a fairy, and although that fairy had been his mother, I feared it might be enchanted, so I quickly handed it back to him. Nevertheless, that ring verified for me that all his words were true.

While listening to your father's marvelous tale, I had felt as overcome with anxiety as he must have felt when he first learned of his family's origins. When he had finished, had he not been so terribly handsome that I could not help but like him, I don't know what I would have said, for his story was strange and marvelous and somewhat frightening because it was true, but most of all, I admired the bravery he had expressed and how his determination to be a great knight was written across his noble brow.

And so, after a moment of trying to take in everything he had said, and then to find the courage to ask him for his assistance, I ventured to make my request.

"Good, Sir Milon," I began, "there will be a great tournament tomorrow."

"Yes, milady," he replied, "and I hope to participate in it."

"I wish for you to be my champion in the tournament," I continued, "and if you succeed, I wish you to become my permanent champion."

"It would be my honor, milady," he agreed.

He did not hesitate in his answer, although to be the champion of a princess was no light matter. Nor do I think he would have refused me if at that point he had already known why I asked. In fact, I admit I was beginning to think that Milon would make a wonderful husband, whatever his family's monstrous origins, for as far as I could see, he was in every way not only flawless but exceeding all other men in appearance and courage.

I did not tell him more then, though I feared he might hear of my pending nuptials from others that evening, but I was convinced that, regardless, his heart would be true to me.

The next morning, however, I thought better of it and sought him out before the tournament.

"Sir Milon," I said, "forgive me for extracting a promise from you while withholding circumstances. No doubt by now you know the king wishes me to marry your opponent, Duke Ganelon, yet I have refused to obey my brother's command."

He nodded to confirm that he fully understood my request that he be my champion.

"Sir Milon," I continued, "despite my deceit, I beg you not to refuse me now. I have no liking for Duke Ganelon, and you will do me a great favor in taking my side against him. I cannot love him, whatever his and my brother's wishes. Please do not forsake me in my hour of need. I know you to be good and noble, and you have not yet made any pledge to serve my brother. Please keep your promise to be my champion in this tournament."

He looked deeply troubled by my words, but he agreed to keep his promise. Then I felt both relieved and guilty, for he had come to Aix to become one of the king's peers, and instead, I was setting him on a path of destruction by causing him to anger my brother. Nevertheless, I selfishly allowed him to serve as my champion, and I was not disappointed.

Roland, I wish you could have witnessed the great skill and strength that your valiant father displayed that day. Not only did he serve me well as a champion, but he defeated every knight who challenged him, including Duke Ganelon, who in the jousting, not only was thrown from his horse but crashed into the stands, dislocated his shoulder, and spent the last hour of the jousting having his arm set by the physician.

And when Milon had defeated the sixth and last knight for that day, everyone in the crowd then jumped to his feet, exclaiming in awe over Milon's prowess: "Why, he is like the great Sir Tristram or Sir Bedwyr risen from the grave!"

Seated beside my brother at the tournament, I feared his wrath, but he only turned to me and said, "You have chosen well your champion, Sister, although I daresay Sir Ganelon does not think so."

"I would only have the best," I replied, meaning more by my words than was readily apparent, but my brother did not pick up on the nuance.

"Who is this valiant knight?" Charles then asked me.

"He is a brave young knight of great and ancient lineage," I replied.

"He is of the House of Lusignan and brother to Sir Geoffrey Great-Tooth, the famed giant-killer."

I watched my brother's face closely as his expression turned into a great smile. "Why, I am charmed by such a novelty. I did not know Geoffrey had a brother, and he has not been to court since I was a boy, though I remember well how he could defeat half-a-dozen knights in the tournaments in one day."

Then Charles called to have Sir Milon brought to him, and he presented him with the purse himself for winning the tournament.

When Milon removed his helmet to bow to my brother the king, his dark hair flowed down to his shoulders and his handsome ruddy face, so like your own, Roland, despite the heat of battle, was more handsome than anything I had ever seen, and even Charles, I believe, looked on him and instantly felt that your father had to be the most glorious knight he had ever seen, perhaps even greater than himself, so he said to him, "Sir Milon, I know from my sister that you are of great lineage, and you have here today made your ancestors proud of you. I have witnessed many tournaments, yet I know of no knight who could have fought so well as you have today; it was a truly marvelous sight. This purse of gold is small reward for such skill as yours. I wish to make you, this day, one of my peers, and I will grant you any other wish you may have."

And then, Roland, your father broke into a great, dazzling smile, and without a moment's hesitation, he replied, "My lord king, I accept with all humility to become one of your peers, and if you truly mean I may have any other wish, then I ask of you the great kindness and honor of bestowing upon me the hand of your beautiful sister, Princess Bertha."

Instantly, the entire crowd gasped; then everyone began to mutter and whisper to one another, but no one was more surprised than I, for although I admit to having considered Milon a possible husband, I did not expect such boldness from him. After another minute, a great silence fell as all eyes turned toward Charles to see how he would respond.

And as we waited, out of the corner of my eye, I saw Duke Ganelon approach with his sword drawn in his right hand, while his left shoulder was newly wrapped in a sling. And only then did Charles speak.

"Guards, unarm Sir Ganelon."

Immediately was it done, and Ganelon looked sorely displeased to have his sword taken from him, for I do not doubt he meant Milon harm.

Then Charles looked Milon straight in the eye and said, "Sir Knight, my sister is already engaged to marry Sir Ganelon, Duke of Mayence, and that agreement will not be broken. Despite your noble lineage, you are not one to aspire to the hand of a princess, and I find your remarks intolerable. I have offered you a token of friendship and a place among my men, and yet you mock my hospitality by seeking to come into my house like a thief in the night to take my choicest prize. Such behavior is insufferable. You have until dawn to leave Aix."

"I am no thief in the night, my lord king!" Milon exclaimed, causing the crowd to gasp at his fearlessness in even daring to reply. "It is you who speak like a thief, for you have just offered to fulfill any request I might make, but in the next minute, you take it from me. That is unworthy of the king I would serve."

Then before Charles could find words, Milon turned and left the tournament grounds, the crowd making way for him.

"I ought to have his head," Charles said, turning to me. "Such impudence. What made him dare to presume himself worthy of my sister?"

"He is noble and good, my lord," I replied, hesitating, but feeling uncontrollable emotion surging up in me. "I…I love him, Charles. I—"

"Love him!" exclaimed Charles, so loud that everyone must have heard. "Love a common knight whose lineage we have not even verified!"

"He is a son of Lusignan," I asserted.

"Fie!" spat Charles. "I have never heard that Geoffrey of Lusignan had a brother, save the monk whose death he caused, and even if this knight should be whom he claims, do you think I would wed my sister, my flesh and blood, to the son of the serpent-woman Melusine? Do not talk foolish, Bertha, or you will find yourself locked away in a nunnery rather than married to the greatest peer in the land."

I burst into tears at this speech, and quickly I rose and ran from the dais where we were seated. I made my way to my chamber, my lady-in-waiting following close behind me, and once there, I wept for hours.

I could not understand how this turn of events had taken place, for I'd had no inclination that Sir Milon felt anything for me. Doubtless, he was impudent, I thought, but he knew if he did not speak, I would soon be wed to Ganelon. I could not help wondering whether he truly loved me or he was merely seeking a great dynastic marriage. Still, my heart told me he was true and honest, and when I recalled the look on his face when he asked for my hand, I felt certain his request had been inspired by far more than simple material remuneration. But now my brother had banned him from the court, and within a few days, I would be married to the man I despised, the man who, had my brother not forbade it, would have attempted to slay the man I loved before my very eyes.

I wept that entire evening, and it was not until I was preparing to go to sleep that my maid came to me.

"Milady, you have a visitor," she announced.

"At this hour?" I said, for I was already in my nightshift. "Who could it be?"

"It's a man, milady," she replied.

"Oh, give me a minute then," I said, finding a robe to put over me so I did not appear too unseemly. I dared not ask her what man it was, for if she had known the man, I expected she would have told me his identity; therefore, I could only hope it was Sir Milon, come to rescue me. It was forward of him to come to my rooms in the evening, but I could think of no other man who would be so brave, save my brother.

I was surprised instead when a minute later my maid showed Bishop Turpin into my chamber.

"Leave us," I then told her, for if any man in France could be trusted to enter a maiden's chamber at night, it was Bishop Turpin.

"What can I do for you, your Excellency?" I asked.

"Milady," he replied, "I am sorely grieved by the king's treatment of that brave and gallant knight at the tournament this afternoon."

"As am I, your Excellency," I replied.

"Milady, if it be not too presumptuous, I would know whether you return the affection he has for you?"

I so quickly blushed at this question that he could see there was no need for me to answer.

"I suspect you have no love in your heart for Duke Ganelon," Bishop Turpin continued. "Am I correct in that surmise?"

"Truth be told, your Excellency, I loathe the very sight of him," I admitted. "I do not understand how my brother could wish such a marriage for me. I know a princess is not supposed to love, but instead, she must marry for the benefit of her country, but I love Sir Milon. I do not know him well, it is true, but I feel like I have known him forever and that I can look into his very soul and see it is good and true, and I have no doubt he will be as great an ally to my brother as any duke, even if he be only a knight, for he is descended from great kings, I believe."

"Yes, I have heard the stories of his family, especially of his mother. Despite the rumors about her that seem so difficult to believe, for I am no believer in superstition, it is said she was the daughter of the King of Albany; therefore, he is more than worthy of your hand in marriage, being a king's grandson, while Duke Ganelon has no royal lineage to which he can lay claim."

"My own royal lineage is no great thing," I admitted, "for my father's father was not a king, but Lord Mayor of the Palace, and it is only by the good favor of the Pope that my family has succeeded to the throne of France."

"This I know well, also, my lady, for I am old enough to remember the beginnings of your father's reign. I even can remember that once in my youth I saw the great Lady Melusine herself when she visited the court of King Theuderic IV, and a most gracious and remarkable lady she was, so I cannot believe the evil that has been spread about her and her heirs. Sometimes, I fear the Holy Mother Church has those within it who spread such tales for their own agendas, for they do not like the old ways of the pagans, despite the fact that so much of what we believe has been borrowed from them and disguised as something unique to us. But forgive me, milady, for these theological arguments are complex and not fit to be discussed in the hearing of female ears, especially when we have so little time to act."

"Little time?" I asked.

"Yes, Sir Milon waits in the chapel. I made inquiries and sought him out after the tournament, and then he confessed to me his great love for you. He said it was love at first sight, so he feels it is God's very desire that he be with you, although he cannot explain why he feels such an overwhelming passion. While I do not understand it myself, it is sufficient for me to believe that your marriage to such a pure-hearted knight will be better for this country than should you wed Ganelon, for the thought of putting the duke a step closer to the line of succession, while I cannot explain it, causes a chill to run through me."

I did not know what to say. Was it possible that I was to marry the handsome, brave, undefeatable Sir Milon?

"What do you say, milady?" Bishop Turpin pressed. "We have not much time. Will you marry Sir Milon this evening? It would mean that you would have to flee from Aix until your brother's anger cools, but if you truly love Sir Milon, I will do all I can to make King Charles see the sense of this marriage and forgive you."

I stepped toward Bishop Turpin then, and taking his hands in my own, I said, "Your Excellency, you will forever be my friend, and if ever I can repay this favor, I will gladly do so. Go to my beloved knight and tell him I will join him in half an hour. I just need time to dress for the wedding ceremony and to collect enough of my belongings that we may leave directly after."

"I will do as you bid, my child," Bishop Turpin replied, bowing, and then he left me. I immediately called my lady-in-waiting back to my room, swore her to secrecy, and then dressed for my wedding while she collected what of my belongings could easily be borne away with me.

In half an hour, I was in the chapel with my lady-in-waiting for a witness. Bishop Turpin was already there, and when I entered, Milon stepped from behind a pillar. We immediately placed our hands in one another's, and we did not once cease looking in each other's eyes throughout the ceremony. Afterwards, we often questioned how such love could have come about so quickly, but we always agreed that we had made the right decision, and in the years that followed, despite all the hardships we faced, we never for a moment wished it had been otherwise.

Within the hour, I found myself on my own palfrey, riding beside Milon, my lady-in-waiting following behind with my possessions, for she refused to be parted from me. We traveled all that night until daybreak when we found an inn; there we stayed the entire day so we would not be seen in the daylight.

What followed would make for a long tale, Roland. It's sufficient to say that we traveled many days, moving from place to place so we would not be captured by my brother's men. We soon heard rumors of how angry Charles was. He had offered a great reward for Milon's capture, dead or alive, and my own return, although alive, of course. Nevertheless, I feared he would accuse me of treason, of a crime against the crown, for he was not yet wed, nor had children, so any child I gave birth to would be heir to the throne; therefore, in his eyes, we were endangering the succession by marrying without his permission.

Often we hid in churches, having carried with us a letter from Bishop Turpin, asking that we be given sanctuary, though we feared everyone we spoke to might be endangered, or worse, betray us. When we learned a price was on Milon's head, we quickly made our way to Italy. We dared not even go to Milon's brother Geoffrey from fear that Charles would wreak revenge on him. I insisted my lady-in-waiting leave me at this point and return to her brother's barony where she would be safe, for I no longer wished to endanger her. By then, Charles was quite furious; we continually heard stories of how he intended to end Milon's life and carry me back to France to marry me to Ganelon. At one point, your father and I had to disguise ourselves as beggars and wander for days from town to town so we would not be recognized. At last we came to Sutri, tired and footsore, and unable to go any farther. And when none would take us into their homes, we found shelter in this wretched cave, which we hoped would serve as a home for us only for a short time, until Charles' anger would soften and we could obtain his forgiveness.

Then soon after you were born, Roland, the Saracens crossed the sea and came into Italy, threatening Rome itself. Your father, remembering his knightly vows, once more donned his armor, and taking his lance and shield, he went out to do battle for King Charles and the Holy Church, never seeking recognition for his work, and even fighting beside Charles when he came with his army to defend Rome, although never revealing his identity. But while your father hoped his valor would help to bring about Charles' forgiveness when the war had ended, he instead was slain by the foe, dying valiantly for king and church. Since then, as you know, we have lived these long, weary years in this wretched cell, dependent on our kind neighbors' assistance and what little work I could do. I have hoped always for brighter and better days, but I little expected that today would be the start of them. This very hour, however, I feel deep inside me that your destiny is calling.

And so, Roland, now you have learned the story of your birth and your kinship, and you know the destiny that is yours if you but do your part. The blood that flows in your veins is the blood of heroes, and it will not belie itself. You have seen your uncle, King Charles, and before he leaves Sutri, you must convince him to acknowledge you as his nephew and take you as a squire into his court. Take this golden ring, the very ring that was your father's and that he received from his mother, the great Lady Melusine. Had he carried it with him when he went to fight the Saracens, he doubtless would be with us still, but he left it with me because he knew it would secure you your birthright when the time came, both to be recognized as the king's nephew and also so you could someday go to your Uncle Geoffrey and claim your right as the Lord of Lusignan, for Geoffrey yet lives and has no children of his own, so you are his heir. Tonight, you must take it with you when you go to see the king so he will recognize you as the son of Sir Milon and his own nephew.

CHAPTER 5

ROLAND'S TALE CONTINUES

I REMEMBER FULL well how I took the ring my mother gave me that evening, and how I looked at it long, marveling at its beauty in the light of the declining sun, until finally she said to me, "Go now. It is evening and there will be a banquet and a great celebration at the castle. Ask your friend Oliver to assist you in making your way before my brother Charles so you may proclaim your lineage and your right to serve him or one of his knights as a squire."

I did as my mother bid. I changed into my finest and only other suit of clothing, and then I kissed my mother on the cheek, and with the ring on my finger—it was a ring for a man's hand, but even my mother was impressed by how well it fit me—I made my way to the castle. Within the hour, I was outside the banquet hall, and although a guard tried to stop me, I said, "Make way. I am the king's nephew. He will know me once he sees the ring I wear," and although the guard would hush me, King Charles heard my words and had the guard bring me forth, and there I boldly told him, "I am your nephew, Roland, son of your sister, the Princess Bertha, and her husband, the brave

Sir Milon. I have with me this ring of the House of Lusignan as proof of my birthright, and even now, my mother waits in our home just outside the city to welcome her brother."

At these words, everyone in the crowd expressed astonishment; I could hear their gasps and whispers of "Such insolence" and laughs at my poor clothing, but I ignored them and looked straight at King Charles, who sat stony-faced for a moment. But then a smile spread across his cheeks, and he said, "You certainly have the courage demonstrated by my family. Step forward and show me this ring." And so I did, standing before him at table and removing it from my finger to hand to him. He held and looked at it for a minute, and then he said, "I have never seen this ring, but I have heard of the rings Melusine left her children, and this ring, indeed, fits their description. And if you are whom you claim, then your mother's face will confirm it. Lead me to her."

Then a great uproar of surprise came from the crowd as King Charles stood up, ordered his horse, and completely interrupted the banquet. In a few minutes, I found myself seated on his steed before him and we galloped out of the city gates to the grotto where my mother and I lived, followed by several members of the court, including Bishop Turpin, whom I could see was very pleased by the reunion scene that followed.

In a moment, my uncle and mother had forgiven each other all their past wrongs, and then King Charles told her to prepare to leave. He was traveling to Rome to see the Pope, but he would return in a few days time to bring us back to Aix with him. Indeed, he wanted us to take up lodgings in the castle at Sutri in the meantime, but my mother refused, saying she needed a few days to prepare and say goodbye to her old life.

And good as his word, before the week was over, King Charles returned to Sutri and bore my mother and me back to Aix, and there I grew into manhood in his court, first as a squire to his peer Duke Namon, and then as one of his peers myself. And somehow in all of the excitement of those years, I never again thought to question my mother further about my father's family.

Now, riding beside Merlin, could I even be sure that all I thought I remembered my mother telling me was accurate? It had been so many years ago, and I had scarcely given it a thought since—in truth I was afraid to think of it, at least the part where I was the grandson of Melusine, the fairy serpent—and much of what I did remember my mother telling me was what my father had told her before I was even born, and most of his information he had gained from his nurse or his brother Geoffrey. And what of Geoffrey? He was my uncle, and still famous enough for having slain a giant that I had heard of him. I knew he yet lived at Lusignan, but I had never sought him out. Yet now I was to learn all from my grandfather, Raimond, once Count of Forez and Poitou and husband to the Lady Melusine of Lusignan. It was hard to believe my grandfather could even still be alive, for my father had been his youngest son while Geoffrey must have been twenty years older than my father. That would mean my grandfather must be well past his eightieth year by now.

Just what was I now to learn? And why was Merlin, the great enchanter, involved in it? He alone must be three centuries old. The whole matter was almost impossible for me to believe, as impossible to believe as that my grandmother had transformed herself into a flying serpent. But if that were true, my grandfather would certainly be able to tell me so.

And what about the magical ring? Was it truly magical? Perhaps so, for I had carried it with me in all my battles and never been defeated, although I liked to believe that was due to my own prowess and skill. Nor did I consider the last battle at Roncesvaux Pass a defeat since Ganelon's treachery had caused my downfall, for I knew full well he had always hated me and must have arranged the ambush. I only hoped that King Charles would discover Ganelon's treachery and destroy him. And the ring was still on my finger—apparently the traitor had failed to find my body or I do not doubt he would have taken it from me out of spite, if not greed or curiosity.

Why had I ever consented to my mother marrying Ganelon once we returned to court? I had, in truth, been still too young to object, and I knew she did it as a sign of reconciliation to her brother. Nor did she feel repulsion toward the duke then, for her beauty and youth had faded, she had already known romance in her life, and she had acknowledged he would make her a good husband. Yet he and I had never seen eye to eye. Then he truly grew to hate me after my mother gave birth to my half-brother, Baldwin, for he feared the king would favor me over Baldwin since I was the older nephew, and older even than the king's own sons, but none of that was my fault. I could not help it if my uncle the king loved me, and I deserved that love, for I did everything I could to serve him well.

I did try to be a dutiful stepson, and I loved my little brother until he became old enough to mimic his father's hateful ways. But I could never accept Ganelon in the role of father to me, not when my own father, although I had never known him, had been the embodiment of knightly virtue and courage from all I had heard of him.

Still, it was strange that I did not know anything of my father's family for certain. I had never even met a relative of his. And now, here I was, just hours away from seeing my grandfather where he lived among the hermits.

As if meeting my grandfather would not be surprising enough, just coming to Montserrat was an overwhelming experience. We arrived late the next evening at the foot of the mountain where perched the monastery. The sun was just setting, and the sight was one of astonishment. I, who had lived in King Charles' palace and worshiped in the Cathedral at Aix and the other great cathedrals of the day, had never seen anything to equal my first sight of Montserrat. No, it was not overly large or awe-inspiring—it had no grand towers or balconies, no ornate decoration, nor pillars, stained glass windows, or golden crucifixes. But its serene mountaintop setting made it unlike any other location I had ever laid eyes upon.

Somehow, Montserrat seemed a fitting place to learn of my origins. I had been resurrected, it seemed, and now I was approaching the closest place to Heaven that I had ever seen on the earth, and there I hoped to find answers to my questions, including not only the story of my father's family's past, but also why it was that Merlin— whose presence was perhaps the most mysterious part of this entire experience—should choose me for a quest whose purpose I could not even begin to imagine.

At that time, Montserrat did not even have a great monastery as it would in later centuries; only a grouping of small hermitages filled the mountaintop—just a few monks living together in each structure like small families. Already as my and Merlin's horses began to climb the mountain's steep foothills, I sensed the peace of this place, its mountaintop almost hidden in the clouds, the evening sun setting it aglow as if God Himself were shining a great light upon it, claiming it as His Holy House.

"We will sleep here tonight," Merlin said as we came to the mountain's base. "It's a long hike up and too steep for the horses, and it's dangerous to walk up that winding road in the dark, even for one of my youth and agility."

I was not sure whether he was joking about his youthfulness, considering he had brought me back to life; how was I to know whether beneath his great snow white beard a youthful face of twenty was not to be seen?

I quickly got off my horse and helped Merlin to make camp, which didn't take much effort. He had a small bedroll with him, which he somehow managed to unroll and turn into a giant tent, fit for King Charles himself, and from out of nowhere, he filled the tent with two beds, a chair, a table, and blankets. Then he instructed me to collect wood for a fire. I looked around for several minutes to gather sticks and branches, but I had only found a few when he hollered for me to come back.

"I only found these little twigs," I said, returning with them to him.

"These will do," Merlin replied, taking them from me and muttering in a language I did not understand. The next thing I knew, the twigs expanded in his hand, and then he dropped them to the earth and we both stepped back as they grew into large logs—so much wood that we had enough easily to burn someone at the stake with it. Then Merlin uttered another incantation, and little balls of fire sprung to life, igniting all the wood.

"Now go catch us something to eat," Merlin told me.

I quickly did his bidding, stunned by what I had seen him do. I had heard many tales of Merlin, but I had never witnessed magic of this magnitude. In fact, I had often thought the old tales of his magic had simply been made up, or at least exaggerated. In afteryears, I heard many tales of magic told of Charlemagne and his court, but they were mostly the fancies of men, none of them ever true. Even Maugris, the chief magician of Charlemagne's court, who claimed to be a great wizard and raised by the fairies, was never someone anyone had seen work true magic, and I suspect the stories about him were all rumors he had spread about himself while he used his dwarf stature only to add to his mysteriousness. Consequently, I was both in awe and fear of Merlin when I saw him do such great and true sorcery.

As for finding us dinner, I had no weapon but my sword. I had no bow and arrow, no spear, no snare, but I dared not oppose Merlin's command from fear he would become angry and throw a ball of fire at me—not that I had yet seen him betray any anger, but if he did grow angry, it might be too late for me to know how far his wrath might reach.

After a few moments, I spied a squirrel, his claws clutched into a tree trunk, watching me, uncertain whether he should remain hidden behind the trunk or flee. Before he could decide, I swung my sword and chopped off his head with one blow. I had found our dinner.

"Very good," said Merlin when I brought the decapitated squirrel back to him. A few minutes later, working remarkably fast, Merlin had it skinned and roasting over the fire. It was a puny little beast and hardly a meal for one man, much less two, but somehow, I managed to eat until I was well past full, and Merlin miraculously had seconds.

"Time to get some sleep now," he said, for it was long past dark. "It's a long hike up the mountain so we want to start at the first glimmer of dawn."

"All right," I said, not sleepy yet, but knowing it best to obey him.

Once we were in the tent and in our beds, however, I could not help but pester him with some of the multitude of questions burning in my brain.

"Sir," I asked, "why must we go to visit my grandfather?"

"That will all be explained to you tomorrow," he replied. "There is a long story you must know, and it is not fit for me to tell it. Your grandfather will enlighten you on all these things."

"But is it true," I continued, "that my grandmother was a fairy or a serpent of some sort?"

"Again," Merlin repeated, "it is a long tale and your grandfather will explain it all to you tomorrow."

"Why must we pretend that I am dead?" I continued. "Will I ever get to return to my uncle's court or see my companions again?"

"No, you will not return to the court; however, as I have told you before, you will see your friend Ogier the Dane again if all goes according to plan."

"And what would that plan be?" I persisted.

"Again, that will be explained to you tomorrow. Now go to sleep. At my age, I need all the rest I can get."

My curiosity overly piqued, I dared ask one last question.

"Just how old are you?" Then fearing his anger, I added, "I am sorry to ask, but you have to understand this whole experience is beyond human belief for me."

"I am hundreds of years old," Merlin replied, "as you already know. The exact number of my years is unimportant; to say it is around eight centuries or thereabouts is sufficient."

"Eight centuries!" I exclaimed. "But—"

"No more questions or we will be up all night and you will be too sleepy to listen to what you must be told in the morning."

Duly hushed, I asked no more, but I could not help muttering to myself, "Eight centuries old...." I was no great scholar, but I had learned to read a bit at my uncle's court, and the good court scholar Alcuin had instructed me a little in history. I knew King Arthur had lived in the years following the fall of the Roman Empire, and I knew the empire had fallen about three hundred years ago. I had always understood that Merlin was an old man at King Arthur's court, but even taking that into consideration, he should not exceed four hundred years old, yet he claimed to be double that. How could that be? How was it possible for anyone even to live beyond one hundred? It was so marvelous and difficult to believe that I could not even begin to imagine what additional wonders I would learn on the morrow.

It was hours before I slept, and sleep came fitfully then, perhaps because of Merlin's snoring. But finally, when it felt as if I had just drifted off, I found Merlin shaking me awake as the first glimmer of dawn rose over the landscape.

When Merlin woke me, I did not feel well-rested at all, but the cool mountain air quickly brought me to my senses. And after I emerged from the tent and walked away just a few feet to relieve myself, I turned around to find Merlin had completely packed up the camp and was waiting on his horse for me.

"Hurry; we are wasting time," he said.

Before I could even mount my own steed, his was galloping off.

Quickly bolting onto my horse, I chased after him, shouting, "What? No breakfast?"

But I was less hungry than surprised by his behavior. He was well ahead of me and his horse raced like none I had ever seen—not even the great Bayard that the dwarf Maugris had ridden, although doubtless Maugris' small stature had made it easier for a horse to carry him.

I had to ride about a mile up the mountain path before I caught up with Merlin, whom I found bartering with an innkeeper to care for our horses until we descended back down the mountain, for the path was steep and rocky and would need to be walked from that point.

As we stepped from the innkeeper's dwelling, I dared ask Merlin, "Why did we not sleep there last night, and what of food? I am famished."

"Fleas in the beds and rat-droppings in the food," Merlin muttered and marched off ahead of me.

My stomach was rumbling with hunger. I felt in no way prepared to climb a mountain in that condition, but I had no choice but to follow Merlin, trying my best to keep up with him, for he walked as swiftly as a youth of twenty, never expressing the slightest sign of fatigue. I had been, if not the greatest, certainly one of the greatest champions at my uncle's court. Only perhaps Ogier the Dane could outfight or outrun me, so I was astonished by the stamina of this man who last night had told me he was eight hundred years old. He truly must have incredible powers, I realized, so I decided it best simply to follow his lead rather than argue with him about having breakfast.

While the mountain itself could not be even a mile high, the path up it wound itself in such a way that I'm sure we walked thrice that distance, and with it all being uphill, even a young man like myself had to be panting a bit by journey's end, but Merlin showed not even a bead of perspiration on his brow when we reached the summit.

Once near the top, with the morning sun now fully risen and lighting the entire hill, I was overwhelmed with the beauty and felt almost as if I were basking in the very light of God, with nothing but the singing of the birds to be heard around me.

"Impressive, isn't it?" said Merlin. "It reminds me of a mountain in Avalon that your grandmother used to climb with her mother when she was a girl, a mountain from which one has the ability to view any part of the world he wishes, but here at Montserrat, why would you wish to view any other place? It is said that God Himself resides here, although I personally believe He resides everywhere and in many forms, including in each of us."

I did not know how to respond to such a remark, nor did I have time to reply, for at that moment, we came over the mountain's summit to find a man sitting on a large stone along the roadside. The moment he saw us, he rose to his feet and stretched his arms toward Merlin.

"Welcome, friend," he said, stepping forward and placing his hands on Merlin's arms. He was an old man, looking as old as the wizard himself, though I daresay Merlin was ten times his age if what he had told me was true, and after the magic I had witnessed the night before, I no longer felt the need to question the truth of anything Merlin told me.

Merlin returned the old man's embrace, and then he turned toward me, redirecting the old man's attention. The stranger looked almost hesitant to behold me as Merlin said, "Raimond, this is your grandson."

"No introduction is necessary," said my grandfather, stepping toward me. Unused to signs of affection, I think I stepped back as he approached, or perhaps I did so from fear now that my family's mysterious origins were to be explained to me. Surely, what I had heard of Melusine could not be true, and yet I dreaded it might be.

"Fear not," he said, seeing my hesitation and continuing toward me. "You are most welcome here, son of Arthur, son of Mordred, son of Melusine."

As I tried to understand his words, he clasped my shoulders and looked deeply into my eyes, and I had the uncanny feeling that I was staring at myself—at the man I would be in half a century's time.

"I see astonishment in your eyes," my grandfather told me, "but you show courage in not flinching at my greeting, although I daresay you do not understand it wholly."

"No," I admitted, relieved to have him remove his hand from my shoulder, "but I have recently become accustomed to marvels I do not understand."

"Come," he said, taking my hand and then stepping toward Merlin to clasp his hand as well. "There is much to tell and little time."

I walked in a daze, not having expected my grandfather to be anything except a weak old man, but while he was definitely old, he was spry and stepped quickly. I felt all in a daze while Merlin looked greatly amused and winked at me as we followed my grandfather, strange as it was to think of the old man as such.

In a few minutes, Raimond had led us to a small stone building against the mountainside.

"We will be left alone here," he said, beckoning us inside. Before I entered, I looked about and saw various other hermitages scattered along the mountain—some as small as my grandfather's, others three or four times larger, but all small enough to fit inside my uncle's throne room. None of these buildings hinted at the grandeur of the monastery that would be built upon this mountain a few centuries later.

I had to duck to enter my grandfather's dwelling, and then I found myself inside a cozy little room furnished with simple wooden chairs, a table, and an uncomfortable-looking cot in the corner. The morning sunlight shone into the room, illuminating it, but never once during the conversation that followed did I think to look out the window, for I was soon entranced with what my grandfather told me.

I sat at the table, following my grandfather's gesture to do so.

Merlin turned toward the fireplace, and after muttering some words I could not hear, a fire sprang up in it, and by the time my grandfather had collected a few earthen cups and a jug of water, Merlin had cooked several plates of eggs and even baked a loaf of bread—I knew not how.

"We will eat now," said Merlin, "for what you will be told, Milon, is not fitting to be heard on an empty stomach."

I was starved and gladly took the plate offered me. I quickly gobbled down the meal while Merlin and my grandfather did the same, no one speaking as we ate. Within five minutes, we had rinsed down the food with cups of water, and then I turned to my grandfather, no longer able to withhold my questions.

"I understand, Grandfather," I began, awkward as it was to name him such, "that Melusine was my grandmother and your late wife, but what did you mean when you called me son of Arthur and son of Mordred? You know, surely, that my father's name was Milon since he was your son."

"Yes, my boy, I know that, but while I could give you a quick answer to your question, it would not satisfy you sufficiently, so I will tell you all now, and it will be a long tale so prepare yourself."

He then looked at Merlin, and when I also looked in his direction, the old wizard nodded his approval, and so my grandfather began his tale.

CHAPTER 6

RAIMOND'S TALE

WHERE DO I begin? It is a long tale, and there is so much to tell, so I will not bore you with all the details of my background; rather, I will try quickly to summarize my own past up until that moment when I met your grandmother, the Lady Melusine, for it did not feel as if my life had even begun for me until that moment, and indeed, just the minute prior to my meeting her, I had thought my life was swiftly approaching its end.

As I am sure you already know, your grandmother, Melusine, had her secret, but I had one of my own, which she helped me to keep long before I knew of hers. All I knew then was that your grandmother was the most beautiful being I had ever seen, and she was the source of all my success and all my joy until that fateful day when I made the mistake of defying her and her secret was revealed.

But I am getting ahead of myself already.

I was born the third son of Hervé de Léon, a Count of Brittany and a great favorite of Brittany's king. My father was a wise man and a true friend, so the king and he were the closest of companions. But one day a group of evil men at court, jealous of my father's popularity with the king, and equally hating the king's heir, his nephew, arranged that nephew's death so that it looked as if my father were the murderer. My father, despite his protestations of innocence, was unable to prove he had not committed the murder. The king, although deeply grieved for his nephew, decided that because of his prior love for my father, rather than condemn him to death, he would send him into exile. I tell this story as my father told it to me when I was a boy, although I later learned he left out some important details, as you will eventually hear.

My father left Brittany and travelled through France until he came to the Forest of Forez, and there he used what wealth he had brought with him to purchase land, establish himself as lord of a new castle, and begin his life over.

Because my father was of goodly countenance and pleasant in manner, and because word of his wisdom and counsel to the King of Brittany had spread throughout France, and despite tales of how the King of Brittany's nephew had died, my father was soon befriended by the Count of Poitiers, and after some time, he wed the count's sister. As I said, I was their third born son. My father continued to rise in esteem, and in time, the King of France, who was Childebert III at that time, came to rely upon my father for his wise counsel and raised him to the rank of Count of Forez.

I knew little else about my father's background, for he died when I was yet a young boy. The year of his death, a great sickness spread across the land, and besides my sire, it also took my two older brothers to an early grave. As for my mother, she had died in giving birth to me. Beyond the grief I experienced at finding myself an orphan, this loss meant I would wait many more years before I could learn anything further of my ancestry and its significance.

My maternal uncle, Aymeri, the Count of Poitiers, now took me under his wing to raise me to be worthy of being a count myself. I grew up with my cousins, Bertrand, the future Count of Poitiers, and his sister, the Lady Blanche, and we were all great friends. I adored my uncle and spent every moment I could with him, hoping to learn from him so I might make my father and my brothers proud that I would carry on their legacy when they could not.

Then came the day when my cousin Bertrand and I were made knights, and all the great families from miles and miles around came to the celebration. It should have been the happiest day of my life, but instead, save for the day I lost my beautiful wife, Melusine, it was the worst I have ever experienced.

When the time came that day for the boar hunt, I rode out at my uncle's side into the great forest. Our party soon caught the trail of a hunted beast and we pursued it fiercely until we finally had it cornered. Then the creature became so alarmed at its life being threatened that it violently charged toward our dogs, scaring them back, so that none dared attack it. Even the men on their steeds, though armed with spears and arrows, stood back, wary of approaching close enough to pierce it from fear it would attack them.

When my uncle and I arrived upon the scene, we instantly saw the fear of all the men. My uncle poured his scorn upon them, mocking them for allowing the son of a sow to get the better of them. Wishing to show myself worthy of the knightly spurs I had just earned, I jumped from my horse and ran straight at the boar, ramming my spear between its shoulders before it could make a move.

But it was a tough old beast and quickly ran against me, knocking me to the ground and then tearing off past everyone and into the forest. Although the creature was now wounded, the other men still held back, certain that the beast was only more infuriated and dangerous than before.

Knowing the creature could not live long given how deeply I had speared it, I quickly followed its path through the woods, my uncle riding at my side.

We chased it throughout the evening as the sun set, but when night fell, while our hounds still scented its trail, my uncle said it was perilous to pursue it in the dark. I was headstrong and wanted to continue, so my uncle hesitated, then looked up into the sky to see whether sufficient moonlight would allow our continued pursuit.

All of a sudden, my uncle froze in his saddle, staring up at the evening stars. He did not reply to me when I repeatedly questioned him about what he saw, and his silence soon made me fear he was bewitched.

After a moment, he came to himself, but he was close enough to me that, despite the thickening evening shadows, I could see the look of horror on his face.

"Come, Uncle. I am not a fool to risk my neck in the dark for mere sport," I said, afraid to ask him what was wrong. "We will make camp here. It is getting cool and I will build us a fire."

My uncle dismounted his horse and tied it to a tree; then he sat down upon the ground while I collected wood to burn. He sat there like a man who is dead in his soul after experiencing some great grief. I pretended not to notice and went about my work, although his silence greatly disturbed me. Once I had a fire burning, I walked about half a mile from our camp until I was able to shoot a rabbit with my bow and arrow and bring it back for our supper. Not until I had the rabbit cooked and my uncle had tasted of it did he feel ready to tell me what had troubled him.

"Raimond," he said, "when I looked up into the sky, I saw a terrible sign. The stars foretold my death, and by thy very hand. I know you love me, Raimond, so I did not at first wish to say anything to you, but I do not understand how it can be that you would hurt me so."

"My lord, my dear uncle," I said, tears coming to my eyes at the very thought of my committing such an unthinkable deed, "you know I love you as if you were my father. You have taken me in and treated me as well as you treat my cousin, Bertrand, your own son. Do not think I would ever do such a deed."

"The stars also foretold," continued my uncle, as if he had not even heard me, "that you will profit greatly from my death. I do not know how, for though I love you, all I have will go to your cousin."

"Nor do I wish any profit from your death, my lord," I assured him. "I have my own portion from my father. Perhaps you misread the stars. It cannot be possible what you claim you saw."

"The stars do not lie," my uncle replied. "I wish I were wrong, but I stood looking at them for a long time, and I know not how, but they seemed to move about the heavens until they formed horrible images of my death, and you standing over me with—"

Suddenly, a great rustling was heard in the nearby thicket, and before we could move, out burst the wounded boar, my spear still in him. He must have been mad with pain by that point, for he came charging at us. I had only a second to grab my bow while my uncle jumped to his feet, trying to pull forth his sword, but before he could do so, the boar was upon him, and without second-guessing myself, I sent an arrow flying at the beast. But the creature's hide was so tough that my arrow only bounced off his skin and flew backwards, piercing straight into my uncle's heart.

A second later, the horrible creature had disappeared again into the forest, and my uncle lay crumpled upon the ground. I fell beside him, weeping and wanting to pull out the arrow, but his hands were clasped tightly around it while his eyes stared accusingly at me and blood poured forth from his lips. My uncle, Count Aymeri of Poitiers, was dead, with not a final word for me, but knowing that the prophecy foretold by the stars had been fulfilled.

I cannot describe the grief, the fear, the anger and despair that came over me. My rage caused me to see red, and overcome with madness, I ran in circles about the clearing and even through the fire, seeking to destroy my pain. But the skies parted at that moment and sent down a torrent of rain, clenching the flames before they could do more than singe my clothes, as if God himself would not let me be relieved from my punishment. Then I screamed and ranted at the heavens for betraying me, and I know not how long it was before reason seeped back into my brain.

Finally, I realized that my uncle's death looked like murder, and once the other courtiers found us, I would be blamed for this deed, accused of treason to my lord, my beloved uncle. Perhaps I would even be hunted by my own cousin Bertrand as he sought revenge for his father's death.

Desperate, fearful, I raced into the forest, not knowing where I was going or where I wished to go. I do not know how I survived that night. I only remember running, stumbling over roots, falling to my knees in tears, only to rise and run again. Could I have found a way to destroy myself, I have no doubt I would have, but in my agony and thoughtlessness, I had left behind my weapons with my uncle's body. I ran to rid myself of my agony, caring not that I was becoming lost in the forest or whether some wild beast should find and tear me apart. Most horrible of all was the thought that if I did not destroy myself, the rest of the prophecy my uncle had seen in the stars might come true—namely, that I would profit greatly from his death.

Exhausted, thirsty, my sobs and tears having drained my body of fluid, at last I came to a forest clearing. There I saw, as if by a miracle, a fountain of water springing up from the ground and flowing into a stream that led through the forest. Remembering the story in the Bible of Hagar—of how God had made a fountain burst from the earth to give her and Ishmael water—I thought perhaps this fountain was meant as a comforting sign from God that I was not to die, that I was to drink and live. Recalling my uncle's prophecy that great good would come to me as a result of his death, I began to think that perhaps that good was part of God's plan, for after all, did not God Himself put the stars in the sky to foretell the prophecy?

But before I could think more, with my body drooping, my feet sore from running, I managed to struggle to the stream and drink to restore my spirits. I drank long and greedily and soon felt the joy of restored strength from the cool clear water.

Only after I had drunk my fill did I sit up on my knees to look about me. That was when I saw, standing just a few feet from me, the most beautiful woman I had ever seen. It was dawn now, and the morning sun lit her red hair so that it shone like gold, while her green eyes were as cool and inviting as a forest glade, and her gown was rich, yet simple, as if she were more a woodland sprite than the great lady she surely must be.

The sun had only just broken forth as I had drunk, and so I thought she must have been hidden in the forest's shadows when I first approached the fountain. But now she stood so close to me that I could not imagine how I had not heard her step.

"Milady, my pardon," I said, kneeling again. "I did not see you approach."

"Do not be afraid," she replied, her face all kindness. "I have been waiting for you."

"For me, my lady?" I said. "I am sorry, but I do not believe we have ever met, for surely, I would remember one so beautiful."

"No, we have not met before," she replied, "but I have heard of your great prowess in the hunt, your wisdom inherited from your father, your loyal nature to your uncle, and I knew that you were in this wood, so I have waited for you to arrive, Raimond, nephew to the late Count of Poitiers, and Count of Forez in your own right."

"Then you know what has happened to my uncle?" I asked. "You know it was an accident—that I did not mean to kill him?" As I spoke, I wondered how she could know such a thing and whether I had not just incriminated myself through my speech.

"Hush," she said, and stepping closer to me, where I remained upon my knees, she took my head in her arms and pressed it against her breasts. "Hush," she repeated. "Everyone in France knows how well you loved your uncle and how he loved you and that nothing but amity ever existed between the two of you."

"But that he should die at my hand!" I cried into her breast.

"No one will think that either," she replied, stroking my hair, and while I found this all incredible and strange, I could not pull myself away from her comfort. "It was clearly an accident," she soothed me. "They will know that when they find the body. You need not fear."

I was stunned by her words, but I managed to ask, "But, milady, if the body has not yet been found, how do you know this?"

She laughed, laughter as musical as a bubbling spring, and it gave me instant comfort and a sense that I had nothing to fear. Then she replied, "You are so exhausted that you forget you just told me that your uncle has died and that somehow you slew him accidentally. All I said was that I knew you were out hunting in the forest."

My mind felt so muddled with grief and with the wonder of seeing the fountain and this beautiful lady that I thought perhaps I could not clearly remember what I had said. I had no reason to think she did not speak the truth, and I felt I could trust her, even when she said what seemed impossible for her to know. She was so beautiful that she inspired trust in me, and her countenance glowed like that of the Virgin Mary in paintings I had seen—filled with love and compassion. And as my head continued to rest against her breast, I began crying— crying for my father and brothers and even my mother, and of course, for my uncle. I let pour forth all the pain and anguish from all the fear and confusion and grief that I had felt over the course of a lifetime.

And when I had finished my tears, I felt radiating from this fair lady's breast such warmth and goodness that it was as if I were being made whole and complete and fully well again. Then a sense of vivacity and wonder for the miracle of life filled me in a manner I had not felt since my earliest childhood.

"Come; it has been a long night and you are tired," she finally said. "Come and eat." And drawing me to my feet, she walked me a short distance to where a table was set with a veritable feast upon it, and two young maidens emerged from the wood to serve us.

I was equally astonished by this sight. I could only think that she had set out that morning on a picnic with her ladies and that she must be the daughter of some great lord who lived nearby.

"Eat to your heart's content," she told me, and I did so, yet there was so much food on the table that it did not seem to diminish at all as we dined until I began to think she must be some magical being, a fairy, or perhaps an angel sent to me from God in my distress.

When we had finished eating and I had thanked her, she surprised me yet again.

"It is time, Raimond of Forez," she told me, "that you take to yourself a wife."

"My uncle told me that I should wait another year or two," I replied, "and that he would negotiate for the hand of one of the many fine ladies in the neighboring provinces for me. But now...well, what woman would want me when I will be known as the murderer of my uncle?"

"I have already chosen you, Raimond," she replied, both astonishing and pleasing me. "Your uncle foresaw greatness for you upon his death, and I will be the one who will bring about that greatness for you."

Had I told her about my uncle's prophecy? I did not recall having done so. How could she know what he had said the stars prophesied?

"Do not be afraid, Raimond," she continued, looking me straight in the eye as if reading my very thoughts. "I have only love for you. Do you love me?"

"Milady," I said, fumbling for words, unused to women addressing me in such a manner that would have been unseemly in any other female. "Milady, I do not know you or your name. I know nothing of you, though you are so fine and lovely that I suspect you must be a princess. Nor do I know how you know of me, but yes, I do love you, for you have shown me such kindness and mercy and forgiveness as I cannot imagine any other woman would do, and you…you are so very beautiful."

She laughed for a moment and then replied, "You have no need to fear, and I appreciate your honesty. I promise you I am a lady of noble lineage, the daughter of a king, and I will show you kindness all your life, Count Raimond, if you will marry me."

"Milady," I pled, though I desired her with all my heart, "I am not of the blood royal. I am not worthy to marry you."

"I daresay," she replied, "that I know more of your lineage than you do yourself, Raimond, and I promise you that there is no man of more noble stock whom I could ever desire for my husband. I promise that if you marry me, you shall never want for any material thing for the rest of your life, for I am wealthy beyond your imagining, and more to the purpose, I promise you will never want for love all your years, and I promise you children and everything else that a man could desire. Are you agreeable to these terms for our marriage?"

"Yes, indeed, milady," I replied. "How could I refuse them?"

"There is only one condition," she replied, her face growing serious, "and you must never ask me the reason for it. Every Saturday, I am to have the day to myself. On that day, you are not to see me nor to enter my chamber. I will give of myself to you six days a week, but on that seventh day, as in keeping with the Lord's commands, I am to rest."

I did not know why she would choose Saturday as her day to rest; I feared this decision suggested she was not a Christian but a Jewess, but I also knew that I would marry her even if she were a Moor, although she was far too fair, her hair too golden in the early morning sunshine, for me to believe she was any virgin daughter of a Mahometan.

"Will you agree to this condition, Raimond?" she asked, her eyes searching my own. "Will you solemnly swear to it?"

"I will, milady," I replied.

"Then I will wed you, Raimond of Forez, and we will have many happy years together as we reestablish the greatness of both our families."

"Milady, forgive my rudeness," I replied, "but you have not yet told me your name."

"I am Melusine, eldest daughter to the late King Elynas of Albany," she replied. "I am of noble birth like yourself, but now your humble wife and servant if you will have it so."

"That I will, my fair Melusine," I said, overcome with infatuation as I rose from the table and knelt at her feet. "It is my dearest wish, and this the happiest day of my life, save for that day we shall be wed."

I cannot begin to describe for you, Roland, how I felt at that moment. Just an hour before, I had been heartbroken and wishing the very ground would open to swallow me, yet now I was to marry the loveliest creature in all the world, and a king's daughter, no less, who promised me wealth, and children, and most of all, love, something I especially craved, having now lost all my family save for my cousin, the new Count of Poitiers, and his sister, both of whom perhaps would now hate me and seek vengeance because they would think I had slain their father.

"Yes, Raimond," Melusine continued, "we shall be wed. I must go now to prepare for our wedding, and you must return to your uncle's castle, for by the time you return, his body will have been found and brought back. You must join your cousins in mourning your uncle's death, and when seven days have passed, invite them to your wedding. We will hold it in the grounds surrounding your father's castle. The castle is badly in need of repair, having been vacant all these years while you have served at your uncle's side, but I will prepare it for the celebration of our nuptials while you complete your time of mourning. Do you understand all this, Raimond?"

"I can scarcely believe," I replied, "that the Lord, my God, would provide such blessings to me as you have brought to me this day, milady, but yes, I understand it."

"It is good that you are thankful to God," she replied, "for I seek to fulfill His will in all I do, and in our marriage, Raimond, we will go a good way toward fulfilling it. Go now. I will see you again in a week's time when I come to you as your bride."

A week passed, during which time we buried my uncle, and I did what I could to comfort my cousins, who accepted my explanation as to my uncle's death, knowing full well how I had loved him. Their compassion toward my own grief showed me just how easily I had allowed my fears to overcome my reason.

Then on the eve of the seventh day, although I found myself still astonished by all that had happened, I kept my promise to the beautiful Lady Melusine by telling my cousins that I was to be married.

"Married?" Bertrand exclaimed. "How is it that this is the first we have heard of it? Did my father know of this intended marriage?"

So I told Bertrand and Blanche how I had met the fair lady Melusine at the forest fountain the morning after I had spent the night lost in my grief over my uncle's death.

"But who is her family?" Bertrand demanded. "I have heard of the King of Albany, although I do not know his name, but if she is his daughter, what is she doing here in France?"

Embarrassed, I admitted that I could not answer his question, but I told him that I knew Melusine was very rich and would bring with her a great dowry. I also repeated how beautiful she was, but my cousins seemed more interested in her wealth and lineage than her beauty or kindness. Still, I was certain they would instantly be won over by her, just as I had been, once they met her.

The next morning we set out for my father's castle of Forez, but although I had lived there during my childhood and occasionally visited it since my father's death, I was astonished to find how the road to it had changed past all recognition. Instead of a dark country road winding through the forest, it was a grand promenade, lined with towering trees, leading to the castle. Even the castle itself I could scarcely recognize, for it had grown to be six times its size, with more towers and turrets than I had ever seen before, and it looked newly constructed save for the original structure, which stood off to the side like a kitchen added to a palace.

"Cousin Raimond," asked Bertrand, "when did all this change come about?"

"I told you my wife is of great wealth," I replied, "and she has prepared the castle for our home."

"But in just seven days' time?" gasped Bertrand.

"If the Lord God could create the earth in six days," I said, smiling to hide my own dismay, "surely a castle can be constructed in half a fortnight."

But despite my words, I was equally stunned by the sight before me, nor did I suspect how the marvels of that day had only just begun.

The road dipped down into a valley before it approached the castle, and at the bottom of the valley was a meadow in which several large silk tents were raised like none I had ever seen. You would have thought a great festival were to be held there, for everywhere could be seen knights and their ladies, squires and maidens, as well as their horses of every color and kind, from palfreys to warhorses, and both coursers and destriers. Among the tents were set up kitchen grills and fire-pits to provide food for all this multitude of people whom I did not even know, yet all of them had apparently been invited as wedding guests. And here I came simply with my cousins Bertrand and Blanche, their mother, and a handful of Bertrand's knights, no more than half a score in our party by comparison to the several hundred who were already gathered about my father's castle.

But perhaps most marvelous of all was the large and gracious stone chapel that I knew for certain had not been there before; surely it would have taken a good year to build, yet there it stood, and I was to be married inside it. And despite my astonishment to see it, I admit it was a great relief to me, for I had felt some doubts whether my bride was truly a good Christian, considering how she seemed to have wisdom beyond mortal ken. I had secretly feared perhaps she was some sorceress in the dark arts, though repeatedly, I had tried to push this fear from my mind as I recalled her great warmth, her gentleness, and her kind and soothing ways of comforting me, yet the thought had pestered me until this moment when I saw we were to be wed within the Holy Church.

As my cousins and I approached, a band of men came forward to greet us, blowing on trumpets, and then lining the way to announce our presence, and in another minute, as we came into the grounds for the celebration, everyone present stood and cheered my entrance. Soon I found myself being led on my horse to a great dais, as would hold a king's throne at a tournament, where was seated my beautiful bride. She came down its stairs in an entrancing gown of white with gold trim, a gold tiara in her hair worthy of the princess she was, and rich jewels inlaid in gold around her ivory neck and arms. Later, my cousin Blanche would remark that she did not think any woman in the world could have such fine or so many jewels as did my bride. Truly, Melusine looked like a radiant angel that day.

"Welcome, Raimond, my love!" Melusine greeted me once I had dismounted from my horse.

I quickly introduced her to my cousins, and she graciously welcomed them. Then without ado, Melusine said, "Come. We have much to celebrate, but first, we must be wed."

She took my hand and led me toward the chapel, and I, overcome by her beauty and unable to think, much less speak, as the crowd cheered loudly, simply followed her. The noise of the wedding guests quickly lessened as musicians began to play outside the chapel, and I then entered inside the House of God with my bride while my relatives and my lady's attendants trailed in behind us.

Although not as large as a cathedral, the chapel had the most exquisite stained glass windows I had ever seen, so beautiful that I could not help looking at them in wonder with one eye while keeping the other on my fair bride's face as we walked up the church aisle. And then we were before the altar, and there stood the Bishop of Poitiers to wed us.

We stopped just far enough from the bishop that while the guests seated themselves, Melusine could turn and whisper to me without anyone hearing, "Raimond, this is the happiest day of my life."

"And mine also," I replied.

"I am glad," she said, "but it will not be happy if you break your promise to me. Do you remember your promise?"

Caught off-guard, I needed a moment to remember just what I had promised. "That I will always love you until death do us part?" I guessed.

"You promised," her voice gently reprimanded me, "not to seek me out on Saturdays. If you break that promise, great ill will befall us. I will be forced to leave you that same day, and it will bring me great heartbreak. You made me this promise, Raimond. Before we go further with this ceremony, you must be certain you are able to keep it."

"Dearly beloved," began the bishop, before I could think what to say, before I could ask why I must keep such an unusual oath, "we are gathered here today to witness the marriage of Melusine, daughter of the King of Albany, to Raimond, Count of Forez."

I could not disappoint all these people gathered here, and I was willing to promise anything to possess this beautiful creature as my wife. I could only imagine all the ways she would make me happy.

"I promise," I whispered back to her.

She smiled and turned her attention to the bishop. As he spoke, however, I never once took my eyes off Melusine, and at one point during the ceremony, I thought I saw a hint of worry on her face, as if she did not fully trust me. I could not help but wonder what it truly meant that she had demanded this promise from me. What man was not allowed to see his wife for one whole day each week? What if she were an angel, or a fairy, or...or something even more unthinkable...?

But when the time came to exchange our vows, I said, "I do."

Then came the time to exchange the rings. At that moment, I nearly panicked, for I had not thought about needing a wedding ring, but an attendant came forth with two rich gold rings of fine and ancient workmanship. They were carved into the images of serpents swallowing their tails, so finely carved that the serpents seemed nearly to come to life as we placed the rings upon our fingers, and again I marveled, and for a moment, I felt a bit of fear as well, until Melusine smiled upon me and relieved me from all feelings save love and joy.

Once the rings were exchanged, the wedding Mass concluded with Communion. When Melusine took the Blessed Sacrament into her mouth just like the rest of us, it confirmed for me that I had nothing to fear, for I knew she must be a Christian like myself or God would strike her dead for taking the Sacrament; therefore, if as I suspected, she did have magical powers, they were surely ordained by God.

And then great shouting and cheering followed as I walked my bride down the aisle and back outside where her countless servants had prepared a tremendous feast for us. I was now introduced to dozens of people whose names and titles astonished me, for surely all the royalty of Christendom seemed gathered there that day, and yet, I could not imagine why they all would have come, or how Melusine could have gathered them all together on such short notice.

Once during the celebrations, I left my bride's side momentarily because I had drunk too much wine, and as I passed through one of the many festive tents, I heard the guests whispering among themselves. "Who is she? She says she is a Scottish princess, but how can that be?" "Were we led here under false pretenses?" asked another. "But she must be someone important," said a third, "for she sent the most magnificent and impossibly swift ship to bring us here." "That is nothing," said another, "for we came in the finest carriage I have ever seen, and the horses raced so fast that we were here in just hours though I think we must be in the very center of France, and I came all the way from Hungary." "And I from Armenia," said a fourth, "arriving within a day, though it should be several weeks' journey." And then one old woman made the sign against the evil eye while a couple of other ladies made the Sign of the Cross.

But I quickly forgot all these fears once I was back at Melusine's side. She might be a sorceress, or even some sort of fairy, but I could not believe her anything but good, and the way my heart leapt at the sight of her was sufficient to make me think that if she were evil, then sin must be bliss.

You look pale, Roland, at those words. You need not worry, for I have been here for many years at Montserrat praying for my soul and I trust my sins have been forgiven. I only say such things so you will understand the power that your grandmother, the beautiful Princess

Melusine, had over my very heart and soul, such that had she wished, she doubtless could have led me into sin and shown no mercy toward me, but despite the stories you may have heard about her, I never had anything to fear at her hands, save loss of her love if I broke the promise I had made her, which I was determined I would never do, for I knew from that day that I could not bear ever to be parted from her.

All that afternoon and evening we celebrated. A great joust was held, and there was much feasting, and music, and dancing, and all manner of merriment such as I had never seen before nor ever have experienced since, and all those present agreed that never before had there been such a celebration in the history of all mankind.

And then darkness began to fall, and my cousins Bertrand and Blanche came to bid me farewell and return to their own castle. Melusine thanked them graciously for attending her wedding feast and for the privilege of aligning with their House, and she gave to Bertrand a mighty jeweled sword worthy of an emperor and a hunting horn made of ivory and one of her servants came forth with a great black Arabian horse complete with a rich saddle for him. For my cousin, the Lady Blanche, there was a string of the finest pearls I had ever seen, and a great necklace of emeralds, and a chest filled with gowns made of silk, satin, and the finest lace. And for their mother was reserved a collection of rings—garnets, diamonds, rubies, amethysts, and every other gem and precious stone imaginable, such that she could wear a different one on each of her ten fingers and change them every day and never have to repeat wearing one for an entire month. Both my cousins and aunt were astonished by all these priceless gifts and they thanked my bride profusely. Finally, Melusine bowed to Bertrand and he kissed her hand, and then she kissed Blanche and her mother on their cheeks, and after many well wishes between us all, my relatives made their departure.

Melusine next led all the visiting dignitaries into the castle where several dozen servants showed them to their rooms and cared for all their needs.

Once inside, I was astonished by the castle's size, as well as how it was richly furnished with tapestries and good oak furniture, gold and silver candelabras, silk cushions on the chairs, great Oriental rugs on the floors, and all manner of other finery.

My wife led me up a grand staircase and finally to an enormous bedchamber that she said was ours. I asked whether we would each have our own chambers, and she said that yes, she had her own that she would use on Saturdays, but the rest of the time, she would lay with me as my wife, which was only proper for she loved me dearly and intended to give me a large family.

I was struck by such bold talk that seemed unseemly for a maiden, but I reasoned that perhaps it was not unusual from a princess who was used to having her own way and knew her duty was to produce an heir.

I took her in my arms then, and I was about to kiss her and take her to bed and enjoy the greatest bliss that a wedding day can bring when she pulled away from me.

"Raimond, I must remind you of your promise now," she said. "You will promise not to see me ever on a Saturday, for if you do, such great sorrow shall befall you that it will only be surpassed by the greater sorrow that will be caused to me. You understand that promise fully, do you not?"

I was surprised by her continually reminding me of this promise. I could see how very serious she was about it, and I would have trembled at the thought of breaking it were I not already trembling at the prospect, at the deep hope, that we would now consummate the marriage. Any other bridegroom would have considered it his right and taken his bride at that moment, but somehow, I felt Melusine had the upper hand, and I was so enamored with her gracious manners, her stunning beauty, and her deep sense of wisdom, that I was more than willing to be her slave and do her bidding.

"I promise," I repeated.

And then I was barely able to conceal my excitement as she disrobed and allowed me to see her in the fullness of her beauty—a beauty the goddess Aphrodite herself would have envied. I felt almost guilty of a sin for gazing upon something so lovely, and I cannot begin to express my emotions when she then allowed me to take full possession of it.

I had heard tales of what became of men who loved fairies, and even in that moment of passion, the notion that she could be such would not quite leave my thoughts. I partially feared I would wake the next morning to find myself living in the next century, an aged and crippled man with only hours left to live, but in that moment, even such an end felt a worthy barter in exchange for an hour spent in the fair Melusine's embrace.

The following morning, I still had my youth and strength, and I remained quite amorous, and every night after that, I was blessed with holding Melusine to me, and loving her dearly, and feeling completely safe and comforted in her love when we were together.

And yet, in the weeks and months that followed, in the back of my mind there remained doubt—doubt especially on those Saturdays when I never saw her, when I would wake in the morning to find my bed empty save for myself. But on Saturday evening, just a minute after midnight, she would return to me and love me as amorously as every night prior. In time, this pattern became so familiar that my fear and questioning diminished and I accepted the situation as normal and routine. But never was the lovemaking normal or routine, for each time it felt as if I were again possessing a goddess for the first time.

Not long after we were married, my beautiful bride began to build a great castle a few miles from the enlarged Castle of Forez. She insisted that the improvements made to my father's castle had been made quickly and were only intended to serve until there was time to build us a proper home, one befitting such a great lord as myself. I did not know what to say to her in response to this statement, for despite my father being made a count by the king, he was among the poorest of the nobility, and I had no delusions that I was a great lord. But Melusine thought otherwise, and before I knew it, a tremendous castle was being constructed, so large that both the Castle of Forez and the Castle of Poitiers easily would have fit inside it with room to spare.

Melusine had found hundreds of workers to build this palace— from where I never knew. Even more astonishing was what must have been the cost for the materials, but she told me I need never worry about money for she had no lack of it, and as time went on, our wealth grew to astronomical proportions such as I doubt any man on this earth will ever know again.

When this first and greatest of Melusine's castles was nearly completed, my cousin Bertrand came to visit us. He could scarcely believe his eyes at the sight of our dwelling. As you well know, Roland, the Castle of Lusignan is still the largest castle in all of France, and the most magnificent as well—not even your uncle Charles can boast of possessing anything to rival it, and Melusine herself named it.

Nor was one magnificent castle enough for her. We soon owned so much land that she kept building us castles throughout the kingdom so we could travel about for our pleasure as well as to visit all the property she purchased for us. She built castles at Vouvant and Mervent, and the town and tower of St. Maixent, and the castle and town at Ainnelle. And besides indulging in this odd architectural hobby for a woman, she was gracious and kind to all, giving to the poor, often going out to feed the hungry in the town where we would be staying, and urging the other nobles to do the same. I don't think anyone could have disliked her when she was so generous, and she had a way of winning over any who might have envied her until they longed only to be her greatest friends.

Melusine was the epitome of everything a woman should and can be, and yet she was wholly unlike any other woman I have ever met. I would be hard pressed to think the great Cleopatra or even the Queen of Sheba could have rivaled her. And when she began to present me with children, well, there was nothing more any man could have wanted. I felt like the happiest man on earth in those days, and I could not imagine any greater fortune could exist. Indeed, we were happy for so very many years that my grief over the loss of my parents, brothers, and uncle was healed as my children began to fill the empty place in my heart.

Now, I understand many stories have been told of my and Melusine's children, and while I do not in this retreat hear all the gossip of the outer world, occasionally a traveler has revealed to us here the tales that men tell. Almost all of those stories of my family are lies, and some of them quite spiteful, but most are just misunderstandings. It is exaggerated how many children Melusine and I had and all the great deeds they accomplished. You would not think in the short number of years since Melusine left me that already such exaggerated tales would be told, but men's memories are short, and people prefer to hear of the remarkable and the superstitious over the commonplace. The better of these stories are about what great knights our sons became, how brave they were, and what great deeds they accomplished, but the worst stories tell of how our children were terribly deformed and horrible creatures, and while I admit some grain of truth lies beneath these tales, for the most part they are only grossly distorted fancies.

CHAPTER 7

MERLIN INTERRUPTS

"**FRIEND RAIMOND,**" MERLIN interrupted, "I appreciate that as you speak all your past comes back to you as if it were only yesterday, but it's past the noon hour now, and at this rate, we'll never get the full story told, and we only have today, for Roland must set off on his quest tomorrow."

For a moment, my grandfather stared at Merlin, as if in a trance. In truth, as my grandfather had spoken, his eyes had often glazed over as if fully lost in the past. Save for the occasional mention of my name, he might have been telling the story to himself. Now after a minute, he lifted his eyes away from Merlin's to look into the fire.

"I am sorry," he finally replied. "I know time is of the essence, but it is hard to summarize. I find so much feeling rises up in the telling, and therein lies the magic of the story. Surely, you understand that, Merlin."

"I do," Merlin replied. "But we don't need every little detail—how many rings Melusine gave your aunt at your wedding, for example. Now that you have told us how you married her, get to the main point.

You've built up the mystery well enough, so it's time to reveal the secret."

I wanted to know the secret as well, but my bladder was ready to burst.

"Let us pause for just a minute," I said. "I need to relieve myself."

"I suppose you're hungry as well," said Merlin. "You young people can never sit still for more than an hour."

"I have been sitting here for four hours listening," I replied, and then I rose and went outside and behind the building, all the while thinking over everything my grandfather had said. I found his tale to be absolutely beyond belief, and yet, I could see that he was completely sincere. But while I wanted to know more about my grandmother, Melusine, I also wanted to know what Merlin had meant by my going on a quest, and I was beginning to have my doubts about my being here. What right had Merlin to take me from the battlefield, to let the world think I was dead? Granted, he had healed my wounds, and perhaps I would have died otherwise. But did I really owe him my life? And what of Alda, my betrothed? Merlin said she would die of a broken heart? Could I not leave now and return to my uncle's court before it was too late for her? And even if Alda should not die, how could I live with myself, knowing the grief she would feel to think I was dead, not to mention the pain my mother would feel, and my good uncle, the king, and my many other loyal companions?

I decided enough was enough. What right had Merlin to bring me on such a journey without asking me my thoughts about it, or even telling me my purpose?

As I returned to the hovel that served as my grandfather's home, I was determined to ask about my journey's purpose before I would spend another minute listening to stories, but before I could utter a word, Merlin told me, "Sit down and have something to eat."

"I want to—" I tried to say, but he instantly hushed me.

"You have questions," Merlin said, looking up from the grapes he was picking apart, "and your grandfather and I have the answers, but you will not know the proper questions to ask until you already have the answers, and as I said a few minutes ago, you young people are much too impatient. Sit down and eat."

I pulled out my chair, but I also began to say, "I want to—"

"I eat very little," my grandfather interrupted me, "so I will continue to talk while you dine, and I will try to tell the rest of the story so it will be finished by nightfall; that way you may get a good night's rest before continuing your journey."

I was going to object, but Merlin gave me a piercing look that convinced me to continue listening, while I hoped my grandfather would get to his point before another hour had passed. That was as long as I would wait, I told myself, little suspecting how mesmerizing I would find the rest of his tale.

CHAPTER 8

RAIMOND'S TALE CONTINUES

S I WAS saying, Melusine and I had children, but the stories about those children are highly exaggerated. We did not have as many as it is claimed— some storytellers say we had as many as ten— but in truth, we only had four sons, and so all the tales of those other sons' great deeds and their becoming kings of foreign lands and such is all nonsense as well.

Our firstborn son was Geoffrey—today he is called Geoffrey Great-Tooth and Geoffrey the Giant-Killer, and he is the current Count of Lusignan. It is true he killed a giant—I'll get to that story shortly—but first, let me dismiss the falsehoods. The bards say—although he yet lives and any who look upon his face could see it is false—that he had teeth like a great boar, and that those teeth were the sign of a curse upon me, a sign of my guilt over my uncle's death and the boar associated with it, for even though Melusine never told a soul what I had confessed about my uncle's death, and my cousin told me he knew it was not my fault, even if the arrow that killed his father was mine, still idle tongues will wag, and so stories circulated and mountains were made out of molehills. Yes, Geoffrey had a bit of what you might call buck teeth, but not the curving tusk-like teeth that gossips claim. And he did become a great knight and perform many feats of strength and daring, that much is certainly true.

Our second son was Fromont, and he was always a gentle soul. Melusine saw that all our children were raised up in the ways of the Holy Mother Church and that they received the Sacraments, and it is not at all uncommon anywhere in Christendom for a second son to take Holy Orders, so in time, Fromont decided he would enter a monastery. And yes, his older brother was opposed to this decision, as I'll explain.

Our third son is known by the lying storytellers as "Horrible"—as if Melusine and I could ever have named a child such. It is a gross lie, that name. His real name was Raimond, named for me. He was quite large and strong for his age, and yes, he was slow-witted and born with a deformity. He also had a blemish on the side of his face that looked like an eyelid that had grown shut. Rumor said he had a third eye, but the physician said it was a hole in his skull, a soft spot in his head. The physician also told me it was not uncommon for one deformed child to be born in every family. Out of four boys, I would say it was good odds that one would be so born. And because Raimond was slow-witted, he did not know right from wrong, so one day he threw a rock out of a window that killed one of the servants. He also bit his nurse while she was suckling him. She quit right away, but I think she was mentally unstable anyway. Another of the nurses—she whom I understand kidnapped your father, Roland—she was always argumentative, and I am sure she helped to spread these lies about our family; she even had the nerve to tell me to my face that Raimond was a monster child, and that Melusine and I should have had him drowned when he was born, but we could not do so. Then one night, little Raimond came down with a terrible fever, and by morning, he was dead. Melusine and I were both heartbroken. We had a quiet funeral for him, but when he was seen no more, superstitious people spread stories that he ran away in the night and that he lives yet today, hiding in the forest, eating children, and I don't know all what sort of other disgusting and sick lies they have spread—they are the ones who are sick, to make up such tales.

After Raimond's death, we feared to have more children, not wanting to go through the pain of losing another. It was many more years before Melusine gave birth to our last son, Milon, who was just an infant of a few months when the horrid events happened that destroyed our family.

I'm getting to the point now, Merlin, so quit looking so impatient.

I mentioned, Roland, that your uncle Geoffrey was a giant-killer. The world has become skeptical since those days that giants ever existed, for decades have now passed since Geoffrey's great deeds. Yet I assure you that there once were many giants upon this earth, and I believe your uncle killed the last of them; and while the giants were evil and deserving of it, it is a shame, for they possessed much ancient lore and knowledge, most of them having lived for centuries compared to us humans who consider ourselves extremely fortunate to reach our eightieth year.

I hear you sigh, Merlin, and I trust it is because you grieve with me over the loss of the giants' knowledge and not from further impatience. Nor is this the appropriate place for me to tell of the giants' lore, for I knew nothing of it until later when Melusine made it known to me, as I will explain in its proper place, but for now, I must keep the story moving forward before Merlin casts a spell upon me to speed up my tongue.

Until that time in my life, I had occasionally heard rumors of giants, but the only one I knew for certain had lived had been in Brittany a couple of centuries prior—the giant whom, as the bards sing, King Arthur slew so he could rescue the niece of his cousin, Duke Hoel. Sadly, Arthur was too late to rescue the lady, but he certainly destroyed the giant. And then one day, word came to me that a giant was harassing people in my own dominions, and it was this giant that my son Geoffrey went to fight.

Melusine was away at that time, building yet another of her castles. When a group of villagers came to Lusignan with news of the giant, they begged an audience with Geoffrey, who was already renowned for his great strength and the swiftness of his sword. He had fought against the Moors in Spain and taken on many other adventures; he was acknowledged as the greatest warrior in France at the time, and consequently, many a person had sought him out to right a wrong over the years, and he had always been quick to do so. But now he was being asked by these people to fight a giant—a non-mortal. That was more than any man should have been asked, and yet, Geoffrey was always headstrong and his bravery knew no limits, so he accepted this quest.

I begged Geoffrey not to go; I tried to convince him he would break his mother's heart if harm came to him, but he would not heed my words. He insisted he would destroy the giant, who was preying upon the villagers' cattle, before it began to prey upon the villagers themselves; indeed, the giant had extracted homage from the villagers in livestock, and now that almost all their sheep and cows were gone, they feared he would eat them next.

I was terribly worried, and yet, what could I do? Even though Geoffrey was my oldest son and my heir, I could not stop him, and so he rode off with his comrades, who worshiped him as their leader, to right yet another wrong.

I was in daily fear of the mortal danger my eldest son would face, but little did I suspect that his brother Fromont's innocent request to me would soon bring far greater disaster to our family.

Fromont had always been a bit different. He was a quiet and studious child; I had never seen any great value in reading when there were jousting tournaments to compete in, and castles to build, and beautiful women to love, but Melusine insisted that our children be taught to read and write and have all manner of august education, for only then, she said, would they be able to reason and properly discern right from wrong. Despite a mother's best efforts, Geoffrey was headstrong, and while he excelled in sports and athletic feats, he could barely read as well as I could, and that is not saying much. Indeed, I am the only hermit here not to be entrusted with making illuminated manuscripts for I mix up my Ds and Bs, never able to remember which one should face which way, and I would make a mess of other such trivialities.

But Fromont took after his mother. Not only did he learn the Frankish tongue, but also the Breton tongue of my ancestors, and Latin and even Greek and Hebrew. He was always spouting out some information about the wisdom of Solomon or how Roman aqueducts had been built, or about the wars of Julius Caesar, or the genealogy of King Arthur, and I know not all what else. When I heard Fromont philosophize, his wisdom would go in one ear and come out the other for me, and more than once, Geoffrey would mock him, telling him that his muscles were turning to mush while he filled his head with such nonsense. Indeed, I sensed Geoffrey was ashamed of Fromont, who despite being trained in knightly deeds as a young squire, could scarcely swing a sword to defend himself; instead, the boy would repeatedly sneak away from the training fields to climb a tree with a book or scroll—I still don't know how he kept acquiring books, but his mother must have somehow supplied him with them. When he was twelve, he had first visited the monks at Maillezais Abbey because he wanted to learn the secrets of bookmaking and they were great producers of illuminated manuscripts.

Geoffrey was disgusted with Fromont's lack of interest in manly pursuits, and he never failed to let him know it; in front of Fromont, his tongue would ceaselessly mock the monks and all scholars.

Doubtless, it was because of Geoffrey's absence that Fromont now felt it best to come to me with his request. I was surprised he did not wait until his mother came home, for she planned to return on Friday and to spend her Saturday in rest and seclusion as always. But for whatever reason, Fromont decided it best to come to me alone that day. And then he told me how he wanted to take Holy Orders so he could go live with the monks.

All I could reply was, "Do you really want to become a monk when you could be a great warrior like your brother, who even now is off to rescue a village from a giant and win great fame for his prowess? You would throw away such glory to be a monk?"

"The monks are good and holy men, Father," was his simple reply.

"I do not deny that," I said. "Only, I do not understand why you would wish to join them. Why coop yourself up behind abbey walls when you could be out on a horse, fighting battles and serving your king, or winning a fair maiden for your wife?"

"Those are deeds of earthly glory, Father," he replied. "There is other work to do besides slaying giants and stealing women's maidenhood— God's work that must be done, and neither of those activities you mention does God favor."

"There is nothing wrong with either of them," I replied. "A young man should be out and sowing his wild oats." Remember, I was still young and foolish in those days, only just barely having reached my fortieth year, and I was full of vigor and lusty happiness and always eager for my beautiful wife; the great calamity of my life had not yet come upon me to make me more serious-minded and dismissive of the ways of the flesh. When my uncle the earl had died, I should have learned, but so much good and happiness had come to me since then that I thought it foolish not to be relishing the present life rather than longing for the afterlife. Yet, Fromont, unlike me, was introspective from birth, and he remained insistent on joining the monastery.

"Father," he told me, "I wish to work as a scribe, to copy manuscripts—the wisdom of Rome and Athens and Jerusalem and Alexandria—it must be preserved, and it is a long and laborious task to copy out just one book. Yet all of culture and civilization is dependent upon our doing so."

I hemmed and hawed and made some half-derogatory remarks about reading and the clergy, but I loved my son too much to oppose him for long.

"What will your mother say?" I asked, slowly beginning to give way to him.

"Mother has always supported the Holy Church. She will be proud of me. I know she will," Fromont replied.

"And what of your brother, Geoffrey?" I asked.

"I do not belong to Geoffrey, Father. I belong to God. Geoffrey will be Count of Lusignan and Forez when you are gone. He will have everything he needs, so what does it matter to him how I choose to spend my days?"

"But why join the humble monks?" I persisted. "I could use my position at court for you to be made a bishop, or at least I could persuade the local bishop to make you an abbot. I could ask his majesty to speak to the Pope—you could perhaps in time even be a cardinal."

"I am not a seeker after worldly gain or recognition," Fromont replied. "I just want to read and write, to learn the wisdom of the ancients, and to look after what is best for my soul."

I wished then his mother were present, for perhaps she could have talked some sense into his head, but I also feared she would only side with him. I could have had him thrown into the dungeon until he changed his mind, but I knew he was headstrong like his mother and older brother, and so he would inevitably have his way, even if it were not a way I could understand.

Finally, when I did not speak for a minute, Fromont said, "I am going tomorrow, Father. I will take with me only the clothes on my back. I need no worldly goods to follow the Lord."

"Go then…" I said, finding the words difficult to speak, "and my blessing goes with you, but do not be surprised if your mother or brother comes to the abbey to try to convince you otherwise. They may not give up as easily as I have."

"Yes, Father," he replied, "but I will be ready for them, and I will not be dissuaded, for you see, it is not my decision, but God's decision, and so I must obey."

I said nothing. I had tried all my life to be a good Christian—I went to Mass, I tried to keep the Ten Commandments and to love my neighbor as myself—but I had never felt a call from God—I could not understand what that must be like, and yet, here was my son having such an experience.

That next morning, Fromont departed. I saw him off, promising to come and visit him at the abbey in a fortnight once he had settled into his new life. And that evening, Melusine came home. When I told her what Fromont had decided, she spent the evening trying to comfort me. "We have other sons to do great deeds of valor," she said. "Geoffrey will succeed in slaying his giant—I just know he will—and young Milon sleeps in his crib now, but in not too many years, he will be a hero as well, and I am not old yet. Other children may yet come to us."

I was surprised that she was not more upset over Fromont's decision when I was so upset about it. I think it was because I knew Geoffrey had always scorned the local monks, claiming they were corrupt and lazy, living off alms and the donations of good Christians so they could lead lazy lives of reading books all day, which he had little use for. Not being much of a reader myself, although not as adamant about the matter as Geoffrey, I still had to side with him. What was this strange love of learning that my son Fromont had? Why did he want to fill his head with books when there was men's work to be done—castles to build, giants to slay, kingdoms to rule? But I could not argue further about it, not when Melusine had given her consent.

"Fromont has made a wise choice," she assured me. "If everyone chose the same occupation in this world, not only would the earth be a dull place, but much that is needed would never be accomplished. Do not let his decision trouble you."

But it did trouble me, the more so because I now feared I would lose two sons, one to a giant and the other to the Church, for I knew Fromont would now obey his abbot or bishop or the Pope, but never again his father.

It was with great relief that a few days later I received word that Geoffrey had successfully slain the giant. The young messenger who came to give me the news was overwhelmed with joy and told me he had seen the battle with his own eyes. Geoffrey had fought valiantly, avoiding the giant's club and swinging his sword at the giant's legs until the monster fell to the ground, and then before the creature could get up, Geoffrey ran up to it and sliced off its head. The entire village had taken up feasting to celebrate its salvation through my son's victory.

Pleased beyond words, I had the following message sent to Geoffrey: "Hurry home so we may celebrate. I am lonely since your brother left to join the monks at Maillezais."

To be lonely might have sounded foolish considering I had my beautiful wife, and it had only been a few days since Fromont had departed, but secretly, since Melusine would not side with me, I hoped to get Geoffrey to come home and persuade his brother to leave the monastery before he had taken his final vows.

A couple of more days passed, but no response came from Geoffrey. I felt very depressed by the time the next Saturday approached. I knew I would have to spend that day alone, for Milon did little but sleep in his crib, and Melusine would be away from me all day, and now my two oldest sons, who were all I lived for besides my beautiful wife, were both gone away.

When I woke that Saturday morning, I could not foresee what tragedies would befall me. I went downstairs to have breakfast alone. I did not have to explain to the servants that their mistress would not join me for breakfast that morning, for by now they knew well the routine, although they knew not the reason for it. I had grown so accustomed to such behavior from Melusine that I had ceased to question it, yet every now and then on a Saturday, I would come upon the servants whispering, and then I knew they wondered why Melusine hid herself away every seventh day.

In truth, I had now and then wondered the same, but I had always quickly pushed the thoughts away from me; I had only one reason to worry—that Melusine might be unfaithful to me. My cousin Bertrand had hinted at such a possibility to me early in my marriage, but I had quickly told him to hold his tongue or there would be no friendship left between us, so he never spoke of it again. Yet the thought still troubled me enough that about a year after we were married, I had a female spy conceal herself outside the door of the chamber where Melusine went every Saturday to be certain no one else entered the room while she occupied it. This maid watched the room from early Friday until late Sunday and assured me that no one but Melusine had come or gone from the chamber. Nevertheless, I had this woman watch for three consecutive Saturdays to be certain, and when each time the answer was the same, I grew convinced that my beautiful wife was faithful to me. For the twenty or so years since then, I had trusted that whatever my beloved's reasons were for hiding from me every seventh day, it had nothing to do with her being unfaithful.

Yes, I had my questions about some other things—where our great wealth came from, where she found all the servants and laborers for our castles, and why if she were the King of Albany's daughter, I had never met any of her relatives—yet, I loved her so well that I could not ask her such questions from fear they would make her sad and cause her to believe I did not trust her. I did trust her in all things—perhaps not at first, but by this time in our marriage, I knew her to be the very soul of honesty, integrity, and goodness. She was kind and generous to all, charitable to the poor, one who always championed the wronged, and a benefactor who helped the good and wise to prosper. I could find no fault in her.

I tried to tell myself that morning as I ate breakfast that it was only one day alone, and on the morrow, Melusine would join me as usual when we went to Mass, and that surely today I would receive a message from Geoffrey, if he himself did not return. I told myself there was no reason for the sense of dread I felt creeping over me that morning other than a ridiculous and unwarranted sense of loneliness; surely I could be alone for one day, and after all, the servants were still about.

Then as I was rising from the breakfast table, my steward appeared to tell me a messenger had arrived. For a second, I rejoiced to think Geoffrey was coming home, but then my steward added, "My lord, prepare yourself. He brings ill tidings."

And before I could speak, the steward had shown the messenger into the room. The man was no ordinary messenger. It was a monk—one I recognized as being from the monastery at Maillezais. Instantly, I realized the news must concern my son Fromont and not Geoffrey.

"What is wrong, man?" I demanded of him. "What is it? Is Fromont ill?"

The man struggled to speak as I watched his face contort into all sorts of hideous and fearful expressions.

"Speak, man!" I demanded. "What is it?"

And then I noticed how filthy he was. He had ash or soot of some sort upon his brow, and his cloak was torn and muddied.

"What is it?" I repeated.

"My lord," he spoke slowly, "your son, Fromont, is dead, as are all but a handful of the monks from Maillezais."

"Dead?" I muttered. "How?"

"The abbey has been burnt down. It was done intentionally, my lord. It was your son Geoffrey; he erupted into a great rage over his brother becoming a monk and he took it upon himself to burn down the monastery. He demanded his brother come out to speak with him, but when Fromont refused, fearing his brother's great anger, my lord Geoffrey lost all control and ordered his men to torch the building. Only I and two others escaped, and I have come to you to ask for reparation so we might rebuild the monastery and to beg your protection lest your son Geoffrey hunt down and kill those of us who remain."

I stood frozen in shock as the monk spoke these words. I could not believe such a turn of events. How could my own flesh and blood do such a thing, and to his own flesh and blood? Such terrible emotion raced through me, quickly changing from shock to anger to unbearable grief. I had feared losing one son to a giant, only instead to lose another to his own brother!

"Where...where is my son Geoffrey?" I demanded. "Did he bury his brother?"

"No, my lord; the fire was so terrible we cannot even identify the remains of our brother monks. As for my lord Geoffrey, as the abbey was burning, he received a summons from a village in Northumberland in Britain that is being persecuted by a giant. The villagers there, having heard of how he saved a village here in France, begged him to come to their rescue as well. He departed this morning for Northumberland; only then did I think it safe to come out of hiding so I could tell you this woeful news."

I did not know what to say. How could Geoffrey casually go off to fight another giant after having killed his own brother, as well as a few dozen gentle monks? I might not have wanted Fromont to join the abbey at Maillezais, but that did not mean I wished the holy brothers any ill, and certainly, I did not wish for my son's death!

"My lord, forgive me," begged the monk, "but I am exhausted. May I be excused?"

"Yes, of course," I said. "My apologies." I called for my steward and ordered him to take the monk to a private chamber, to draw him a bath and provide him with new clothes, and then I commanded another servant to set out to find the other surviving monks and bring them to Lusignan where they might also recover from any injuries and have shelter until the abbey could be rebuilt.

My servants now sought to comfort me in my grief, but I asked that they leave and not disturb me. I remained there alone at the table where just moments before I had been eating breakfast and hoping for my son Geoffrey's return.

I was beside myself with shock. I could not believe such a chain of events could be true. I could not believe that Geoffrey, as hotheaded as he had always been, could commit such a crime.

What kind of madman would do such a thing—to kill holy men and his own brother, and then rush off to aid strangers? And his going to help others was not even an act of kindness but of hubris for Geoffrey—a means to accomplish his desire for fame and glory. But what good are fame and glory when you become the enemy of God, destroying His house and slaying His children? How could it be possible that my own son would commit such a crime, such an act as that of Cain against Abel and, ultimately, against God?

I was overcome with dismay, frustration, anger, and grief. I swore and raged and threw my plate across the room until the servants came in to see what was wrong, only to run and hide from my fury, and then after several minutes, my anger exhausted, I was overtaken with grief.

I sank to the floor and wept and wept, until I felt completely drained. I thought of Fromont as a child, how I had cuddled with him, played with him, how Melusine and I had held his hands as he took his first steps, how he had loved his books while I had only ignored him and felt ignored by him because he was constantly reading, but now I wished I could tell him how proud I was of him for his dedication to learning. I remembered his smile, the sound of his laughter, and how he would defend himself when his cruel older brother would tease and bully him. How could I now love my eldest son after what he had done? I had wanted Geoffrey to come home, but now I told myself, "Damn him! I hope I never see him again." But I also knew his mother would not want that. Somehow, I suspected she was of a more forgiving nature than I.

But she did not even yet know what a calamity had befallen us!

And then, without giving it thought, I got up from the floor and went to our chamber, and when I did not find her there, I remembered that it was Saturday, and although for more than twenty years, I had never once disobeyed her rule that I not disturb her on the seventh day, I did not think that today of all days that condition could be upheld— or that she would expect me to uphold it.

And so I went to the chamber where my beloved Melusine locked herself up each Saturday—actually, I should not say locked herself up, for I had never tested the door to see whether it was locked, for I had vowed not to disobey her.

But today my great sorrow was so unbearable that I felt compelled to tell her the horror as quickly as possible—so I could relieve myself of the worst news, so she also could move past the shock all the sooner, and so then we could comfort one another. In my anguish, I did not even think to knock when I reached her private room. I simply pulled open the door, not pausing with surprise to find it unlocked, and I burst into the room, expecting to see her immediately and to tell her all the agony of our family's shame.

Instead, I saw before me what I could not believe. The chroniclers and the troubadours would have it that I spied on Melusine through the keyhole and that I was shocked and did not tell her what I had seen until days later, but that is all just their way to create suspense for a fairytale they have created from our lives. The truth is that I entered the room immediately, and while I was shocked by what I saw, it was not the shock of horror, but rather the awe of seeing sheer and exquisite beauty like no mortal man ever gazed upon before.

This beautiful woman, whom I loved more than anything else in all of God's creation, was completely naked and swimming in a giant pool, like a Roman bath, a pool I did not even know we had in our castle. When I entered the room, her full torso was above the water so that her large, luscious, goddess-like breasts were wet, causing them to sparkle in the sunlight that was pouring in through beautiful stained glass windows above the pool. Later, I would gaze at those windows and realize they were far more beautiful than any other windows in France, yet the colored glass was pale and ugly compared to my lovely wife. For at that moment, all I could do was gaze upon her perfect God-given beauty.

Melusine now looked at me, and I looked at her, and she allowed me for a moment, an unforgettable moment, to gaze at all her feminine loveliness.

Her hair was a beautiful rich, red color with a spot of gold like a halo where the sun struck it. Her eyes were a deep green, her breasts tremendously full and luscious. For a moment, she allowed me to admire her, for my mind, body, and soul to worship her, and then she smiled and dove beneath the water, and I had the shock of my life, for in a moment, breaking above the water was a tail like that of a giant fish, with blue and silver scales, the very colors she had chosen for Lusignan's shields and banners.

I stood in disbelief as I watched her swim back and forth beneath the water's surface. I stood there for several minutes as I realized why she had always forbidden me to see her on Saturdays. She had a secret she had kept from me—a secret that she was different, perhaps not human, perhaps enchanted, perhaps a fairy, or perhaps a monster. I had sometimes dared to wonder whether she might be a fairy...but how could anyone so beautiful be a monster? I immediately drove the thought from me.

I felt wholly entranced by her beauty—truly more enchanted even than when I had first seen her so many years ago in the forest and she had comforted me and quickly won my love. She had been so beautiful that day, but all the rich gowns and jewels in the world could not now compete with the beauty of her mermaid form. Is that what she was? A mermaid. A radiantly beautiful mermaid. I did not care what she was. She was beautiful beyond belief, a very goddess, the most attractive and stimulating and awe-inspiring creature I had ever seen.

I could not control my desire for her. Not half-knowing what drove me on, I stepped farther into the room, and lest someone else discover her secret, I shut and locked the door behind me. She had forbidden me to enter, and I feared I had embarrassed her, which is why she had dove under the water, but she had not hissed at me, nor screamed, nor ordered me to leave.

Now, I found myself longing for her as I had never longed for anything in my life. I found myself removing all my garments, and then wholly naked myself, I descended the steps into the pool, and just as I was waist deep, she swam up to me, took my hands in her own, and pulled me under the water. For just a moment, I felt a twinge of fear, but then her body gently pressed against my own, and we swam through the pool, she deftly controlling our movements, our lips firmly pressed to each other, our limbs entwined, fast in one another's embrace, as we coupled beneath the water.

I felt as if I had traveled to another world. I felt she had taken me to a kingdom beneath the sea, to a wonderful, glorious land I had never imagined. I know not how else to describe that heavenly experience. With my eyes closed, I journeyed in my mind to beautiful, fabled, underwater lands. I traveled through a blinding golden light. I felt as if my very soul were preparing to leave my body because of the intense pleasure I experienced with her. I do not even know how what we did was possible since her legs had disappeared, but I felt as if I were making love to a goddess, to Aphrodite herself—but not even Aphrodite could possibly be so beautiful as my Melusine, my dear, beloved wife.

And then I found myself waking upon the floor beside the pool. I do not remember leaving the water; I do not remember us parting. I woke to find my undergarment placed around my waist and the chamber lit by candlelight. My beloved was standing above me, fully clothed, and now completely human in form, for I could see her slippered feet beneath her gown.

And I heard myself ask, "Did I dream?"

"No," Melusine told me. "Raimond, my love, you are the dearest, sweetest man in all the world, and I do not know why you have betrayed me, but—"

Before she could finish, I rose to my knees and begged her forgiveness.

"I am so sorry, my beloved. I do not know why you have a secret, but I love you. You are my faithful and true wife, the mother of my children, my very soul and my lifeblood. Despite your secret, I will love and protect you and defend you and serve you and anything else that you need or command. Do not be angry with me, please, for I cannot bear it."

"I warned you many years ago, Raimond, before we ever married, against betraying me," she replied. "You promised me you would never come to me on a Saturday. I am not angry with you, for I know you did not do it to hurt me. I understand human curiosity, but I know you would not even betray my trust out of curiosity. You must have a truly good reason. But no matter how unfair it may seem, whatever your reason, I must leave you now."

"No," I cried, wrapping my arms about her legs while kneeling before her and laying my head against her stomach. "You cannot leave me. You cannot. I am truly sorry, but enough sadness and pain has occurred for me this day. Do not betray me by forsaking me."

"What sadness and pain has occurred?" she asked, beginning to stroke my hair. "What is wrong?"

"My love," I cried, "I would never betray you, never do anything to hurt you, but this day, a horrible deed has been wrought against our flesh and blood, and in the most horrible way, by our own flesh and blood. I—"

But I could say no more. My grief overcame me whereas just moments before I had known great joy with her as if I had not a care in the world. I had made love to her, and it had been the most beautiful expression of our love we had ever shared, and yet now I feared it was a sign of our farewell. And if she left me, I would have nothing left in this world to bring me joy or even solace.

"Come," she said. "I need not leave until the dawn. Tell me what has happened."

"Geoffrey—he—he—you know his rashness and anger. You know our son Fromont's good heart and his desire to join the holy brothers at Maillezais. When Geoffrey learned that Fromont had gone to the monastery, he went into a rage. I—I can't—"

"Raimond, my love, tell me. Tell me," she cried. "The night is passing and there is much I must tell you as well before I depart, so be quick in your speech."

With a great sob, I looked up at her and exclaimed, "Our son is dead! Fromont is dead. Geoffrey burned down the monastery and killed Fromont and most of the other monks inside it."

The look of horror on Melusine's face was indescribable. I had never seen her appear so miserable—her terrified expression was as extreme as the intensity of her beauty when I had first entered the room.

"Oh, my dear boy," Melusine sighed. "My dear boy."

And then she knelt upon the floor beside me, and we held each other, and we wept for the longest time.

"Raimond, my love," she finally said. "I do not know why this horrible event has happened. I wish it had never happened, and I wish you had never come to see me this day. But I know not how I could have prevented it. All I know is that God will somehow make right what we cannot. You must trust me in that regard; you must trust Him."

"God?" I said, feeling anger rise up in me. "God? How can God make right what is no more? Fromont is dead. He sought to serve God and this is how he is repaid."

"Do not blame God for man's misdeeds," Melusine warned me. "God did not burn down the monastery."

"But...what...? I do not understand," I admitted, my thoughts all a muddle. "You speak of God as if you are certain. But...what...? Forgive me, my love, but what are you? You are not human, are you? Are you enchanted, or are you a fairy of some sort? Are you cursed—but how could that be when I know you have magical powers I have never dared to question you about...but now you tell me you are to leave me, and...I don't even know what to say—I have had so many questions I have never asked of you, even when my cousins pressed me for answers, even when I myself was frightened by how you seemed to know things that could not be known. I...I only want—"

"Hush now," she said, placing her finger upon my lips. "I do not know all. I do not have all the answers to why God works His will the way He does. But I do know that while I have lived here in this human world, I have seen little more than fear among you humans. You speak of evil. Your priests talk of sin. But all those concepts are based in simple fear. You humans behave in unseemly ways that hurt others, and you even hurt yourselves because you live in fear. That's all it is—fear. It is fear of not understanding Fromont's reasons that caused Geoffrey to destroy his brother. It was fear that drove you nearly mad when your uncle died. It is fear that now fills your soul when I tell you I am to leave you. I did not always understand fear, for I grew up in a place where fear was not something I knew, but now having lived with you all these years, I feel such sorrow over the power and extent of your fearful thoughts."

"I am afraid," I confessed. "But how am I to understand all this? What life is left to me when one son kills another, and now the woman I love says she will leave me?"

"I will leave you, Raimond," she said gently. "In that, I have no choice. It is not because I do not love you. You must not argue with me about it, for it cannot be undone, but I will explain to you the reason. You must put yourself in a frame of mind to hear many explanations before this night is over. But first, you must promise me that you will take no revenge upon Geoffrey, that you will love him as our son, despite what he has done. And you forget that we have one other child, our newborn Milon. There is no reason not to believe that he might yet be the son you were meant to sire—the great champion who will restore order—he whose birth our love has been meant to bring about."

"I do not understand," I said, fighting back my tears. "What do you mean by a champion?"

"If you will listen," she replied, "and promise not to interrupt me, for I have little time left, I will tell you all, Raimond. Prepare yourself for an unusual tale like none you have ever heard before, for I promise you will find this tale very difficult to believe."

"I don't know that anything could be harder to believe than what I have seen and learned today," I replied. "But no matter how astonishing it might be, I will keep my promise and remain silent until you are finished."

"Oh, my dear Raimond," Melusine said, actually laughing, despite all the grief that had come upon us that day, "you have no idea how I am about to stretch your beliefs and understanding. I will tell you the story of my life, but in doing so, many other mysteries of this world will be revealed to you. And while I have never wished to leave you, I assure you everything that has happened was all meant to be and is part of God's plan, for it is time now that certain knowledge be given to you and our descendants. And the pain you will experience will not come from some wrong you or I or anyone has committed, but simply in the parting of two who have loved one another so very deeply as we have."

CHAPTER 9

ROLAND INTERRUPTS

"**H**OLD," **I SAID.** "I cannot hear any more. I need some fresh air, a chance to catch my breath. The things you are saying are just too incredible to be true, and as amazing as they are, well, a man does not want to hear about his grandparents coupling."

Merlin let out a roar of laugher when I made this comment, but then he grimaced, saying, "I need to take a piss and I better do it now."

He stood up and waddled outside, looking like he would barely make it in time.

I was left staring at my grandfather.

"We must continue the tale," said Raimond. "Night is falling, and there is still much to tell unless you do not want to hear what your grandmother told me. Sometimes, I wish I had not heard it myself, for they say ignorance is bliss, but it is knowledge the world should hear, for in time, the human race will be better for knowing it."

"Then why have you withheld it so long?" I asked. "All you have so far told me is marvelous to hear, and yet, lies have spread all over the land about Melusine, and you have done nothing to counter them."

"Not lies, Roland," he replied. "They were not told to slander your grandmother. People simply have active imaginations, and they make up stories to try to explain what they do not understand; some have even out of pride made up other children for me, to link themselves to my line because they secretly find it attractive, and some others perhaps even know of our great lineage, which I have yet to explain to you."

"But why," I asked, "would people want to pretend to be related to us if they feared Melusine was a serpent?"

"That I can't quite say," said my grandfather. "I guess because they want the best of both worlds. They can be afraid of her and call her a serpent, but they can also wish a bit of fame for themselves in being connected with her legend and all the great and good things she did. Is it any different a situation than the relationship we humans have with God? We both fear and love Him. Or what of a king? Plenty a man will disparage his king, but that same man will stand by the road and cheer the king when he passes through his village."

"I suppose," I said, "but I think I need some fresh air before I hear more. Excuse me."

I did not mean to be rude, but what was I supposed to think? How was I supposed to respond when I had felt myself become aroused just listening to my grandfather's sexual experience with Melusine in the pool. I feared and yet longed for such an experience with a woman— once, I had dared think I might have such with Alda, though I had tried not to dishonor her with such thoughts. But now, what woman would I ever find when I was instead on this strange quest? Merlin had himself called it a quest, and yet, I still did not know what I was to do or why it required my hearing this long, convoluted, and even disturbing family history. But...that my grandparents had loved each other so deeply—that was nothing to be ashamed of in my family background.

I stepped outside and looked up at the first star appearing in the night sky, and its sight carried my thoughts to my grandfather's uncle, the Count of Poitiers, who had predicted the future—his very own death—in the stars. I did not long for death, but I certainly wished I could see the future and where this adventure was to take me. I missed the warmth of my chambers in my uncle the king's castle, and I was sad to think I would never be with Alda in the way a man longs to be with a woman—the way my grandfather had been with Melusine. I was angry to think that Alda would die of grief. I was angry that I was here. Why had Merlin brought me here? Why couldn't I have been told all this years ago? Why now must I be made aware of it?

"Better get back inside," said Merlin, coming around the corner of the house and looking much refreshed.

"Give me a minute," I snapped at him, and I turned to walk around the side of the hovel so I could at least relieve my bladder, since I had no release yet for my frustrations and anxieties.

A few minutes later, dreading to go back, yet knowing I could not resist the chance to hear what Melusine had told my grandfather, I returned inside. I found a bowl of fruit on the table, wine poured into goblets, bread and cheese on a platter, and plates filled with meat and vegetables.

"Eat," said Merlin. "You'll feel better, and you won't want to hear all that is to follow on an empty stomach."

"Thank you," I said.

"I know it is a hard tale to swallow," my grandfather said. "You can only imagine how much harder it was for me to hear it from my wife's lips—from a woman I thought I knew, only to discover she had an entire past I knew nothing about and that she was even a different kind of creature from me."

"It is surprising, but I will hear the rest," I replied softly, feeling some pity for the old man, and realizing he had been innocent in all the events that had happened. Nor was he the one holding me hostage with his story, but rather, Merlin was orchestrating all these events. Even that fact I had difficulty wrapping my head around, for how could I believe I was associating with a man who claimed he was eight hundred years old, who could do magic, and whose deeds had been sung by bards throughout Christendom for centuries? And what surprises still awaited me I could not imagine, for I had yet to learn what the quest would be that I was to undertake.

"Continue," said Merlin, nodding to my grandfather.

"I will," he replied. "I will, to the best of my memory, relate now the next part of the tale as I heard it from Melusine. A word or two here and there may have changed in my memory, but the essence of it all will be true, and the truth—well, the Gospel says the truth will set us free, but I'll leave that for you to determine after you've heard the amazing things Melusine told me in her own words."

CHAPTER 10

MELUSINE'S TALE

MY EARLIEST MEMORIES are of my mother, and by "mother," I do not mean Pressyne, the woman who gave me life, nor even Morgan le Fay, who took me under her wing and understood me when my own mother could not. By Mother, I mean Avalon, the Holy Isle. She was my first friend—even more so than my sisters—my lasting friend, my teacher, my solace, my refuge. She has met all my needs, and now she will be my home again because your breaking your promise, Raimond, will cast me from the mortal world.

Do not cry, Raimond. I know you regret what you have done, and I do not blame you, but it just simply must be, for there is fear in your world that makes men act violently toward what they do not understand, and so my leaving is for my and your safety, but also, so I may aid you in new ways. Never fear that I completely forsake you; I will always watch over you even if I am not by your side. But for now, listen to my story, for we have little time, and there is much I have to tell you.

I think my first memory is simply of lying on the grassy lawn at

Avalon near where we had our little cottage; it was early morning and the ground was covered with dew, and I was surprised and delighted by its coolness. In my memory, I lay there a long time, watching the sunrise—I'd like to say it was a deeply meaningful moment, that I remember it clearly, but it's only an early memory and a dim one at that.

My sisters and I were triplets. I was the first born, but within the hour, Melior and then Palatyne followed, so my sisters and I fill each other's earliest memories. I can still see us running across the fields at dusk, chasing the fireflies—we wanted to believe they were fairies—we never saw any real fairies—no pixies or any beings of that sort—but it hardly mattered. We pretended the fireflies were fairies, and the mushrooms were fairy houses. The countless fairy stories our mother first told us and many others we made up ourselves we came to believe as true—but who is to say our imaginations do not create the fairies anyway and make them real?

And I remember the forest—at least, it did seem like a forest, and a wonderfully large one, protective and never frightening. In reality, it was just acres and acres of apple trees with the occasional odd oak, rowan, or other tree springing up among them. My sisters and I would laugh as we collected apples, toss them at one another, tumble over them, and eat them thoughtlessly. Apples were abundant at Avalon and remain so, for even the mild, short winter there—which gives the island a little variety so the inhabitants will all the more appreciate the otherwise seemingly endless summer—left us with hardly any absence of them, and it allowed for springtime and the return of the beautiful apple blossoms followed by fresh fruit, neither of which we would have traded for anything. I know nothing on this earth so beautiful as when the apple trees blossom in the spring—for even on a timeless island where we have all eternity to live, we find much in the Goddess-God's bounty to make us grateful for all we have.

Unlike mortal man—who is forced to toil so that what little free time he has he can scarcely appreciate or use wisely, we on Avalon had all the time we needed to enjoy everything without the sadness of knowing it would someday end. I will be one of those few residents of Avalon now who will truly understand mankind's sadness because I have lived among humans. Do not look startled, Raimond; you already know I am not fully human. It is sufficient for you to understand me as a fairy—it is too much to explain the details at this time. I am not a spirit, and Avalon is not heaven, nor exactly earth, but an in-between place, a place of special grace and sanctity, perhaps most akin to the biblical Garden of Eden.

I say I have lived among humans because I am not quite human myself. I say I searched for fairies as a child, because at that time, my sisters and I never considered that perhaps the reason why we never found any was because we were fairies ourselves. It is not even fully true to say I am a fairy, and I do not mean to misguide you, but everything at Avalon is so simple, and yet so difficult to explain to a human. For now, so I do not get ahead of myself, it is sufficient to say that as a child, I did not know I was perfectly happy, that any strong longing could lead to heartache; now, having lived as a human all these years, I can understand what a mixed blessing human existence is—for even great pain can be a blessing to you—and all pain passes with time.

Avalon was, and remains, an idyllic place, but childhood is the most idyllic time, and few have known, as did my sisters and myself, such a truly idyllic one. My understanding then of childhood was limited. The great grief and perhaps the great blessing of childhood is that you do not realize you are happy until you have known sorrow to compare with your happiness, and once you have known sorrow, try as you might, happiness may come close to your grasp, but it will always elude you. Once innocence is gone, we can never fully regain the happiness it brings.

I did not know then what a special place Avalon was. I did not know how fortunate my sisters and I were to live there; nor did we think to question why there were no other children on the island, no one closer to our age than a handful of young men and women, who had reached the age of reason, and whose bodies had changed to those of adults; they had been called from throughout the outside world to come and study on the Holy Isle. All others who lived at Avalon were the Blessed— many of them heroes, many more saints of their own faiths, whether it be Christianity, or the Celtic faiths; even Jews, and those of the Norse beliefs, and old believers in the Greek Gods were among us; in my youth, I even saw the first of the Prophet Mohammed's followers come to live there, and many more of them have joined us since as will many of other faiths unknown to those in Christendom at this time. Avalon was the Celtic name for our isle, but it was equally the Greeks' Happy Isles for such as the great hero Achilles, who resided among us, and the Valhalla for those worthy Norsemen who were called to reside there. It is, in a sense, whatever those privileged to come to it desire it to be. But famous men and women of the world are far from the majority of its inhabitants; most of them are simply quiet souls, those who had achieved peace in their hearts, and a sense of oneness with the Goddess-God or whatever name by which the great Supreme Being was known to them—be it the Goddess Ceridwen, or Odin, or Amon Ra, or Zeus, or any other by which He-She has made Him-Herself known to man, although many have misunderstood and distorted Him-Her in their human frailties. But it matters not the name given to the Deity, for in each case, Wisdom, the great Guiding Force of the universe, has guided those blessed of many faiths until they were ready to come to us at Avalon.

As girls, my sisters and I knew of these inhabitants—many of the blessed women were constantly among us. We seldom saw the men, although, of course, we knew their names. A great castle stands on one end of the island where we were told King Arthur resided, and Morgan le Fay, who lived among us, would go there often to visit and consult with him, for he was her brother. I never met him during those early years, but I knew him from the tales of traveling bards who were occasionally allowed to visit Avalon.

I did not realize then that these blessed mortals who resided at Avalon were different from my sisters and me; they were blessed indeed, but not all of them were sprung from the bloodline of Avalon, though many might be counted as distant cousins of a sort.

Others there were of equal greatness to King Arthur, but there is no purpose in my listing them, for you would not know most of their names—they were ancient kings and queens, warriors, druid priests, all of ancient times before the Christians began recording history from their perspective, and before the bards and later troubadours quit singing the tales of those famous men and women. Just because their names are mostly forgotten today does not mean their lives were not significant or influential to the course of human history and mankind's wellbeing.

In those days, my sisters and I, as mere children, were allowed to roam and play about the island as we pleased. We had no fear and knew no one would harm us—we could not even yet conceive, I do not think, of what harm was. We were taught our letters and to read, to write, to sing, and we were taught to follow the rituals and traditions of Avalon, but these lessons that gave our days structure took up only a few hours then; our schooling did not begin in earnest until we were on the verge of womanhood—and then my mother told us we were to join the acolytes, who had come from the world of man, to train with them in the mysteries of Avalon.

Years before we joined them, we knew of the acolytes—they were like a great group of older cousins, always there, but their identities a bit blurred to us since they were outside of our immediate family circle.

However, there was one young lady, named Grainne, who questioned me one day when I had just turned five, about how my sisters and I had come to be raised in Avalon. She had come to study at Avalon from Eire, and she thought it odd that my sisters and I should be raised in Avalon when there were no other children about. When she asked me of my life in Avalon, I could scarcely answer her other than to say our mother had brought us, and when I told her my mother's name, she asked whether my father were not King Elynas of Albany; I said I believed my father's name was Elynas, for I had heard my mother and Morgan le Fay discussing various matters, which I did not understand, and I had heard his name mentioned once or twice. But I bit my tongue before I should confess to Grainne that I had not known my father was a king or that I had never heard of a land called Albany. At that time, I thought nothing of not having my father around, for my sisters and I, being the only children on Avalon, did not realize most children lived with both parents, and we scarcely thought of our father since we had never consciously known him.

"They say," Grainne told me—to this day I remain amazed that a first year acolyte like her should be so bold and crude to upset a child with her questioning—"that your mother cursed your father for breaking his promise to her. They say she then left him in anger."

"What promise? What curse?" I asked, for I knew nothing of this story.

"They say when your mother married King Elynas, that she made him promise not to visit her during childbirth or when she nursed her children, but he broke that promise and entered the room right after you and your sisters were born, when your mother was feeding you, and when he did so, your mother was so angry that she left him."

This was all news to me. I had never heard such a thing, nor could I imagine why there would be such secrecy over my sisters and I being nursed or fed. *How could Grainne make up such a foolish story?* I asked myself.

"That makes no sense," I replied. "Why would my mother become angry over such a silly thing?"

"Because she had a great secret. Because she was not human but part witch, and she did not want your father to know her secret—that is what the stories say."

I was stunned, but I felt the color rising up in me, my blood beginning to boil, and then I shouted out, "It's a lie! My mother is not a witch! What a stupid, foolish story. It is all lies! It never happened, at least not that way."

"Ask anyone," Grainne replied. "Don't be mad at me. Everyone knows that is what happened and why your mother came to Avalon. She was ashamed and afraid of what would happen to her if King Elynas' people found out she was a witch. I can't even understand why Lady Morgana allowed her to set foot on the Holy Isle."

"She is not a witch," I declared. "It isn't true!"

And then I saw our teacher coming toward us to see why I was shouting. Before she came close enough to speak to me, I ran off home to ask my mother to tell me the truth.

When I entered our small cottage, my sisters were playing on the floor with their dolls, and my mother sat rocking in a chair by the fire as she stitched a gown for one of us to wear—which one of us it did not matter; my sisters and I often shared our clothes, thinking nothing of it. We knew nothing of jealousy, for Mother made certain all our needs were met, and we had no outside influences to make us feel we were lacking in anything. At least not until now, when I suddenly felt we were lacking in a father.

"What is it, Melusine?" my mother asked when she looked up and saw me standing before her, half out of breath. When I did not reply, she persisted, "What is troubling you? Your face is all flushed."

I didn't know what to say. I wasn't sure what it was I should ask her. How do you ask your mother whether she is a witch?

My mother put down her work, and reaching out her arms, she called my name.

Her gentle tone made my sisters look up, wondering what was wrong; I saw their questioning faces from the corner of my eye as I went into my mother's arms.

"Melusine, dear, you're crying," my mother said, as I felt the first tear trickle down my face. "What has upset you so much?"

"Grainne," I said.

"That girl!" my mother hissed, much to my surprise. More to herself than to me, she added, "I knew she never should have been allowed here." I sensed something was terribly wrong then, for my mother was always so even-tempered, and I could hear her heart starting to race as my head rested on her breast. Finally, she demanded, "What has that girl said to you?"

I could not face my mother as I said it. I buried my face in her breast and sobbed out the words so that I'm surprised now that she even understood me.

"She called you a witch."

"A witch?" My mother sounded both surprised and troubled. "What made her say such a thing?"

"Oh, Mother, she's an awful person," I said, pulling back now to look into her flaring eyes. "She said terrible things about you...and... and about our father. She said you're a witch and...that you were keeping a secret from Father, and that's why we don't have a father... because he didn't like that you were a witch."

I was finding it hard to explain, and the anger in her eyes was intimidating. But something else in my mother's manner, in the way her nose twitched as if she were holding back tears, made me fear Grainne's words were true.

"That girl doesn't know what she speaks of," my mother replied.

"Then you're not a witch?" I asked. "I told her you weren't. You're not a witch—are you?"

"No, I'm not a witch—not in that sense at least. I'm—well, you might call me a wise woman, I suppose, but not a witch."

"She said it's because you're a witch that Father doesn't want us with him."

"No, that's not true, dear," my mother replied, squeezing me in a hug so that I lay my head against her breast again, but I did not bury my face there this time. "Your father loves you very much—all of you," she added. I looked toward Melior and Palatyne then and saw they were watching us and listening to her as well.

"Then why aren't we with Father?" I asked.

I had never thought to ask until that moment and neither had my sisters, but now they got up from the floor and came to my mother, staring at her questioningly.

"Oh dear," said Mother. "I wanted to wait until you were older to tell you all about your father. But let me tell you this—your father loves you girls very much, and the only reason why you are not with him is because it would not be safe for you to be so."

"Not safe?" I asked. "Is Father a bad man?"

"No, my dear, no," she said, pulling me up on her lap while my sisters came and leaned against her knees. As she spoke, she took turns stroking our hair. "No, your father is a good man, but he's a very important one. He is the King of Albany, and for that reason, we must keep you safe because there are bad men who might like to kidnap little princesses. I don't say that to frighten you. You have no reason to be frightened, for you are perfectly safe here in Avalon, but that is why we are here instead of with your father."

"We're princesses?" asked Melior. "Like in the stories?"

"Yes, my dear. Like in the stories," Mother replied.

"Will we marry princes?" Palatyne asked.

"And grow up to be queens?" added Melior.

"Well, I can't say for sure," Mother replied, "but it's very likely; you'll at least marry men of noble birth."

"Will we ever get to see our father?" I asked.

"In time," said Mother, "when you are of age; it's very possible, at least. Then, I'm sure, he will want to be involved in making great marriages for his daughters."

"But why doesn't he at least come to visit us?" Melior asked.

"My dear, if he did, the bad men might follow him," said Mother. "He loves you so much that he is willing to bear the pain of being separated from you to keep you safe. That is great love indeed, and you must be proud of it."

"Mother," I asked, "where is Albany? Is it near Avalon?"

"Nothing is near to Avalon, my dear, and yet everything is. It is hard to explain, but if you like, I will show you tomorrow where Albany is."

My sisters and I all agreed that we wanted to see Albany, where our father was king, so the next day, our mother took us for a long walk, so long that if we had not been so eager to see Albany, I think our little legs would scarcely have made it up the high hill she had us climb, a hill on Avalon that we had never visited before. We climbed for what seemed like hours; it probably only seemed long because we were still children, but I know it was a great effort for us; my sisters were ready to quit halfway, but my mother and I urged them along, and I was insistent on going to the top so I could see my father's country. I could not explain the need I had to see it since I had never given much thought to our father before, but I desperately wanted to understand this piece to the puzzle of my existence, and even at such a young age, I sensed my mother was withholding something from us.

Finally, we came to the top of a great hill—a small mountain really—and when we looked out, we saw the sea surrounding Avalon, and across the sea, a great land, rich with green meadows, rocky with large mountains, and filled with abundant lochs and trees and wildflowers and heather. Never have I felt that I stood at such a high elevation or that I could see so far. We even saw little towns and villages, and on a steep hill, a great castle.

"That is your father's castle," said my mother. "It is there you were all born on the same day. And there were great celebrations held, for never had triplets been born in the land to anyone's knowledge—the silly priest said it was a sign of God's favor that you be born in the image of the Trinity, but I told him it was more likely you were born in the image of the Goddess-God and His-Her companion Wisdom."

At the time, my mother's comparison of Christianity to our ancient religion at Avalon hardly registered in my youthful mind. I knew then only one thing. As I stood there, looking out at that land so grand and rich, as large and almost as beautiful as Avalon itself, I knew that someday I would go to Albany to see my father, the great King Elynas—and if my mother would not tell me the full truth of our separation, I would learn it from him.

I will not burden you with more details of my youth in Avalon, for the next ten years of my life were still happiness and contentment, save for the occasional longing to see my father and a couple of significant events that made me realize another world existed outside of the Holy Isle.

One such event was less an event than a passing occasional glimpse of the great King Arthur. Even in Avalon, his praises were sung, and we learned the tales of the Knights of the Round Table, of Queen Guinevere and Sir Bedwyr, of Prince Mordred and the Pretender Constantine, of Merlin and Morgan le Fay. These tales drifted to us from the outside world—brought now and then by an acolyte or a bard granted special permission to visit us. Sometimes the people of Avalon laughed at the tales for how distorted they were from the truth; sometimes our friends in Avalon even showed a spark of anger at the lies told, and now and then, I saw a moment of deep thought, longing, or even a nostalgic tear among them for a past that many at Avalon had known and a few had even participated in to some degree.

By that time, nearly two centuries had passed since the fatal Battle of Camlann, where good King Arthur had been defeated, but already the truth of those tales had been forgotten by the outside world. Still, to me, it seemed like Camelot's days of glory had been just yesterday, just a few days before I was born. After all, King Arthur was a very real person to me, for after the Battle of Camlann, Morgan le Fay had brought him to Avalon, where he had resided in his own castle ever since—a castle the folk of Avalon had allowed him to build while he was still fairly young, and where his sons lay buried. Only a very select few are chosen to live beyond the length of mortal years, and most of those of Arthur's past—Guinevere, Bedwyr, Mordred—had all passed on, but Morgan le Fay, his sister, whom we knew as Lady Morgana, still lived, and some said the great Merlin yet lived as well, although I had never seen him; the stories that came to us from Britain and France told of how he lay trapped in a cave in the Forest of Broceliande, but Morgan le Fay told me that story was a fantasy made up by men who knew not what they spoke of; however, when I then asked her where Merlin was, she would not tell me, for she said it was not time for me or even her to know, but that I could be certain he was about the business of serving mankind.

Now and then, we had a bard come to sing other tales to us. Songs of the Trojan War were quite common, as were tales of Aeneas and the founding of Rome, but these interested me little compared to the tales of King Arthur. We had no end of insufferable stories of the Romans—of Cleopatra and Julius Caesar's love for each other as well as Cleopatra's love for Marc Antony—I found such romances distasteful, for it seemed to me that Cleopatra should not have given herself to such men, making them higher than herself. And we heard the songs of Ireland—among my favorites was that of the Star-Eyed Deirdre, and also of the Children of Lir, and so many other stories that if I mentioned them here, they would mean nothing to you because they have been forgotten by the mortal world. But always, it was the tales of Arthur I appreciated most.

I will never forget one day when my mother and sisters and I were invited to Morgan le Fay's palace, which had a large audience chamber where she often hosted the traveling bards and others who provided entertainment; Morgan le Fay would invite all the people of Avalon to hear these beautiful songs. My sisters and I had rarely been allowed to attend because of our youth, but we were thirteen by this time. At the concert, not only were all of the young acolytes of the Goddess-God present, but so were many of those worthies who had been granted extended lives upon Avalon, and among them was my hero, the once great High King of Britain himself.

I had caught glimpses of King Arthur now and then, but I had never been close enough to speak to him; not that it mattered—I never would have dared to say a single word to such a famous and imposing figure. He must have stood over six feet tall, and although his beard had as much grey as any other color in it, one could see he was as strong as any man alive, and no king since has been his equal.

That evening during the concert, I found myself watching King Arthur more than the bard we were both listening to; besides, the bard was singing of Beowulf, and I could never understand why Morgan le Fay or King Arthur would agree to listen to it since it was a Saxon song, while they were Britons. It was far more pleasant to gaze upon the great King Arthur than to hear of the hideous Grendel or his even more disgusting mother. What a thrill it was the couple of times during the performance when, from across the room, King Arthur caught my eye. In embarrassment, I would quickly turn my head, but I was thrilled beyond words by his attention. At that time, I truly believed myself in love with him, and I'll admit I envied Queen Guinevere—I was glad later to learn that the tales of how she had loved other men were all false, for I could not imagine how any other man could hold her heart when she had such a handsome, brave, and strong man as King Arthur for her husband and lord.

When the song was finished and we were preparing to leave the gathering, my mother stopped to thank Lady Morgana for inviting us. As I waited for them to finish talking, no one less than King Arthur himself came up to me and said, "So, Melusine, what did you think of the bard's song?"

Never would I have even guessed that King Arthur knew my name; it took me a second to recover from my surprise before I could respond. "It was well enough," I said, "but it was nothing compared to the wonderful tales told of you and your knights at Camelot, Your Majesty."

King Arthur laughed and then replied, "Don't believe everything you hear, my girl."

I must have looked puzzled, for after a moment, he said, "My dear, it's been two centuries since Camelot fell, and in that time, much more has been made up about me than has been remembered, and at the rate these storytellers are going, I wouldn't be surprised if someday they even change my name in the stories."

"Oh, sir," I replied, "how could anyone change the stories when they are so wonderful already?"

"Someday you will understand," he said, "for I imagine in time that tales will be told of you as well. If someday you should leave Avalon and live among mortal men, be prepared for how they lie—or at least elaborate upon the truth—and for how faulty their memories are."

Lady Morgana then called to King Arthur. He excused himself and went to join her while my sisters came up and squeezed my hands, nearly as thrilled as I that I'd had the chance to speak to the legendary king.

But King Arthur's words had troubled me, and I often pondered over them in the days that followed, for I did not want to believe that the tales I had heard of him were not all true—and perhaps, even more, I feared that men would someday spread lies of me.

Not long after, I came to understand better my role and why in time I would be called upon to live among mortal men. By then, I had begun to spend considerable time with Lady Morgana. When my sisters and I turned fourteen, we were told that when we celebrated our next birthday, we would be ready to take upon ourselves our adult roles either in Avalon or in the mortal world, and so we had one last year to prepare ourselves. During this final year, we were each assigned to learn from an elder wise woman. Many ladies at Avalon, including my mother now that her young daughters no longer needed her constant supervision, had an acolyte to mentor, and my sisters and I were now included among the acolytes. My sisters each served under a lady whose name would mean little to mortals, but I am proud to say that perhaps because I was first born of triplets, I was chosen to serve under the Lady Morgana herself.

The hierarchy of Avalon, if it can even be called such, is difficult to explain, and certainly there were those at Avalon far older than Lady Morgana, but she had been chosen by Merlin himself to become the Lady of Avalon, successor to Nimue, and she had a talent far beyond any others at Avalon, a talent that superseded any level of training or years of study. We all acknowledged her as the most powerful and magnificent of all those among us who served the Goddess-God, and we all adored and respected her so that never was any envy shown toward her or her great abilities. Although jealousy exists in the outside world, and hierarchy and pride have even marred the good intended by the Christian Church, at Avalon, we all served the same purpose—

we all lived to do the will of the Goddess-God.

Nevertheless, I could not help but feel that for me to be chosen by Lady Morgana as her pupil was a high honor indeed, and I found myself unable not to express my exuberance over being so chosen. But my mother warned me, "Don't let it go to your head, Melusine. She had to choose someone, and one of the first signs of wisdom is humility, not pride."

I then suppressed my pride, and I soon realized that the depth and degree of knowledge and wisdom I must acquire was so vast and mind-bending that while to study under Lady Morgana was an honor, it was equally a great task, almost a burden, to learn and take on the responsibility of serving the Goddess-God—and especially when it also meant service to mortals, who were cantankerous and ungrateful most of the time.

I learned so much as Lady Morgana's acolyte that it would take years to explain it all to you in full detail, Raimond, and most of it would not interest you, much less concern you, but one question I always had that I finally could not help but ask. I wanted to know how it was that the world had come to be divided into regular mortals and those privileged others, often believed to be fairies by the mortals themselves, who dwelt at Avalon and the few other Holy Places throughout the world that I learned existed.

"Ah, you have a love for history, Melusine," Morgana replied when I asked her how this state of affairs had come to be. "It is important that you know this information, and I have been waiting for you to ask. You are old enough and wise enough now to know the truth and to differentiate that truth from the myths men tell themselves about the world's origins, myths mankind creates because humans have short memories; in truth, only in recent generations have mortals begun to record their history. As for Avalon's history, that is a tale almost as old as man's existence itself, and I will tell it to you."

I felt myself trembling with excitement at the prospect of learning such important information.

"What do you know of the origins of the world?" Lady Morgana began.

"Only what a couple of the acolytes have told me they learned as Christians," I confessed. "That there was a Garden where God placed man and woman, and they ate the fruit of a tree, even though it had been forbidden them, and for that transgression, God cast them from the Garden. Ever since, they and all their descendants have been forced to toil, although Christ the Savior finally freed them from sin and death."

"Yes, that is the story the Christians believe," Morgana agreed. "But there is far more to it, and it did not happen quite that way."

"Tell me the truth then," I said. "I am ready to hear it."

And so Morgana told me of the world's origins, which have been largely forgotten and much distorted because of man's inability to remember, but they have been preserved, regardless, in the wisdom of Avalon. I was so fascinated by what Morgana told me that day that I remember every word she said, and I will recite it to you now, Raimond, as I heard it from her lips.

CHAPTER 11

MORGAN LE FAY'S TALE

T HE HISTORY OF Avalon is linked to mankind's origins. But while time has separated man from his ancestors by hundreds of generations, we of the true blood of Avalon are not removed by nearly that many.

I daresay, Melusine, you know that in the mortal world I am known as Morgan le Fay—Morgan the Fairy—for men understand not my powers, which are not so much my own powers, but those of Nature and the wisdom derived from studying it. I and you and all the people of Avalon are not rightly fairies, but we are of a special lineage. Many others come here to study and then to return into the mortal world to serve as druids, as priestesses, as wise women and counselors, but they are fewer and fewer as the years pass by. We are lucky if half a dozen at a time come to us now, but in the generations before my time, often several hundred acolytes would come to Avalon each year. That change has been brought about by the coming of Christianity to Britain and Eire and Albany, but it is not a change for us to weep over, for the Goddess-God, the Source of All, has His-Her ways of manifesting and ordering all things to their appropriate time and season as needed for the good of all.

We of the ancient blood of Avalon will continue for centuries yet to come, as I have been privileged to foresee in the Holy Pool.

When I say I am not Fay, it stands to reason then that I must be mortal, yet I am more than mortal, for I have been nourished by the royal honey of Avalon. We call it royal honey or royal jelly, for it is not unlike that substance that the honey bees make to feed their baby queens, although it has additional ingredients only known to a select few of us, and just as it alters the bees so they become queens, so we are altered so that we become not immortals but perhaps hybrids, super-mortals, you might say, at least in terms of our longevity. The secret of the royal honey is an ancient one and must not fall into the hands of mankind—for that reason, only a few of the lineage know of it, and we must be careful regarding to whom it is fed. Is it elitist? Yes, perhaps, but it is not necessarily a blessing, for the extension of life can cause much pain when all those whom you love pass away and you are left behind, but in time, we grow used to losing the beloved mortals in our lives, and rather than mourn, we find comfort in enjoying the time we have with them and then moving on to their successive generations.

I know, Melusine, that you are very familiar with the songs men sing about my brother Arthur, and also the muddle of conflicting stories they have told about me. That is because already men have forgotten Avalon's purpose, and even the acolytes who come here are now given a watered down version of our history and our teachings from fear our knowledge could fall into the wrong hands, for those who are truly wise among men are few and often overshadowed and overpowered by the greedy and the feeble-minded.

You know Arthur and I are only half-siblings. We had different fathers, both of whom were mere mortals, although his father, King Uther Pendragon, did number among his ancestors a daughter of the Goddess-God, a daughter who, in the mess of history that the humans keep, has become known as Aphrodite; I'll explain more about her later in my story. As for my own father, he was Gorlois, Duke of Cornwall. My and Arthur's mother was the Lady Igraine; she chose to live among the mortals, but she was herself descended from the ancient House of Avallach. And your own mother, Pressyne, is also descended from that line, and so, Melusine, you are my cousin of a sort.

Living on Avalon is a blessing for we who minister to humans. Most of us know how much of a blessing it is, for we have either left Avalon to minister, or we have begun our journeys in the mortal world and then later been brought here.

Our bloodline is kept lean, only a handful being born to each generation, and so we must align ourselves with human men and women from time to time, and in those cases, we leave children behind in the mortal world, who because of our blood in them, often rise above the average abilities of mortal man, and now and then, children are also born whom at some point in their lives are fed the royal jelly and allowed to become numbered among Avalon's permanent residents when their time in the mortal world has ended. Both Arthur and I were such children, a rarity indeed, although I did not taste of the jelly until Merlin brought me to Avalon when I was a woman, and Arthur did not taste of it until I gave it to him after the Battle of Camlann to heal him of his wound and prevent his death. And you, Melusine, are such a one, though you tasted of the royal jelly from earliest childhood, but I will leave that tale for your mother to explain to you, and it is much for a young girl your age to take in. I'll simply say that you were chosen with your sisters—for triplets are a rare blessing—to receive such a designation, and while it is destined for you all to enter the mortal world, in time you will all return to Avalon. But for now, my purpose in telling you this history is so you may understand the mortals among whom you will soon reside.

Remember, we do not claim to be immortal; the royal jelly allows our lives to be extended, but we can die by accident or violence among the humans, and occasionally, one of us chooses to leave this life—such happened to my predecessor as Lady of Avalon, Nimue, who was my mother's cousin and chose to surrender her post to me, for she could no longer bear to watch the mortals and serve them after all the pain she witnessed following the Fall of Rome, the hoards of Huns and Vandals and Visigoths slaying people, and the bloodshed and darkness that fell upon mankind these last few centuries as humans forgot most of the knowledge it took them centuries to acquire. Her loss was an additional blow to our people, but we know she works with the Goddess-God in another realm now and continues to serve Avalon in her own way. In the two centuries since her departure, I have done my best to fulfill the role and purpose of the Lady of Avalon in keeping with the traditions and wisdom of my predecessors.

I see sadness in your eyes for mankind, for their mortality, but it is that very sadness, that compassion that has led to your being chosen as one who will remain at Avalon for generations to come, although not until after you fulfill your purpose in the greater mortal world.

It is up to us at Avalon to keep wisdom alive, to keep the human spirit alive when it falters, causing fear and despair to settle in the soul. That is when we go, unseen, and whisper in human ears while they sleep, causing people to dream of greatness, of a better world, of a golden age of mankind that once existed or might exist again. They may not remember such dreams, but the seeds are then planted.

You see, humans are filled with fear. Their greatest fault is not their anger, their greed, their violence, their lies, or their treachery to one another. No, for all of those evil behaviors are the results of their fear—fear of death, fear of being unloved, and fear of not having enough, whether it be food, water, money, land, or more trivial items they mistakenly deem necessary to survive. And that fear is at the very heart of all their wrongs toward one another and most of all toward themselves. Man's greatest sin is his belief in sin, his belief that he is not worthy, that he must somehow redeem himself when in truth the Goddess-God blessed man and woman both with worthiness from the moment of their creation. It is only when people doubt themselves, when they give into fear and self-loathing, that evil develops.

Christianity has overtaken much of the world now, and Islam and Judaism also have great power over men, and all three hearken back to that much distorted tale of the Garden of Eden where Adam and Eve were warned not to eat of the fruit of the Tree of Knowledge, but they disobeyed and were then cast from the Garden.

Mortals believe this tale to explain their unhappiness when in truth they are the source of their own unhappiness, and not because they committed sin, but because they doubt their worthiness, which leads them to act in all manner of ways, which may be termed sin, but it is not the same as that sin they falsely believe they were born with, making them unworthy from the moment of their origins.

The truth is that none of us here at Avalon know what happened in the Garden of Eden—it has been lost to the ages and hidden behind centuries of pain and fear that have distorted the tale. I know only that no loving God would put a tree in a garden, tell His children not to eat from it, and then when they do, cast them forth. That would be like a mother throwing her child out of the house for eating a sweet she told him he could not have. What mother would be so cruel? The Goddess-God is not cruel, Melusine; rather, He-She is the source of Love and Creation. Nor is it in any manner evil to desire Knowledge. Never think otherwise.

There is one still alive who does know the truth of what happened in the Garden of Eden. Her name is Lilith, and someday when you are ready, you will learn about her, for she is our ancient enemy, but our battle with her is not one you are yet prepared to face, although you shall play a role in it when the time comes.

Do not waste time now on fears of the future. I only mention Lilith so you understand that parts of the Garden story as men know it are true, but not all the parts, for the Christians and Jews have written Lilith out of their stories so she is barely more than a wives' tale now. But for today, let me tell you how Avalon came to be, and how we of Avalon have always sought to help the sons and daughters of Adam and Eve.

I am sure you are familiar with the Bible, for we value all mankind's knowledge and wisdom here at Avalon; its origin stories were written by people thousands of years removed from the truth of what happened, so mistakes in those retellings were bound to happen, but nevertheless, the writing of it was a noble attempt to get at the truth.

Perhaps you may remember in the Book of Genesis how the Sons of God coupled with the Daughters of Men to create the race of giants, the Nephilim. Another race of giants also existed, the Anakim, the children of Lilith. The Nephilim were good and benevolent toward mankind while the Anakim, because they were filled with Lilith's spite, sought to destroy the race of man.

For many years, war existed between the Anakim and mankind.

The Nephilim continually came to mankind's aid in this struggle, and as a result, I fear the Nephilim tended to have the worst of it, for mankind was no match for giants, and in trying to protect the weaker race, the Nephilim were forced to put themselves in danger time and again. I will not go into detail of all the events of those early centuries of human history; it is sufficient to say that many members of all three races died in these wars, but in the end, while many of the Anakim and the humans survived, only two Nephilim, the brothers Albion and Avallach, remained. Fortunately, these brothers were among the wisest and most skilled of their race and would survive for many years to come.

By this time, one man, Nimrod, was proclaimed the first king, as the result of his pledge to the people that because he was a great warrior and wiser and stronger than all other men, he would devise a means to protect humanity from the Anakim.

However, Nimrod's speeches were filled with grandiose rather than wise words, and while he was a great hunter and warrior, he could not possibly slay all the Anakim on his own, for the Anakim moved with great stealth, attacking human villages at night when their immense size was hidden by darkness so they could sneak up on their victims.

Fearing that the people would turn against him if he did not fulfill his promises, Nimrod went to the Nephilim brothers, Avallach and Albion, and asked for their aid. He initially expected the Nephilim, the only creatures of great size and strength equal to that of the Anakim, to fight his giant enemies, but the brothers were peace-loving and refused to war against the Anakim; in fact, the wars the Nephilim had fought in the past had all been in self-defense and to assist mankind, but never had the Nephilim taken the offensive in the battles, their pacifism, I fear, driving their race to near-extinction. Nimrod fell into despair at the brothers' refusal. He feared the Anakim would soon outnumber humanity and their great strength would quickly lead to the human race's destruction. After Nimrod made repeated pleadings with the brothers, however, they came to a compromise.

You doubtless know of the Tower of Babel, but probably only from what is told in the Bible, which leaves out many details. The full story must be known by you if you are to understand Avalon's history. You see, the Nephilim brothers helped Nimrod to build the Tower of Babel. Man did not have the skills or tools in those days to construct such a wonder. The Nephilim brothers, by comparison, possessed sophisticated building skills, and their stature assisted them tremendously in the process, for they were able to lift items of extreme weight and place them easily at great heights, all of which would have been a tremendous struggle for any mere man. Albion and Avallach also possessed many powers beyond those of humans by virtue of their descent from the Sons of God—powers you are not yet ready to understand, but some of them surely lie dormant in your blood, and for all we know, you might become a great architect, a builder, artist, or some other type of great creator because of that strain within you, for Avallach numbers among your ancestors.

In any case, the result of Avallach and Albion's great masonry and artisan skills was the fabulous tower they built for King Nimrod. It was a structure like none the earth had ever seen before or has since. It is prophesied that in another twelve or so centuries, humans will again build such magnificent structures as was the Tower of Babel, but I doubt any building will be so stunningly beautiful.

Now the Bible says that Nimrod's Tower was built so that man might reach the heavens and thus conquer God, but anyone with an ounce of sense would know that Nimrod would have been a fool to think such was possible. Sadly, the humans have come to equate his name with being a fool for that reason. Similarly, the tale that the Goddess-God caused the humans to speak in a babble of languages is a thoughtless story. Is it not common sense that as people moved away from one another, they would develop their own languages independently?

No, the Tower was built to make the Anakim realize they could not harm the humans so they would leave them alone. It was so tall a Tower that even the Anakim were dwarfed by it. It was large and strong enough that all the human race could fit inside it if the Anakim threatened, and it was high enough that it served as a watchtower should the Anakim try to approach; that way, plenty of warning could be given to the people to get inside it before the Anakim could attack. Avallach and Albion even made it large enough that they could enter it. The Tower was so impregnable that, ultimately, it was believed the Anakim would give up their harassing behaviors and leave the humans alone. In addition, and against the Nephilim brothers' better judgment, it was equipped with weapons—bows and arrows to shoot, hot oil to pour down, and balls of fire to hurl at attackers.

Before long, the Tower's purpose was achieved. The Anakim attacked the Tower and were driven away by the arrows shot forth from it. But they came back better protected, this time trying to topple it, break into it, even dig beneath it, but they could not breach it, and after several failed attempts, they became bored and migrated away in hopes of finding other victims to torment. They and their descendants spread to Europe and the Mediterranean areas while the humans were left in peace.

But humans can never remain at peace for long. When they no longer had a mutual enemy, they began bickering first among themselves and then with the Nephilim brothers, accusing them of having more than their fair share of food because of their size, and all other manner of ridiculous and petty arguments, which showed their ingratitude. Despite this behavior, Albion and Avallach felt they were bound to stay and protect the humans in case the Anakim should return, but they would have been better off if they had abandoned mankind. For a long time, Nimrod managed to maintain the peace among his people, but as the years went by, new generations of humans claimed stories of the Anakim were just lies told by their elders, and their selfish greed caused them to part ways with one another, expanding their boundaries, moving outward, and forming their own kingdoms—not until they came in contact with the Anakim would they realize how mistaken they had been.

Then King Nimrod died in a hunting accident, and with his death, all peace between the humans and the Nephilim brothers ceased. Avallach and Albion were accused of trying to imprison humans within the Tower and even of manipulating Nimrod into doing their will. The people would no longer abide the brothers' counsel or even their presence. The Bible says the Tower was destroyed by God, but the Goddess-God had no need to take such action, for humans will often bring about their own destruction.

Realizing their lives were in danger at the hands of those they had long served, Albion and Avallach locked themselves inside the Tower for their own protection. But the Tower was no longer formidable now that human technology had advanced so that weapons of great destruction were created—gunpowder, catapults, siege towers, and all sorts of horrible things. These ungrateful humans finally succeeded in weakening one of the Tower's walls, and Avallach and Albion barely escaped with their lives as the Tower toppled over, killing most of the humans who had tried to destroy it, and in the process, erasing from mankind's memory the knowledge of how to build such formidable weapons so that it will yet be many centuries before they acquire such knowledge again.

Of course, the Bible's authors composed their tales centuries later, so they did not witness the destruction of the Tower or know what had truly happened; the tales passed down had become muddled over the generations, so the Bible's writers drew their own conclusions, placing the blame for the Tower's destruction upon a jealous God who barely resembled the good Goddess-God.

Meanwhile, Albion and Avallach washed their hands of humanity. They traveled to the sea, journeying far until they found a beautiful island completely uninhabited, the island now known as Britain, which at that time came to be named Albion for its first resident, while Avallach contented himself with a nearby smaller island, the name of which over the years has become Avalon. Avallach brought with him to this island an apple seed he had saved from the Tree of Wisdom in the Garden of Eden, a garden and a tree that the humans in their hatred and fear had since destroyed, having harvested the trees to build their weapons to war with one another. From that apple seed grew the first apple tree of Avalon, from which in turn grew many apples with seeds that have resulted in our beautiful apple orchards, and which give those of us at Avalon wisdom beyond that of humanity.

The Nephilim brothers were alone in Britain at that time, for the humans had not yet come, and no Anakim had reached Britain's shores, but more importantly, there were none of their own kind for the brothers to associate with. Seeing their loneliness, one of the Daughters of the Goddess-God took pity upon the brothers' loneliness and sorrow in knowing they were the last of their kind. This Daughter was named

Brigantia, and in time, she mated with Avallach. Their descendants were the Brigantes people of Britain, and from their line comes also the people of Avalon. While Avallach was of gigantic stature, his children by Brigantia were not quite so tall, and over time and through the use of natural magic, and eventually through intermarrying with the humans who later came to Britain, our race has now grown to normal human size; today, most of us have more human blood in us than we do the ancient blood of Avallach and Brigantia. Nevertheless, it is our descent from them that allows us to have many powers over the natural world, which humans call "magic," but which is simply knowledge of the workings of the elements and the invisible forces set up by the Goddess-God for the world's functioning. Our abilities, such as telepathic skills, foresight into the future, and many others, are as natural to us as is spinning a web for a spider or flying to a bird.

In time, Albion also wed, surprisingly enough, to an Anakim woman named Chelah, who had been cast from among her people for her great ugliness. When she made her way to Britain's shore, out of loneliness and pity for her, Albion took her for his wife, but it would have been better had he never done so for she was a spiteful, miserable creature who stirred great strife between the brothers until Avallach permanently isolated himself to the Isle of Avalon while Albion remained on the isle that bore his name. Chelah gave birth to Gog and Magog, giants who found for themselves Anakim brides, and in time, a race of giants came to populate Britain. They were all quarrelsome creatures, taking after their Anakim ancestors, but only harming themselves in their disputes.

Then came the human invasion of Britain. I know you have heard the songs of the Fall of Troy, and perhaps even of Prince Aeneas and how he fled Troy and managed to reach Italy, where eventually his descendants would found Rome. Aeneas was himself the son to Aphrodite and Prince Anchises of Troy. Aphrodite was one of the daughters of Zeus, or so the Greeks knew her, when in truth she was one of the Daughters of the Goddess-God, like those who gave birth to the Nephilim. Only now, so many generations after the Garden of Eden, the human bloodline was stronger, so Aphrodite and Anchises' mating did not result in a giant child, though Aeneas was still a great hero in his own right because of his immortal mother.

Years later, Aeneas' great-grandson, Brutus, accidentally slew his own father, and as punishment, was exiled from his home. After many travels, Brutus and his companions arrived in Albion, and immediately, they began to wage war upon Albion's descendants. By that time, Albion had passed away, but Chelah still lived, and she egged on her sons, Gog and Magog, to wage war against the humans; the result was both sons being killed in battle. Brutus' arrival to Britain caused the fiercest slaughter of giants ever to take place, for he and his men came bearing razor-sharp swords, something Albion and his descendants had never conceived of creating, for they had no need of them in their island home. Consequently, despite their great size, the descendants of Albion were no match for mankind, and like their Anakim cousins in other parts of the world, they were slowly being exterminated until today only a handful of giants remain upon the face of the earth. In fact, Melusine, I have foreseen that among your progeny shall be a great giant-slayer who will help to free mankind from what remains of their oppression. It is a shame that the descendants of Albion should be included in this extinction, but while humans are far from flawless, the giants, by virtue of the blood they gained from their ancient mother Lilith, are far more evil.

As you know, Brutus became the first human king of Britain and the island was renamed for him. He, in turn, became the ancestor of Uther Pendragon, my brother Arthur's father. Our ancestors of Avalon in time came in contact with Brutus and his descendants, but using his creative arts, Avallach protected the island from human entry, inviting only those judged worthy to learn from him the old ways of Wisdom and ancient times. Among those most deemed worthy was Joseph of Arimathea, who came to Britain first with his nephew, the Christ. Later, Joseph returned with his daughter Anna, who married Bran the Blessed, one of Avallach's giant descendants. My own mother, Igraine, and your mother, Pressyne, descend from this couple. I need not tell you the history of Avalon since then, for you know of how Igraine bore Uther Pendragon's son, my brother Arthur, and how later Arthur and I mated, giving birth to Mordred, whom we hoped would be next High King of Britain, but it was not to be. Yet my and Arthur's bloodline survives, and as I will explain to you someday soon, Melusine, your destiny lies intertwined with this bloodline.

I have far more to tell you, but I shall end my tale here for today, for it is a great amount of information to take in and muse over. If you learn nothing else from it, realize that mankind has always acted out of fear throughout its history. It was fear that has caused men and women to believe themselves unworthy of the Goddess-God's love, and ultimately, it is fear that caused them to leave the Garden of Eden. Fear caused them to quarrel with the Nephilim who sought only to help them; they feared not having enough if they shared what they had with the Nephilim, and they feared sharing what they had with one another, and so they have always warred with their brothers. Some say that even the wars with the Anakim were the result of a wrong Adam and Eve did to Lilith, again based in fear, but the truths that underlie that supposition have been lost to time and are known by one only—Lilith herself. Yes, as I said, she still lives, but we will discuss her another day.

What is important for you to understand now is that mankind is far more capable than it gives itself credit for. Humans' abilities would be limitless if only they would believe in themselves and in the innate goodness that the Goddess-God granted them at the Creation. We of Avalon must, as our duty and in our compassion, do whatever is possible to change that fear that keeps humans from attaining their full glory.

Do you understand, Melusine, all that I have told you? What questions do you have? I will answer them all, for it is important that you be clear on these matters before I explain to you your own role in helping to continue Arthur's bloodline, and in that process, assist the human race in achieving its destiny.

CHAPTER 12

MELUSINE'S TALE CONTINUES

I WAS SO stunned by all that I had just heard from Lady Morgana's lips that it took me a moment before I could respond.

"Yes, I understand," I finally said.

"Do you?" Lady Morgana repeated, not doubting me but wanting to make certain. "Have you ever suspected then, Melusine, why you were chosen to be my acolyte?"

"No-o," I said. "I admit I've wondered why I was chosen over either of my sisters or the other acolytes here at Avalon, but I don't know why such an honor should have been bestowed upon me."

"That is good to hear," she replied. "You are not prideful then, but we cannot have you unaware of your powers. You have a skill, a talent of which you are scarcely aware. Do you have any idea what it might be?"

"No, my lady," I said, surprised.

"You, Melusine, are a creator. Many are called to serve, but few are blessed with true creative powers. It takes a special talent, the gift of imagination, to create."

I was pleased by her words—pleased by her praise—but I did not understand yet what her words truly meant.

"Milady, I don't understand what you mean by a creator," I admitted. "I have not created anything."

"Ah, but you have," she replied. "You have vision. I have seen it when you and your sisters have been at play—when on the shore you have built sandcastles. Melior and Palatyne stacked mud upon mud, but you were artistic, creating elaborate cities, temples, and palaces. I've seen it as well when you have drawn pictures, for you have an eye for detail. I have seen it even when you have stitched your gowns— how you let not the least important detail of the task escape you. Your mother has told me how you will stay up half the night to finish some personal project when your sisters have long since tired of a task. You are a perfectionist in your creations, and more importantly, a visionary. You have imagination, which is the greatest gift anyone can have, for by it all things become possible—it is what forms dreams, visions, and ultimately, what leads to mankind's reality, for all of reality was a dream first. Having such a vision is what changes the world. Brute force in itself is stupid and only causes pain. A warrior is weak. An artist is strong. Warriors mostly seek to destroy; even when they seek to protect, they do so through destruction of their enemies. But the visionary is the one who creates—creates music, art, poetry, all the things that inspire mankind to achieve its greatest good. Now do you understand?"

"I am pleased, milady, that you think so highly of me," I replied, speaking slowly, for my heart raced with excitement as she spoke; my soul acknowledged the truth of her words, but what she said also frightened me, for if I were a creator, was that not dangerously close to being like the greatest creator, the Goddess-God? What role then was

I to play for mankind? "Lady Morgana," I continued, "I know you are far wiser than I, so if you believe I have such talent, I will believe you, but I do not understand why I have it or how."

"Many have talent to some degree," Morgana replied. "Your sisters have some, your mother a great deal; I have a fair share of it myself. At times, it skips a generation, sometimes several, but then it manifests itself again, for it is in our bloodlines. It is the architectural creative skill that our ancestor Avallach had—that which was able to build the great Tower of Babel, that which later came and raised the great temples at Stonehenge and Avebury that mankind now scarcely remember because they lie in ruins, but their greatness was once nearly unsurpassed. The creative power of the Nephilim flowed in the veins of those men who built the pyramids in Egypt, and it led to the existence of this sanctuary here at Avalon, including all the wonderful palaces you see on our sacred isle. Would you not like to be such a creator, Melusine? To build great palaces, homes for humans that will inspire them to reimagine what their world might be, to make them feel grander, to think loftier thoughts because they see such beauty that they aspire to creating it themselves, to becoming beautiful people, not only on the outside but on the inside as well?"

"Yes, milady," I replied. "I would greatly enjoy that. It would be a thousand times more fun than it ever was to build sandcastles, and it would be purposeful as well."

"Good. Good," said Lady Morgana. "There is one other calling that you have, but we shall save that until another time. For now, we shall study the skills you must learn—how to move stones with vibrational power, how to build domes that shall not collapse, how to make impregnable walls, and also how to create beauty in all that you build so you shall be remembered, and more importantly, so men shall look upon your work in wonder and feel a longing to be better, to aspire to such greatness themselves. Someday, many a great builder will see one of your creations and realize what is possible when one has vision and takes joy in the creative spirit, thus inspiring him to create as well; such beauty as what you create will help to unleash repressed powers of the human mind and lead mankind to explore beyond its current grasp."

"It feels like such a blessing," I replied, "to think I might do such things—things that could make such a difference."

"It is, but it will have its difficulties too—be aware of that, although the specifics of those difficulties must wait until you are more thoroughly trained. Go home now and we will continue your studies tomorrow."

I thanked her once more and returned to my family, my head filled with lofty thoughts I had never before imagined.

In the months that followed, I learned much from Lady Morgana. She taught me many spells and incantations; we studied herbs and the ways of the forest; we studied the elements and how to master them so we might use their power for good. And I was even allowed to build a palace at Avalon with Lady Morgana's help, although by the time we finished it, I was astounded to discover that I had surpassed my instructor in my abilities as an architect as well as a mason. I could even cause stones to levitate so I might move them far more easily than she could, and while such work left her exhausted, it did not tire me at all.

And then came the day when Lady Morgana told me, "You have

done well, Melusine. You have exceeded my expectations. I have only one thing left to teach you. One part of Avalon and mankind's history I have not yet told you, and it will greatly affect your future more than any other information. It has to do with your direct mission to humanity, but before I can give you that information, you must learn what it is to love a human, for in such love can be inconceivable joy, but it can also lead to much heartache because of the fickle nature of man, which results from his fear and self-doubt. Do you believe yourself ready for this calling, Melusine?"

"Milady," I humbly replied, "I do not think it matters whether or not I believe myself ready because doubtless I must fulfill what is my destiny."

"That is true, my dear, but I wish to prepare you. I send you back now to your mother. She has long dreaded this day, but she has something she must tell you before we can begin this last lesson of your training."

"My mother?" I said with surprise.

"Yes, your mother. She has knowledge—a story rather, of your family's past—that it is now time for you and your sisters to understand in detail. Go home tonight and ask your mother once more to tell you of her and your father's romance. I do not doubt she has told you the tale before, but tonight she will tell it to you differently; she has not been exactly untruthful to you, but she has withheld information from you until she knew you would be prepared to hear it and have it serve you in your future mission. Now that time is come."

"Yes, milady," I replied, knowing it better not to question her if my mother were to provide the answers I sought.

I quickly took my departure then, my head spinning as I pondered what my mother might say. I found myself thinking back to that day so many years earlier when I had come home, upset after Grainne had called my mother a witch, saying that was why my parents had parted; I remembered my mother correcting this story by saying we had left my father simply to keep us safe from those who would harm us because we were princesses of Albany. But after all the months I had spent studying with Lady Morgana, it became apparent to me that it was always planned for my sisters and me to study at Avalon, and that had made me wonder whether there were not another reason why we had left my father. Was it because we were special and had to be raised in Avalon? Did my father have any choice in the matter?

How was I even to ask my mother such a question?

I waited until after supper—when my sisters had gone outside to read in the cool summer evening air and I was helping my mother to wash up the dishes. I never did understand why she would wash the dishes when my sisters and I would have done it for her, or she could have had a servant to do it, but she was stubborn and preferred to do everything for herself.

"I am not a queen," she often would say when I would question her on such matters, but it was only now as I assisted her that I truly understood how this remark was a reference to her past. "But you were a queen once," I replied. "Did you not like being a queen?"

She looked at me oddly and then went back to washing a cup. I tried to think what to say next, but after a moment, she added, "I enjoyed being married to your father, but I did not marry him because he was a king. I endured being a queen for his sake."

"Then did you marry him for love?" I asked, hopeful.

"I married him because it was so destined for me. I married him so I might have my children."

"But you did love him, didn't you?"

She looked troubled and stopped washing the cup in her hand. Then sighing, she said, "I loved him dearly, but not at first. In the beginning, I thought I was just fulfilling my destiny."

"Mother," I said, seeing she seemed more willing tonight to talk of her past than usual. "Why did you leave, Father? You have always told us it was so we would be safe, but I have learned from Lady Morgana that there was more to it than that; she told me it is up to you to tell me, but that the time has now come for us to be told."

My mother did not look at me but rinsed off the cup and handed it to me to dry. Then she took a plate from the stack and began to wash it.

I waited, expecting her to say something to change the subject, but instead, she finished washing the plates without speaking another word.

When she handed me the last plate to dry, finally she said, "When you are finished with that, go sit outside with your sisters. Tell them I have something important to say and I will join you in a few minutes."

"Thank you, Mother," I replied. And then she went to her room.

I finished wiping the dishes and then joined my sisters outside.

"Mother has something to tell us," I said, sitting down beside them.

Melior looked up from her book, but Palatyne continued to read.

"It's important," I told them. "It's about our father. She said she'd be out in a minute."

Palatyne then closed her book and set it aside and Melior did the same.

Both of them looked at me questioningly.

"Lady Morgana told me today," I explained, "that it is time we know the full truth of our parents' pasts, so I was to ask Mother to tell us. And so I have."

And then we waited in silence a couple of minutes more, my sisters' eyes as big with questions as I felt my own must be.

Finally, Mother emerged from the house. I noticed her eyes were red when she sat down beside Palatyne on the bench outside our door.

Palatyne took her hand. "You've been crying, Mother," she said.

Mother made a gesture as if it were nothing, and then taking a deep breath, she tried to find words to tell her story.

"I never wished to deceive you, my girls," she said. Mother could often be severe, but when she called us "my girls," we knew she was at her most loving. "Do not be angry with me," she continued, "for I hope you will understand why I did what I did when you were but a few days old. I did it to protect you, and I have only waited to tell you until you were old enough to understand the truth."

"Go ahead, Mother," said Melior. "We love you. You need not fear our anger."

Trying to smile, she began.

CHAPTER 13

PRESSYNE'S TALE

I SUSPECT, MELUSINE, that Lady Morgana told you of our bloodline—that we are of the ancient line of Avalon, and that Lady Morgana and myself are cousins of a sort. I do not know, Melior and Palatyne, whether your tutors have given you the same information, but it is so, and therefore, you need not wonder why, when I left your father, I chose to come here to Avalon because Avalon has always been my home.

But even as I girl, I knew the day would come when I would leave Avalon, when I would go forth into the world of men to serve them.

I did not wish to leave Avalon, for I knew no other life than what I had experienced here, and my own parents had long ago passed away, my father having been human, and although my mother was of Avalon and she had brought me here as a girl after my father's death, she had left a few years later to return to the world, hoping to prevent a war among the humans, which happened regardless and resulted in her own death. Consequently, I was nervous to venture forth from the Holy Isle, but Morgana assured me I would be safe in the mortal world, and I felt it my duty to keep our bloodline alive for the good of the human race and to bring mankind what wisdom I could if only people would listen and be open to my influence.

Morgana told me I was to marry a great man and thereby influence him, and through him, make the lives of many people better, which I was more than willing to do. The only danger the situation presented for me, she said, would be if my husband should see me feeding my children. She said it was vital not to let the humans know about the royal jelly we feed our children, which keeps them immune from disease so their lives are extended, allowing them to grow wise and better assist mankind. This jelly, as you know, you were yourselves fed as girls.

I knew the condition set upon me and my future husband upon my entering the mortal world, and I was determined not to let it be broken. I also knew the evil of men, considering how my own mother had died during a war. I was determined then not to trust my husband with my secret, but simply to raise up my children so they could help mankind.

But I had no idea what a fine and handsome man my husband would be, for I had seen few men at Avalon, and those like King Arthur, whom I knew, were old, although I always thought Arthur extremely handsome and distinguished, perhaps precisely because of his grey hairs.

Now my daughters, you will be surprised, but the husband originally chosen for me was not your father. Other plans were made for me, and your father, though I loved him no less for it, ended up becoming my husband by default, and here is how it happened.

The man chosen for me by my elders here at Avalon was Hervé de Léon; he was a count in Brittany and very close to the King of Brittany at the time. He was a great warrior and counselor and had been instrumental in Brittany's efforts to remain an independent kingdom against the rising power of the Franks, who today rule all of Gaul save Brittany, and now they have lent their name to the country as France. While Hervé sounded like a fine man, I was surprised I was chosen to marry only a count and not a king. Morgana then told me, "Do not give any value to the titles men bear, for many are true kings by their blood and their noble hearts, whether or not they hold crowns. The current King of Brittany is descended from Duke Hoel of Brittany, who was cousin to King Arthur, and is himself a cousin of sorts to Hervé de Léon; more importantly, Hervé may only be a count in the eyes of men, who have forgotten his lineage, but he is the heir to King Arthur, a descendant of Arthur's son Mordred, and I might add, my own descendant as well."

I was stunned by this statement, for like yourself, I had heard the tales of King Arthur and Camelot that the bards sing, and I had taken them for truth, assuming that Arthur had been betrayed by his son Mordred and both had fallen at the Battle of Camlann, leaving the kingdom to Arthur's distant relative Constantine of Cornwall. I later learned all the details of that stunning story, but they are too cumbersome to tell here. It is enough to say that Constantine of Cornwall was the instigator of the events that led to Camelot's downfall, along with an evil woman named Gwenhwyvach, who was herself Queen Guinevere's half-sister. They had long plotted revenge against Arthur and Guinevere for an imagined offense. After Mordred died and Arthur was brought here to Avalon, Constantine had their names blackened throughout history. Mordred's sons, Princes Meleon and Morgant, then rose up against the usurper, but Constantine also defeated them and had them slain. However, Prince Meleon had secretly wed Lady Rachel of Rheged who was pregnant with his child. She managed to flee to Arthur's relatives in Brittany where she gave birth to a son, who in time was given lands in Brittany and made a knight and count. Rachel named her son Arthur for his illustrious great-grandfather, but many in those days were named after Arthur, so the boy thought nothing of it and his true lineage was always kept a secret to protect him. Morgana herself told me all this history, she having witnessed much of it firsthand, and she concluded by telling me, "This child of Meleon and Rachel grew up and had children of his own until now many generations have passed. Hervé de Léon is the direct descendant and very heir of King Arthur. It is he whom you shall wed with the purpose to bring forth as your children great leaders among men who will help the human race to advance."

You can imagine how my heart leapt at these words. Who would not wish to marry the descendant of King Arthur, the most noble king who had ever lived? I immediately and enthusiastically agreed to the match, but Lady Morgana warned me that Hervé himself did not know of his ancestry from King Arthur, for several generations had now passed, and while at some point, Arthur's kingdom would be restored to his descendants, until it was determined that the time was right, Hervé was not to be told of his lineage. I solemnly swore that I would keep the secret until I was told to do otherwise. I then made my preparations to travel to Brittany.

I traveled through a portal in the Holy Well here at Avalon to a well in the Forest of Broceliande, not far from the King of Brittany's castle. It was there in the heat of the sun that I met Hervé, who had stopped to fetch a drink. He was struck by my beauty at once, and while I knew any number of men might stop by the well, I recognized him instantly as my future husband because of his grace and bearing, his manly physique, and his handsome face. He was the most handsome man I have ever seen; I mean no injustice to your father when I say that, for your father was very handsome himself, but there could have been no comparison between Hervé and any other man who was alive at the time.

When Hervé asked me how it came to be that I should be alone by a well, I replied that I was of a noble house, but I was there to fetch water for the sisters of a nearby convent where I was living and that it was my intention to take the veil.

"You can do no such thing!" he declared. "You would deprive all the world of such loveliness and such beautiful children that you would bear. You cannot be serious."

"I wish to devote my life to God," I replied, which was not wholly untrue since I was intent on doing the Goddess-God's work in marrying him.

"There are other ways to serve God," he said, "and one way would be to make happy your fellow men, for I am all alone in the world, my parents both deceased, and I have found no woman until now whom I thought fair enough to be my bride."

"You are far too handsome not to have a bride," I replied, and I batted my eyes—I won't deny it—for I knew I must win him and win him quickly before his brain began to question the love stirring in his heart. "You are the only man handsome enough to make me reconsider my vows."

"Come with me," he said, reaching out his hand. "Ride with me upon my horse for a time, and then we shall see at the end of the day how you feel about taking the veil."

I accepted his hand and he lifted me with one arm up onto his horse. He was so strong, his waist so firm as I wrapped my arms around it, his back so broad, his whole bearing so very noble, that I felt overwhelmed with desire for him.

"If you wish to marry me," I said, "pray make it happen this very day, for now that I am beside you, I do not believe I can bear that we be parted."

"So be it," he said, laughing. "You are so beautiful that I cannot deny you anything, although I fear you may be one of those dangerous fairies I have heard tell of who will carry a man away to her land where what seems like only an hour will be spent in lovemaking, but he will wake the next morning to find his entire life has passed. Still, if I could spend one hour in lovemaking with you, it would be worth giving up a lifetime."

I felt such love, such an affinity for him. I could not explain it, but my heart told me we were born to spend our lives together, to be soul mates, and I could only wonder whether Morgana knew this, or whether it were just my good fortune that such an arrangement should also lead to my happiness. We rode to the nearest village, and there the parish priest married us within the hour, he not daring to ask any questions because it was apparent Hervé was not only a great lord but also a gallant knight whom one did not question.

Once the vows were said and the sealing kiss exchanged, Hervé told me, "I have never been happier in all my life." And then he rode with me to the castle to introduce me to the King of Brittany, whom he said was his best friend in the world and almost like a father to him. That night, I slept in his bed in the king's castle and we made love until the dawn. My daughters, nothing you will ever experience is as pleasant as the feeling of a man's body pressed against your own, but I warn you that such pleasure is overpowering and might lead you to make foolish decisions. I thought, because I was of the line of Avalon, I was above letting my heart overpower my wisdom, and I continually told myself that I had married Hervé because I had a mission to continue King Arthur's bloodline, but once I was married and had lain with him until my flesh and his were deliciously wrapped together, I forgot all else but that I loved him wholly and would have gladly died for him.

We were blissfully happy together for many months, spending much of our time with the king, who was Hervé's great and good friend, and the rest of our time we lived upon my husband's own estates. I grew to love Hervé deeply, until I felt truly that he was bone of my bone and flesh of my flesh. He was my Adam, the first and only man I ever wanted to be with. I worshiped him, and I know he worshiped me; it was as if we were the only beings on the earth, and there was nothing we would not have done for each other. There are times even now when I can get caught up in daydreaming about those days and lose myself for hours, although when I wake from such memories, the world is painful to me. Not that I would change any of it, for then I would not have my dear sweet girls, but if I could be with Hervé still, I would be. I only trust that in some other world, we will somehow be reunited.

But our happiness was not to last. One wicked man chose to interfere in our lives. At that time, the King of Brittany had a nephew, Perard, whom it was said the king loved as much as his own son. Perard was a few years younger than Hervé, barely more than a boy, but he thought himself a man, and he lorded it over everyone that if his sickly cousin the prince should die, then someday soon he would be king. His uncle reprimanded him for his bullying of other men and his backstabbing ways, but he loved Perard too well to punish him. Finally, Perard's taunts and disparaging words became so intolerable to all the court that Hervé went to the king and warned him that if his nephew did not learn to hold his tongue, the king's knights might teach him to do so. Hervé wished to keep peace in the kingdom, but the king, though frustrated with his nephew's behavior, was unwilling to curb it; instead, he took out his anger on Hervé, telling him not to interfere in the affairs of his betters.

Hervé was greatly hurt by such words when the king had always treated him as one of his own household, but he could do nothing but obey the king and allow Perard to continue running his tongue to the disgust of all.

Not long after, Perard began plotting against his uncle and cousin. For his ally, he enlisted the Duke of Mayence, one of the great nobles of the Franks and a close friend of Pepin of Herstal, who at the time was Mayor of the Palace; it was rumored that Pepin had his eye on the Frankish throne for himself and his sons. Whether or not this was true, he had succeeded in subduing the Alemanni, Frisians, and Franconians and bringing them under Frankish rule, and now he secretly plotted to conquer Brittany and make it part of France as well. The Bretons have always been proud and have successfully stood against the Franks, despite their greater numbers, so Perard truly showed what a fool he was when he decided to plot with the Franks to overthrow his uncle and cousin and seat himself on Brittany's throne. Both the Duke of Mayence and Pepin knew they could make Perard a puppet vassal to the Frankish king if only the King of Brittany were out of the way.

Hervé suspected a plot was afoot, so in private, he confronted Perard, not wishing to go to the king and have the old man's heart broken from learning his nephew had betrayed him. Perard first tried to deny his betrayal, but when Hervé presented evidence of the plot, he grew violent and pulled a knife on Hervé. In the struggle that ensued,

Hervé got the upper hand, and although he did not mean to hurt his opponent, the knife turned the wrong way and Perard was fatally wounded. If only the villain had died instantly, I might have lived out the rest of my days with my husband, but Perard screamed like a little girl when the blade entered his chest, causing the guards to rush into the room and instantly arrest Hervé for slaying the king's nephew. Minutes later, Perard was dead, but not before he told the guards that he had tried to stop Hervé from committing treason against the king.

The king was greatly grieved and demanded an explanation, but Hervé refused to tell the king the reason for the fight, not wishing to speak ill of the dead. And so, the king presumed Hervé was at fault since he had previously borne a grudge against Perard.

You can imagine how I feared that Hervé would be put to death, but there was nothing I could do. Lady Morgana had told me I was forbidden to interfere in the affairs of men—my only duty was to bear Hervé's children and influence him by modeling kindness and goodness; I was not to give him counsel, but how could I fulfill my other duties if he were to be killed?

At the last minute, the king settled simply for banishing Hervé. My husband, cloaked in sorrow and shame, was sent from the kingdom. I begged to go with him, but Hervé refused to let me, telling the king to hold me back, saying he would not make his shame my own. I cried and pled, but my own husband told me he never wished to see my face again. I know he said it out of love for me, but what kind of life did he think I could have if I were not to be with him?

I was left alone, my husband's lands and possessions taken by the crown, and my husband departed into the Frankish lands. The king was kind to me, believing me innocent, but soon after, a marriage proposal was made to me by the Duke of Mayence, who served the

Frankish king. I absolutely refused this proposal, but then the King of Brittany told me that since I was now his ward in principle, if not in actuality, he would dispose of me as he pleased and that such an alliance with one of the great Frankish lords would ensure peace between the Franks and Bretons. I was appalled. The duke disgusted me for the role he had played in the events that caused my husband's banishment, so it was impossible that I could stomach being married to him. The king arranged for my marriage to be annulled on reasons of desertion by my husband; then he ordered me to marry the duke and told me the wedding would happen swiftly. Eventually, I consented only so I would be less suspect when I tried to escape and search for Hervé.

Fortunately, the night before the wedding, Lady Morgana sent two male acolytes from Avalon to help me escape. We found our way from the castle to the forest well where I had first met Hervé, and although heartbroken that I was separated from the man I loved, I was grateful to return through the well's portal back to Avalon.

You can imagine how devastated I was at parting from Hervé. When I returned to Avalon, I was like one truly numb and dead to the world. I thought I would die from the pain. I could not eat, and I cried and cried for days, and even after my tears finally dried up, the ache in my heart would not be quenched.

Finally, after many, many months, Lady Morgana called me to her. She told me that it had been decided that the only way my broken heart could ever be healed was if I were to find a new love to replace the old one. That was the worst possible solution in my opinion, but she and all the people of Avalon continued trying to persuade me to love again. They told me they would find me a good and noble man, and that by him I would have many children, one of whom could complete my mission by marrying the child of Hervé. They had learned that Hervé had since married a mortal woman, who was now pregnant with his child.

I was even more heartbroken to think my beloved had married another, but I was told he had done so to find solace for his great sorrow over losing me, and that I should do the same. I now realized that I could never have Hervé back, despite the longing in my heart, so I started to think of my future.

After spending many days considering the alternative of remaining at Avalon and being miserable, I found some solace in the thought that my and Hervé's blood could yet be mingled in a union between our children, and so finally, I consented to marry again.

Morgana told me that my future husband had again been chosen for me. This time, he was to be Elynas, King of Albany. Elynas' first wife had recently died, and he was grieving and seeking solace. I consented to this marriage, thinking that since I was also heartbroken, we could comfort one another, although I would have to present myself in the guise of a widow to him. Because Elynas already had a son, Prince Nasciens, by his first wife, I knew my children would never rule his kingdom, but that would not stop me from having a daughter to marry Hervé's future son. Furthermore, Elynas was himself of an ancient and noble lineage that had done much to advance mankind's wellbeing in the islands of Britain and Ireland.

And so, I prepared to marry again. As I had with Hervé, I went into the forest by a well, and there, one day when he was out hunting with his courtiers, Elynas arrived. He was parched with thirst, so I gave him water to drink, and as I did so, I said to him.... Forgive me, my girls, for my tears, but I did love him dearly. I won't be able to tell you all the words that passed between us, but I did tell him that I was of noble lineage; I told him my late husband's lands had been taken from him unjustly, and in fighting for them, he had been killed, leaving me a widow without a protector or a penny in the world. Elynas wished to right this wrong immediately, but I asked him solely to give me shelter, and so I ended up returning with him to the castle. Of course, I did everything in my power to make him fall in love with me, which was not difficult really because he sought comfort from a woman and he already had an heir, so marrying a widow of unknown lineage did not concern him. Indeed, I knew he was intoxicated by my beauty, and since he was so very handsome and manly, I felt love reawakening in my breast.

In a short time, Elynas proposed, and I consented on one condition—that he promise never to disturb me while I was feeding my children, for you know I had to feed the royal jelly to you, and it would be fatal if that secret be discovered by men who would use it for all kinds of breeding purposes to develop a race of powerful but evil men who could use their advanced age and other abilities to acquire great wisdom and power and then dominate others—a purpose directly in opposition to the good for which we of Avalon used the jelly.

Your father agreed to this condition, but your half-brother, Nasciens, who was at the age of reason by that point, did not understand it. He was a boy who was approaching manhood at an alarmingly fast rate, and he was very curious, and...I hesitate to tell you this part, but you would not understand what followed otherwise; you see I was a young and beautiful woman, not many years older than Nasciens in appearance, although in truth, being raised in Avalon, I was a few decades older than his father. In any case, Nasciens had a great desire to learn more about women; he was a young boy with stronger desires than most his age, but lanky, awkward, and ill-mannered so that the young ladies at court were more prone to laugh at than kiss him.

Nor do I like to think ill of anyone, but Nasciens' sexual urges were not natural for one so young. I can only think it was from such desires that he decided to peep at his stepmother while she fed her children— from a desire to see a woman's naked breasts.

In secret, your half-brother dug a small hole into the wall separating my room from another, and then one day, just a few days after your births, when I was feeding the three of you, he spied upon me. Now, I am very intuitive, as are most women from Avalon, so I instantly sensed that something was wrong, and when I scanned the room while feeding you, Melusine, at my breast, I saw his eye peeping through the hole. You can imagine that when I saw his eye watching me, I was so startled that I let out a scream.

Your father happened to be walking down the passageway at that moment. When he heard my cry, he immediately burst into the room with his sword drawn, from fear I was in danger.

There before him was not only his wife with one daughter at her breast, but his other daughters sitting and eating with spoons from a jar filled with the royal jelly. (Perhaps you don't remember, but you were all genetically advanced and as large as one year olds, though but a few days old, so you were quite capable of feeding yourselves.) I quickly tried to divert your father's attention from the three of you by explaining why I had screamed. Your father then promised he would punish Nasciens, who had run and hid as soon as I cried out. But he could not help remarking with surprise on how his children were able to eat on their own. For a moment, he stood there, awestruck, and then he stepped closer and looked at the sticky golden liquid in the jar and asked, "What are you feeding them?" Before I knew what to reply, he repeated the question, and then he called for a guard to go fetch the court physician.

I tried to lie and say you were eating just normal honey mixed with some fruit, but he said, "Honey and fruit do not make children grow this strong and able so quickly." When the court physician arrived, he looked frightened to see the jelly, especially when he was told to taste it. I think he faked doing so, for he was so fearful, but I was not surprised when he declared, "It is poison, my lord. What kind of woman feeds poison to her children?"

"What kind of monster," then roared your father, turning on me, "have I married that she would seek to poison my children?"

I—oh, the pain of that day still hurts almost as much after all these years. I—I don't know what more to say than that he would not listen to me. I reminded him that he had promised not to disturb me when I was feeding my children, and I berated him for breaking his promise, although I could not really blame him in my heart, for he had only broken into the room to aid me when he heard my scream.

But now, your father refused to listen to any explanations from me, and I knew not how to explain a secret I could not reveal. The physician urged him to cast me into prison so I might be tried for witchcraft, and he demanded that I immediately be separated from my children from fear they would be stained with my sins; indeed, he even insinuated it might be safest if we had you destroyed, for surely you were demon children if you could eat with spoons at such a young age.

It was a horrible, miserable hour for me, and I have no doubt that your father, enraged and aghast at the incident, might well have acted on the physician's recommendations had I remained. But in desperation, I quickly grabbed all three of you into my arms, refusing to let you be separated from me. At that moment, fortunately, Lady Morgana was watching us in the reflection of the Holy Well, and seeing my predicament, she instantly cast a spell to return us all to Avalon before the guards could lay hands upon us.

To this day, I imagine your father has always questioned what became of us. He must have seen us disappear before his very eyes, which must have unnerved him a great deal. I do know that he never wed again, and I have always feared that I brought greater heartache to him than the grief I first sought to soothe when I married him.

So you see, I did leave to protect you. In fact, I had no choice, for Morgana made the decision to rescue me, but I knew it was for the best. Later, I learned that the physician had the bottles of royal jelly thrown into the sea, which was for the best because then no one could investigate their ingredients; had the jelly fallen into the wrong hands, I hate to think what powers it might have provided unsuspecting mortals who innocently ate it—powers of telepathy or physical strength that might have been used for harm rather than good.

Please, my girls, understand that I loved your father, and I never would have left him for any reason other than to protect Avalon and its magic. I could not risk staying and having him question me from fear I would give away Avalon's secrets. Men have always been capable of the worst crimes against one another, and no doubt, some human would have sought to use that forbidden knowledge to gain power over others and harm them.

I hated to leave your father; I loved him more than life itself, but I knew that he was only human, and that at some point, if I told him the truth, he would give away my secret; he would confide in someone he should not, and then you and I would have trouble. Furthermore, in just the short year I was married to your father, I had grown increasingly frightened of Nasciens. He was a horrid boy, not only for peeping at me in my nakedness, but because he was one to bully children smaller than himself, to torment small animals, and always to threaten adults with his father's punishment if they did not do what he wanted, so that soon no one dared to stand up to or discipline him. And your father, despite even my urgings, would give into him on all matters, feeling he must be soft with Nasciens because he had lost his mother. Had I remained and Nasciens obtained possession of the royal jelly, I dread to think what he might have done with it, for he might have become powerful enough to make entire nations obey him, setting himself up as the next great emperor. I could see only grief, only bloodshed and misery for humanity if that should happen, and I simply could not risk it.

Once I had safely returned home, I spent many hours discussing and debating all these matters with Lady Morgana and many of the wise women of Avalon, but in the end, I had to agree with them that it was best I stay here on the Holy Isle to raise you away from your father and all mankind. I wanted to write to your father to tell him I forgave him, but I could not even do that. "You must not have any contact with him, as much for his safety as your own," Morgana told me, "for if he tried to trace the letter and reach you, he might try to force you to return, and that would result in an invasion of the Holy Isle and war between us and mankind, which would be devastating to the human race and detrimental to our benevolent purposes."

And so that, my girls, is the truth about your parents and your birth. I am sorry it is not a happier tale. I am sorry you did not have a father to take joy in your growing up. I have no doubt your father loved you, for he was truly horrified at the thought that I might be hurting his children. I hope you can find it in your hearts to understand why your removal here to Avalon had to be. And I hope it will be a good lesson to you when you venture into the human world, so you will realize that while men are often well-intentioned, they are weak and easily give way to their fears when they are faced with situations they cannot understand.

CHAPTER 14

MELUSINE'S TALE CONTINUES

"**M**Y FATHER BETRAYED you," I said to my mother after she had finished her tale. "Were you not greatly angry?"

"No, Melusine, it was not like that," she replied.

"But you warned him and he agreed—he promised not to interrupt you when you were feeding us, and yet he did what you told him not to do. Is that not betrayal?"

"Yes, a human would see it that way," she replied, "and since you are part human, though your words surprise me, perhaps that is why you see it that way too, but you must understand human nature. Your father loved me, and I have no doubt he loved you girls from the way I watched him treat you the few days he was with you, but humans find it difficult to control their natures. That is why they have so many laws and commandments—to keep them from doing what it is in their natures to do, and each human almost always in some way or other breaks every law made except perhaps the most severe one of murder, and yet you'd be hard-pressed to find one among them who has never had a murderous thought. It is certainly rare to find a human who has never stolen something at least once in his life, and almost impossible to find one who has never told a lie, and while perhaps the majority have not physically committed adultery, I doubt there are many who have not done so in their hearts. Human nature is weak and mankind knows it; both men and women are continually struggling to repress their desires, and for that reason, we must take pity on them. And in this case, though your father broke his promise to me, he did so out of great curiosity and from fear that harm was being done to me or you girls when he heard my scream. And then his wish to punish me was only from fear I was harming you when he saw what he could not understand. But it was Nasciens who initially led him to believe ill of me."

"But what of Father now?" I demanded. "Will we never get to see him?"

"My dear, no good can come of such a meeting," said Mother. "It would only break his heart and remind him of what he has lost. Besides, you will have your own work to do in the world, so do not concern yourself with the past."

"Might we not see him," asked Melior, "without his seeing us?"

"Yes, please, Mother," Palatyne begged, "just so we may look upon him once to know the man who is our sire."

"No, it will only bring you all pain," said Mother. "I forbid you to do so for your own good. Now, it is almost time for evening prayers. Go and get ready. We mustn't be late."

Mother urged us to hurry, and soon we accompanied her to the sacred grove for the ritual prayers to the Goddess-God. But while my heart spoke those prayers that evening, my heart and thoughts were not in them; instead, I was scheming how I might get a glimpse of my father. I knew my sisters desired it as much as I did, so I was certain they would aid me, for we had always thought alike, although I fancied myself the leader since I was the eldest by a few minutes.

The next morning when the three of us were out walking together, I told my sisters that despite our mother's command, I still wished to see our father.

"But do we dare to disobey Mother?" Palatyne asked, although I could tell she wished to see our father as much as I did.

"What would she do to us?" Melior replied. "She loves us, so she will understand why we feel the need to see Father, even if it displeases her."

"It isn't right that we've been kept from him," I argued. "I know Mother means it for the good, but our father did nothing so terrible that he deserved to lose all three of his children."

"But perhaps he does not even want us any longer," suggested Palatyne, "especially since Mother said he already has a son."

"He must want us," I replied, "or he would be an unnatural father, which would not be like him from what Mother told us, and perhaps our brother would also welcome his sisters, for as females, we would be no threat to him taking the throne."

"But Nasciens—he seems like such a nasty boy," Palatyne objected.

"He was just a boy back then," I said. "I'm sure he's grown into a fine and noble man now."

"I don't know," Palatyne said, continuing to look fearful.

"We can debate all we want whether or not it is right," I stated, "but we will not know whether Father or Nasciens care about us until we try to make contact with them."

"But are we prepared for Father's possible rejection?" asked Palatyne.

"We must be," I said. "I imagine we are less prepared to go through life wondering whether our father loves us and always fearing to know the truth."

"I am certain he loves us," said Melior, "and loves Mother as well, and that he understands she did what was best for us."

"I do not know that he is that wise," I replied. "But as you say, we cannot know without trying."

The next question then was how we would go about finding our father. Since that first day when we were still children, Mother had often led us up the mountain to look at Father's land, and even his castle, and we all agreed she would not have done so if she did not want us to know of Father and feel affection for him.

"But how do we leave Avalon so we may travel to Albany?" asked Melior.

"I know how," said Palatyne. "I read it in a book I borrowed from Lady Morgana a year ago, and I have been dying ever since to practice it."

Palatyne's eyes lit up as she spoke, which confirmed for me that while her questions had made her seem the least willing of the three of us, she was now ready to force herself from the security of Avalon to seek the outer world.

"Go ahead," I said. "Teach us."

"We must climb up the mountain overlooking our father's land so we can see where he lives, and then I can cast the spell that will take us there," she replied.

We were all in agreement to take this step, but we had not time to go that morning, and we knew we would be called upon for various duties throughout the day, so we decided that the next day we would depart our home an hour before sunrise to reach the mountain at daybreak, and from there, we would make our journey to Albany.

"Mother will be worried," Palatyne said.

"We can leave her a note," said Melior.

"No," I replied, "for she might pursue us if we tell her where we have gone."

"We can just leave a note for her saying that we are well and will return in a day or two," Melior said.

"Will we return that quickly?" asked Palatyne. "How do we know we will be safe in the world of mortals?"

"If we stay together, we will have nothing to fear," I replied. "We are all attune to different magic that will protect us—spells we can cast to stop anyone from harming us."

"Will we make ourselves known to Father?" Melior asked.

"If we do, what if he does not want us?" Palatyne added.

"We cannot know the consequences of that until we see him," I replied. "We should prepare ourselves for such an outcome, but we should not worry over it until it happens. I think we should first get a sense of Father's character, and then we can determine whether to reveal ourselves to him."

"I am sure he will welcome us," Melior said. "He could not possibly be our father and not love us."

Palatyne and I did not share Melior's confidence, but we had made our decision to go through with our plan. I admit I scarcely slept all that night from anxiety. We left early the next morning before Mother was awake. In the dim morning light, we climbed the mountain, the sun rising just as we reached the peak.

"There is Albany," said Melior, pointing to the rocky, yet lush landscape in the distance. "Isn't it beautiful?"

"Not as beautiful as Avalon," said Palatyne.

"True," I added, "but our future lies in the lands of men. Mother has said we will have missions among the mortals, and I think it only right that our first mission should be to heal the pain in our father's heart."

My sisters agreed with me, and so without further ado, Melior asked us to join hands and to envision ourselves before the gates of our father's castle in Albany. Then she spoke the words that would allow our intent to become truth. We closed our eyes as she spoke, concentrating on the vision, and then we experienced—or at least I know I did—a certain lightheadedness before I felt my feet leave the earth, and though I dared not open my eyes, I could feel myself floating through the air for about thirty seconds before my feet again touched firm ground and I realized my sister had quit speaking.

"Oh, Melior, you succeeded!" shouted Palatyne, who must have been first to open her eyes. At her words, I also opened mine and saw that we stood on a hilltop with our father's castle a good couple of miles in the distance.

"I had intended to set us down before the castle gates," she replied, seeming disappointed, "but I guess this is close enough."

"It is," I said, looking down at the town surrounding the castle, through whose streets we must walk. "We need to think what we will say when people speak to us, and the castle guards, from all I have read of kings and castles, will not allow us to enter through the gates without questioning our purpose in coming."

"Why, we will say we are King Elynas' daughters come from Avalon to visit him," said Palatyne.

"Don't be ridiculous!" I snapped, nervous and, therefore, irritable over the prospect of meeting our father.

Palatyne looked at me as if not understanding what she had said wrong.

"Melusine is right," said Melior. "These people may have forgotten the king ever had daughters, and even if they do remember, they may well laugh or sneer at us, thinking we are impostors."

"That is true," I said. "We are obviously sisters from our appearance, but we still must bear some token to prove our identity."

"I know," said Palatyne. "My scrying mirror—it will allow the king to see our mother in it, and then he will know we come from his true wife and are his daughters."

"That should work," Melior agreed.

"But only for our father," I said. "How do we first get past the guards to be shown into Father's presence?"

None of us had an answer to that question.

"Let us just walk toward the castle," Melior said after a moment, "and perhaps an answer will come to us before we get there."

We agreed to follow Melior's suggestion, and within a few minutes, we had walked down the hill. Just as we were about to enter the town, I had an idea. "I know what we could do—King Arthur often had damsels in distress come to him to request he right the wrongs done to them. Perhaps we could do the same—say we come seeking relief from some distress, some sort of persecutor."

"But what will we tell the guards to make them believe us?" asked Palatyne.

"Leave it to me," I replied. "It's best we not discuss it any further since the townsfolk may overhear us."

I was noticing people looking at us as we entered the town, perhaps simply because we were strangers, but I think also because they were struck by our beauty. Men and women both stopped to stare as we approached them, and they stepped aside to let us pass in the market streets. We were not dressed so grandly as to inspire awe, wearing our simple light blue acolyte robes—we had not thought to wear anything more suitable to match the fashions of the townsfolk, or anything that would proclaim us to be princesses. But we could see our robes still raised curiosity as people shot us strange looks, then turned to mutter among themselves. One or two men gazed on us with obvious lust—a look I did not know then, but soon would understand once I had spent more time among men. But all looked at us with a sense of awe or respect, especially when they saw we were headed to the castle. When we stood at the gate, even the guards seemed uncertain how to address us, and it was a moment before the captain of the guard emerged from a small gatekeeper's lodge to question our coming.

"Fair ladies," he asked, "what business have you with the royal court of Albany?"

"We are three sisters," said I, "and we have been sorely misused by a knight who has stolen our land, which is ours by our birthright. We wish the king to hear our grievances and redress our wrongs."

"Have you no father, no husbands, no brothers to settle this matter for you?" he asked.

"Alas, no," I replied. "We are all maidens and our father's only children, and now our father is an old man, too old to defend us, but perhaps if his majesty should send a knight to our rescue, I shall give myself to that knight as his wife."

"A good reward," smiled the captain. "I wish then I were not married myself. Follow me, please, ladies."

The captain turned on his heel and ordered the guard to open the castle gate. In a few more seconds, he was leading us into the castle courtyard.

Melior gripped my hand, as if to say, "That was easy enough," but I remained uncertain how I would explain who we were to our father once we were in his presence.

We crossed the courtyard and arrived at a door that led into the castle's great hall. I nearly had to pull Palatyne across the courtyard because she kept stopping to gaze about her, although I could not blame her, for everything about the castle was astounding. From the hill, the castle had looked only as large as King Arthur's castle on Avalon, but that was simply a large home for King Arthur since he had no need at Avalon of attendants, guards, and countless servants. Here, the castle walls went on and on for hundreds of yards, and the courtyard was filled with soldiers while more were patrolling the walls, and a few servants, most carrying buckets of water or bundles of firewood, scurried about. Squires were walking together and laughing, and even a priest or two strolled past us, but it would not be until I grew more accustomed to being among men that I really knew what all these people's positions were, so all their various costumes denoting their different ranks were a wonderment to us.

Once we entered the building housing the great hall, we were taken into a small antechamber where a scribe asked our names and our business. Before Melior could stop herself, she replied, "We are Melusine, Melior, and Palatyne, princesses of Avalon and Albany."

The scribe looked at us, first speechless and then tongue-tied, trying to ask for an explanation. Seeing quick action was needed before his astonishment turned to doubt, I commanded, "Show us to our father, the king. We will not be kept waiting."

"Yes, milady," he said, looking at me as if he thought I might be insane so it would be best to humor me. "But is your father expecting you? Let me announce you in private."

I feared any delay would result in us being turned away, so before the guards could bar our entrance, I pushed past him, with my sisters quickly following. Suddenly, I found myself in our father's great throne room. I had moved quickly enough to make a stir and cause all those assembled to turn and stare at us. Instantly, Palatyne hissed at the scribe, who had hurried after us, "Announce us!"

"But—" said the scribe, at a loss for the delicate words he needed in his fear that we were impostors. Unwilling to wait for him to cease bumbling, I took the lead.

"My Lord King!" I shouted. "We are the Princesses Melusine, Melior, and Palatyne of Albany and Avalon, your own royal daughters. We bring you greeting."

A hundred pairs of eyes stared at me with astonishment, but I ignored all the noble men and ladies in attendance and approached the throne. As I stepped forward, my father turned to speak to a young man standing beside him. I was struck by this young man's countenance before I even got a good look at my father. At first, I thought they might be brothers, for both looked so young, but then I realized the young man must be our brother, Nasciens, for he looked to be about thirty, and I knew he was many years our senior since he was the son of our father's first wife.

I stopped a half-dozen yards from my father and waited a moment for him to turn his attention back to us. I was stunned to see that when he beckoned us forth with a faint gesture of his hand, a look of dread was spreading across his face. Our brother was beardless, but our father had a reddish brown beard and I noticed his bright green eyes as I drew closer. I could see that he must be fifty years of age, with just the first touch of grey in his beard; wisdom shone in his eyes, but also a hint of pain that I hoped was regret for having been parted from us so long.

"Step closer," he said when I stopped less than five feet from his throne. I heard my sisters stop behind me, but they did not advance when I went to the raised platform and knelt on the steps before him. He then leaned forward, and taking my face in his hands, he said, "I see your mother in your features, but which one of you is which?"

"Your majesty, I am Melusine, your eldest daughter," I replied. "And this is Melior." I turned back to refer to each of them; they remained standing a few feet behind me as I spoke. "And this is Palatyne, your youngest, although as you know, we were all born just minutes apart."

"I know," he replied, "for I remember well that day, as does your brother, Nasciens, here, for he was a boy of nearly fifteen when you were born."

I stood now beside my sisters and bowed to my brother, but he only tilted his head, scowling, making it clear that our presence did not please him.

"Can it be that you really are my daughters?" asked the king, still trying to take in this moment.

"Father, it is true—" I began.

"Stop!" exclaimed Nasciens. "No one addresses the king in such a familiar way. Not even myself. Sire, you must not be taken in by these women until we have true proof they are my half-sisters."

"The proof lies in their faces," our father replied. "How old are you, my dears?"

"We are fifteen," Melior replied. "Our birthday is May 1st."

"Yes, exactly," my father replied, and he turned to our brother as if to say, "See, did I not tell you?"

"That is no proof," Nasciens declared. "It is well known that my stepmother stole away with her children in the night, just days after they were born. Anyone in the kingdom would know these details."

As my father looked at my brother, his features hardened. Nasciens bent down to his ear and whispered, but my acute hearing easily heard his words. "Father, these women could be tricksters out to do you harm. You know you have enemies among the Picts, and even among your own people. Do not make the mistake of acknowledging them until you are certain of their identities. Send them from the throne room to where they may be questioned in private."

My father nodded, considering the wisdom of this response. Before I could speak again, he said, "Guards, show these young ladies to a private bedchamber and keep them under guard until I can speak to them further."

"We are not 'young ladies,'" I snapped. "We are princesses of Avalon and Albany and your daughters, and our mother will not be pleased by your response."

"See, Sire; already she threatens us with witchcraft and sorcery!" Nasciens exclaimed.

"If you turn our father against us, *Brother*," I said, spitting out the last word, "you will bear the brunt of any sorcery I use. But as our father's son and heir, you should have nothing to fear from three women who seek only affection from their kin."

"Melusine, we will speak more later," my father said as the guards made it clear, by stepping before the throne and forcing us back, that we were now to be constrained by them.

"Speak we shall," added Nasciens.

"Make sure that your tongue be smoother when we do," I warned him before we were led away.

I was fuming inside. Palatyne appeared afraid, but Melior just sighed with sadness as we followed the guards. We now had two armed men both before and after us so we could not easily escape. We were led through another large chamber, then up a staircase and down a long corridor. When we crossed the castle rampart, I thought how I could have flown away if I had the skill—something I intended to insist on being taught once I returned to Avalon, in case I should ever be in such a predicament again. Next, we entered a tower, went up a flight of stairs, and were placed inside a small bedchamber where one bed, large enough for two, but not three, filled most of the room.

"The king will summon you again at his pleasure," said one of the guards in a surly tone, and then the door was slammed in my face as I called out, "This is an outrage!"

"Are we prisoners?" Palatyne asked.

"Obviously," I said, looking through the door's small peephole. "The guards are standing outside to make sure we cannot escape."

Nor did we have any means of escape save a barred window; even if I could have flown, I could not have gotten past the bars.

"We just need to give Father time," said Melior. "He has a kind face. It is a shock for him to see us again."

"That is no excuse for such treatment," I replied.

"It is our brother's doing," Palatyne stated.

"He's no brother to us," I said.

"Oh, Melusine, you know how humans fight," said Melior. "We cannot expect otherwise when Nasciens, for whatever reason, feels threatened by us. We know from all the tales we have heard of mortals that fathers and sons quarrel, and so do brothers and sisters. If we give Father a little time, perhaps he will come to his senses."

"But what if he doesn't?" asked Palatyne.

"I still have my scrying mirror," said Melior. "It will take us back to Avalon."

"If we can use it at the right moment," I said, "and not when we are in a moment of conflict."

"Let us use it now," said Palatyne.

"No," said Melior. "Let us give Father some time."

"How much time?" I asked.

"He knows we are his children," Melior said calmly, sitting down on the bed. "I suspect he will come to us before nightfall."

"If he doesn't, I hope he has nightmares," I said, and then we decided we would lie down on the bed, one of us keeping watch out the window to see whether we could learn anything since the bed would not hold all of us.

As it turned out, Melior was wrong about our father. She thought better of him than he deserved—although all these years later, I understand it was not because he did not love us, but because he was too weak to stand up for himself, too weak to stand up to a son who had grown to be taller and stronger than him and apparently inclined to bullying. And because bullies are always cowards, I have no doubt Nasciens feared we would take his place in our father's affections. His fears were groundless, however—after all, he was our father's only son and heir. But we'd made a bad start with our brother, and I doubted it would get better.

By the time darkness fell, Palatyne was too worried to sleep, but Melior wrapped her arms around her to soothe her. I stayed awake, fearing our brother would try to murder us in our bed, and once Melior and Palatyne finally did fall asleep, I remained by the barred window, looking up at the stars and wondering what was to become of us. I did not feel afraid since Melior had the skills to return us to Avalon, but I imagined Mother was now worried about us. I did not know whether she had any power that would allow her to see where we were or whether she would seek help from Lady Morgana or someone else at Avalon. I only knew I was severely disappointed by my father.

Just as I was watching the first traces of dawn through the window, our prison door opened, startling my sisters awake, and suddenly, our father was in the room.

We all stood looking at him, unsure what to say. I only hoped he had come to his senses.

By the light of the torch he carried, our father looked into our questioning eyes and said, "I could not sleep from what you revealed to me today. I apologize for your treatment. I was just too stunned to know how to respond. All these years I have wondered what became of you and your mother—I did not know whether you were dead or alive. Tell me; is your mother well?"

"She is quite well, sir," said Melior, "although she does not know we've come here so she is doubtless worried about us. We had expected you to be surprised, but not that we would be held as prisoners."

"You are not prisoners; you are free to go," he replied.

"Free to go?" I said. "Is that all you have to say? That you want us to go, after you have not seen us for fifteen years?"

Pain creased his brow. For a moment, I thought he would cry, but then he replied, "I am sorry. I am not well. My strength is rapidly declining, and my physicians cannot tell what is wrong with me. My mind is sometimes too tired to make the best decisions. I—no, I do not want you to go, but you must; you are in danger here—Nasciens will soon be king, and then you will not be safe."

"Why does Nasciens hate us so much?" Melior asked.

"He hates everyone," our father replied. "I don't think he ever recovered from his mother's death, despite how I tried to love him in her place. Her loss was terrible for him. She died giving birth to his little sister, who also died. When I married your mother, she also tried to win his affections, and for a time, I thought she would, but when the three of you were born, he was enraged, ranting about how it was not fair that your mother should live and have three daughters when his mother died and could not even have one. He hated you from that moment. He knew, because I warned him, that he was not to disturb your mother when she was feeding you. I made him make the same promise to me that I had to her, but he was a headstrong boy, and you must understand, I acted instinctively and without thought when I burst into the room, hearing your mother's screams. I only did it to protect her from harm, not yet knowing the cause of her alarm. And then, to see you, just a handful of days after your birth, eating with spoons as if you were two or three years old—you have to understand what a shock that was—and that it frightened your brother as much as me.

"Nasciens threatened me then, perhaps fearing that otherwise I would punish him for spying on your mother; he warned me that he would tell all the court what he had seen and declare your mother a witch and the court physician sided with him. I knew I could not silence his tongue save to have it cut out, and I could hardly do that to my own heir. But then it did not matter because your mother took you away, caused you all to disappear so suddenly. I told everyone she had gone to visit her family, although even I did not know where she came from—I concocted the story that she was a Saxon princess from a land far to the south so my people would be pleased that she was of royal blood, but when she did not return after a time, such stories of her being a witch or an evil fairy were bound to spread, especially when it was known the three of you were also missing. Nasciens was convinced your mother held some dark secret; that she was something unnatural. Nor did I know the reason for her secret—I only know I broke my promise and it resulted in great misery for me.

"I never wanted to lose you girls, and now I should be delighted to have you return, but I have been under Nasciens' grip too long. A stronger king could have borne it, but I have been so sunk in grief all these years that I have let Nasciens have his way too often, and now that I am dying, what can I do except let him continue to have his way? My only hope is that in time he will remember what love I showed him after I am gone, and that will inspire him to be a good king."

"Somehow, I don't think that will happen," I said, feeling little sympathy for my father or my brother's weaknesses.

"No, Melusine, neither do I think so," my father admitted. "I want to believe it will, but Nasciens has been difficult since he was a little boy. His mother was a shrewish woman who, despite my being a king, always thought herself superior, claiming to be of more ancient bloodline than myself, descended from the old High Kings of Britain in the days before the Saxons invaded, including some fierce but forgotten queen she said was named Gwenhwyvach who had lived not long after Rome fell. In truth, her father was merely a baron to the King of Lothian, but I was taken by her beauty when I visited that king's court, and I was the one who raised her to so high a station by marrying her. Only after our wedding did her true temperament shine through. Unlike your mother, who was both beautiful and kind, Nasciens' mother led me a horrid life until the day she died. Then when I met your mother, I thought I had finally found happiness, only to have it suddenly torn from me. Oh, how I have wished all these years it could have been different. I have wished for so many things to have been different. I especially wish Nasciens took after me more than his mother; I fear he will be a poor king and unable to hold the kingdom against our warring neighbors, the Picts, and even if he does, I have little hope for his two sons who are quarrelsome, spoiled little boys; be grateful you have not yet had to deal with them or their dirty, sticky, thieving little hands; if Nasciens does not destroy this kingdom, then in time, his sons surely will."

I began to feel sorry for my father then. I could see how the blows he had experienced in his past had worn upon him, and although he was not that old in years, he now seemed as haggard in appearance as a man two or three decades older.

"Father, we came simply because we wanted to see you—to know the father we have never known," said Palatyne. "We are sorry our brother has brought you no joy, but somehow, perhaps we can provide you with some happiness in your last years."

"The only thing you'll be providing," exclaimed Nasciens, bursting in through the still open door, "is food for the fishes!" Stunned by his entrance, I wondered how long he had been listening outside, but before we could say anything, he reached out and grabbed my wrist.

"Nasciens, what are you doing?" demanded our father.

"I'll not have anyone threatening me or speaking against me—not even you, old man," he replied. "I am tired of enduring your abuse, your complaints that I have never been good enough for you when, if you had ever been a father to me, rather than chasing after trollops like the mother of these girls, I might have known a father's love and learned how to become a great king."

"You still have that opportunity, son," said Father. "You cannot blame me for your faults. You are old enough now to decide that your future can be better than the past."

"Yes," Nasciens replied, "and I decide that no other children of yours will be part of my future. I do not need sisters who try to turn you against me or try to take my throne. I saw how their mother stole your affection from me, and I won't see these whores do the same."

"You will watch your tongue and remember that I am still the king," said our father, boldly stepping up to him.

"You were the king. My men wait in the next corridor, ready to hail me as their liege lord. Meanwhile, you," said Nasciens, poking his father in the chest, "you will join your daughters, feeding the fish in the moat."

"How dare you!" my father exclaimed, and in a surprising move, he pulled the crown from his head and smashed it against Nasciens' skull.

Stunned, Nasciens' face went white while my father stepped into the hall, exclaiming, "Quickly, my girls, before his ruffians are upon us!"

Frightened, my sisters and I raced from the room and down the tower stairs, only to hear an armed guard fast on our heels.

"This way!" our father cried. We followed him down the corridor and to another stairway. "We must make it to the throne room where my guards will protect us!" he shouted.

"Run, old man!" screamed Nasciens, his men now behind him and all of them about to descend the stairs we were halfway down. "Run all you want, but the entire castle is mine. Your most loyal men have turned against you."

Our father did run, and we ran behind him. When we reached the bottom of the stairs, we followed him down another hallway. Rather than turn toward the throne room, we followed him to the next corridor, and then we came to what appeared to be a dead end. But in a second, he had loosed some hidden lever and the wall swung open, disclosing a dark tunnel.

"Hurry!" he exclaimed as we entered, although I did not like to enter what looked like little more than a cave. In the chaos of our running, his torch had fallen and none of us had stopped to pick it up. I was thinking now how Melior could transport us to safety in Avalon at any time, but we would be severely punished if we brought our father back with us; yet we could not leave him behind in this desperate moment.

My father closed the passage behind us, but he said Nasciens would know how to enter it, so it would only give us a few seconds of extra time. In the dark, we could not run but only walk forward, groping with our hands. After we had gone about fifty feet in the dark, a large hole in the cave's roof admitted a great deal of light, but this opening was too high up for us to escape through it. A large boulder sat in the middle of the cavern, the result of the roof caving in at that location.

"Help me," begged our father, quickly trying to push the stone so it would roll and block our pursuers.

Instantly, we joined him, all our weight forcing the stone to move. We could not get it to block the entrance completely, but we moved it enough that a grown man would have great difficulty sliding between it and the cavern wall.

"Quickly, grab those rocks," our father said, gesturing to some small loose stones lying about. Knowing the enemy would be upon us in a second, I cast a spell, causing the stones to roll into the open crevice to seal it.

My father looked astonished to see the stones fly up and place themselves one upon the other.

"It—what? How did—oh my God? Are you truly witches after all?" he asked, his face turning white.

"No, Father, no, simply your daughters who seek your love," said Palatyne.

"Do not fear, Father. We will do you no harm, we swear," Melior added.

"There isn't time to explain now," I said. "Nasciens will be upon us before we know it. Come! Which way, Father?"

"Please tell us we are not trapped inside here," Palatyne begged.

"This way," said my father, shaking his head again, ready to plunge back into the tunnel's darkness.

"Wait," said Palatyne, casting a spell that caused a ball of fire to appear in her hand; it served us as a torch, yet did not burn her flesh.

"Why didn't you think of that earlier?" I asked her.

"The light might have shown Nasciens where we were when we first entered," she replied.

My father now looked ready to faint from shock. I stepped between him and Palatyne to block his view of the fireball and asked, "Father, where does this tunnel lead?"

"Into a mountain," he said, shaking his head as if to regain his wits, "but it comes out through the other side; it winds about in a maze so that I doubt anyone else remembers after all these years how to get through it."

"We must hurry," I said, for already we could hear Nasciens' henchmen pushing the stones out of the crevice. In another minute, they would be in the chamber, and it would be impossible for three girls and a sick man to outrun them once they had broken through.

We rushed forward, stumbling over rocks that lay randomly scattered in the mountain cavern, and not a few times, one of us fell down. Before long, our father stumbled and let out a cry.

"I think I twisted my ankle," he exclaimed when we turned back to aid him.

"Here, we will help you," said Melior, trying fruitlessly to lift him by one arm while I grabbed the other.

After several moments of increased anxiety, we got him to his feet, but he could not walk on his ankle. He hobbled along with my and

Melior's assistance while Palatyne lit the way with her fireball. But after about a hundred yards, he lost his grip on our shoulders and fell to the ground.

"I can't go on," he said, his face writhing in pain.

"We must find a way to bear you," I said. "What can we make a litter from?"

But his injury had already slowed us down enough that now we could hear Nasciens' men in the cave behind us.

"We only have a few minutes before they find their way through this maze," said my father. "There is no hope. You must leave me, my girls. You must save yourselves."

"No, Father," cried Palatyne, sitting down beside him and placing her head on his chest.

"Yes, my dear. My life has been empty without you, and Nasciens has brought me nothing but grief. In a few more minutes, he will kill me. But in my last moments, let me think that I at least had three daughters who loved their father and will live on after me."

"Father, we are sorry for all this trouble," said Melior. "We never meant to bring it upon you."

"You have done no wrong," he replied. "Your brother is the monster who has caused this tragedy. It would have happened in time even without your presence."

"We will not let him kill you," I protested. "There must be some other way."

But the guards' shouts grew louder, and a holler of "This way!" was quickly followed by the increased clamoring of armored men approaching us.

"What can we do?" asked Palatyne, rising to her feet, her eyes pleading with me.

I knew she wished to transport Father back to Avalon with us, but I also knew that to do so would threaten the safety of the Holy Isle. No matter how much we loved our father, he had broken his vow to our mother so we could not trust him completely. All that remained was for us to show him mercy.

The clanging of armor and shouts of men now filled the cavern; then around a turn in the corridor, the soldiers burst into sight, not fifty feet away.

"Melusine!" cried Palatyne.

"Run, my girls! Save yourself!" shouted my father, and in their terror, my sisters obeyed him, racing past me. "I love you, my girls!" Father shouted. "Tell your mother I always loved her!"

"We love you too, Father," I said, and then I whispered a spell to make the cave walls quake. Instantly, rocks fell from the ceiling, plummeting down upon the enemy, but also upon our father, one giant stone striking him in the skull and immediately killing him, but protecting him from a worse fate. I regretted his death as I regret that of any human life, but most of all, I regretted that I had not seen my cowardly brother leading his men in the charge, but rather standing back, and therefore, not dying when the roof caved in.

"Melusine, hurry!" screamed Palatyne as the rocks began to fall.

The second I saw my father's face go white, assuring me that his suffering had ended, I turned and was at my sisters' heels.

"Melior, cast the spell to take us home," I told her, and as we ran, we linked hands. Not ten seconds after our father's death, we disappeared from the cave.

In a split second, we found ourselves back in Avalon, on the patch of land we had departed from just twenty-four hours before.

"Mother need never know we were gone," I said.

Palatyne looked at me and said, "Our father is dead. Surely, we have to tell her that."

"If we do," I replied, "she will not be pleased to know we disobeyed her and left Avalon to find him."

"Still, Melusine," Melior said, "we have to tell her. She loved Father. She has a right to mourn his loss."

"No," I said. "We need not tell her. Not now. Let some time pass by at least."

Then saddened, barely able to suppress our sobs, we slowly walked home.

"Father did love us," said Palatyne.

"Yes," said Melior. "Did you hear how he called us 'my girls'?"

"He was a good man," I said. "I hate to think what will become of his kingdom now. I am certain Nasciens did not die during the cave-in, and I hate to think of him ruling Albany."

"We must avenge Father somehow," said Melior. "We can't allow such an evil man to rule a kingdom."

"But how?" asked Palatyne.

"I don't know," said Melior.

"Perhaps when we have finished our training," I said, "we will have learned a way, but I do not think revenge is in keeping with the ideals of Avalon. Furthermore, I suspect Nasciens is perfectly capable of destroying himself without our aid."

"I hope so," Palatyne muttered.

"But think of his poor people," added Melior.

By now, we could see a light shining in our house and smoke coming up from the chimney. We all looked forward to returning to the coziness of home.

"We'll just tell Mother we wandered too far from home yesterday and slept in the forest," said Palatyne, and we all agreed to this falsehood. But when we opened the door, Mother, who was standing by the fire, instantly turned toward us, her eyes flashing with fire.

"You would not listen to me, would you?" she demanded. "You could not leave well enough alone."

There was no point in lying. It was obvious she knew all.

"Mother, we thought—" began Melior.

"You thought?" Mother interrupted. "Did you think I wouldn't find out what you had done? Lady Morgana saw it in the Holy Well and came to tell me immediately. Do you not think I have many a time looked after your father, watching him and aiding him however I might? Did you seriously think you could do anything to remedy the past?"

"We didn't want to *do* anything, Mother," said Melior. "We just wanted to *know* Father—and to know his love."

"And are you satisfied now?" Mother demanded.

"Yes," said Palatyne. "We are sorry to lose him, but we know he did indeed love us."

"And he wanted us to tell you," I added, daring to approach her, "that he always loved you."

And that was enough. The moment the words left my mouth, a strange look came over Mother's face, and then she broke into tears and I led her to a chair.

"I never ceased loving him," she said after she was able to quit sobbing. "He was a good man. It was not his fault he had a frail human nature like so many other men. I just—it's foolish; I knew it could never be—but I just wanted to let him know I loved him one last time before he died."

"He knew, Mother," said Palatyne, seating herself at our mother's knee and laying her head in Mother's lap.

"Mother, we are sorry," said Melior. "We did not mean any harm. We just wanted a father like anyone else would."

Mother sighed and was silent for a moment before saying, "He was sick. I knew and feared he would experience great pain; I'm sure his death saved him from more agony later. If it were not for Nasciens now ruling, I would say it is all for the best."

The rest of that evening, Mother's tongue rattled on, telling us many endearing stories about Father until gradually we all fell asleep on the floor by the hearth, listening to the soothing tone of her voice, our last thoughts that day being prayers for Father's soul.

Only in the morning did Mother tell us that while we slept, she had traveled to the cave in Albany where Father had died. There she paid her last respects to him and gave him a proper burial.

"It is all for the best," she repeated. "Now he will not have to suffer."

"We are sorry, nevertheless, Mother," said Melior.

"I know, my girls," she replied. "Actually, I long ago suspected you would seek out your father once you knew the full truth. That was partly why I kept the story from you for so long. I just wanted it to be a better experience for your father and all of you when you met. You see, when I told you the story, I purposely forbade you to go see him precisely because I knew if I did, you would be disobedient; I know your natures, perhaps better than you know them yourselves, and you all have a bit of human stubbornness in you that you inherited from your father; I did not expect your disobedience to result in your father's death, but I did know that without being disobedient, you could never learn the consequences of it."

"I'm not sure," I said, "what it is we were to learn, except perhaps that to interfere in the affairs of men is a delicate business, and we cannot force humans to change or do anything they do not wish. Is that it?"

"Yes," said Mother. "As your father told you, Nasciens would have been king in time anyway, and it is not unlikely that he would have eventually killed your father to make that happen sooner. Your actions were, despite good intentions, basically selfish, and they only sped up what ultimately would have happened."

"We have learned our lesson," Palatyne assured her.

"But some good has come from this experience as well," Mother continued, her voice gentler now. "There is good in everything."

"How was there good in this?" Melior asked.

"As I said earlier, by causing your father's death, you saved him from further suffering due to his illness, but more importantly, he died knowing he was loved—something he could not have known otherwise."

"Then," I dared suggest, "is part of what we should have learned... is it that things will work out for the best no matter what happens or what we try to do? Does it mean there is a reason for everything regardless of whether we can see it at the time?"

"Yes," said Mother. "We must accept that when we act, we should first look at our intentions and make sure they are fully good and not based in selfishness, and we must never act from a desire to control things we cannot. We must accept that the Goddess-God orders all things properly. Understanding and trusting in that is the beginning of wisdom. And while we should always strive to do good, whatever happens—even if it is contrary to what we want or we intended—it is what is best for us in the long run. And now through your own disobedience, you understand the human need to be disobedient, so you understand human nature better and will be better able to help humans without trying to force them to do what you think is best—for trying to control others, even for their own good, will only backfire upon them and you. Our goal is to further mankind's spiritual evolution and the spiritual evolution of all Creation, while understanding that we cannot force that evolution; we must not forget, either, that the universe and mankind will evolve regardless of us. We can only help human evolution along in the same way we help a plant to grow when we water a seed. We can give the seed what it needs, but we cannot make it grow. Growth is inherent in its nature and will happen when it is ready."

I admit, dear Raimond, that I had difficulty wrapping my mind around this notion, and I pondered it many times before I chose any action in all the years that followed. I do not doubt you have difficulty understanding it as well, for you humans and your religions and governments are all built around trying to see rigid codes of right and wrong, good and bad, God and Satan, Heaven and Hell, but it is not so simple—everything, whether it seems malicious or benevolent, is all for the greater glory of the Goddess-God, the increase of Wisdom, and the growth of the human soul and the souls of all creatures.

And so, that is the tale of my life up until the time you knew me, Raimond. Soon after my father's death, I left Avalon and intentionally met you beside the well. I have no doubt that in future ages, they will say that my beautiful, frolicsome mermaid tail you have seen was the result of a curse my mother placed on me for my father's death. People will claim—because they are unable to believe that anything different from them can be good—that I purposely killed my father, but do not listen when you hear such tales. The truth is that my beautiful mermaid tail is my own creation, and I have it simply because it is beautiful and it brings me great joy to splash it about in the water. I have other creative shape-shifting abilities that I enjoy indulging in for my own amusement. I am filled with so much creative energy that if I were to bottle it up, it would cause me to wilt inside and eat away at my spirit, and so I must use it to create, and when I do so, it evolves and develops so that my talent and spirit are nurtured. I would not be a daughter of Avalon if I did not find the greatest joy and pleasure within life and its possibilities.

Therefore, if you remember nothing else that I have told you, understand this: There is no curse, and there is no forbidden knowledge. There is simply good in the universe, and joy and pleasure, laughter and love. At times, humans let their fears block such joy and love from themselves, but joy and love are the guiding forces of the universe that the Goddess-God and Wisdom set up in the beginning to be our tools, our playthings, and to bring happiness to us all.

And now I am at the end of my tale, and I imagine you are no longer surprised to have had me as your wife, for you understand that your father Hervé's first wife was my mother and their marriage was intended to give birth to a special child, the very heir in blood, if not in title, to King Arthur, from whom your father descended. Due to unexpected circumstances, however, the honor of giving birth to that child fell to you and me; that is why I initially married you, but nevertheless, I have loved you greatly, dearly, in a way I don't believe I could have ever loved any other man.

In the days to come, you may wonder whether our love was enough, considering what has happened to our sons, but do not despair. You might have put all your hope for our family's future in Geoffrey or Fromont, but do not forget that it is usually the last who shall come first.

Now my beloved, my handsome, my good and noble husband and

helpmate, my very life's soul, my Raimond, I must leave you. Do not weep. I leave because I love you so dearly. You see, my life will continue on for centuries after yours has ended, and so, I wish to leave you before you enter old age, for I could never bear to see you grow old, to decay and become feeble. I want always to remember you the way you are. I am sorry to leave you at this time when you suffer grief over Fromont's death, but I cannot remain now that you know my secret; should you unintentionally let it slip from your lips, you would endanger me and yourself. Nevertheless, I promise you that in the end all shall be well. This world's troubles mean little over the course of time. It is not what happens, not even to those we love most dearly, that most matters, but how we learn and grow from it, how our own souls are tried and strengthened as a result of our trials.

I ask you to do only two things if you truly love me. First, spend more time in prayer. Mortal man scarcely knows what great power resides in prayer and how it moves the forces of the universe to bring about greater good. More is accomplished by prayer than all the great schemes of man, all the wars, all the fights, all the philosophical treatises, and all the courts that seek to control that which could simply be made right if men only focused their minds upon the holy and the good. So pray daily, not as one begging for mercy, but with a belief in the overall goodness of everything and a trust that all will be made right in its time; use your imagination to picture complete peace and happiness, and when you believe it possible, it will happen, for imagination is the great power that propels our prayers into becoming our future reality, as accorded by the Goddess-God's eternal plan.

Secondly, I leave you our two wedding rings—one you already wear upon your finger, and I know you have never for a moment parted with it since I gave it to you on our wedding day. And now I also give you my own ring to show that our time together is ended, but it never will be forgotten, and our love never betrayed by either of us. Pass these rings on to our children. They are powerful rings that were given to me by Lady Morgana herself, and she told me they are destined to belong to our descendants. They are the very rings that Wisdom gave to Adam and Eve when they were married at the beginning of the Creation in the Garden of Eden. They are incredibly powerful rings, their power to be preserved until the hour it will most be needed. They are the greatest gift I can leave you. Whoever wears them—provided he or she be of our line, the line of Arthur and Avalon that has passed through us—will never be defeated in battle or in law throughout the generations, and ultimately, these rings will display far greater powers than you will witness in your lifetime.

Farewell now, my Raimond. I love you forever.

CHAPTER 15

RAIMOND'S TALE CONTINUES

ND WITH THAT, and before I could even prepare myself for what was next to happen, Melusine ascended up into the air, great gossamer wings miraculously spreading out from her back, and after blowing me a kiss, she flew out the window. I was too stunned to run to the window to watch her fly away, and it was many moments before I even felt able to move.

I would later hear that many of the townsfolk saw her flight. I do not doubt she intended such a sighting in the hopes it would make them realize that greater beings than humans were watching over them, but as she had said, man is ever filled with fear, and it did not take long before people began to spread horrible rumors about my beloved Melusine.

I felt so overwhelmed by all these events that after Melusine left, I sat there for the longest time. I had been in a daze all the while she told her tale, ever in wonder, never thinking of my human body, the pain of being seated for so long, or the call of nature, and when I finally stood and stretched forth my legs, I found it to be the middle of the night, and only later, did I realize that a whole day had passed while she told me her tale. But at that moment, it was all I could do to make it to my room and collapse upon my bed.

I must have slept for a full day and night, and when I woke, my first thought was about the rings, our wedding rings, the rings that she had told me had once belonged to Adam and Eve. I was to pass them to my children, she had said.

My own ring remained on my finger. I would save it for Geoffrey. The other ring I planned to give to Milon. I had left it on the table beside my bed when I had gone to sleep, but before I was out of bed, I reached for it, only to find it gone.

Roland Interrupts

"Oh! The nurse!" I exclaimed. "But she claimed that my grandmother gave the ring to her to give to my father. That Melusine appeared to her that same evening."

Raimond's Tale Continues

In truth, Roland, I believe the nurse stole it. I do not know that Melusine ever appeared to her. I truly doubt such a story. In any case, just minutes after I left my bed that morning, my steward came to tell me that my son and the nurse were missing, and so when later I thought of the ring and could not find it beside my bed where I had left it that night, I knew she must have taken it. I had never trusted that nurse with her sharp tongue, and now, although I had all the kingdom searched, we never were able to find a sign of her. Yet, in the end, it all worked out, for as you know, after the nurse's death, your father,

Milon, went to Lusignan and trained with his brother Geoffrey to become a great knight, and when Geoffrey sent word to me of Milon's return, I was grateful, although I was never to see Milon again before he departed this world so bravely fighting the Saracens. I had waited decades, my dear Roland, to be reunited with your father, but it was never to be. Still, it does my heart good to see you, my grandson—the only grandchild I have. It is a blessing from God to know you exist—to know that my line will not die out, although I know our time together is already coming to a close.

Merlin, I thank you for your patience; remember, it took my dear Melusine a whole day to tell me her tale, yet I have told it to you all in one night, doubtless forgetting parts, but I am certain the important parts I have revealed to you. I can see dawn already starting to spread its light across the sky, so let me finish my story quickly now.

I was sorely depressed for many months after the loss of my wife and then the disappearance of Milon. I fear I would have lost my mind or sought to kill myself had I not now and then remembered how Melusine had told me not to lose hope, and that I must give the rings to my children, and that I must pray. And so I waited to learn how to give the rings to sons who were far from me, and I prayed a great deal, and finally, after several months, a peace settled over me and I knew what I must do.

Soon after, Geoffrey returned to me. When I told him all that had happened between his mother and me, he confirmed for me that every word of it must be true, for he had learned more about our family when he had gone to Northumberland to slay the giant. Upon seeing Geoffrey, the giant had fled from him, having heard of how Geoffrey had killed another giant on the continent. Geoffrey pursued him into Albany and eventually chased him into a cave where he slew him, freeing the people from their oppression.

But, remarkably, in that same cave, Geoffrey stumbled upon a large chamber bathed in a warm glow without any source for the light being visible. The walls were plated in gold and studded with jewels, and in the middle of the chamber was a great gold tomb with the figure of a king at rest upon it. Engraved upon the tomb's side were the following words—I know them by heart for Geoffrey—who barely learned to write his name—was so stunned by them that he repeated them over and over to himself and then found a priest to write it all down for me, and I have pondered over it many a time:

Here lies the noble King Elynas, who by his own misfortune, lost me.

This noble king was my husband, who swore to me upon our marriage never to interrupt me upon giving birth or when feeding my children, but when I gave birth to our three beautiful daughters, Melusine, Melior, and Palatyne, he broke his promise, through no fault of his own, but the treachery of his son, Nasciens. Nevertheless, I needed to abandon him.

I then took my daughters to Avalon where I raised them and they grew to be beautiful and wise.

When they were fifteen years of age, I told them what had happened between their father and me. They then journeyed to Albany to find their father, and through misfortune, and again by Nasciens' treachery, they lost their father when the roof of this cave fell upon him.

This tomb I have erected to Elynas' memory for the great love I bore him. Be it known that none shall enter here again unless he or she be of my own lineage.

I am Pressyne of Avalon, mother of Melusine, Melior, and Palatyne, and ever in my heart the wife to noble Elynas, whom I never ceased to love despite his mortal weakness.

After Geoffrey and I shared our stories, I gave him my wedding ring, for Melusine had said it was to go to one of our sons, and I trusted the other ring in time would be found and become Milon's property if he yet lived, as you know did happen.

By this time, I was hearing rumors that Melusine had been seen flying about the countryside, and I even heard she had been sighted as far away as the monastery at Montserrat on the other side of the Pyrenees. I knew rumors were seldom based in truth, and I could not imagine my beloved would fly about, haunting the countryside, to fan those rumors. These tales only affirmed for me what Melusine had said—how fearful humans are and how they hurt themselves because of that fear, and my heart felt great pity as a result for all the human race.

I then recalled how Melusine had so strongly urged me to pray, and when I did so, I began to feel better, more at peace with myself and no longer as concerned about the state of my property, the crops, my serfs, the Church's wellbeing, or any of the other issues that one of my status must worry over. Instead, I sensed the time had arrived to pass on my title to my son and to make my peace with God.

And so I made a pilgrimage to Rome and received through the Pope himself forgiveness for my sins, and then I travelled here to Montserrat, to spend the rest of my days with the monks, seeking the wellbeing of my soul and praying for my fellow men. The monks have been so good to me, so patient, and they have helped me to be at peace with this world. So in the end, much as I loved Melusine, I feel that

I have found here the place where I have always belonged, for I have never felt so at peace anywhere else, nor at any other time in my life.

Once I came here, I relinquished any further expectations for my life until one day, a mere fortnight ago, when Merlin appeared at my door and startled me by the revelation of who he was. My first thought, upon seeing him, was that he was yet another old man come to spend his remaining days seeking God. Little was I prepared for the honor bestowed on me when he revealed to me his illustrious name. Nor will I forget how he addressed me: "Raimond, Count of Lusignan, spouse to her ladyship, Melusine of Avalon, and grandfather to the paladin Roland, who is nephew to King Charles of the Franks, I have come to visit you, for I have great tidings to bring you."

Part of my surprise was due to only half-understanding his words, for I knew nothing any longer of what occurred in the outside world. Some years before, word had come to us that King Charles now ruled over the Franks, but I had departed the world in the days when the Merovingian dynasty still ruled; we receive no news here at Montserrat of the deeds of King Charles or his men, and it was only when Merlin explained it all to me that I understood that you, Roland, the great hero of the Franks, are my own grandson. Then Merlin told me it was time that I bring about great good by telling my story, and to that purpose, that he would soon be bringing you to me. Since then, I have waited and rehearsed the telling of my tale over and over so I would tell it to you correctly, and yet, I fear I have made a muddle of parts of it. But now it has been said and I can be silent. I will leave it to Merlin to explain to you why you need to know this long and convoluted, yet fascinating story of your origins, for even I do not know what great good he thinks may come from it.

CHAPTER 16

MERLIN ILLUMINATES

THANK YOU, BROTHER Raimond. You have certainly taken your time in the telling, but I admit I could not have told the story any better myself, for I was not present to witness all the events you have described. I could have told Roland the facts and the gist of it in a much shorter time, but the meat of the tale is not in the facts, but in the emotion of it, in what it meant to you to live and experience it, and you have told that part of it very well. Few things in this world are more important than a story well told, especially one that describes our relationships with our fellow beings, for the whole purpose of this life is to learn from our relationships; how we interact with our fellow human beings is what creates the contrasts that stir our souls, not only into love or anger or countless other emotions, but to make us focus and determine what we want and what we will and will not be.

However, some points of your tale I fear may not be so clear, and perhaps you yourself, Raimond, are unclear about them. Let me say it straight out, Roland, that your grandmother Melusine was a remarkable woman, and she always strove with great success to provide the very best life for your grandfather and your father and uncles. No failure is to be attributed to her, for even when we believe we have failed, all these things have been worked out prior to our entering these lives to bring about the very best results in the end, even though we cannot foresee it at the time. If we could foresee the end, we would want to skip ahead to that happy ending and leave off the pain, the confusion, and the struggle, but it is in the struggle that we gain because there everything is to be learned.

You, Roland, are now in the midst of that confusion and struggle. You are doubtless wondering why you have been subjected to hearing this long and rambling tale. You also must wonder why your life was spared in the recent ambush when many of your comrades were slain.

You know I saved your life, and no doubt you realize you were betrayed since you and your men, the very rearguard of the army, were trapped in the pass after you were told it was safe to march through it. And I suspect you can guess who among your company did the betraying. Yes, I can see it now in your eyes—you know instantly who would betray you. The name is forming on your lips, although you wish not to believe such evil of him.

Your own stepfather, Ganelon, Duke of Mayence, your mother's husband, is your betrayer. You have long known he hated you, and you suspect it is because you have won such favor with your uncle the king, and perhaps even more so, because your father, Milon, ran off with your mother many years ago when Ganelon was to wed her. Doubtless, those are reasons enough for Ganelon to hate you, even though they are unreasonable, but the angry, vengeful, and selfish heart knows not logic.

But an even greater reason exists for Ganelon's hatred toward you and all your family. A reason that goes back for centuries—a longstanding feud between your family and Ganelon's. You heard mention that your great-grandfather, Hervé, was cast out of Brittany for slaying the King of Brittany's nephew, Perard, but you also doubtless caught that Perard's rebellion against his uncle was backed by the Duke of Mayence. That duke was Ganelon's grandfather, and he sought the destruction of your great-grandfather Hervé and his family. That Duke of Mayence had a double-grudge against your family, both your mother's side and your father's. He was in fact the brother to the first wife of Elynas, King of Albany, she who was mother of Nasciens, Melusine's treacherous half-brother.

As your grandfather explained, he is born of that secret line of King Arthur that was preserved and went into hiding after Arthur's fall at the Battle of Camlann. Ganelon's family—his ancestors for centuries back—have long hated all those descended from Arthur and those linked to Avalon. They have sought to find, persecute, and ultimately, kill Arthur's descendants ever since the Battle of Camlann.

Today, the legends tell of how Arthur was betrayed by his own son, Mordred, and how they slew one another at Camlann, but as you have heard today, the truth is that Mordred and Arthur were never enemies but fought on the same side against the usurper, Constantine. Today and for centuries to come, Constantine will be known simply as Arthur's successor, but such a whitewashed version of history is a travesty. Nevertheless, history is always recorded by the conqueror, so Constantine and his supporters were able to twist the truth how they pleased. You might be surprised when I refer to Constantine as "the conqueror," but the truth is that he did manage to conquer Arthur's kingdom in the most wicked act of betrayal imaginable, and then he laid the blame on the head of the good and noble Prince Mordred, who was the truest of sons to his father, King Arthur.

Not only was Constantine the actual betrayer, but after Mordred died at Camlann and Arthur was wounded, Constantine became King of Britain and suppressed all further efforts to restore the crown to the rightful heirs of Arthur, including personally slaying Mordred's sons within a church where they had sought sanctuary. But Mordred's oldest son Meleon had secretly married Princess Rachel, daughter of King Uriens of Rheged, and she fled with their newborn child to Brittany where Arthur's cousin, Duke Hoel, granted her sanctuary. The family tried for a long time to keep the child's survival quiet, but in time, Constantine's descendants learned the truth and continued to persecute Arthur's family in small and subtle ways.

Constantine also failed to give credit in history to his great ally, one who was an even greater persecutor of Arthur and his line. Constantine died only a few years after ascending the throne, leaving it to his nephew. But Constantine had a son with this ally, the evil witch Gwenhwyvach, who is known in legend as the "False Guinevere" for she was Queen Guinevere's half-sister and tried to pass herself off as Guinevere on Arthur's wedding night. When Arthur discovered the truth, he had her imprisoned, but in time, she escaped and won Constantine to her side to work her evil.

After Constantine succeeded in conquering Britain, he sought to have Gwenhwyvach killed, but she fled to Scotland where she raised their son. She passed onto this child all the vile wickedness and knowledge of witchcraft she had learned, and she made him swear at a young age to seek the destruction of Arthur's descendants, for she had discovered through her wicked arts that Arthur's great-grandson had survived. Since that time, I and Lady Morgana of Avalon have made it our purpose to protect Arthur's bloodline, although now and then Gwenhwyvach's descendants have won a battle against us, as they did when they succeeded in having Hervé banished—yet they would have had him killed if we had not intervened in time. They did succeed in killing others of your line, wiping out various branches whenever more than one child was born per generation, but we have always succeeded in preserving Arthur's male line of succession. We have also striven to make sure the bloodline continues by sending the priestesses of Avalon to mate with Arthur's descendants whenever we could, as was the case with your great-grandmother Pressyne, who was intended to bear Hervé's son, but when those plans were thwarted, her daughter Melusine was sent to mate with your grandfather Raimond.

Equally Constantine and Gwenhwyvach's descendants have tried to breed to gain power. Nasciens' mother was such a one, which is why she married King Elynas; she hoped to control the throne of Albany through her children and then wage war upon Brittany. She died before that deed could be accomplished, but not before she could pass her evil venom on to her son Nasciens. Although he was a mere boy, his mother taught him well, and he suspected early on who Pressyne was—his spying on her was not from natural sexual curiosity but to affirm his belief that she was of the enemy's party—and when he sought to kill his father, he also sought not to kill his sisters but to capture them—he would doubtless have forced into marriage or even raped your grandmother Melusine had he been able to hold her hostage any longer than he did; then he would have been able to breed on her what he would have considered a super-child of sorts, one of greater abilities than most humans, and also one who would corrupt the inherent goodness in Arthur's line.

Nasciens' line has now died out, but his maternal uncle's descendants became the Dukes of Mayence, as I have said. And so, because of this old blood feud, your stepfather, Ganelon, Duke of Mayence, sought to kill your father, Milon; he would have convinced your uncle the king to do so had Milon and your mother been found after their marriage. Had your uncle, King Charles, not been so kindhearted, Ganelon might even have succeeded in framing you, Roland, in some way as a traitor and had you killed as well. But no matter what action the members of this evil family take, in the end, they have always received their just deserts. You will be happy to know that Ganelon's betrayal is already known, and very soon your uncle, King Charles, will have him ripped limb from limb by wild horses for his treachery.

Such an end would be a reason to celebrate except that your grandmother left behind two magical rings of equal power. You have one such ring in your possession. The other ring, until now, has been in the possession of your uncle Geoffrey. Unfortunately, that ring has fallen into the wrong hands. In his old age and dotage, your uncle has made a disastrous marriage, and I fear the ring will become the possession of his evil witch of a wife. I wish I could interfere and take the ring myself, but as you know, I and those of Avalon are to guide but not directly interfere with human destiny. Should Geoffrey's new wife learn how to wield the power of that ring, there is no telling what evil she could do. Should you learn to wield the power of your ring, you would only be equal to her, and in your opposition, the two of you could work great destruction before one or the other succeeds. That said, the rings have limited power unless they are used together. In any case, I cannot share with you the secret power of the rings for fear it be misused.

But it is crucial that you gain the other ring back from Geoffrey's wife. Do not forget those rings were given to Adam and Eve at their marriage, so they represent the greatest love that two people can know. We cannot allow one or both of them to be used for evil. Do you understand now why you have been told all this long story and what the task before you must be?

CHAPTER 17

ROLAND REPLIES

"**I AM AMAZED** beyond belief," I told Merlin and my grandfather, "by everything I have heard this night, and while I do not pretend to understand it all, I feel in my heart that every word is true. And there are coincidences that amaze me—to think my great-grandfather Hervé de Léon was from Brittany and his ancestors for generations—it makes me believe it was no accident that my uncle the king made me Prefect of the Marches with Brittany and why I was the first of the Frankish people able to create peaceful communication with the Britons there—because I always felt so akin to them, and that is because I am of their blood.

"And I have always, more so I believe than any other at King Charles' court, been a lover of the songs of King Arthur, so to discover I am not only descended from him, but if I understand you correctly, I am his heir...it is amazing and gratifying...and it explains why I must reclaim the ring for my family and pass it down to my descendants—Arthur's descendants.

"I have no wife, for you tell me my fianceé, Alda, will die of a broken heart over hearing of my death, but I am still a fairly young man, so I trust I shall have children yet and pass these rings on through my family until the time when they are needed again; is that correct? Am I close to guessing your purpose?"

"Yes," said Merlin. "You shall live to have descendants. I have a great plan for that, and it requires you to reunite with one of your old friends, whom I told you would be the only one of King Charles' court you should see again, that friend being Ogier, son to the King of Denmark and the greatest of King Charles' paladins, save for yourself. He shall help you recover the ring and also help you in your quest to acquire the Holy Lance."

"Ogier?" I replied. "But what does he have to do with my finding a wife and having children, or of regaining my family's rings? And what is this Holy Lance that you speak of?"

Merlin replied, "You will understand all when—"

EPILOGUE

LUSIGNAN, FRANCE
JUNE, 1995

THE RINGING PHONE woke Adam from his sleep and his dream of Roland.

It took him a minute to wake, to realize what the ringing noise was, and as he woke, he remembered the creep who had broken into the room, and then he recalled that Anne was not with him. Jumping from the bed, he scrambled to grab the phone, desperate to find out whether it was Anne calling him.

"Hello," Adam said, frantically picking up the receiver.

"Adam? Adam, is that you?"

Disoriented, Adam didn't know at first who was speaking. "Anne, is that you?" he asked.

"Anne? No. Adam, it's your mother. You have to come home. You, oh God, you have to come home right away!"

Mary Morgan was screaming into the phone between heart-wrenching sobs.

"Mom, what's wrong? What's happened?" Adam asked, hearing fear and confusion in her tone.

"It's the twins!" Mary cried. "Oh, God. Adam, it's—they—they took them. I don't know who or how, but someone kidnapped them. Lance and Tristan, your precious boys, they're—they're gone. I don't know how this happened. Who could do it? I—"

As his mother continued to scream, Adam felt his whole body turning numb. He sat down on the bed, tears already making their way to his eyes as he shouted, "What do you mean, 'kidnapped'? What happened?"

"We put them to bed in the nursery," said Mary, pausing to catch her breath, "and a couple of hours later, I went to check on them and they were gone. I called the police instantly—detectives have been here all night asking questions and investigating. Someone came in through the upstairs window, although we don't know how anyone could have. Whoever it was kidnapped them. But how do you carry away two babies from the second floor of a stone house? I—oh, come home, Adam. Come home. I'm so sorry. It's all my fault, I—"

"Mom! Mom!" Adam shouted, trying to stop her hysteria so he could talk to her, but he could get little more sense out of her. It would be easier to go home—to talk to the police and to get more information. But how could this be? How could this have happened, and who would want to hurt him like this? His children had been kidnapped! How would he tell Anne?

Anne! He had to go find her.

"Mom, calm down," he said, although frantic himself. "Listen to me. Anne and I will leave now. We'll be home in, oh, I don't know how many hours it will take, but we'll drive until we get there—this afternoon or somewhere around then, I guess. We'll be there by suppertime. We'll call you when we get into England. We'll...."

He didn't even know what he was saying. Where was Anne?

"Mom, I have to go. I'll see you soon."

"Oh, hurry, Adam. I'm so sorry. I love you. Don't blame me; I—"

"Just try to calm down, Mom. It'll be okay. I'll talk to you soon. Bye."

He hung up the phone, feeling his life would never be okay again. Then he grabbed his clothes and put them on, slid into his shoes, and within less than a minute of hanging up the phone, was opening the motel room door, about to run into the night to find his wife when, instead, he found Anne standing there as if she were just about to turn the doorknob.

"Adam, I just had the strangest experience," she said, her face pale. "I had this unbelievable dream, and...and I woke up sleeping in the park. I don't know how I got there. I—"

"Anne, honey, I know. I know what happened to you," said Adam, grabbing her shoulders, relieved to see her. "We can talk about it on the way home."

"Home?" she said, looking puzzled. "We were going to—"

"The boys have been kidnapped. We have to go home," he said, wrapping his arms around her. In another moment, the shock of his words struck her and her sobs broke forth.

AN INTERVIEW WITH TYLER R. TICHELAAR ABOUT

MELUSINE'S GIFT

MELUSINE'S GIFT IS the second book in The Children of Arthur series, and some readers may find it a surprising continuation. Most Arthurian fiction series focus solely on King Arthur, so what made you decide to link the legend of Melusine to that of King Arthur?

I was already aware of the connections between the Arthurian and Charlemagne legends. Let me explain those connections first, and then how I fit Melusine's legend between them. In the Charlemagne legends, Merlin is held prisoner in a cave in the Forest of Broceliande, and the dwarf Maugris, a wizard at Charlemagne's court, listens at this cave and talks to Merlin. I never bought into the idea that Merlin would let a young woman trap him in a cave, but I saw no reason why Merlin couldn't be in France centuries after the time of King Arthur. Secondly, Morgan le Fay ties into the Charlemagne legends, playing a villainess as is typical for portrayals of her. While she makes a brief appearance in *Melusine's Gift*, Morgana's connections to the

Charlemagne stories—and particularly Ogier the Dane—will be treated more fully in the next novel in the series.

My idea to attach Melusine to the Charlemagne legends, making her Roland's grandmother, comes from my reading several pseudo-history books that claimed Charlemagne's sister, Bertha, married Milo or Milon, Roland's father, and that Milon was the son of Melusine. There is no record in the Melusine legend of such a son, yet these pseudo-historians want to claim Melusine and this genealogy are all true; regardless, I decided such a connection would make great fiction. As for connecting Melusine to the Arthurian legends, the legends of Melusine say she was raised in Avalon, and since King Arthur lived there, I thought it only plausible she would have known him and Morgan le Fay. But if Melusine were from Avalon, why did she enter the real world? I decided early on she couldn't possibly be a witch or some evil spirit but simply must be a misunderstood being, and so the ideas referred to in the novel that she was cursed by her mother I have dismissed as human gossip and misunderstandings to show she had a much greater mission that in a sense furthers King Arthur's mission.

Of course, I have completely fabricated the descendants Arthur has in the novel, although many royal and noble families have claimed descent from Arthur just like they have from Melusine. Still, while there are medieval sources for Mordred having sons, that's as far as the line goes. I decided that Arthur's grandson, Meleon, would have a son also named Arthur, who would grow up in Brittany, since it was Britain's colony, more or less, and consequently, a likely place for Arthur's descendants to live, and then I worked in the connection so that Raimond is descended from Arthur. I think it was serendipity that the Melusine legends do state that Raimond's father Hervé came from Brittany. That was a sign to me that I was on to something—or maybe in some way I was channeling the past and what really did happen and has been lost to history.

When did you first become interested in Melusine?

When I was a teenager, I subscribed to the Time-Life Book series *The Enchanted World*, which retold numerous fairy tales, myths, and legends, and Melusine's story was one of them. I kind of forgot about her, however, until I became interested in genealogy and discovered that among my ancestors were the Plantagenet royal family of England. I then began reading a lot about the Plantagenets and learned that they claimed descent from Melusine. That made me wonder exactly how she was their—and my—ancestor. Actually, a lot of medieval noble and royal houses claimed her for an ancestor, and there were several women named Melusine in the Middles Ages who have been confused with her. I have never seen a legitimate genealogy that connects her to any of these noble houses. However, what interested me was that if, as legend said, she were a cursed fairy and she had all of these deformed children, then why did so many prominent families want to claim descent from her? I don't know that there is a good answer for that, other than that there must have been some historical person named Melusine who was of some significance, the truth of her story lost to time. I couldn't help wondering and trying to imagine who that important woman could have been, so eventually, I decided to tell her story as it might have been, making her more real than just a stereotypical witch or demon.

You have set Melusine's story in the eighth century, so if you aren't sure she's really historical, how did you decide on that time

period for the novel's setting?

When Melusine lived is not really clear and I haven't been able to pinpoint an exact time frame for her. My novel is largely based on the supposition that she was the grandmother of Roland, Charlemagne's nephew, but even then pinpointing a time is nearly impossible because the Charlemagne legends themselves play fast and loose with history, and if everything included in them really happened, Charlemagne would have needed to live a much longer life than he did. The historical Charlemagne was born in 742 and became co-ruler of France with his brother in 768 and then sole ruler in 771. He was crowned Holy Roman Emperor by the Pope in 800, and he died in 814. Roland, however, is traditionally said to have died at the Battle of Roncesvaux Pass in 778. Roland himself is not likely historical and Charlemagne did not have a sister named Bertha that we know of, but that aside, Roland is a grown man when he dies, so at the very latest he would have had to have been born in the early to mid-750s, yet Charlemagne is already king of France in the legends when Roland was born, which is impossible unless Roland died far later than the traditional date of his death. I decided despite these chronological issues that the Battle of Roncesvaux Pass would happen in 778, which would mean Roland was born around 755 and his father Milon was about twenty when he was born, and Milon's brother Geoffrey was twenty years older than him, so Geoffrey would have been born about 715 and Melusine probably somewhere around 695. I have made some loose references in the novel to other historical figures, such as Merovingian kings of the time, to make this time frame seem realistic in the novel.

As for the genealogy of Roland, there is no legitimate source that links him to Melusine. Pseudo-historians claim his father Milon is Melusine's son, but I have been unable to determine where this fanciful idea originated. That said, it made sense to me that Milon being the son of the notorious serpent fairy woman might be a reason why Charlemagne would oppose his sister's marriage to him, so from there, my story began to develop, although I included as part of the reason for Charlemagne's opposition to the marriage his wishing to wed Bertha to Ganelon, Duke of Mayence, a union she does not favor.

If people wish to read more about Melusine, what books would you recommend?

Unfortunately, there isn't much to read. I suspect there might be more texts in French I am not aware of, but the first written version of the legend we know of was by Jean d'Arras, written about 1382-1394. Later an author named Coudrette wrote *The Romans of Partenay or of Lusignen: Otherwise known as the Tale of Melusine* between 1401 and 1405. Coudrette's book was my primary source, and it is the most complete one. I had difficulty finding anything in the way of scholarly works on the legend, but Gareth Knight has written some interesting books that summarize and try to explain the legend from a metaphysical and psychological point of view. Then there is the modern novel *The Wandering Unicorn* (1965) by Manuel Mujica Láinez which is told by Melusine during the time of the Crusades and focuses on her watching her descendants during that period—including those who would become the Kings of Jerusalem and were a branch of the Plantagenets. The legend has also received attention in A.S. Byatt's novel *Possession* (1990). A few other historical novelists writing about the Plantagenets have included mention of her, notably Philippa Gregory in her *The Cousins' War* series (2009-2014) about the Wars of the Roses.

Melusine has received nowhere near the degree of popularity that King Arthur has received, with thousands of books written about him. When I mentioned to people that I was writing about Melusine, no one I told even knew who she was. Most people fail to recognize she is the inspiration behind the mermaid on the Starbucks Coffee logo. Yet in the Middle Ages, I daresay among legends, hers may have been the most famous after King Arthur's.

What major liberties would you say you took in retelling Melusine's story?

The biggest liberty is that I wished in this book and all those in The Children of Arthur series to rewrite the past and remove all the sin and guilt and curses from it. I refused to have Melusine's mother curse her for her role in her father's death resulting in her need to hide herself away every Saturday when she changes her form. Instead, I decided her mermaid and flying serpent appearances were the result of her own creative energy and playfulness. In the legends, Melusine does amazing things such as building giant castles; she also raises a large family and is very loving to her husband. Even when Raimond betrayed her, the legends say how sad she was to leave him. Like Morgan le Fay, she is a confusing character who seems to be both good and bad, suggesting much has been forgotten about her original story. I couldn't just simply let her be evil. I made her good, but hopefully in a complex way.

Speaking of retelling stories, you have also rewritten part of the Bible in this book. What made you decide to retell the story of the Tower of Babel?

I knew that Avalon was named for Avallach and Albion (Britain) was named for a giant by that name. I realized there are some other giants in Arthurian tales—Arthur is said to have slain a giant that kidnapped his cousin Hoel's niece, and Melusine's son Geoffrey also is a giant-killer. So I wondered how I could work those giants into the story and explain how they could exist historically. I wanted to answer that question so my story would be plausible since Geoffrey's killing a giant is a big part of the Melusine story. The Bible tells of giants called the Nephilim and the Anakim, and the old British legends tell of giants named Albion, Gog, and Magog, so I decided to create a genealogy for these giants going back to the Bible, and I figured if Albion were a giant, then so was Avallach, for whom Avalon was named.

There is no biblical tradition that mentions Avallach and Albion, but such powerful beings needed some ancient origins. Let me forewarn readers now that I will be doing more rewriting of the Bible in future volumes in the series—after all, I have to explain more about Adam and Eve's wedding rings that I've referenced in the series and which will come to play a key role in the upcoming novels; any discerning reader will realize that means a rewriting of the Garden of Eden story is yet to come.

Also, I'd like to say that writing anything that derives from Christianity and the Bible is very difficult for me since it requires me often to go against the orthodox versions of Christianity and its theology. But I hope my novels separate truth from the dressings of religion. I just can't be a believer in sin and damnation. I think all the ill behavior of mankind arises from fear, not original sin, and the best thing we can do is raise humans' self-esteem so they believe themselves to be chosen and loved sons and daughters of God, not cursed children.

I also loved the magical elements of these legends too much to make the novels realistic historical fiction; instead, I consider them to be historical fantasies, and that gives me license to rewrite these mythologies as if they were an alternate human history, and one that I hope pushes against the tiresome good vs. evil paradigm that confines too many of our stories. There is a good vs. evil story developing as this series goes along as will be made more apparent in the next book, but in the end, I don't believe in evil as embodied by some Satan figure, and that's why I reject the idea of ills coming from curses or eating of forbidden apples or breaking a prohibition by spying on your wife. I hope my readers will suspend their disbelief a little and read with an open mind to understand my theme that we can rise above our troublesome human fears. Consider this: What if these stories were true as I have written them? Why couldn't there be a little magic in the world, a little extra power that makes us special, but which we have blocked from our understanding? How might human history have been different if these stories were true and we discovered someone we feared, like a half-serpent, half-mermaid woman, was actually a benevolent spirit seeking to help the human race?

Your stories do read like a continual revelation of human history, especially in this novel, since you tell stories within stories. What made you decide to use this narrative format?

The story within the story format goes back at least to *The Arabian Nights*, and it was also very popular among the great Gothic novelists of the late eighteenth and early nineteenth centuries, such as Matthew Lewis in *The Monk* (1795) and Mary Shelley in *Frankenstein* (1818). I am a huge fan and student of the Gothic, as evidenced by my book

The Gothic Wanderer: From Transgression to Redemption, a study of Gothic nineteenth century British literature, so obviously the Gothic novel has influenced my writing. I also played with this story within a story form in my previous novel *Spirit of the North: a paranormal romance*.

It seemed appropriate to me to use the story within a story format because in *The Arabian Nights*, many of the stories concern Haroun al-Rashid, who was the Caliph of the Abbasid Empire in the eighth century. Charlemagne and Haroun al-Rashid even had contact with one another. And in the next book in this series, *Ogier's Prayer*, Haroun al-Rashid will appear as a character, giving the book much of an Arabian Nights feel to it.

As for the Gothic, you'll find it has its connections to the series more overtly in the fourth volume of the series, *Lilith's Love*, with its take on the Dracula legend. The Gothic continually is about family secrets, characters finding lost manuscripts that make stunning revelations, and all manner of transgressions that need redemption. I thought a Gothic narrative structure was perfect for these novels since it allows for the past to be revealed to Adam and Anne, and the family secrets they discover are also the secrets of the entire human race's past, and the whole Garden of Eden tale has always been about transgressors, redeemed through Christ's sacrifice—what could be more Gothic than that? But in the end, I hope what seems Gothic about life is revealed not to be terrifying at all when we truly understand our past, aside from the fear we have allowed to distort it.

Given the name of the next book in the series, *Ogier's Prayer*, and that at the end of *Melusine's Gift*, Merlin tells Roland that he will meet up with his old companion Ogier the Dane in the quest to

recover the ring, what role can we expect Ogier the Dane to play in the next novel, and why did you choose him to be a main character in the series?

I won't give away too much here, but I did earlier mention that Morgan le Fay plays a role in the Charlemagne legends, and in those legends, her role is intertwined with Ogier the Dane's story, so expect more Arthurian as well as biblical stories being reworked into the storyline in the next book. If you can't wait, then I encourage you to read the legends of Charlemagne yourself. An excellent place to start is James Baldwin's *The Story of Roland*, which was my own first introduction to these incredibly rich stories.

I promise many more surprises before The Children of Arthur series is complete.

For the latest updates, visit my website and blog at:

www.ChildrenofArthur.com

ACKNOWLEDGMENTS

I WOULD LIKE to extend my thanks to the following people for their help and support in the writing of *Melusine's Gift*:

Diana DeLuca and Rosalyn Hurley for reading and providing invaluable feedback on the rough drafts of this book. Thank you for going on the quest with me.

Lee Brown, Gene Stroobants, and other members of the Writers Ink group in Marquette, Michigan, for listening to me read portions of this novel at our meetings and providing support and suggestions.

Scott Pavelle, who shared his timelines, maps, and enthusiasm for the legends of Charlemagne with me.

Dana Moran for her encouraging comments and listening to me discuss the novel.

Jenifer Brady for reading the final draft with an eagle eye and an accomplished writer's expertise, as well as for being an enthusiastic reader and supporter of all my books.

Larry Alexander for the beautiful interior book and cover designs for this and all the books in The Children of Arthur series as well as his excellent work in designing my website, www.ChildrenofArthur.com.

In addition, I thank my literary predecessors, especially James Baldwin for first introducing me to the legends of Charlemagne, and Time-Life Books where I first read the legend of Melusine, as well as Jean d'Arras and Coudrette for their early books of the legend, and Gareth Knight for his books that try to explain and analyze the Melusine legend.

And most importantly, I thank the real Melusine, whoever she was...or is....

THE CHILDREN OF ARTHUR SERIES

continues in:

OGIER'S PRAYER

THE CHILDREN OF ARTHUR

BOOK THREE

BY

TYLER R. TICHELAAR

WHEN THEIR CHILDREN are kidnapped from the family castle, Adam and Anne Delaney race back to England from their vacation in France. Assuming their children will be held for ransom,

the couple are ill-prepared for the truth about who has kidnapped their boys. Secrets about both of their families will be revealed as a result.

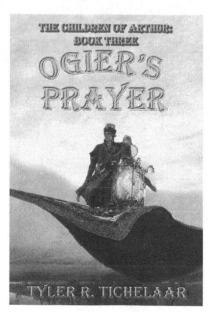

When the great wizard Merlin mysteriously reappears in their lives, Adam and Anne hope he can help with the investigation. But Merlin is more concerned with sharing yet another story about one of their ancestors, this time Ogier the Dane, a great knight of Charlemagne's court, a pagan among Christians who went on a fabulous journey to the East. Ogier's story will enlighten Adam and Anne about an ancient evil soon to be unleashed on the world—an evil that only they may be capable of defeating.

Ogier's Prayer, the third volume in Tyler R. Tichelaar's The Children of Arthur series, will take readers on a magic carpet ride reminiscent of the Arabian Nights as Tichelaar weaves stories within stories in a manner to rival Scheherazade herself.

Be sure not to miss any of The Children of Arthur series:

ARTHUR'S LEGACY: THE CHILDREN OF ARTHUR, BOOK ONE

MELUSINE'S GIFT: THE CHILDREN OF ARTHUR, BOOK TWO

OGIER'S PRAYER: THE CHILDREN OF ARTHUR, BOOK THREE

LILITH'S LOVE: THE CHILDREN OF ARTHUR, BOOK FOUR

ARTHUR'S BOSOM: THE CHILDREN OF ARTHUR, BOOK FIVE

and you might also enjoy Tyler's nonfiction study of the Arthurian legend:

KING ARTHUR'S CHILDREN:
A STUDY IN FICTION AND TRADITION

For the latest information, release dates, and to purchase books, visit:

www.ChildrenofArthur.com

A Sneak Peek at *Ogier's Prayer: The Children of Arthur, Book Three*
the next volume in
The Children of Arthur series:

OGIER'S PRAYER

PROLOGUE

803 A.D.
YEAR 187 BY THE MUSLIM CALENDAR

HAROUN AL-RASHID—sovereign over half the known world as ruler of the Abbasid Caliphate, which stretched from Arabia's southern deserts to the great Caspian Sea, and from the Mediterranean's easternmost reaches to the borders of India, so that all the world knew his fame and feared him, yet marveled at his magnificence and admired his wisdom and prowess—was terribly bored.

The mighty caliph sat in his sumptuous palace in his glorious capital city of Baghdad and wondered whether there was anything at all left in the world that could possibly give him a few hours' amusement. He had engaged in all manner of sport, warfare, and love during his youth. He was honored and esteemed above all in his domains and over all princes and heads of state outside the borders of his empire. Not even Charlemagne of the Franks himself could rival the caliph in any way. And now as the great caliph approached his fortieth year, he felt that everything there was to see and do, had been seen and done, and so being a great ruler was a sorry position to hold in life, for all manner of amusement had always been readily available to him, all his desires quickly and easily fulfilled, and only great boredom had resulted from all his prosperity and success.

Today, this mighty potentate was in a miserable, listless mood which not even wine nor song nor women nor games could dispel. Such was his mood when Giafar, the grand-vizier, and Haroun al-Rashid's old and tried friend, entered his chamber. Bowing low, Giafar waited, as was his duty, till his master spoke, but Haroun-al-Rashid merely turned his head and looked at his friend, and then sank back into his former weary posture of being slumped in his chair. After a moment, he sighed in a manner that asked Giafar, without the actual use of words, "What is it this time?"

Now, Giafar had something of importance to say to the caliph, and he had no intention of being put off by mere silence, so taking Haroun al-Rashid's sigh for permission, he made another low bow in front of the throne and began to speak.

"Commander of the Faithful," said Giafar, "I have come to remind your eminence of how you have undertaken to observe, secretly and for yourself, the manner in which justice is done and order is kept throughout your great capital city. For that very reason, you came to Baghdad from your palace in Ar-Raqqah. And today is the day you have set apart to devote to this purpose, and perhaps in fulfilling this duty, you may find some distraction from the melancholy that I perceive is so strongly overpowering you."

"Giafar, you are right!" exclaimed the caliph, suddenly stirred with a renewed interest in life. "Thank goodness you reminded me. I always find my people amusing, and at times, I have been able to right a wrong, punish an evildoer, and even gain some wisdom from the common folk. But what are you waiting for? Go, find our disguises, and we will walk among the common people as if we were one—or rather two—of them."

Giafar bowed and quickly obeyed. Five minutes later, he returned with two disguises, and after assisting his master, within a few moments, they were both dressed as foreign merchants.

And in another minute, the caliph and vizier had passed through a secret door in Haroun al-Rashid's private chamber that took them through a long and twisting tunnel beneath the palace. Soon they emerged outside through a hidden door in a city wall covered by a great shrubbery. Quickly, they merged with the crowds, as if it were an everyday ordinary activity for them to walk the streets of Baghdad, bartering in the bazaar, giving alms to beggars, and stopping to kneel when the call to prayer was sounded.

So disguised, Haroun al-Rashid was able to find some pleasure in this great joke that freed him from the burdens of statecraft. Often, he considered that he might so remain in such a disguise, with the intent to slip away from the palace and Baghdad and his own high position, so that he might forget all his cares, for the ruling of an empire was no light matter. But he also knew that his wife, Zubadai, and his children, as well as the many millions of his subjects, depended on him. Should he disappear, his absence would cause all kinds of problems for the empire and lead to rumors of his death, suspicions of foul-play, and even civil war. No, he had a duty to his people and could not forsake it, but it did not hurt to fulfill that duty now and then by pretending to be one of the people so he could better understand those whom he ruled.

Despite the diversion of pretending to be a foreign merchant, today the great caliph found no amusement in the streets capable of diverting him from his melancholy and boredom. He was pleased to see the peace and good order of the city; his people appeared content, and he could observe that the city was prosperous. Even the blind beggar he passed had a smile on his face.

"Blind one," he stopped to inquire, "what reason gives you cause to be smiling?"

The beggar's smile only grew wider at the question, and looking over the caliph's shoulder, he pointed up into the sky.

"He is not blind!" exclaimed Giafar. "Blind men do not point at the sky!"

But the blind man continued to point, and his dishonesty was quickly forgotten when Giafar and Haroun al-Rashid both turned to discover what so commanded the beggar's attention.

Soon everyone in the street was also staring—and pointing, and gasping, and exclaiming, "Is it a genie? An evil sorcerer? It can't be real! Am I seeing things?"

Haroun al-Rashid had never in his life doubted his own vision, but at that moment, he came very close to it.

"A genuine magical flying carpet!" exclaimed Giafar.

"It is indeed!" Haroun al-Rashid agreed. "The stuff of genie tales."

The carpet was floating over the city, just perhaps fifty feet above it, slowly growing closer and gently descending. For a good five minutes, everyone in the streets of Baghdad stared up at it, murmuring in astonishment, and children crawled up onto their parents' shoulders so they might see it better.

In a little while, the carpet descended so that it landed on the flat roof of a house. And when the man, who had previously sat cross-legged upon it and whose appearance had been difficult until now to see clearly, stood up, even more gasps filled the street.

This man was no native of the city, nor even of any city or property in all the great Abbasid Caliphate. This man had a light complexion like no one in Baghdad had ever seen. His hair looked to have been spun from gold, and he was clad in shining silver armor that sparkled in the sun.

"Is it a god?" cried one woman.

"Blasphemy!" a man replied.

"It must be a Christian," said another man. "For look at his pale skin—and a Christian is the farthest thing from a god that anyone could be!"

The golden-haired man was beautiful, however, tall and finely formed, and dazzling even without a smile, for he looked uncertain, looking down first upon the crowd, and then at the magic carpet beneath his feet, as if willing it to fly back up into the air.

And then the magic moment was broken as three soldiers stormed into the house, upon the roof of which the golden-haired man stood.

In another minute, the soldiers had arrived on the roof, and the Christian knight, if that is what he was, had drawn his sword, ready to do battle.

"Drop your sword! You are under arrest by order of his great majesty, Caliph Haroun al-Rashid!" cried one soldier.

The caliph heard his name invoked, but he made no move, not wishing to reveal his true identity, but even more so, wishing to see how this fight would turn out.

The golden-haired stranger, instead of dropping his sword, charged toward his assailants, and within a minute, the three soldiers found their own weapons struck from their hands and sent flying into the street, the crowd quickly dodging them. One man, in the fight that ensued, stumbled over the roof's edge and went crashing into the crowd, causing a bystander a broken bone. Another, in fear, jumped onto a neighboring roof, while the third soldier fell to his knees, begging mercy from the golden-haired, godlike warrior who had so mysteriously appeared in their city.

"Now!" exclaimed the stranger, "you may take me to your king, but I go as his guest, and not as a prisoner to any man."

After recovering from his astonishment, the kneeling soldier regained his feet and did as he was bid, leading the way back down through the house. The stranger stopped a moment to put his sword back into its sheath, then bend down to gather up the magic carpet, roll it, and tuck it under his arm, before descending through the house.

As the crowd waited in astonishment to see this amazing warrior enter the street, Haroun al-Rashid said to Giafar, "Quickly. We must return." And elbowing their way through the clamoring crowd of men, women, and children, all seeking to get a glimpse of, or even better, to touch the mysterious stranger, the caliph and his grand vizier made their way back to the secret tunnel that would allow them to return to the palace.

Within half an hour, they were once again in the caliph's private chamber, and immediately, they heard a rapid, insistent pounding on the door from the servants who repeatedly cried, "My caliph, are you there? Please, a great marvel has happened. Come quickly!"

"I will be there in a moment!" the caliph shouted, perturbed by his servants' impatience; they should know better than to harangue him.

Then there was silence, for once confirmation was heard of their master's presence, his servants dared not anger him.

Giafar quickly helped his master change out of the merchant's clothing and back into robes suitable for a great ruler to receive an esteemed visitor.

Then Haroun al-Rashid stepped toward the door and placed his fingers around the handle to open it, but first he turned back and said to Giafar, "Have that deceitful blind beggar found and thrown into prison for his falsehood." When the caliph did open the door, dozens of servants, his wife, children, and ministers all bowed before him and created a path so he could pass through. Haroun al-Rashid ignored them all and strode through the palace to his throne room where he intended to receive his illustrious guest.

Once seated, with a wave of his hand, the caliph ordered the guards to open the door. Then in strode the golden-haired man, taller than everyone else in the room, and escorted by six more soldiers, whom no doubt he could have easily divested of their swords if he had so wished, but instead, he had willingly given up his own sword, his air of confidence and bearing declaring he felt no need for it.

The mysterious stranger came to a stop a few feet before Haroun al-Rashid's throne, and after bowing, he awaited permission to speak.

"Stranger," said the caliph, "we have seen with our own eyes your amazing entry into our great city. We would know your name and your purpose here."

"Great Caliph," said the golden-haired giant of a man, "I am Ogier the Dane, one of the paladins to the great Charles, King of the Franks, and in my own right, Prince of Denmark. I am a stranger here in your domain, it is true, but I come in peace on a mission I can share with your ears alone. I beg a private audience with your majesty."

By then, the multitude of the royal household had crowded into the throne room. They now all gasped at such a bold demand from a stranger.

Haroun al-Rashid waited a moment as everyone reacted to this unusual request, and then, clapping his hands together, he ordered, "Silence!"

The room became still as Haroun al-Rashid looked deep into Ogier the Dane's eyes, searching as if to read his very soul. After a moment, he rose from his throne and stepped forward.

The silence was broken when he placed his hand on Ogier's

shoulder, a familiarity he had never shown in public to any man, not even to Giafar.

"Come," said Haroun al-Rashid. "I have been sorely bored, and you have brought me pleasure in the unexpectedness of your visit. Your words speak truth, for you look to be one of noble breeding, and your eyes bespeak suffering but also wisdom. I will hear your tale, but first, we will have you properly bathed and fed."

And then leading the way, Haroun al-Rashid personally escorted the stranger to his own private bathing pool where he left him under the care of his servants, saying to Ogier, "Please refresh yourself, and then my servants will bring you to me to dine. Over our meal, I will hear with great pleasure all you have to say."

And so it was, in an hour's time, that Ogier the Dane, Prince of Denmark, thousands of miles from the cold northern climes where he had been raised, found himself dining with Haroun al-Rashid, the Caliph of the Abbasid Empire, the most powerful man in the world.

Seated at a table, the caliph ordered wine for his guest, and all manner of sweetmeats and fruits and vegetables, every delicacy known within his great empire, and as they began to eat, the caliph said, "Now, I wish to hear your tale, for I have no doubt it is a marvelous one."

Ogier the Dane nodded in agreement and said, "My lord, I will be most pleased to tell you my story, and perhaps when I have finished, you will be good enough to aid me, though I am but a humble knight of Charles the Great, King of the Franks."

"We are good friends with King Charles," replied the caliph, "although he now calls himself an emperor, so I am surprised you do not show him the respect he deserves with that title."

"Emperor?" muttered Ogier. "Emperor of what?"

"He was crowned as Holy Roman Emperor by the pope. Did you

not know this? It has been two or three years now since it happened."

"No, I...I—"

"It seems you have been journeying far from home for a long time then, Prince Ogier."

"I believe so, your majesty," replied the Dane.

"Come. Tell me all about it. When did you leave King Charles' court, and how did you come to be in my domains?"

"That is a long, long tale, Great Caliph, and I find it not easy to know where to start. I do not wish to weary you, but I fear we must begin just a few days after my birth."

"I am prepared for a tale as long as you have to tell," Haroun al-Rashid replied, "and we have all night for the telling."

"I fear it will take at least that long if not longer," Ogier began, "but I am happy to obey your command to hear it, and I hope that in my words you will find the entertainment you seek."

ABOUT THE AUTHOR

TYLER R. TICHELAAR holds a Ph.D. in Literature from Western Michigan University, and Bachelor and Master's Degrees in English from Northern Michigan University. He is the owner of his own publishing company, Marquette Fiction, and of Superior Book Productions, a professional book review, editing, proofreading, book design, and web design service.

Tyler is the author of numerous historical novels, including *The Marquette Trilogy* (composed of *Iron Pioneers*, *The Queen City*, and *Superior Heritage*), *Narrow Lives*, *The Only Thing That Lasts*, *Spirit of the North: a paranormal romance*, and *The Best Place*. He has also authored non-fiction titles that include *My Marquette*, *The Gothic Wanderer: From Transgression to Redemption*, and *King Arthur's Children: A Study in Fiction and Tradition*. An avid genealogist, Tyler has been fascinated by the Arthurian legend and medieval history since childhood.

Visit Tyler at:
www.MarquetteFiction.com
www.GothicWanderer.com
www.ChildrenofArthur.com

Made in the USA
Columbia, SC
03 December 2017